Déjà Moo

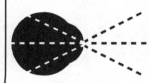

A PERFECTLY PROPER PARANORMAL MUSEUM MYSTERY

DÉJÀ MOO

KIRSTEN WEISS

WHEELER PUBLISHING

A part of Gale, a Cengage Company

Farmington Hills, Mich • San Francisco • New York • Waterville, Maine
Meriden, Conn • Mason, Ohio • Chicago

Wheeler Publishing Large Print Cozy Mystery.
The text of this Large Print edition is unabridged.
Other aspects of the book may vary from the original edition.
Set in 16 pt. Plantin.

LIBRARY OF CONGRESS CIP DATA ON FILE.
CATALOGUING IN PUBLICATION FOR THIS BOOK
IS AVAILABLE FROM THE LIBRARY OF CONGRESS

ISBN-13: 978-1-4328-5444-7 (softcover)

Published in 2018 by arrangement with Midnight Ink, an imprint of Llewelyn Publications, Woodbury, MN 55125-2989 USA

Printed in Mexico
1 2 3 4 5 6 7 22 21 20 19 18

To Alice

ONE

I aimed the flashlight beneath the hood of my vintage pickup and frowned at the tangle of wires.

The night was cold and still, aside from the occasional metallic squeak of my feet on the chrome bumper. No breeze rustled the dying vines in the nearby vineyard or stirred the bare branches of the apple orchard on the other side of the road. Stars blazed brittle and cold, undimmed by the lights of nearby Sacramento.

Rubbing my arms, I regretted my wardrobe choice. My jeans, Henley, and electric-blue down vest weren't enough for winter in central California. I undid my ponytail, letting my wavy brown hair fall around my shoulders for warmth.

I tugged lightly on a cable leading to something I couldn't name. Yep, it was still attached. So why had my truck died?

True, the red pickup was over fifty years

old. But my dad had babied it like a prize heifer. After my dad died, my now-ex boyfriend Mason had made sure the truck continued running like a dream.

I hopped off the bumper, thudded hard to the uneven ground, stumbled, and winced. The drop would have been lighter if I'd ever been able to lose those last ten pounds. But blue eyed and freckled, I seemed doomed to be shaped like my central European peasant ancestors.

Something rustled in the vineyard. Giving a little jump, I turned my flashlight in that direction. The unsteady beam elongated the shadows of hunched and twisted grapevines, their gnarled arms reaching.

Shivering, I turned back to my pickup. I'd promised to help my mother guard San Benedetto's most sacred bovine — the Christmas Cow — and I was an hour late. Every year, a committee of representatives from local government, the Ladies Aid Society, and the Dairy Association built a thirty-foot straw cow, and every year, someone set it on fire. Well, nearly every year. It got run down by an RV once. Now people placed bets on the cow's fate.

Twin headlights appeared on the arrow-straight road.

I swallowed, remembering every single

urban legend about bad things and dark crossroads. Striding to the driver's side of my truck, I opened the door and tried to remember where I'd put my phone.

The headlights grew larger.

Movements jerky, I scrabbled in my purse on the passenger seat. So what if the road was deserted? San Benedetto wasn't the scary big city. I was safe. Totally, totally safe.

The driver was probably a farmer on his way home. Or a tourist who'd waited to sober up after too much wine tasting before getting in his car. It wasn't a psycho killer armed with an ax and creepy clown mask.

"Totally safe," I muttered.

The car roared closer, its lights blinding. I could tell by the wide-set headlights that it was big, a sedan with ample trunk room for bodies.

The car slowed. The driver had spotted me.

Heart rabbiting, I turned my purse upside down on the seat. A wallet, breath mints, a candy wrapper, museum brochures, and my phone tumbled out. My phone skidded sideways, fell to the floor, and bounced beneath my seat. Stooping, I rummaged for it.

A window whirred down. "Maddie?" a man asked.

Phone in hand, I jerked upright and gasped with relief. "Detective Slate?" Jason Slate was one of our local cops, and a good one.

"What's going on? Car trouble?" He unfolded himself from the car, his shadow long on the asphalt. Tall, dark, and handsome, with broad shoulders and narrow hips, Detective Slate stood somewhere over six feet tall. He was in a suit, so I guessed he'd just gotten off work on the wrong side of midnight.

And even though I knew he wasn't going to dismember me and fertilize the vineyard with ground-Maddie, my heart beat more quickly. I had a crush on the African-American cop.

"The engine died. I was about to call my mom," I said, my cheeks warming. "And then a tow truck." It wasn't like I went running to mommy *every* time something went wrong.

"Is she guarding the cow tonight?"

I bumped against the open truck door. "Yes, and I'm late." My mother did not tolerate late.

Slate grinned. "No one's been able to really explain that tradition to me. What does a straw cow have to do with Christmas?"

10

"It's Swedish."

"So I've been told, and why Swedish?" he asked. "San Benedetto was founded by Italians."

"Because of the great Swedish influx of 1908. That's when the Jorgensen family arrived."

"One family makes an influx?"

Leaves rustled on dry earth and I glanced at the vineyard. "It did in 1908 San Benedetto."

"Now I know you're pulling my leg."

"Nope. Serious. It was a really big family."

"Did they force-feed local history to you in grade school?"

If they had, I couldn't remember it. "I researched Swedish Christmas traditions as part of my Paranormal Christmas exhibit at the museum." The phone buzzed in my hand and I checked the screen. "That's my mom now. Do you mind?"

"Go ahead."

"Hi —"

"Madelyn, this is your mother," she said, terse. "Don't come. I repeat, do not come."

My scalp prickled. "What — ?"

"The cow is under attack."

"Attack?" My grip tightened on the phone. "What's happening?"

11

Slate straightened. "Maddie?"

"Oh my God. The gingerbread men!" she shrieked, and the phone disconnected.

"Mom? Mom!" I shouted into the dial tone. Oh-my-God-oh-my-God-oh-my-God. My mom is never flustered. She's known for always being perfectly, terrifyingly in control right down to her ironed jeans. But her voice had held an unmistakable thread of panic.

"What's happening?" Slate asked, his tone hard and brisk.

"The Christmas Cow's under attack. My mom's there!"

"Get in."

But I was already sliding into the passenger side of his sedan. The attackers were probably trying to set the cow on fire. What if my mom tried to stop them or attempted to put out the flames herself?

Slate revved the engine. Spitting gravel, we tore onto the road. He grabbed the radio between us and shouted numbers to the dispatcher.

I buckled up and grasped the dashboard, straining forward as if that would make us go faster.

He flicked a switch and a siren wailed. "There are always two people on guard, aren't there?" he asked.

"Usually. But my mom didn't think the other guard tonight would be much help, so she asked me to stop by." It was nearly two a.m., the end of my mom's shift.

"Who's her partner?"

"Some guy from the Dairy Association."

"She'll be okay," Slate said. "Those farmers are tougher than they look."

My fingertips whitened on the dash. "Can you go any faster?"

He accelerated. "And since the cow attacks began . . . what was it, thirty years ago?"

"It was 1988." You never forget your first straw cow conflagration.

"Since then, these cow arsonists have never hurt anyone. They're probably just kids. I'm sure your mom is okay."

I gasped. Ahead, an orange glow lit the night sky. "The cow!"

My mom had failed, and like my truck, my mom never failed. Had we reached the end times? Had my broken-down pickup been an omen? Not that I believe in omens. Just because I own a paranormal museum doesn't mean I have to believe in all things supernatural. True, I'd seen some odd stuff at the museum. But nothing I couldn't attribute to a trick of the light or . . . something.

13

The edge of the phone bit into my palm. Hands shaking, I dialed my mom. The call went to voicemail.

We roared through the adobe arch that proclaimed *Welcome to San Benedetto*. Clouds of black smoke billowed down the street.

We passed the brick bank and the local microbrewery, their windows dark for the night. I glanced at the dash clock. It was two fifteen in the morning, and San Benedetto sidewalks rolled up at eleven. The arsonists had timed their attack well. As usual.

Other sirens wailed, red and blue lights flashing through the roiling smoke.

We screeched to a halt beside the park, and I gaped. The thirty-foot cow was now just a metal skeleton atop a smoldering ash heap.

Firemen piled from their trucks.

A slender figure staggered through the ashes.

I leapt from the sedan. "Mom!" I raced to her. "Mom, are you okay?"

Blue eyes wide, she stared through me. "Gingerbread men," she moaned.

"What happened?" I clutched her shoulders, assuring myself she was in one piece. Her cropped, silvery-blond hair stood up in

14

places. Her orange safety-fleece jacket was gritty with ash.

Slate jogged across the park to us. "Mrs. Kosloski, are you hurt?"

She gulped, shook her head, straightened. "I'm fine. There was a gang. They shot flaming arrows into the cow. Flaming arrows!" She grasped my wrist. "Arrows!"

"Can you describe the people who did this?" Slate asked.

Anger flashed across her soot-stained face. "Right down to the icing. They were dressed as gingerbread men with candy buttons and . . . and . . ." Her lips quivered.

"What?" he prodded gently.

"Santa Claus," she whispered. "He was involved."

"No," I said, shocked. Christmas was my mother's favorite holiday, and Saint Nicholas her favorite saint. And she wasn't even Catholic.

She actually had a Santa Claus toilet seat cover. If the seat's up, Santa covers his eyes with his mittens. When I was a kid, the wealth of tinsel and glitter in our house made the holidays magical. As an adult . . . heck, I still loved it.

"What will the children think?" My mother clutched Slate's arm. "There must be a way to . . ." She shook her head. "No,

15

we won't be able to keep Santa's involvement out of the papers, not with the webcams."

"Webcams?" The detective's golden-brown eyes narrowed.

"Webcam," I said. "Singular. Leo helped them rig one this year so other townsfolk could help guard the cow from their computers." My assistant at the Paranormal Museum was versatile.

"And the video feed is recorded?" Slate asked.

"It's on three-second intervals," I said.

"I'll need to see that video," he said.

My mother buried her head in her hands. "It's probably all over the Internet by now," she wailed. "What will the children think?"

"How many attackers were involved?" Slate asked.

"It's hard to say. They were all moving so quickly, and it was dark. I think there were four gingerbread men plus Santa."

"Where's the guy who's supposed to be helping you guard?" I asked.

"Bill." Her lip curled. "Since he's president of the Dairy Association, he thinks he's too good for guard duty."

"But where is he?" Slate asked. "He didn't go after the arsonists, did he?"

She motioned vaguely at the park, the

16

burnt metal skeleton, the gazebo. "I don't know. We agreed to guard opposite sides of the cow. I had the street side, and he had the creek. And then I was surrounded by laughing gingerbread men and flaming arrows were flying everywhere. It happened so fast."

"Thanks," Slate said and walked toward the creek.

My mother and I looked at each other, then followed him past the gazebo.

Firemen showered water on the ashes. A jet of water hit a white canvas sign and sent it flying to the ground.

"I knew we shouldn't have built the Christmas Cow this year," my mother said, edging around a park bench. "This always happens. And the worst of it is, I really think people look forward to the fire more than the cow!"

I knew they did, but I patted her on the back. "It's okay."

"No, it isn't. San Benedetto has changed, Madelyn. Murders. Flaming arrows!"

"At least we haven't had a murder with a flaming arrow."

"That isn't funny."

"No." I sighed. "I'm sorry."

Slate shuffled sideways down the creek bank.

17

"Do you think Bill went after the miscreants?" she asked me. "I hope he's not hurt."

I shook my head and watched Slate pick his way down the uneven slope. The creek ran low in December, but its bank was filled with prickly bushes that plucked at the detective's suit. I turned toward the gazebo. "Which way did the gingerbread men go?"

"Everywhere," she said. "They scattered. Laughing. As if arson was a joke!"

"They were probably kids. To them, a giant flaming cow *is* funny. And no one got . . . . hurt." I cocked my head. A dark pile of rags lay slumped over the rear gazebo steps. Dread slowed my breath. "What's that?"

My mother's face paled. She hurried forward. "Bill?"

I trotted to catch up, then stumbled to a halt.

A middle-aged man lay sprawled on the gazebo steps, his eyes wide, staring. An arrow stuck upright from his chest.

TWO

Dead. A man was dead. My brain tilt-a-whirled, my stomach twisting. Getting a grip on myself, I raced to the top of the gully and stumbled over a loose rock in the darkness. Slate's flashlight beam bobbed on the opposite side of the low creek.

"Detective Slate!"

The light swiveled, hitting me in the chest. "I found tracks leading across the stream," he said. "I think they go to the high school." He sloshed back across the creek. "What did you find?"

"Bill Eldrich," I said, voice splintering. "He's . . . he's dead."

"Where?" Bent low for balance, the detective ran up the slope toward me.

"The gazebo." I nodded in that direction.

My mother had backed away from the body. Two firemen in helmets and sturdy coats knelt beside the lump on the gazebo steps. I rubbed my chest.

Slate strode past me to the gazebo.

I stood paralyzed. The creek splashed against the rocks below. Radios crackled. A man shouted.

I dug into my down vest and pulled out my cell phone, called Leo.

After a few rings, my museum assistant picked up. "Maddie?" Loud music blared in the background.

"Hi, Leo. You're not in a bar, are you?" My sole employee wasn't yet twenty-one, but he was on his own in the world. I couldn't help worrying about him.

He laughed. "I get enough mothering from Mrs. Gale. And no, I'm not in a bar. I'm at a party. What's up?"

"The cow burned down."

"No way! Hold on." He shouted something, and there was the sound of cheers and whooping. "I always miss the action," he said into the phone. "Were you there? Did you see it go up?"

"No, but my mom was. The police want to see a copy of the webcam footage."

"Oh," he said, sobering. "Is your mom okay? She wasn't hurt, was she?"

"No, but the police need to see that footage."

"You mean . . . now?"

"Now."

"Are you at the cow?"

I stared at the pile of sopping ashes beneath the metal frame. "What's left of it." The firemen had done a thorough job killing the embers. The park stank of smoke and wet straw.

"I'll get to the museum and post it on YouTube, then —"

"No." My grip tightened on the phone. "Don't."

Sirens wailed in the distance.

"Why not?" Leo asked. "That's what the plan was."

"I know, but . . . Don't tell anyone, but the Dairy Association president was killed." I probably shouldn't have told him this, but he'd hear about it soon enough. And I trusted him not to blab the news at the party.

Leo sucked in his breath. "Damn. But your mom's okay?"

"She is. Can you email the video to Detective Slate? I'll explain everything tomorrow."

"Sure. What's his address?"

I recited it, shouting above the blaring sirens, then scrunched my brows. Even to me it seemed odd that I had a detective's email address memorized. In my defense, it was an easy one to remember. Plus, Slate had helped me research objects in my

21

museum connected to local historical crimes.

And in the past, I might have been peripherally involved in a crime or two.

A blue Mustang with flashing lights screeched to a halt by the park. An Amazon with short blond hair emerged and surveyed the scene, fists on the hips of her tight pantsuit.

My shoulders hunched.

"If the police are still there," Leo said, "I can come and bring the file."

Leery, I eyed the newcomer, Slate's partner Detective Laurel Hammer. "Uh, no thanks. That's okay."

"Are those sirens? The cow's not still on fire, is it?"

"No, it's out. There mustn't be much happening tonight, so the entire fire and police departments are here."

Laurel spotted me. Nostrils flaring, she stormed across the remains of the cow.

Discretion being the better part of valor, I hustled toward my mother, who was speaking with Detective Slate beside the gazebo.

"Kosloski!" Laurel shouted. "Halt!"

My mother turned.

I kept moving, head down, phone pressed to my ear. "Gotta go. I'll tell Slate to expect that email." I hung up.

"Leo's going to email you the video file from the webcam," I said brightly. "I told him it was urgent."

Slate nodded.

"Kosloski!"

My mother waved. "Over here, Detective Hammer."

"I can see where you are," Laurel snarled. "What I don't understand is why your daughter didn't stop when I told her to."

"Oh," my mother said, "Madelyn never does what she's told anymore. It's strange, since she was such a well-behaved child."

A muscle beat in Laurel's jaw. "What happened?"

"Mr. William Eldrich is dead." Slate pointed to the body with his pen. "Apparently killed by one of the Christmas Cow attackers. Mrs. Kosloski was in the middle of telling me what she witnessed. We've got webcam footage being emailed to the station. Mrs. Kosloski, would you mind repeating what you told me?"

My mother nodded, her silver earrings swaying. "Certainly. As you know, the Christmas Cow is a long-standing tradition in San Benedetto and a tribute to our sister city in Sweden. Only they have a giant goat. I'm sure you also know that nearly every year someone sets our cow on fire."

Laurel shifted, scowling.

"Except for that year it got hit by the RV and knocked into the creek," I said, enjoying the history because Laurel was not. She already knew the legend of the Christmas Cow. The whole state did.

"And the cow survived '86, '98, '04, and '05," my mom said.

Three police cars roared by and came to a stop. The uniformed officers leapt out and converged on us.

"The body is on the rear gazebo steps," Slate said to them. "You know what to do."

The uniformed cops nodded and hurried to the gazebo.

"And tonight?" Laurel prompted.

My mother drew a long, shuddering breath. "Mr. Eldrich, who's the president of the Dairy Association, and I were guarding the Christmas Cow. We'd agreed to man opposite sides for better coverage. I was near the street. He took the creek side, thinking any potential arsonists might attack from the direction of the high school." Her breath hitched. "We were both right. They came from all directions, yelling and whooping and shooting flaming arrows. The monsters were everywhere! There was nothing I could do to stop them. We were fools to try," she said, mournful.

"But you had time to call your daughter," Slate said.

I shot him a dark look. What was he implying? This was my mother, President of Ladies Aid he was talking about!

"I'd begun dialing right before the attack began. Madelyn was late —"

Laurel snorted.

"— and I wondered what had happened to her. Then the arrows started flying, and all I could think was to tell her to stay away."

"When was the last time you saw Mr. Eldrich alive?" Slate asked.

My mom's cheeks pinked. "Our shift began at ten o'clock. He was late. I think he arrived around ten thirty. I'm afraid I was rather severe with him."

"You argued?" Laurel asked sharply.

"Of course not," I said.

"Oh, no, Madelyn," my mother said. "We had strong words."

My stomach bottomed. What was she doing? You *never* tell the cops you had a motive to kill someone. Not that anyone could seriously think my mother was involved, especially not anyone as smart as Detective Slate.

"He thought being president of the Dairy Association meant he didn't have to pitch in on projects like these," my mother said.

25

"But when you're president, it's important to set a good example. If you don't care about the project, then why should you expect anyone else to? Unfortunately, Bill had such an unpleasant attitude that I didn't explain my philosophy as calmly as I could have."

"How did you explain it?" Laurel asked.

"What does it matter?" I asked. "My mom didn't shoot an arrow through him because he was late for guard duty."

Laurel eyed me. "All right, Kosloski. Why don't you come over here and tell me what you saw?"

Now they were separating the witnesses? I knew what this meant. Laurel thought my mother might actually have something to do with the murder. I shifted my weight and something cracked beneath my foot. I lifted my tennis shoe. A broken arrow lay in the straw, the wood cracked like a number two pencil after the SATs.

Whoops. "Sorry," I said.

Laurel growled, stepping closer.

"Miss Kosloski was with me," Slate said, his tone mild.

Laurel sucked in her cheeks and took a step backward.

"Her truck was stalled on the side of the road," he said. "I'd pulled over to assist

26

when the call came in from her mother. We drove here together."

"Maddie!" a woman shouted.

Laurel hissed, "Finkielkraut."

I turned. One of my best friends, Adele Nakamoto, was hurrying across the park. Her boyfriend, Dieter Finkielkraut, loped beside her. The two were a classic example of opposites attracting: Adele's parents owned a vineyard; she owned a hoity-toity tea room, which had the misfortune of being next to my low-brow paranormal museum; and she had a penchant for Jackie Kennedy–style suits, though tonight she was dressed like a pink snow bunny in a furry parka and white jeans. Dieter was a shaggy-haired, devil-may-care contractor, who worked to ski and ran a bookie business on the side.

My eyes narrowed. Dieter specialized in odd bets, such as when and if the Christmas Cow would burn. No wonder they'd turned up.

"Look what the cat dragged in," Laurel said. "Fancy finding you here, Finkielkraut."

He grinned and saluted with one finger.

"There's smoke drifting down Main Street," Adele said. "I thought my tea room might be on fire. Maddie, what are you doing here? Are you all right?"

"My mom was on Christmas Cow duty."

"Oh no!" Adele's eyes widened. "Mrs. Kosloski, were you hurt? You're covered in soot."

"Am I?" My mom brushed off her pressed jeans. "No, I'm fine, Adele. Thank you for asking."

Laurel smiled unpleasantly. "It's nearly three a.m. What were you two doing on Main Street? Nothing's open at this hour."

Dieter looped a muscular arm around Adele. "We just got back from Tahoe."

"On a Thursday morning," Laurel said, voice flat and disbelieving.

"It was so romantic," Adele said, her breath visible in the chill night air. "We snowshoed through the forest at night and picnicked in a clearing overlooking the lake."

And even though it was totally inappropriate for me to feel a twinge of jealousy, I did. It had only been two months since my boyfriend Mason and I broke up. I'd gotten past the hurt, but I was keenly aware of my single status.

Slate cleared his throat. "All right. I need to speak with Mrs. Kosloski alone. Laurel?"

Laurel marched the rest of us across the street, and we dutifully lined up beside my mother's butter-colored Lincoln. After pinning us in place with a glare, she strode back across the park toward the gazebo.

"Wow," Adele said. "The police are really taking this year's cow burning seriously."

"That's because it's more than arson," I said in a low voice. "The other guard, Mr. Eldrich from the Dairy Association, was killed."

Adele gasped.

Dieter hugged her shoulders more tightly. "Killed?"

"They attacked with flaming arrows," I said. "Mr. Eldrich was hit."

"Oh my God." Adele pressed a hand to her mouth. "Your mother could have been killed. I always thought the annual Christmas Cow shenanigans were funny. But this is terrible. We knew Mr. Eldrich."

"We did?" I asked blankly. I'd spent most of my adult life overseas, only coming home last year. I was still getting reacquainted with my hometown.

"Remember?" Adele said. "We took a school trip to visit his dairy farm. Harper got to milk a cow."

"Oh, right." I'd gotten chased through a field by a cow, scrambled over a fence to escape, caught my shirt on a post, and exposed myself to the entire fifth grade. No wonder I'd blotted out the memory. "Did he have any family?"

Adele shook her head. "Not anymore. His wife died five years ago. They never had children."

"It must have been an accident," Dieter muttered. "Kids with arrows, lots of chaos . . ."

"Dieter," I said, "were you taking bets on the cow this year?"

He glanced toward the gazebo and Laurel and the milling cops. "I can't talk about it here."

I crossed my arms. "Dieter —"

"I've kept Adele out too late as it is. She's got to open the tea room in the morning. Come on, Adele. Let me get you home."

"We can't leave Maddie here alone," Adele said.

"No," I said, "it's okay. I'm not alone. My mom's here. You and Dieter go on." I gave her what I hoped was a significant look: *And wheedle what you can from him about the Christmas Cow betting.*

She nodded and yawned. "I'll see you in the morning. If you need anything, call."

"Thanks."

They piled into Dieter's rickety pickup and drove off, tools and construction equipment rattling in the bed.

Turning toward the park again, I watched and waited. Watched and waited while Slate interrogated my mother. Watched and waited while the cops unrolled yellow police tape around the gazebo. Watched and waited and felt Laurel's gaze on me the whole time. She and I had a history that went back to junior high. And though I wanted to repair it — we were both adults now — everything I'd tried had made things worse.

My mother walked across the park toward me and I straightened off her Lincoln. If they weren't taking her into the station for questioning, then she wasn't a serious suspect. But who could really suspect my mom, president of the San Benedetto Ladies Aid Society, mother of three, and doer of good deeds?

"Where's your truck?" she asked.

"Stalled on Euclid Road by Rift Vineyards."

"Stalled? Your father's truck never stalls." She pursed her lips. "But thank goodness it did or you would have been here on time. You might have been hurt too."

"I don't need that kind of good luck."

Her jaw tightened. "Have you called for a tow?"

"I was about to when Detective Slate drove up. And then you called and we drove here together."

She patted my shoulder. "The detective's

31

a good man. Get in. I'll drive you to your truck and we'll wait for a tow together."

"You don't have to wait with me. You must be exhausted."

She unlocked the doors and walked to the driver's side. "Actually, I feel strangely exhilarated."

"Exhilarated?" I slid inside.

"And angry. This will not stand."

Uneasy, I twisted the seat belt. "What won't stand?"

"The attack on the cow. The murder. I've had enough. It's one thing for people to kill each other in Sacramento, but this is San Benedetto. The reason people live here is because it's a nice, quiet sort of place without big city problems."

"I doubt people in big cities like crime any more than we do."

"But don't you see what's happening?" My mom started the car and we glided from the curb.

"Kids set the Christmas Cow on fire, like they did last year and the year before that. Flaming arrows probably seemed a fun twist. The cow's such a big target that even if you don't know what you're doing — and I'll bet none of those gingerbread men did — someone is bound to hit it. It's horrible that one went astray and hit Mr. Eldrich, but it was an accident," I said, trying to convince myself. Knobs of anxiety formed in my stomach. It *had* been an accident, right?

"That was no accident, Madelyn."

I edged sideways on the front seat and pressed my back against the door, the better to study her. "What are you talking about?"

"Santa Claus."

My eyebrows scrunched together. "Santa Claus?"

"Bill had enemies. When you're the president of an organization like the Dairy Association . . . or Ladies Aid for that matter . . . you're bound to attract them. But Bill delighted in rubbing people the wrong way."

"Yeah, but accidents *do* happen to annoying people. And what does that have to do with Santa Claus?"

"All the other attackers were dressed as gingerbread men. Why add a Santa?" My mother piloted the car beneath the adobe arch. The distance between the low brick buildings grew wider.

"Maybe the costume shop ran out of gingerbread men." Did San Benedetto have a costume shop? Would the Christmas Cow attackers have been stupid enough to rent their costumes?

"Good point. I'll have to figure out where the costumes came from."

"What do you mean, *you'll* have to figure out?" My voice jumped an octave.

"You've taught me a thing or two since you've been home."

"I have?" I gripped the seat belt across my chest.

"I've always had confidence in your ability to unravel any problem. Why, look at what you've done with that paranormal museum. And you've done a marvelous job solving all those murders."

I squirmed. "I wouldn't go so far as *marvelous.*"

"But tonight a man was killed under my watch. Mine. Enough is enough."

"Detective Slate knows what he's doing. And the police have resources you don't."

"But I have resources they don't."

"You do?" I squeaked, not liking the direction this conversation was going.

She didn't respond, her knuckles whitening on the steering wheel.

A tense silence filled the car.

The Lincoln purred along the grid of roads, its headlights turning the shadows of the grapevines into wraiths. She pulled up behind my red pickup.

"I'll call for a tow," I said. I should have called while we were driving, but I'd been too busy thinking of ways to dissuade my mom from doing what I feared she was going to do — play amateur crime-solver. And yes, I'd been guilty of exactly the same thing in the past, but it hadn't been by choice.

"Why don't you try the ignition again?" she asked. "You never know with these old trucks."

Too tired to argue, I brushed aside the detritus from my overturned purse and turned the key in the ignition.

The truck roared to life.

I pursed my lips. What. The. Heck?

My mother slammed shut the hood of the truck and walked to my open door. "At least that's one problem solved. I'll follow you home. Just to make sure it doesn't stall out again."

"Thanks," I said, puzzled. I'd still have to take the pickup into the garage. It had stalled for a reason.

She followed me to my garage apartment beside my aunt's house and waited in the driveway until I'd unlocked the upstairs door and trudged inside.

Through the window, I watched her drive away, a roller-coastery, fluttery feeling in

35

my stomach. It didn't take a fortune teller to predict life was about to go sideways.

THREE

I yawned, flipped the *Closed* sign to *Open*, and slumped behind the paranormal museum's glass counter. Frost laced the windows overlooking the sidewalk, empty of shoppers at nine a.m.

Grabbing a feather duster from a hook beneath the register, I did a quick walk-through, making sure I hadn't missed anything that needed cleaning. But no spider webs hung from the glossy black crown molding. No dust bunnies congregated on the checkerboard linoleum floor. No haunted photos tilted, askew, on the wall. The secret bookcase door was firmly closed.

I flipped on the twinkle lights in the Gallery room. Since it was the holiday season, I'd switched my sales inventory to relevant paranormal-themed items, namely holiday fairies. They hung from the ceilings on gauzy wings, perched in the windows on piles of fake snow, posed on tall, black-painted pedestals.

Walking beneath the mistletoe into the Fortune Telling Room, I straightened an antique Ouija board on the circular table. I unlatched the door of the spirit cabinet that could hold two grown men, and the hinges squeaked alarmingly.

Hands on my hips, I turned slowly, satisfied. Vintage tarot cards, their colors faded by time, lay artfully spread beneath a glass case. I whisked the duster over the antique Houdini poster.

We were ready for business.

Returning to my post behind the counter, I stared at my computer screen and yawned again. It's all well and good to be running around at three a.m. until you have to go to work the next morning — technically, the same morning.

I pressed *play* for the nth time and watched the burning of the Christmas Cow. The webcams had been on time lapse, so it was a case of now you see it, now you don't. One moment, there was the Christmas Cow, a big red bow and papier-mâché cowbell around its neck. A blur of action. Then fire. Lots of fire. The cow builders had doused the straw with some sort of fire-retardant, but the cow had gone up fast anyway.

GD Cat sauntered across the keyboard and lashed his ebony tail in my face.

"Oh, come on. You only do this when I'm looking at something important." I lifted him off the computer.

He whipped his head around and bit my hand, but only lightly. It was a reminder that he was boss, even if I was the one who filled his kibble bowl.

"Go chase a ghost," I said. "GD" stands for ghost detecting. The cat and the museum had been a package deal. Our relationship was wary, but the customers liked him, so in spite of his bad attitude he got to stay.

The black cat hissed and leapt off the counter. Tail high, he stalked to the giant papier-mâché cave Leo and I had built in one corner of the room. Gryla the Icelandic Christmas Ogre peered menacingly through a crack in the cave wall.

Leo and I had gone all-out with displays of paranormal holiday traditions. The only way I was going to earn a decent living off this museum was if I got repeat customers. And that meant I had to change up the exhibits.

To the main room, I'd added a display of vintage postcards featuring Krampus the Christmas Demon, a collection of antique Italian Christmas Witch marionettes, and the pièce de résistance . . . San Benedetto's haunted cowbells. They hung on an iron frame in a triangular, almost Christmas-tree shape on the wall between the Fortune Telling Room and the Gallery. The bells were reputed to bring death to those who heard their ringing. Getting my hands on them had been a major score.

I returned to the beginning of the webcam video and clicked *play/pause, play/pause* in quick succession to try to catch the gingerbread men in action. But all I saw were quickly vanishing silhouettes. Even Santa was elusive. The webcam had been set on a pole above the gazebo, so there were no images of Mr. Eldrich's murder. Part of me was relieved, because I really didn't want to watch someone die. The other part of me was annoyed the video wasn't more helpful.

On the positive side, my mom was in full view of the webcam the whole time. So at least she was off the hook for the murder.

The bell over the door jingled, and I looked up.

Two youngish women wearing long red Santa Hats with bells on the ends stood grinning in front of the counter.

I adjusted my *Paranormal Museum* hoodie. "Welcome to the paranormal museum."

"Two tickets please," one said, glancing

40

around. "Where's the cat?"

I pointed to the "cave," where GD huddled at Gryla's feet. He rolled onto his back, stretching with that eerie plasticity cats have, and then walked to the door of the Fortune Telling Room. He paused, one paw raised, and his ears swiveled. I sighed. The show-off.

The good-for-business show-off.

"Oooh." One of the women forked over the cash. "Does he see a ghost?"

"Cats are believed to be able to see spirits," I said, vague. I was agnostic about GD's abilities. How do you prove a cat is looking at a ghost anyway? It was *possible* ghosts existed, but I hadn't seen strong evidence. Though weird things did go on at the museum that I couldn't explain. Truthfully, I didn't want to explain the phenomena. The mystery is what makes the paranormal fun.

Giggling, the two women hurried after GD.

I scrubbed my hands across my face, trying to wake myself up.

The bookcase between the museum and Fox and Fennel, Adele's tea room next door, swiveled open. Adele minced in, carrying a delicate cup of tea.

She set the tea on the counter and ad-

41

justed the top of her pristine white apron. "I thought you could use some caffeine after last night."

"I thought tea didn't have much caffeine."

"It depends on the tea. I loaded yours with sugar."

"You are a true friend." I took a sip and grimaced, feeling my teeth rotting. "I take it you couldn't get anything out of Dieter."

She jammed her fists on the hips of her powder-blue skirt. "He wouldn't say a word. Can you believe it? To me! He went on and on about confidentiality and the sacredness of the bet."

"Give it time. You'll make him crack."

"I'm not so sure. How's your mom doing?" Then Adele blinked, looking past my shoulder, and I followed her gaze to the window.

My ex, Mason, walked by on the sidewalk outside. Smiling, he looped one brawny arm around the shoulders of a slim woman with long titian locks. His other hand clasped a young boy's, and I felt my own smile waver.

"Are you all right?" Adele asked quietly.

"Sure I am."

"Because you don't look all right."

"No, really, I'm fine." I blew out my breath. "Mason and I are over. We did the right thing, and I'm happy for him — for all

42

of them. It's just . . ." Elbows braced on the counter, I smushed my head into my hands. "This is so embarrassing."

"I doubt that."

"It's only . . . I don't know. Am I doomed to die alone? I'm over thirty. My odds of finding someone are smaller than they are of getting killed by a terrorist."

Outside, Mason paused on the sidewalk and said something to Jordan and his mother.

"First," Adele said, "that statistic has been thoroughly debunked. Second, you're not quoting it right even if it were true. And third, since when did anything you did ever follow the statistical norm?" She laid her hand on mine. "It's normal to feel this way after a breakup. But you'll move on."

"I have moved on. I'm not pining for Mason. I just haven't . . ." I gestured helplessly. "Moved *on.*" It was the holly jolly season, my favorite time of year. My mother was safe and my museum was booming. So why was dread dripping off me like the Ghost of Christmas Doom?

"I can ask Dieter to set you up with one of his friends."

I made a face. "No thanks." I'd met Dieter's friends. Most were red-nosed octogenarians whose greatest passion was the track.

Mason, now alone on the sidewalk, turned toward the museum and nodded to me through the glass.

My heart jumped, and I gave him a small wave.

"Then you're going to have to stop feeling sorry for yourself and get out there," she said, frowning at the window.

"Thanks for the pep talk."

"You're welcome." Casting one last glance at the window, Adele turned on her heel and slipped through the bookcase. It glided shut.

Mason strode into the museum, his brow furrowed with concern. "I heard about your mom. Is she okay?" His broad shoulders strained the seams of his vintage motorcycle jacket. With his blond hair in a ponytail, he looked the part of a biker.

"More angry than scared," I said, happier than I wanted to admit that he'd stopped in. "She wasn't hurt."

"How are you doing?" His Nordic-blue eyes bored into mine, and his voice seemed to deepen.

"I'm a little worried about my mom. You remember what happened the last time she found a body."

One corner of his mouth curved upward.

44

"If memory serves, *you* found that body at the harvest fair."

"The point is," I said quickly, "I'm afraid she might get involved and put herself in danger."

One of his pale brows lifted. "So you're going to do it for her?"

"I didn't say that," I said primly.

Mason shook his head. "Don't make me worry about you. This has been hard enough."

Warmth crept up my cheeks. "How are things with Belle?"

"She's helping me out at the shop when she's not working at the salon. She's determined to earn enough money to move out."

I straightened. "She's leaving?" Had I made a mistake breaking up with him because of Anabelle, his blast-from-the-past ex-girlfriend and the mother of his newly discovered child? No, I hadn't. We'd needed to step apart to gain perspective. I didn't regret that.

"Belle and I aren't a couple, you know," he said. "Even though we're living together."

"Would you like to be?" And why had I asked that? I fought the desire to squirm.

He looked out the window. "We could be."

My heart meteored to earth.

He met my gaze. "But I can't help thinking about someone else."

And then my pulse began banging double-time. "Oh." We'd broken up to get clarity, and now I was more confused than ever. *No regrets, no regrets.* "Well. I'm sure things will work out for the best."

He hesitated, as if struggling for something to say. "How's your old truck doing lately?"

"Great." It wasn't really a lie. My truck had worked fine that morning. Things were complicated enough without Mason doing work on my vintage pickup. But I didn't want to talk about that, so I changed the subject to the first thing I could think of. "How did you and Belle meet, anyway?"

He smiled. "She was trying to steal my car."

"You're joking," I said, laughing in spite of myself.

"Nope. We were both pretty young and not too smart. Fortunately, neither of us are those people anymore."

"None of us are."

"Let me know if you need anything. Anything," he said with quiet emphasis as he left the museum.

The Paranormal Museum was starting to get crowded, and I shook off my funk. Life was good. My Christmas exhibit was draw-ing in the customers and it was only Thursday. Typically, things didn't really start to hop until Fridays and weekends, when people were wine tasting.

A woman I recognized from Ladies Aid asked about a set of Christmas ogre salt and pepper shakers. Deeming them reasonably priced, she bought the Icelandic Christmas fiends. I wrapped them in tissue paper. The ogress's black eyes seemed to wink maliciously. Hurriedly, I swaddled her in tissue, tucked her into the bag, and handed the shakers across the glass counter.

The bell over the door jingled and my assistant, Leo, ambled into the museum. A quasi-Goth, today he wore a black motorcycle jacket, black jeans, and a black *Paranormal Museum* T-shirt. He got the tees for free, and he hated doing laundry, so his collection of museum T-shirts was nearly as big as mine.

I sat up straighter on my seat. "What are you doing here today? You're not scheduled to work until tomorrow."

"I'm on winter break, and you promised to give me the low-down on what happened last night." He raked a hand through his lanky, dyed-black hair. "Did you get the webcam video I sent?"

"Yes, thanks. Hopefully the police will be able to get more out of it than I did. All I

47

saw were shadows, and they disappeared as quickly as they appeared."

"There's a good shot of the flaming arrows. So what happened?"

Quickly, I told him about the night of the flaming arrows, which now that I thought about it sounded like a bad Bruce Lee film.

A bell jingled softly, and I glanced toward the door. It was firmly closed. My flesh pebbled.

A flash went off, someone snapping a picture of our cowbell exhibit.

A lean woman in a tracksuit wandered to the counter. She brandished a porcelain fairy ornament. "I'll take it."

"Here," Leo said, "I'll wrap it up." He shot me a sideways glance. "If it's okay with you, I could use the extra hours."

And I could use the extra manpower. The Christmas season was delightfully even busier than I'd expected. I rang up the purchase while Leo wrapped the fairy, set it in its box, and bagged it.

"Thank you," I said to the customer. "Come again!"

"I'm telling all my friends about this place. What fun! And cursed cowbells!" Laughing, she sashayed out the door.

"A lot of people are talking about those cowbells after last night." Leo shifted his weight. "You don't think there's really a curse?"

Seated on the barstool, I gripped my knees. "No, because there's no such thing as curses." Though my truck breaking down had been weird. "And even if there was, Herb did his usual binding spell on the bells. For whatever that's worth."

The bookcase to the tea shop slid open and my other best friend, Harper Caldarelli, strode in, the heels of her boots clicking on the checkerboard floor. She was dressed in her financial adviser gear — a thick wool coat over her navy pinstripe pantsuit. It was all good quality, because her practice was successful. "I heard about the Christmas Cow," she said. "Is your mom okay?"

"She's fine," I said. "She was upset, but she wasn't hurt."

"I can imagine," Harper said. "Especially with the cowbell curse business as well."

"I know." Leo braced his elbows on the counter. "They were just talking about it at the college."

I glanced at him. "I thought you said you wanted extra hours because you're on winter break?"

"I had to stand in line to pick up next semester's schedule," he explained. "Between the Christmas Cow death and the cursed cowbells reappearing after thirty-plus years, there's a major freak-out in progress."

"Guys," I said, "the cowbells are just good fun. And the bells didn't *reappear*. Herb got them at the mayor's charity auction and sold them to me." Unsurprisingly, city hall had lost interest in the bells, which had been gathering dust in a storage room for decades.

Harper shook her head, her long mahogany hair cascading over her slim shoulders. "I'm not so sure about fun. The sound of bells is a classic death omen. You can find it in cultures all over the world."

"But cowbells?" I lowered my voice. "The curse is a good story, and the bells tie in with the Christmas theme —"

"They're not tied to Christmas," Harper insisted.

"The Swedes hung them in that metal frame shaped like a Christmas tree." I motioned toward the bells hanging on the wall. "All bells are holiday-esque. Besides, the Christmas Cow is erected in December, and the cowbells are connected to the cow."

"Right, because every member of the committee that started up the Christmas Cow tradition in San Benedetto back in the '80s died."

"Everyone dies." I dragged my damp palm down the thigh of my jeans. "The mortality rate in San Benedetto and everywhere else is 100 percent."

"But they all died within a year," Leo said. "And according to legend, they all heard the cowbells before they kicked the bucket."

"I know," I said, motioning to the triangle of bells and the small cardboard placard beside them. "I've typed up the story of the curse and the deaths."

I'd been promoting the cowbells like crazy. They'd been donated by our sister city in Sweden to kick off San Benedetto's own Christmas Cow tradition, a misguided homage to our sister city's giant straw Yule goat. One of the committee members had trekked all the way to Sweden to collect the bells, drink mulled wine, and shake hands. This connection of the bells to the cow, which had since become one of San Benedetto's most important tourist attractions, made the cursed cowbells kind of a big deal.

"Hey, have you got a Christmas gift for Adele yet?" Harper asked, her gaze darting to the closed bookcase. "I'm totally stuck. What do you get the woman who has everything?"

I gazed pointedly at Harper's expensive boots, designer suit, perfect hair. She *was* the woman who had everything. "Gee, I don't know."

The wall phone rang. I fumbled it, then managed to get it to my ear. "Good morning! Paranormal Museum."

"Maddie, this is Penny," the president of the Wine and Visitors Bureau whispered.

"What's up?"

"You have to come to the Visitors Bureau. Now."

My brows drew together. "What's wrong?"

"Your mother is here."

I went cold. "Is she all right?"

"She's running amok," Penny hissed. "Get over here. Now!" She hung up.

I stared at the old-fashioned receiver. Running? Amok? Neither sounded like my mother. "Sorry, Harper. I have to go to the Wine and Visitors Bureau. Leo, could you —"

"No problem," he said. "I don't have to be anywhere until three."

I checked my watch. It was eleven thirty. "Thanks." I hurried through the bookcase into the tea room and down the bamboo-plank hallway to the alley. My red pickup sat parked beside a dumpster.

I slid onto its front seat. Murder by arrow, cursed Christmas cowbells, and my mother on some sort of rampage at the Wine and

Visitors Bureau. I gripped the cold steering wheel. What the devil was going on?

The truck turned over smoothly, and I blew out my breath. At least my transportation was working normally again.

I drove down the alley and turned the corner onto Main Street. People milled in the park and ogled the remains of the cow. I wrinkled my nose. Even when reduced to ashes, the stupid cow attracted crowds. I don't believe in magic powers, but mentally I willed the gawkers out of the park and into my museum.

At the edge of downtown, I turned into the parking lot of a brick building twined with grapevines. A miniature "educational" vineyard grew beside the parking lot. A few orange and brown and amber leaves clung to the low vines trained along wires. Past the educational vineyard, San Benedetto's real vineyards spread across the flat-as-a-pancake landscape.

A snowman made of metal wine barrel hoops greeted visitors at the entry to the Bureau. A wreath dripping with miniature wine bottles hung from the arched wooden door.

I walked inside. A dozen middle-aged men and women bellied up to the tasting bar. A man with wispy white hair and a *Visitors*

Bureau apron poured. He kept casting nervous glances at the open office door.

". . . knows you were an almost-Olympic archer." My mother's voice cascaded from the open door. "That doesn't mean you killed the man."

I hustled past round tables filled with wine paraphernalia — cork screws and pewter wine aerators and *Kiss My Glass* T-shirts — and stepped inside Penny's office, closing the door behind me.

Penny, a roundish woman in a Christmas sweater and green Christmas-light earrings, shot me a grateful look. "Maddie! What are you doing here?" Her eyes widened with feigned surprise.

Somehow she'd managed to call me without my mother knowing. Clever.

"I came by for more winery maps," I said. "Hi, Mom."

"Madelyn," my mother said stiffly. She plucked at the white pashmina scarf encircling the collar of her camel-colored pea coat.

"What's going on?" I asked. "I heard something about archery."

Penny exhaled heavily. "As I was explaining to your mother, I have no reason to want Bill dead."

"Of course you don't," my mother said.

54

"I don't." Penny stared over her reading glasses.

"I'm quite certain you didn't kill him," my mom said. "You care about San Benedetto too much. But the investigation will go much quicker if everyone simply lays their motives and whereabouts for last night on the table."

"You're only trying to get me to confess," Penny said. "But I have nothing to confess to. Maddie, tell her."

The two women glared at me.

"I don't . . . um . . . Were you really an Olympic archer?" I asked.

"Almost." The corners of Penny's mouth turned down. "I learned to shoot when I was in scouts and never stopped, but I didn't make the cut. And I certainly didn't assault the Christmas Cow. It's our second biggest attraction next to the wineries!"

Only for one month of the year, I thought sourly. My paranormal museum was second biggest the other eleven months.

"Our bureau paid for a special wine and cow promotion," Penny continued, her frown deepening. "It sounded better when our marketing consultant came up with the idea."

"You were at the planning meetings for the Christmas Cow," my mother said. "And

55

there was definite tension between you and Bill. Why?"

"There's no tension." Penny shook her head. "Or there *was* no tension. Bill was a principled man. Even when I disagreed with him, I respected his thinking. He followed the rules. And there was nothing I disagreed with him enough to kill him over."

"But someone did," I said.

"It must have been a terrible accident," Penny said. "I almost feel sorry for whoever shot him. They'll carry that guilt to their grave." A tall stack of brochures slipped sideways and she made an unsuccessful grab for them. A dozen glossy brochures scattered across the tiled floor.

I bent and picked them up. "Maybe it *was* an accident. But there's a chance it was deliberate — someone could have taken advantage of the chaos." Which meant they'd have to have known when the attack was scheduled to happen. Someone on the inside of the gingerbread gang? I shook my head. An accident did seem more likely.

"If you're looking for suspects," Penny said, "don't look at me. There are plenty of better candidates."

"Oh?" I asked. "Who?"

"Try Dean, for starters."

"Dean Pinkerton?" my mom asked.

56

"You heard about the squabble over Dean selling raw milk?"

My mother nodded.

"Well, guess who was behind the lobbying to shut him down?"

"Bill Eldrich?" I said. "Why would he care if someone was selling raw milk?"

"Rules." Penny sighed. "I only hope they didn't get him killed."

FOUR

I leaned against my truck, enjoying the warmth from the engine. A cold breeze fluttered the dried leaves on the grapevines. Three tore free and whispered across the Wine and Visitors Bureau parking lot.

"I know you said you don't think Penny was involved in Mr. Eldrich's death," I said to my mother. "After all, she's . . . Penny. But could she have done it?"

"Simply because she likes grape-cluster earrings doesn't mean she's incapable of murder." My mother resettled her pashmina beneath the collar of her pea coat. "But no, I don't believe she committed the crime. All the attackers were fairly spry."

"Then why — ?"

"Because I want to know why Bill annoyed Penny. And because she's got her ear to the ground. She did give us that tip on Dean Pinkerton. Now let's go talk to Dieter."

"Adele's working on him."

"Their relationship is new. I wouldn't want our investigation to put pressure on it. No, we'll talk to him."

Mulish, I folded my arms across my chest. "I'm not investigating, and you shouldn't either. Mom, let the police handle this."

"Don't be silly. Now are you coming or not?"

"Not." If I encouraged her, she'd only get herself into more trouble. I climbed into the pickup. "I've got to get back to the museum. And Detective Slate . . ." I turned the key in the ignition.

Nothing happened.

I turned the key again.

"Problem?" my mom asked.

"My truck's not starting." I *knew* I should have taken it to the garage first thing, even though it was working this morning.

She gave me a long look. "I thought you were going to take it to the garage first thing?"

"I was. But then I slept late, and . . ." My stomach rumbled.

She checked her slim gold watch. "Then it looks like you're fated to come with me to the taqueria."

I brightened. "Taqueria?"

"It's Thursday. Dieter will be there."

I slid from the truck and shut the door. "How do you know where Dieter will be on Thursdays?"

"I keep my ear to the ground too. Dieter's installing a new water heater in the kitchen."

As long as there was a burrito in my near future, I didn't care what he was installing. "Fine." I got into my mom's Lincoln and she piloted the car into downtown San Benedetto.

"I know it's superstitious of me," she said, "but I always thought you'd be safe in your father's truck. He loved it and you so much, part of me thinks if he's anywhere, he's watching over you in that truck."

"It hasn't been very lucky lately," I pointed out. But a part of me had thought the same thing. Clearly, I'd been wrong.

We drove past the park. The crowd gaping at the cow's metal frame had, if anything, grown.

"I knew I should have pushed harder not to build the cow this year," my mother fretted. She shook her head, her squash-blossom earrings swaying. Her face was drawn, and I bit my lip, studying her.

"How could you have stopped it?" I asked. "It's tradition."

"That's what Bill Eldrich said. And nearly everyone in Ladies Aid, plus their husbands.

It makes me wonder if the cow is what's really cursed."

My mother didn't believe in curses any more than I did. The attack at the cow must have hit her harder than she'd let on.

We drove past the museum. Three people, blowing into their hands, waited in line outside the door, and my heart leaped. "There's a line in front of the museum!"

"Of course there is, dear. It's your museum, after all. Why wouldn't people stand in line for your Christmas display?"

"Thanks for that, but —"

"The Sacramento paper did list you as the second most unusual Christmas attraction in the area."

Second to the Christmas Cow, naturally. "It's a small paper, and stop changing the subject."

"Changing the subject from what, dear?" she asked innocently.

I twisted in my seat. Yes, they were definitely lined up for the museum and not Mason's motorcycle shop.

A biker with a death wish whipped in front of my mother's car, and she stepped hard on the brake. I gasped, clutching the door handle.

My mother *tsked*. "People really need to be more careful."

61

Gripping the dash, I watched as the biker parked in front of Mason's shop. Motorcycles were Mason's life. He'd tried to teach me to ride but the bike had terrified me, made me feel out of control. It was just one more reason why we were not compatible.

"Does Leo want a burrito?" my mother asked, diverting me.

"Oh, right." I dug my cell phone from my pocket and called him.

"Paranormal Museum," he said, breathless.

"Hi, I just drove past on the way to the taqueria, and I saw the line outside. Should I double back now and help, or do you want me to pick up a burrito for you first?"

"It's cool here. Carnitas burrito, black beans, hot salsa, and a side of that green sauce for my chips."

"Got it. See you soon." I didn't need to write it down. It was Leo's regular order. "I guess we're going to the taqueria," I said to my mom.

She smiled.

It wasn't quite noon when we breezed inside the restaurant, so the line along the glass counter was short. The cramped space smelled of meat and cheese and frying onions. My mouth watered.

My mother hailed the owner behind the

counter, a middle-aged Hispanic woman with freckles and short waves of dark hair. "Good morning, Marta."

Marta smiled sympathetically. "Fran, how are you doing? Terrible news about Bill."

"Tragic," my mother said. "Is Dieter around?"

Marta motioned us behind the counter and toward the open kitchen door. She turned to a customer, then turned back. "Be careful, Fran. They say bad things come in threes."

My mom nodded, grim, and passed through the red-tiled entryway.

There was no way Dieter was going to tell my mother anything. But I followed her into the tiled kitchen because I'd never been in there before, and I was all about new kitchen experiences. Since most of the cooking was done up front, by the counter, I was curious about what was kept in the back.

Two industrial-sized refrigerators lined one wall. A young woman stacked plates in the dishwasher. Dieter lay on his back beside a rusted water heater. His T-shirt had ridden up, exposing a tanned washboard stomach. He wrenched out a pipe.

"Hello, Dieter," my mom said.

He jerked upright and sprang to his feet, tugging down his shirt. "Mrs. Kosloski. Hi.

What are you doing here? Is there a problem with the drainage at the house?"

"It's working like a dream. I need to know if there was anyone who picked last night as the night the Christmas Cow would be set on fire."

Dieter splayed his hand across the chest of his ripped tee. "Mrs. Kosloski, you know I can't talk about my clients."

"A man's been killed," I said. "Don't you want to help solve that crime without getting the police involved?"

He glanced at me and shook his shaggy head. "I'm sorry, but how do I know this won't get back to the police?"

My mother straightened. "Madelyn is not a narc."

My mouth tightened. I so totally was a narc. This was a murder investigation!

Dieter's schoolboy expression turned sorrowful. "Can't risk it. Client confidentiality."

"What a shame." My mother fingered her silver necklace. "I was hoping I wouldn't have to tell Adele about . . ."

He paled. "Mrs. Kosloski. You wouldn't."

"I'd prefer not to."

Tell Adele about what? My gaze ping-ponged between them.

"Please," he said.

"The names?"

His shoulders slumped. "One name. But you can't tell the cops."

My mother smiled. "Of course not. Unless, of course, he's guilty of murder."

"She," Dieter said. "Belle Rodale."

I felt the blood drain from my face. Belle, the mother of Mason's child. The woman we'd broken up over after she'd returned to his life.

"Thank you, Dieter," my mom said. "We'll keep this between us."

Numb, I followed her from the taqueria. "Belle. We can't . . ."

How could I interrogate my ex-boyfriend's once and present girlfriend?

"Mom, we can't talk to her about this."

"I understand this is awkward for you, Madelyn. But we're all adults, and you broke up with Mason for a reason."

Because he'd discovered he had a kid, and the kid and his mother were living out of a van. Of course he'd invited them to move into his house. And then I'd become an interloper; his son deserved a shot at an intact family. But I'd never really explained all that to my mom.

She crossed the street and I trailed after her.

"What do you know about this young

woman?" she asked, brisk.

"She's working at the hair salon." Which apparently my mom already knew, because we were currently beelining for the squat, cinderblock building. The phone rang in my jacket pocket, and I pulled it out.

Leo.

I rolled my eyes toward the gray sky. Augh, I'd forgotten the burritos. "Hi, Leo. Sorry, we got a bit delayed."

"It's okay, the crowd's slowed down. But there's a newspaper reporter here asking about the cowbells."

My mom strode ahead of me.

"Can you talk to him?" I asked. "You know the story of the bells. It's on the placard."

"Are you sure?" he asked.

"Yeah. They're only cowbells. See if you can promote some of the other holiday exhibits."

"Sure thing." He hung up.

I hurried after my mom. If she was going to interrogate poor Belle, I had to run interference. "What do you have over Dieter?" I asked, catching up to her.

"I shouldn't say, and you don't want to know."

"Adele's my friend —"

"And I wouldn't keep a secret that might

66

hurt her. Trust me."

Uncertain, I gnawed my bottom lip. I did trust my mother. Usually. I grabbed the glass door to the salon. "Let me do the talking in there."

My mom's cornflower-blue eyes widened with surprise. "Are you sure?"

No. Heck, no. "Yeah, I'm sure."

I opened the door, and my mom breezed inside.

Hair chemical fumes burned my nostrils, and I blinked rapidly. Half the chairs were filled — two women getting haircuts, another with her hair in strips of silver foil, and two more imprisoned beneath hair dryers. All the ladies, wrapped in black plastic capes, fell silent and stared. At least I think they were silent. All I could hear was the roar of hair dryers.

Belle's long auburn hair was done up in a loose bun. Wisps of hair fell artfully past her slender neck. She wore a pink apron over her jeans and T-shirt. Adjusting the settings on one of the dryers, she glanced up and saw me, and her expression wavered. She pasted on a smile. "Hi! I'll be right with you." She fiddled some more with the dryer, then walked toward us and stopped beside the cashier's desk. "Have you got an appointment?"

"Um," I said, "no. Belle, have you got a minute? It's important."

"Important enough to bring your mother?" she asked, the lines around her eyes deepening.

"It's important," I repeated.

Another stylist looked up from her work on the silver foil. "I've got you."

Belle angled her chin toward a curtained exit. "This way."

We brushed through the pink curtains and into a dingy kitchen area. Belle leaned one hip against the sink. "What's going on?"

I swallowed, heart pounding. Just get it over with. "Word on the street is that you won this year's Christmas Cow bet."

Her expression shuttered. "Did Dieter tell you that?"

"No," I lied. "Who knows how these things get out? So, is it true then?"

She compressed her lips. "No offense, but I don't think my finances are any of your business."

"No," I said. "I guess they aren't. But . . ."

"But what?"

But someone was killed last night. And where were you at the time of the murder? Oh yeah, with my ex-boyfriend. No, this wasn't weird. Not. At. All.

"Look, I know this is awkward," she

continued. "This is a small town, and we're going to keep bumping into each other. And I appreciate the way you stepped out of Mason's life when things were challenging for us. And you've stayed out."

"Belle —"

"But Mason isn't your problem."

My cheeks burned. "That's not why I'm here."

She lifted a single, dark eyebrow. "Then why?"

"Because a man was killed last night at the Christmas Cow, and we need to know . . . if you might have any information."

"I don't."

"Okay." I stared at her, knowing there was more to learn and stumped about how to get it out of her. "Well, sorry I bothered you."

My mom followed me into the salon. "Interesting technique."

"Thanks," I said shortly.

A portly, elderly woman raised her dryer and waggled her fingers at my mother. "Fran!"

"Izzy!" My mom strode to her and clasped her hand. "I heard you were under the weather."

I waited, tapping my foot and smarting

69

with embarrassment. Had I really expected Belle to confide in me?

"I'm feeling better now," the woman beneath the dryer said. "Is it true you were at the Christmas Cow when Bill Eldrich was killed?"

My mom nodded.

"Did you see who did it?"

"I'm afraid they wore masks," my mom said.

"What a terrible thing," Izzy said. "Some high school kid just ruined Bill's life and his own, and his parents' too."

"Or college kid," I said, thoughtful. The gingerbread gang had a certain sophistication beyond your typical high school prank. On the other hand, high school had probably evolved since I'd left it.

The woman in the silver foil swiveled her chair toward us. "Are you involved with the Wine and Visitors Bureau?" she asked me. She looked to be in her mid-forties, but florescent lights and plastic black capes are never flattering. I assumed from the highlighting that she was a blond, though it was tough to tell beneath the hair goo.

"Associate member," I said. "Paranormal Museum."

"Me too!" She stretched out her hand, and I walked across the stained linoleum to shake it. Her grip was crushing, and I schooled myself not to wince. "I'm Kendra. Kendra Breathnach. I just joined. I heard about the cow and the accidental death. Terrible."

"We don't know it's accidental," I said.

"Is that your mother?" She nodded toward my mom, now bent over Izzy.

"Mmm hmm. She was guarding the cow when it happened."

"How awful for her. I can't imagine. I mean, the cow attack — you expect that, don't you? But for someone to get caught in the crossfire."

"You said you're an associate member?" I asked. "If you're not a vintner, what do you do?"

"I'm a developer. My company is building an agrihood."

"An agrihood?"

She laughed. "Sorry about the jargon. An agrihood is a community centered around a working farm. This being San Benedetto, we're building it around a working communal vineyard. So instead of farm to table, it's vineyard to table."

"Wow. That sounds interesting." I would never own a vineyard, but maybe someday I'd be able to move out of my aunt's garage apartment and get a real house. The agrihood idea charmed me.

"The vineyard will be managed by a nonprofit. It will also run educational programs for local students and aspiring vintners. The Wine and Visitors Bureau is helping us out with that side of the project. So I thought, why not become an associate member?"

"Where's this agrihood being built?"

"We just bought the old CW Vineyards. They had an even hundred acres, and it fit well with our needs — not too far out of San Benedetto."

I grimaced. It was stupid to resist change, but I hated seeing vineyards torn down for homes. "CW had a lovely old tasting room," I said. "A Gothic Revival house."

Her expression tightened. "Don't tell me you're one of those no-growth people?"

"I guess I prefer slow growth. It's easier to adapt to."

"And unfair to those who need places to live now. But we'll be keeping the tasting room. The nonprofit will use it as their base of operations." She leaned forward, bracing one elbow on the arm of the swivel chair. "I hear you were the one who solved the crime connected to CW. Is it true?"

My lungs compressed. I'd nearly gotten my two best friends killed in the process. "I only handed over some information to the police."

"Don't tell me you're amateur sleuthing the Christmas Cow death? Because that must have been an accident."

"If so, the kids involved need to come forward."

Kendra sat back in her chair. "Whoever accidentally shot Mr. Eldrich will have to suffer with the weight of that death for the rest of their life. I doubt they'll be a danger to anyone else. Jail seems unnecessary."

"I dunno. I think we need to pay for our mistakes, clean our own slate so we can move forward." If the death was in fact an accident, a part of me felt bad for the person who'd shot that arrow. But I couldn't imagine living with that guilt and not at least trying for absolution.

The fluorescent light glinted off the foil in Kendra's hair. "We all pay, one way or another."

I was afraid she might be right.

FIVE

I was back where I'd started — another morning in the museum. Fog pressed against the windows. Shoppers, shoulders hunched against the chill, hurried past on the sidewalk outside. The holiday rush kept me moving, handing out a steady stream of tickets and brochures.

GD, ambivalent, spent the morning perched on the old-fashioned cash register. His tail lashed the keys whenever I rang up a sale.

I glared at the cat and handed a deck of tarot cards to a college-aged customer. "Happy holidays!" I chirped.

"Thanks," she said. "My roommate will love these." She hesitated. "Why don't you have any exhibits in the museum about Santa? I mean — flying reindeer. Zipping through chimneys. That's totally paranormal, isn't it?"

"Did you see our Norse exhibit?" I

74

pointed to the corner where Gryla the Ogre's red eye peered from her cave. "Santa Claus is believed to have derived from the Norse god, Odin. Children left boots filled with carrots and hay by the chimney for his eight-legged horse. In exchange, Odin left gifts in their boots. It's believed to be one of the origin stories of Santa Claus."

"It's not really Santa, though. And the real Santa flies through the air with magic reindeer!"

"Well, yes, but Odin flew through the sky too."

She shrugged. "Whatever. I still think you should have more Santa."

GD sat up and washed his paws, a sure sign of boredom.

"Thanks for letting me know," I said. "We'll keep that in mind for next year." Note to self: more Santa. But the big guy was everywhere this time of year. His plastic form glowed on rooftops. His paper cutout grinned from windows. Replica Santa hats sprouted from people's heads like sunburnt mushrooms.

The customer left, banging the door shut. GD meowed.

"She couldn't have been that disappointed," I said to the cat and peeled off my down vest. All the visitors in the museum had raised the temperature. I jammed up the sleeves of my long-sleeved *Paranormal Museum* tee. "She bought a tarot deck."

The front door swung open and a narrow, wispy-haired man in a bow tie and coke-bottle glasses sidled into the museum. He peered over the top of the thick striped scarf wrapped high about his chin. His gaze darted nervously around the main room. "Are there any cops around?"

I sighed. "No, Herb. No cops."

Not that the cops had any interest in Herb. He just liked to think he was some Dudley Dangerous, a delusion that had been reinforced several months ago when he'd been questioned about a haunted wine press he'd sold me. Herb was a collector of paranormal items. Judging from his thread-bare clothes and the fact that he still lived with his mother, I didn't imagine it was a lucrative career.

He straightened. "Good. I heard about your involvement in the Christmas Cow investigation."

"I'm not involved in the Christmas Cow investigation."

He pressed a finger to the side of his nose. "Of course you're not."

GD leapt onto the counter and butted his head against Herb's arm. For some wacky reason, the cat loved him.

"So what can I do for you, Herb?" I asked.

A gray-haired woman approached the counter. "Excuse me. How much is that fairy in the window? The one with the sparkly tail?"

I stifled a laugh. Had she meant to riff on a '50s song? "Just a sec." I checked my computer. "It's $34.99."

Herb hissed. "Maddie."

"Why is it always ninety-nine cents?" the woman asked. "Do people think we're too dumb to figure out it's really thirty-five dollars?"

I shrugged. "The marketing gods dictate ninety-nine cents."

"Maddie, this is important." Herb tugged on his striped scarf.

"Sorry, Herb. Let me help this visitor."

She sighed. "All right. I'll take the fairy."

"I'll get it out of the window for you," I said, rising from my barstool.

"No, don't bother," she said. "I want to look around some more. I can get it when I'm ready." She strolled into the Fortune Telling Room.

I turned to Herb. "What's up?"

"It's the cowbells. I'm afraid this may be partially my fault."

"What's your fault?"

"The curse! I did my usual binding spell. But sometimes when you're dealing with really powerful curses or entities, you need to bring in the big guns. Now, I know a very reasonably priced specialist —"

I shook my head. "What are you talking about?"

"The man who was killed. They say he heard cowbells before he died —"

"They say? Who are they?"

Herb stopped petting GD and gripped the top of the register. "The curse has returned. Mr. Eldrich heard cowbells, and they foretold his doom."

"Of course he heard cowbells. He owned a dairy farm."

"But he heard *these* cowbells." Herb's knuckles whitened. "And the thing is . . ." He leaned over the counter and GD rubbed against his arm, depositing ebony hairs on his beige jacket. "Lately, I've been hearing them too."

"Your mother lives next to a cow pasture."

Herb straightened, affronted. "You're not taking this seriously."

I might not believe in curses or binding spells, but Herb did. Nodding, I dragged my attention back from the wandering customers and focused on him. "Okay," I said. "Let's logic this out. You say that the cowbell curse is working again because you didn't do a good enough job with your binding spell."

"My binding spell was fine," he said, his eyes gigantic behind his coke-bottle lenses. "I *said,* sometimes curses are bigger than my binding spells."

I forced myself not to roll my eyes. "But the cowbells weren't cursing anyone recently, even before you put the binding spell on them. So why would they start up now, thirty years after the last deaths and *after* you put on the binding spell?"

"Probably because they're here now, in the museum."

"What's wrong with my museum?"

"It's packed to the rafters with ghosts and haunted objects. They're probably triggering the bells' curse. Now, about that specialist —"

"Herb, thanks but no thanks." I wasn't going to waste my hard-earned ticket money on a bogus curse-removal service. The museum was doing well now, but who knew what sales would be like in January?

"I see," Herb said coldly. "You like having dangerous objects in your museum. They attract customers. But it's reckless. One man is already dead."

"Someone shot him with an arrow. It has

nothing to do with my cowbells."

"In the 1980s, every single member of the original Christmas Cow committee died within a twelve-month span. And each one heard the bells before passing. It's happening again. And your own mother is on the committee this year."

"Trust me. My mother is not going to be taken out by a curse," I said. The woman was unstoppable.

Herb's brows drew together. "I did notice an extra layer of protection in her aura. But that doesn't help the other committee members. What if the curse spreads beyond the committee to innocent San Benedetto civilians? These things have power. They grow." He braced his elbow on the counter and lowered his voice. "I'll make you a deal. If you hire my specialist, he'll owe me a favor, and I'll knock down the price of Dion Fortune's scrying mirror. Twenty-five hundred dollars."

"No, Herb."

"The mirror is a historic relic! Dion Fortune was one of the twentieth century's greatest occultists. Her book *Psychic Self-Defense* is a classic."

I nodded to the narrow, black-painted bookshelf behind me. "I know. I sell her books."

"Think how much more you'd sell if you had her mirror."

I had thought of it, and it still wasn't worth it. "Herb, I'm —"

"I smell bacon!" He scuttled to the bookcase and slipped through the secret door into Adele's tea room.

Nonplussed, I watched the bookcase slide closed.

My front door opened and Detective Slate strode inside. He smiled, putting his hands on his hips and parting his blue wool jacket. "The place looks busy. Am I catching you at a bad time?"

My annoyance vanished in a bubble of warmth. "Not if you don't mind being interrupted by customers."

"My ego can take it."

"What can I help you with?"

"I thought you might need my help."

Biting my lip, I looked away. Crumb. Had he heard about our interrogation-gone-awry at the beauty parlor yesterday? "Your help?"

"The cowbell curse."

His smile set my pulse galloping, but I cocked my head, baffled. Why would he be interested in my exhibit? "Are the police in the curse-removal business now?"

He laughed. "Hardly. But I've helped you crack some cold paranormal cases in the past. I thought the cowbells smelled like another one. Where are they, by the way?"

I pointed to the triangle of bells that hung between the doors to the Fortune Telling and Gallery rooms. He crossed over to them and peered at the placard hanging beside them.

Fairy in hand, the gray-haired woman returned to the counter. "I'll take it."

GD meowed his approval.

I pulled out a box from beneath the counter. "Would you like me to wrap it?"

"No. It's for me."

Slate came to stand behind her. Suddenly clumsy, I rang her up and boxed and bagged the fairy. "Happy holidays!"

We watched her depart.

"It's amazing what you've done with this place," Slate said.

"Thanks, but I had help." Because of Leo's web-building chops, our online business accounted for more than half our sales. But a part of me reveled in the compliment.

"Maddie, there's a rumor going around town that you might be investigating Mr. Eldrich's murder."

"What?" My voice went up two octaves.

"You've had some luck in the past."

Indignant, I pulled back my shoulders. It had been more than luck.

"But you need to stay out of this," he finished.

GD sat on his hind legs and walked his front legs up Slate's coat, leaving dusty paw prints on the navy wool.

"GD!"

The detective ruffled the cat's ebony fur. "It's all right. It's what cats do."

"It's too bad your partner doesn't share that attitude," I said. Detective Laurel Hammer and GD had a hate-hate relationship.

"In fairness," Slate said, "GD did run over her foot with a car."

"I don't think that's what happened."

He raised his brows.

"Well," I said quickly, "it was never proven. And you know that if I ever hear anything about either a hot or a cold case, I tell you. I've done it before." But I couldn't tell him about Belle, because that would mean ratting out Dieter. And besides, I couldn't imagine Belle committing arson just to win a bet. Unless it was a really big bet. She'd had money troubles before. And even if she did commit the arson, that was a far cry from murder. Unless she'd hit Bill Eldrich by accident?

Okay, first I would learn the size of the bet, and then I'd make the decision whether to tell Slate or not. I jammed my hands in the pockets of my *Paranormal Museum* hoodie.

"Riiight." He jerked his thumb toward the cowbells. "All I'm asking is that you confine your investigations to cold cases. And I'm happy to dig into the police files on your behalf."

"Thanks." I think. "You don't have files related to the cowbell curse, do you?"

"My understanding is although everyone on the committee died within a few months of each other, the deaths were all attributed to natural causes. Whether we have a file on any of the deaths would depend on if the police were called to the scene or not."

Those files could be interesting. I mentally shook myself. I was too busy to research cowbell curses. And besides, my wall placard about the historic bells was full enough. "Well, thanks."

"Stay safe." He ambled out the front door.

GD lightly bit my hand.

"Hey!" I rubbed the twin pale white dots on my skin.

The cat dropped from the counter and ducked into Gryla's papier-mâché cave. I'd been dissed and dismissed.

I walked into the Gallery and rearranged the window fairies, posing one blue fairy so it body-surfed down a slope of snow. The front bell jingled, and I hustled into the main room.

Leo squatted beside Gryla's cave and scratched GD behind his ears. He rose, a guilty expression on his young face.

"It's okay," I said. "I know GD likes you better than me." The cat only tolerated me because I fed him.

Leo pulled a rumpled newspaper from the back pocket of his black jeans. "Um, I guess you saw the newspaper article."

I stared at him blankly. "Newspaper article?"

"About the cowbell curse."

"Oh! That. I completely forgot." I needed to pick up a copy of the local paper. "Thanks for doing the interview."

"About that . . ." He handed me the paper and I unfolded it. "Looks like the story got picked up by the AP. It's all over the Internet."

I bounced on my toes. "Seriously?" I didn't know why anyone outside of San Benedetto would care, but the article could only boost our online sales. "I owe you lunch. And dessert."

He pursed his mouth.

"What's wrong?" I asked, scanning the article. "This is great publicity for the museum." We'd gone national!

Leo rubbed his head, ruffling his black hair. "Some people are upset about the article."

"Some people?"

"Mrs. Gale gave me an earful. She said I was making the town look foolish."

"No." I flapped my hand in a dismissive gesture. "The cowbell story is quirky. Maybe it's a bit silly, but the cowbells are an old story. No one believes in the curse today."

He looked hard at the black-and-white linoleum floor.

"What?" I asked.

"The thing is, a lot of people do believe."

A silver-haired tourist couple emerged from the Fortune Telling Room and examined the row of haunted photos, high on the wall.

"And I believe in Santa Claus," I said. "It's harmless fun."

"You believe in Santa?" Leo shook his head. "Never mind. None of my business."

"Not as a guy in red velvet who lives at the North Pole and says *ho-ho-ho*." I jiggled my stomach. "But yeah. I believe in Santa as a spirit of unbridled generosity. It's my single paranormal belief." I needed at least one if I was going to market the museum without feeling like a total fraud.

86

"This is different," he said. "People are freaking out. And the article sort of connects the curse to Bill Eldrich's death."

"Oh." That wasn't quite as much fun. But it explained why the story had been picked up by the AP, even if it was in their Strange News section. I rallied. "It'll blow over. Don't worry about it." I chucked him on the arm with the rolled newspaper. "No publicity is bad publicity, and everyone knows curses aren't real. This town has bigger fish to fry, like figuring out who killed Bill Eldrich."

"I thought it was an accident," Leo said. "Not murder. The police aren't calling it murder, are they?"

I lowered my chin and studied him. "I don't know if they think it was intentional or a college prank gone wrong."

He grimaced.

"A local college," I said. And there was only one local college — the junior college Leo attended. "I know you wouldn't be stupid enough to set the cow on fire, but keeping a secret on campus is pretty impossible. What have you heard?"

The tourist couple paused before a bronzed skull on a pedestal. The silver-haired woman reached for it, caught me watching, and snatched her hand away.

87

Leo raised his hands in a warding gesture. "Look, you're right. I wasn't involved. But if I heard anything, I sure wouldn't tell anyone."

"Leo, a man was killed. Even if it was an accident, the truth needs to come out."

"Yeah, and I know exactly how the police make that happen," he said bitterly. "They thought I was a killer once."

"And they caught the real killer."

He crossed his arms over his chest. "I'm not dealing with the police. Not after the way they treated me."

"Then tell me what you know."

"I like you, Maddie. So, no offense, but you'll just tell Slate."

My neck tensed. I didn't like my new reputation as a tattletale. "No I won't," I said, offended.

He gave me a skeptical look.

"There is such a thing as confidential informants," I said. "If you tell me something useful, sure, I'll pass it on. But I won't tell Slate where I got the information from if you don't want me to."

The tourist couple wandered into the Gallery.

"You swear?" Leo asked.

"Cross my heart, the works."

His shoulders slumped. "All right. But

only because I owe you one."

Leo didn't owe me anything, but now wasn't the time to bring that up.

"I heard there were some guys at school who were planning to take out the cow," he said.

"Any names?"

"Look, I don't know if they actually did it. Only that they were planning to. No one's taken credit for burning the cow."

Well, they wouldn't, since a man died in the process.

"I get it," I assured him. "At this point all we've got is talk, and that could have just been boasting. Or maybe they were really planning to attack the cow but someone else beat them to it. Who are these guys?"

Leo's chest rose, fell. "Craig. Craig Wilde. I don't know who else was in on the plan."

"Where can I find him?"

Leo yelped. "You said —"

"I won't tell him who told me," I said quickly. "Look, if they were involved in an accidental death, then it will be better for them if they come forward voluntarily. Maybe someone needs to tell them that. And if they weren't involved, then we need to know that too."

Leo blew out his breath. "Fine. I went to his house for a study group once. I'll get you the contact info."

"Thanks." I clapped him on his leather-clad shoulder. "We'll sort this out." I hoped. "What's Craig's number?"

Leo dug his phone from the pocket of his motorcycle jacket and scrolled through the contacts. "Here." He handed me the phone. Using my own cell phone, I dialed.

"Yeah?" a young man answered.

"Hi, this is Maddie Kosloski from the Paranormal Museum."

"Yeah?"

"I wanted to ask you about the Christmas Cow. May I —"

He hung up.

I stared at the phone. "Looks like I'll have to go to Plan B."

"What's Plan B?"

"My mom," I said, grim.

SIX

"I'm glad you called." One-handed, my mother zipped the collar of her ice-blue parka higher. She fiddled with the radio. The Lincoln had that new car smell even though it was four years old, and by the sparkle on the dashboard, I guessed it had been recently detailed.

"Umm hmm." I looked out the window, watching for house numbers on the rural road.

She slowed beside a barren orchard. Late morning fog twisted in the tops of the skeletal branches. "For a moment, I didn't think you were taking my investigation seriously."

"It's a murder investigation, and the police here are good at what they do."

"All the police? Or one detective in particular?"

My cheeks burned. "What's that supposed to mean?"

91

"You know quite well what I mean."

"The point is," I said, "if Mr. Eldrich's death was an accident, it's better if any students involved come forward on their own." And there was no one better at making someone squirm than my mother.

She adjusted the seat belt across her chest. "And I suppose it doesn't hurt that I happen to know Craig's parents."

I hadn't known she knew them, but I should have. Ladies Aid had its tentacles everywhere.

"You need me," she said, "especially since that truck of yours has gotten unreliable."

"I just figured you had a bigger stake in this than I did."

"So you *need* me."

"Well, yeah. You don't — there it is." Black numbers on a white fence: 8052.

She turned at the gate and her tires crunched down the gravel drive.

"What can you tell me about Craig?" I asked.

"Not much. I know his parents, not him."

"How do you know them?" We bumped past a pasture and clusters of milling cows.

Her blue eyes widened. "Madelyn, you should know them too. His mother, Tabitha, is on the town council. His father, Tom, is in the Dairy Association. How can you expect your museum to succeed if you don't build relationships within the community?"

"I've been kind of busy with the museum," I muttered, my shoulder bouncing against the car door as she swerved to avoid a rut in the road.

"That isn't enough."

I blew out my breath. "I know, you're right."

"But I will admit, your obsession with the museum is paying off. Your Christmas display was a stroke of genius. Who would have thought those silly cowbells would make national news?"

"So you're not upset about the bells?"

"Why would I be?"

"I heard some people thought the article made the town look foolish."

"Foolishness is ingrained in the human condition. And if it's our turn to be laughed at now, it will be someone else's next."

"Interesting philosophy."

She let up on the accelerator and glided into a circular driveway. A two-story, gabled white farmhouse stood at the end of a path surrounded by walnut trees. A few yellow leaves clung obstinately to the branches. More lay scattered on the ground.

"One should never take oneself too seriously," she said. "This murder, on the other hand . . ." She shook her head. "We need to clear poor Craig."

"But if Craig and his friends did it —"

"Of course they didn't. This was no accident. These kids are being framed."

"How do you figure —"

But she'd stepped out of the Lincoln and was striding down the long straight path to the porch. As usual, she'd parked in the first spot she'd seen, far from the house, though there was plenty of room closer to the porch. I hurried after her.

I wasn't a professional investigator, but even I knew you didn't jump to conclusions at the beginning of a case. Also, I seemed to remember some Agatha Christies where the person who insisted it was murder was the person who got bumped off next. Maybe it was time for my mom to start taking her own safety more seriously.

I trotted up the porch steps, the wood thunking hollowly beneath my tennis shoes.

My mother rang the bell.

The front door swung open, and a man's tall silhouette stood framed behind the screen. Then he pushed that open too.

If someone said the word "dairy farmer," this would be the sort of man I'd picture. Middle-aged, he filled the doorway. His iron-gray hair and broad hands could easily fit around my neck.

I swallowed.

His suntanned face wrinkled in a brief smile. "Fran. Come in. And . . . ?"

"My daughter, Madelyn. She owns the Paranormal Museum," Mom said with a hint of pride. "Madelyn, this is Tom Wilde."

We stepped into a sunlit foyer.

"Is that Fran?" a woman's voice caroled. The woman herself stepped out of the dining room. Her tight, hot pink dress cradled her every curve, and her sky-high black heels matched her dark hair. She smiled broadly, her teeth white against her olive skin, and kissed my mother on the cheek. But her eyes were pink as if she'd been crying. "It's so good to see you again, Fran. And this must be Maddie of the Paranormal Museum. I read the article about those cowbells." She laughed warmly and took my hand. "You must have some PT Barnum in you."

"Nice to meet you, Mrs. Wilde," I said, liking her instantly. There's nothing sexier than confidence, and this woman wore her extra curves with pride.

"Call me Tabitha. Everyone else does. Come in, come in!" She ushered us into a living area with raw wood walls and soft white couches and arrangements of poinsettia around a white-brick fireplace.

Her husband, Tom, dropped into the largest chair and said nothing.

"Can I get you some tea? Coffee?" Tabitha asked, leading us to a couch.

"No, thank you." My mom lowered herself onto a snowy sofa.

"You said you had information about the Christmas Cow," Tabitha said, taking the stuffed chair opposite. "I'm starting to wonder if it's one of those traditions that needs to go away."

"I've been asking myself the same question," my mother said, and I sat beside her.

"If you need my support, I'll be happy to help in any way I can," Tabitha said. "Now that someone's been killed . . ." She blinked rapidly. "It's terrible."

I cleared my throat. "About that. There's talk that a group of kids from the junior college were involved in the attack. Your son attends school there, doesn't he?"

"Craig?" She touched her clavicle. "You think he might know something?"

"I'm afraid he might have been involved with the students who set fire to the cow," my mother said in a low voice. "At least, that's the rumor on campus."

"No." Tabitha shook her head violently. "No, he wouldn't. Not with his parents working with the organizations that plan it. He knows how damaging that would be."

"If the story reached us," I said, "the police are going to hear about it too."

"But Craig had nothing to do with it." Tabitha leaned forward on the couch. "I know my son. He's a good boy."

"If Craig witnessed something, it's better that he comes forward voluntarily," my mom said.

"If he saw something, he would have told me." Tabitha's face suffused with blood. She rose, her black shoes sinking deep into the white carpet.

"We think he's being framed," I blurted out.

Paling, Tabitha sat. "Framed?" Her husband's knuckles whitened on the chair arm.

My mother nodded. "There was a . . ." She winced. "Santa Claus near the gazebo, where Bill was shot. The other attackers were dressed as gingerbread men."

"Someone could have taken advantage of the students' attack and used it as a cover to kill Mr. Eldrich," I explained. Or this was a case of Occam's razor and the simplest explanation — a prank gone awry — was the correct one. "Mr. Wilde," I said, "you were in the Dairy Association with Mr. Eldrich. Did you know him well?"

"He was a tough person to get to know," Tom said carefully. "But he ran the association well. We had rules, and he followed them. Not much else you can ask for in a president."

"He was quite determined to build the Christmas Cow this year," my mother said.

"Well, we do it every year, don't we?" Tom asked.

"Did anyone have any problems with Mr. Eldrich?" I asked.

"Dean Pinkerton," he said.

His wife shook her head. "Tom, we don't know —"

"I heard Dean screaming at him. He was pissed."

"About what?" I asked.

"Dean is a lovely man and an important member of the dairy community," Tabitha said, giving her husband a look. She rose and walked to the white-brick fireplace. Kneeling, she flipped a switch and white lights threaded through the poinsettia winked on.

"Raw milk," Tom said.

"Raw milk?" I braced my elbows on my knees. Penny from the Wine and Visitors Bureau had said something along these lines, but I was curious about the couple's take on the conflict.

"Dean's been selling it," Tom said. "Some organic thing. Milk's supposed to be pasteurized, but he's been selling it privately, slipping through some loophole."

"I wouldn't call it a loophole," Tabitha said, retaking her seat in the fat white chair.

"Bill Eldrich wanted to close it," Tom continued. "Shut him down."

"Why?" I shifted on the couch.

"Why do people like raw milk, or why did Bill want to stop Dean's sales?"

"Both," I said. "I guess."

Tom shrugged. "Raw milk is a health fad. But pasteurization kills e-coli and a lot of other harmful bacteria. If people get sick off of raw milk, they'll just say 'bad milk,' and it'll hurt all the local dairy farmers. Rules are rules, and Bill Eldrich was all about the rules."

"Was Dean angry enough to kill him?" my mom asked.

"He was pretty mad," Tom said. "He's the only farmer selling raw milk within a hundred miles, so he had a lock on the granola-head market."

"Tom . . . We don't call people that," his wife said.

A wintery smile crossed Tom's face. "You don't. CRAIG!!!" he bellowed.

My mom and I started on the couch.

Tabitha glanced toward the ceiling. "I could have gone to get him. He's only upstairs."

"You're not his maid. CRAIG!"

Footsteps thundered down a set of stairs, and Craig slouched into the living room. "Yeah?"

He had his mother's dark hair and skin, and his father's brandy-colored eyes. Catching sight of us, he straightened and glanced toward the entryway.

"What do you know about the Christmas Cow attack?" his father rapped out.

Craig's expression grew sullen. "Nothing."

"I put a lot of hours in putting that stupid cow together," Tom said. "Straw isn't cheap, you know, and neither is fire retardant. Not that it did much good."

Tabitha smiled tightly. "Craig, a man was killed. If it was an accident, then we'll deal with it. But if you know who was involved, then those persons need to come forward."

The young man's dark brows slashed downward. "Why do you think I know? Why am I always the one to blame?"

"You're not," his mother said. "But some kids from your school may have been involved, and —"

"And so you blame me? Thanks a lot." He stormed from the room. The front door slammed. On the mantel, the crimson poinsettia leaves fluttered.

Tabitha stared after him, a pained look on her face. "I can't believe Craig was involved."

"It was probably innocent," I said. "But some kids on campus are saying he was in with the group who set the cow on fire."

"Nothing's innocent about arson," Tom growled. "And like you said, if you two heard the rumors, the police will too." He rose. "Thanks for letting us know. I don't like being caught flatfooted, especially not by the police. If Craig knows anything, we'll get to the bottom of it."

My mom smiled. "I'm sure you will. Now, there are a few details we need to go over about the cow. Some people want to rebuild it. I know the city council is concerned about the cost of another conflagration. What are your thoughts?"

Tom left the room while Tabitha and my mom discussed cow pros and cons for a good fifteen minutes. The only conclusion they came to was that they needed to call a full committee meeting on the matter.

Rising, we muttered our thanks and goodbyes.

My mom and I stopped in their driveway. "That went well," my mother said. "All things considered."

"Considering we practically accused their son of arson, yeah," I said.

"They're good people," my mom said. "They were bound to be defensive about their son, but they understand that the truth has to come out — for his sake. We need to talk to Dean Pinkerton."

I jammed my hands in my pockets. "I don't suppose you know him too?"

"Of course I do. This is a small town, and he's on the Christmas Cow committee this year." She smiled. "I suppose you'd like me to set up a meeting."

Resigned, I moved toward the Lincoln. "I suppose I do." If Slate found out what we were up to . . . But of course he'd find out. And the thought of his upcoming disappointment bothered me more than it should have. But my mother and I were in this together now. I couldn't abandon her.

I paused beneath a walnut tree. "What about Tom Wilde? Is he on the committee?"

"No, but Tabitha is." My mom kept walking and rummaged in her purse for the keys. "There's always someone from the town council involved to help with the permitting. Every time the fire department is called out, it costs the city money."

"Why? They have to pay them whether

102

they're putting out fires or not."

My mom aimed her fob at the Lincoln.

There was a bloom of flames, a rush of heat, and I was flying.

SEVEN

Time slowed. I could see bits of metal flying past me. And then I whumped to the ground and the air slammed from my lungs. I lay for a moment, stunned, and then panic set in.

I scrambled to my feet. "Mom? Mom!" Oh God, where was she? I looked around wildly. The Lincoln was an inferno. "Mom!" I trotted drunkenly, shouting.

"Here," she called, her voice faint.

I found her beside a blackberry bush, her blue eyes wide and dazed. "My Lincoln. I just had it detailed!"

I laughed, an odd shaky sound, and clapped my hands to my mouth. "Are you all right?"

She patted her blue jacket, matted with dirt and leaves. "I think so. I'm a bit sore, but that's all. Have you called 911?"

"Not yet —"

"For heaven's sake —"

"I was looking for you!"

"Well, you've found me. Where's my purse?" She patted the nearby bracken. "I'll make the call."

Tabitha and Tom raced down the porch steps. Tom grabbed a garden hose and turned it on.

In spite of her heels and skin-tight pink dress, Tabitha made good time reaching us. "You're alive. I can't believe it. When I looked out the window and saw . . ." Gulping, she pressed a hand to her chest.

"We're fine." My mom rose and brushed off her jeans, but her hands trembled. "I was just looking for my purse so Madelyn can call 911."

"We've already called them," Tabitha said, gazing in horror at the fire.

Tom sprayed water on it, but the fire blazed merrily, a thick column of black smoke rising into the air.

Tabitha coughed and covered her mouth. "Come inside," she said.

A siren wailed in the distance.

"I really need to find my purse." My mother turned toward the blackberry bushes and peered beneath them.

"I'll look over there," Tabitha said and strode away, scanning the bushes.

"It has to be near where I fell," my mother

said. "Help me look."

On our knees, my mother and I scrounged beneath the vines.

"Here it is!" Triumphant, my mother raised her purse. She frowned. "It's scratched. I won't be able to fix that."

"A scratched purse is the least of our problems," I said.

"I realize you're used to this sort of thing —"

"What? I'm not used to it."

"But my life has been more cloistered." Her blue eyes glinted. "Still, this is invigorating, isn't it?"

"No!"

"Now I understand why you and your brother were always traveling to those scary countries."

Smoke billowed our way, and I coughed. "We found it!" I shouted to Tabitha. She waved to us and walked to her husband, who was still spraying the car.

"We've made someone nervous," my mom said.

The sirens grew louder, and I stared at the burning car, still not quite able to believe what I was seeing. "Yeah. And we haven't spoken with that many people."

"So our attacker is either Penny, one of the Wildes, or Belle. Or the killer is afraid I

106

saw something that night and is stalking me."

That was what I'd figured too, and my stomach knotted with fear. How was I going to keep my mom safe from a deranged killer? She needed police protection. Did San Benedetto even have a big enough department for that?

I rubbed my temple, sickened. A bomb. Someone had actually planted a bomb in my mom's car.

On the bright side, we were alive and unhurt. If we could put someone in blue on my mom's tail, it might keep her nose out of the investigation.

The sirens neared.

"You've been very cool under fire," my mom said. "Your father would be proud."

I didn't feel cool. Nausea clutched my throat. If we'd been inside the Lincoln, or even a few feet closer . . . "I could say the same of you."

"I'm furious," she snapped. "I loved that car. Your father bought it for me."

I swallowed, a lump forming in my throat for a reason that had nothing to do with fear or smoke.

My mother sighed. "But I do have insurance."

A police car roared up and parked well

107

away from the burning Lincoln. Its siren cut. Gun drawn, Laurel Hammer stepped from the car and glared. "Everyone all right?" she shouted.

"We're all fine," my mother hollered back.

"Good." But when she neared us, the blond Amazon looked disappointed. She scanned the area. "Get back! What are you thinking, getting so close to a car on fire?"

We weren't that close. The heat from the fire assured that. But Tom dropped the garden hose, and we migrated toward Laurel's police car.

"What happened?" the detective asked.

I gulped. "I think . . . I think it was a bomb."

"A bomb?" Her expression was skeptical.

"We heard the explosion from inside the house," Tom said. "That gas tank didn't just ignite. It exploded. Look at the shrapnel." He pointed to a fender, high in a walnut tree.

A fire truck roared up. Men in yellow hats leapt from it and moved to secure a hose to the truck.

Laurel whirled on my mother and me. "What are you two doing here?"

"I had business with Mrs. Wilde and thought it was high time Madelyn met her," my mom said. "Shouldn't you be securing the crime scene?"

I cringed.

Laurel stared at us. Behind her, the air rippled with heat, distorting the country house, the trees, the field. "Funny how the Wildes are both connected with the Christmas Cow." Her blue eyes narrowed. "It's almost as if you two are investigating my case. And that would be illegal."

"We needed to decide what to do with the metal skeleton," Tabitha said.

"I do confess, however," my mother chimed in, "that we were distracted by talk of the murder."

"We're not calling it a murder yet," Laurel said.

"I thought since the Wildes' son, Craig, goes to the local junior college, he might have heard something about who was involved in the prank."

Tabitha shot my mother a look.

"But I was mistaken," my mom continued. "And this incident makes it clear that it wasn't a prank at all."

"Does it?" Laurel asked.

Three black-and-white patrol cars pulled up. Uniformed officers piled out.

The detective walked over to her colleagues. "Treat it like a crime scene and include the field." She motioned to the empty land filled with tall brown grass. She pointed to the Wildes. "Go inside, please. I'll talk to you shortly." To one of the policemen, she said, "You. Stay here. Watch these two."

The other officers nodded and hurried off.

"All right," Laurel said to us. "You two stay put until an officer gets a chance to talk to you." She strode down the drive after the Wildes.

"I think she enjoys bossing you around," my mom said in a low voice.

"No kidding."

"You really shouldn't have set her hair on fire that one time."

"I didn't," I huffed, sucking in another lungful of smoke. I was actually sweating, so I unzipped my thick vest. "It was an accident." I hadn't even set that fire. I only ran into it to save a thankless GD, and the detective had followed me.

"And running over her foot?" my mom added, gazing ruefully at her car.

"It's not my fault she didn't set her parking brake."

"She said your cat released the brake."

"Come on. My *cat*? Even if GD was somehow responsible — and I'm not admitting he is — what does he know about how cars work? It couldn't have been intentional." Though now that I thought about it, GD was sort of involved in the bad things that had happened to Laurel recently.

I shifted.

Nah. Coincidence. That was all.

My mother shifted her weight too, her sensible shoes crunching on the gravel driveway. "Still, he *is* your cat."

"I didn't put him up to getting into her car. And cats don't really belong to anybody." GD had made it clear I was his servant, doomed to feed, water, and clean up after him until he got bored with the situation.

"Animals pick up on human emotions. He knows how you feel about Laurel."

"Trust me, Mom. Even if he did, he's not going to exact revenge on my account. He only barely tolerates me."

"And do you want revenge on Laurel?"

For bullying me in high school? For stuffing me half-naked into a gym locker so tightly that the fire department had to cut me out? "Of course not. She was a kid and so was I. None of it matters anymore."

"None of what matters?" Detective Slate asked.

I jumped, yelped.

"Sorry," he said. "I didn't mean to startle you. What happened?"

I stepped closer and my ankle turned on an uneven stone. Slate caught me in his muscular arms, and my breath quickened.

Pulse erratic, ankle throbbing, I stepped away. "Whoops." I wobbled to his nondescript sedan and leaned against it. "We were leaving the Wildes' house, mom hit the fob, and the car just . . . exploded. Detective Hammer was first on the scene. She's talking to the Wildes in the house."

He gazed at the Lincoln, now a smoking black ruin. The firemen continued to train their hoses on it, however.

My mother drew a cell phone from her purse. "I'm calling the insurance company." She walked a little ways away.

"Detective Slate," I said in a low voice, "I'm worried about my mom. Someone is targeting her."

He placed a broad hand on my shoulder, and warmth flowed from his touch. "I'll make sure she's okay," he rumbled. "Did she see anything at the attack on the cow that she hasn't told me about?"

"I don't think so. She takes her civic duty seriously, and she's really upset about the murder."

His dark brows drew downward. "Is that why you two are here?"

My shoulders slumped. I couldn't lie. Not

to him. Not when my mom's life might be at stake. "There's a rumor going around that some kids from the junior college were involved in the attack, and that Craig Wilde might be involved. We thought if this was a prank gone wrong, his parents should have the opportunity to talk him and his buddies into coming forward voluntarily."

"You talked to him?" Slate asked, all business.

I nodded, a dull, weighted feeling spreading through my chest. He had every right to be angry with me. I wanted to take it back, fix things. But I couldn't, so I plowed on. "Mostly we talked to his parents."

"What did Craig say?"

"He denied it and stormed from the house."

"So he could have set the bomb."

"Yes, but —"

"It wasn't Craig," my mother said, returning to us and tucking her phone into the purse.

"Why not?" Slate asked.

"Because we could have been killed," she said. "Craig's either a prankster or he's a killer, not both. If he was involved in the Christmas Cow arson, then it was a prank gone wrong, because he had no reason to kill Bill Eldrich. Setting a bomb in my car was attempted murder."

"I'm sorry to say I agree. But we don't know if it was a bomb yet."

"It was," I said. "Cars don't just blow up on their own."

"May we leave?" my mother asked in an indistinct voice. "This has been very upsetting, and I think I'd like to lie down."

I glanced at her. Her face was pale, the lines deepening around her eyes and mouth. "Mom, are you all right?" I touched her arm.

"Of course, dear. Only tired after all the excitement."

Worry spiraled inside me. I'd already lost one parent. My mother wasn't that old, but getting knocked down by a bomb blast could do anyone in. And she tended to burn the candle at both ends.

"I'll have a patrol car take you home and drop Maddie at the museum," Slate said. "But later we need to talk, Mrs. Kosloski. An officer will stay parked outside to make sure you're safe."

"Thank you, Detective," she said faintly.

"Just a minute." He went to speak to an officer just stepping from his car.

"Well, this is inconvenient," my mother said.

"They're giving us a lift."

"And putting me into protective custody. Bad enough I can't follow up on our latest lead without a car. How am I supposed to do anything if I've got a cop following me?"

"You can't." I smothered a grin. For the afternoon at least, my mom would be out of the line of fire. I, however, wasn't going to let it go. This had become personal. "Look, I'll go talk to Dean Pinkerton by myself. I'll tell you what he says."

"He's not going to speak with you. He doesn't know you."

"I'm not socially inept."

"Of course not. But one must finesse these things. I need to be there. I bring authority."

"If he doesn't take me seriously, then he won't be worried about letting things slip."

"Mmm."

"I've done this before," I said.

She tapped her chin. "You say you'll report back?"

"Of course I will."

She smiled. "Yes, I think that just might work."

"Good," I said, relieved. "I'll go alone and report to you what I learn."

"No, you won't. I have an idea."

My stomach curdled.

EIGHT

Harper rushed from the front door of the museum to the squad car. "Are you all right? What happened?" Her breath left a trail in the air.

"I'm fine," I lied. A low-level fear jangled my nerves, made my pulse throb unevenly. I thanked the cops and they continued on, my mother staring plaintively out the rear window as if she were a prisoner.

"Why are the police driving you to work?" Harper's long navy coat drifted about the ankles of her pinstripe pantsuit. A burgundy scarf was knotted around her neck.

Stopping beside a plum tree, I explained. The afternoon sky was as gloomy as my thoughts, a solid mass of gray.

Harper sucked in her breath. "That's serious. Really serious. You both could have been killed."

"I know. I still can't quite believe it happened." But my mom and I were alive and

116

unhurt, and I'd hang onto that.

"What do the police have to say? Are they giving you protection?"

"They're giving my mom protection. It was her car, and she was the witness at the Christmas Cow attack."

"The killer thinks she saw something." Harper rubbed her face. "Unbelievable. A car bomb in San Benedetto. Are you sure you're all right?"

"I wasn't hurt. It's shaken me up, but that's all. What are you doing here?"

"I stopped by Adele's to drop off a tea recipe. I guess I could have emailed it, but I needed to get out of the office. And I still don't know what to get her for Christmas."

I nodded. Harper was involved in an Italian witch tradition and had amassed an impressive collection of kitchen witch recipes, including teas. "You'll figure something out."

"What are you getting her?"

"A tea-themed tarot deck and a book on the history of tea leaf reading." Also known as tasseomancy.

"Dammit, why didn't I think of that? It's perfect."

Two thirty-something women brushed past us on the brick sidewalk, their arms loaded with shopping bags.

I sighed. "I should help Leo."

"Need anything from the tearoom?" Harper asked. "Soup? Salad? Sandwich?"

"No," I said, "but thanks."

She watched me walk into the museum. It was packed with tipsy middle-aged tourists, sobering up before their next wine tasting.

Leo made change for two customers, then turned to stare out the front window. "Why the cops?"

GD sat on the sill and purred with satisfaction.

My voice hitched. "Someone blew up my mom's car."

He whistled. "Seriously?"

"Seriously. But she's okay." I joined Leo behind the counter and explained about the Wildes.

"What did the police say?"

"They sent a cop home with my mom for protection, at least for today."

He nodded. "So they think —"

A woman with a Santa fairy and a hangdog expression approached the register.

Leo fell silent.

I rang up the fairy and handed her a black gift bag. "Thank you! Happy holidays!"

"So they think the killer's after your mom?" he asked. "This means Bill Eldrich's death had nothing to do with the college."

I wasn't sure that held true, and that worried me. The whole affair was getting more and more confused. If someone had targeted Bill, what were the odds the killer could round up a gang of gingerbread men to join in on the fun? Worse, what were the odds the entire gang would stay quiet? Someone would crack, and the killer had to know that. And I had a hard time imagining our killer lurking by the cow in a Santa suit on the off chance he'd be there when a bunch of students struck.

My cell phone rang in my pocket. I checked the screen. *Mom.*

"Madelyn, this is your mother."

"Are you okay? Has anything happened? Are the police still with you?"

"Stuck on my sidewalk like barnacles. Now listen, I have to tell you the plan."

"Maybe that's not —"

"Since I can't leave without a police escort, and our investigation must remain on the DL, I —"

"DL? Down low?" Had my mom been watching gangster movies again?

"I have a solution," she said triumphantly. "Ladies Aid."

"Ladies Aid?"

"They're fabulously organized and absolutely trustworthy. Cora has arranged a meeting with Dean Pinkerton for the both of you."

"What? When?"

Cora Gale, her long wrap coat floating in her wake, wafted through the museum door. Her silver hair was piled in a loose bun, and goddess earrings dangled from her earlobes.

"Now," my mom said.

My gaze flicked to the ceiling. Now? *Now???* "Thanks for the head's up. She's here."

"What did I tell you?" my mother said, oblivious to my sarcasm. "Absolutely reliable. I'll let you go. You don't want to be late!" She hung up.

"I see you got those extra hours you were hoping for," Mrs. Gale said to Leo.

He colored. "Yeah. Well. Christmas. I could use the cash."

I hoped that wasn't true, since he'd inherited a large sum of money earlier this year. But I was glad the sudden wealth hadn't gone to Leo's head. As much as I fantasized about lottery winnings, work was good for the soul.

Cora scanned the counter. "Where's your motorcycle helmet?" she asked Leo.

He turned an even deeper shade of crimson. "Uh . . ."

"You didn't wear it today, did you?" She

120

scowled. "You may think you're immortal, but if you think I'm going to spend my golden years feeding you through a straw because you were too pig-headed to wear a helmet —"

His shoulders hunched. "It's in my top box on the bike."

I almost smiled. He might actually listen to Cora's safety tips. You never knew when a driver could look the wrong way at the wrong time and plow into you — bad news in a car, worse on a motorcycle.

"Make sure you put it on your thick head when you leave." She turned to me. "Are you ready?"

"Um, yes, we can take my truck."

She raised a brow. "The truck that broke down the other day and you still haven't taken to the repair shop?"

My face warmed. Had my mother told her that as well? "Er . . ."

"We'll take my Cadillac."

I turned to Leo. "It's pretty busy —"

"Go," he said quickly. "I got this."

"Thanks," I said, but my insides twisted with guilt. I hated leaving Leo with the crowd. Given that the mad Robin Hood had switched to bombs, though, maybe me staying away from Leo was a good thing. For him. And the thought of taking action against our attacker made me feel marginally better.

A bomb. A freaking bomb. At the memory, a quiver of panic squeezed my heart. I forced it down and away.

I followed Cora around the block to her black Cadillac, parked beneath a barren cherry tree. Unlit twinkle lights twined through its silver and charcoal branches.

She unlocked the doors and got inside. "I'm thinking of getting a Prius," she said, "but it seems wasteful to get rid of my Cadillac when it's still so new." She pointed. "The button for the seat warmer is there."

I turned it on and settled into the buttery leather seat.

She inched from the curb and cruised down Main Street. "You're not getting Leo involved in this, are you? A bombing is dreadful business. It's a miracle no one was killed."

I craned my neck at the fast-disappearing museum. "No, ma'am. Though he did tell me he thought Craig Wilde, a student at his college, might have been involved."

She frowned. "I certainly hope not. But the alternative, that a cabal of costumed men brutally attacked Bill Eldrich and then set a bomb in your mother's car, is worse. I don't suppose the dairy farmers could have conspired to remove the association president?"

"It doesn't seem likely. Was Bill disliked by the Dairy Association?"

"It's difficult being a leader. I was relieved to give up my role as president of Ladies Aid. The job was tremendously rewarding, of course, but the time it took! And all the silly personal conflicts I had to manage. Your mother, fortunately, is well-organized. The ladies respect her." She drove beneath the San Benedetto arch, and the low buildings gave way to vineyards.

"But Bill?"

"Oh, I suppose he was liked well enough. But in any organization, there are always conflicts."

"Such as?"

"It was a tough election. He had a serious fight on this hands for the president spot. His opponent wasn't a very good loser."

Now that was interesting. Maybe a sore loser would be willing to spill some proverbial beans. "Who was his opponent?"

"Dean Pinkerton."

"I see." Interesting that his name kept cropping up.

We drove past a billboard, a picture of a green vineyard with an open door set into it. *VINEYARD AT YOUR DOOR,* the sign proclaimed. And in smaller print: *Breathnach Estates.* Behind it lay acres of barren and cruelly carved earth. Men in hardhats strolled purposefully about. An earth-mover tore a gash in the ground. Spewing clouds of exhaust, it bumped and turned and unceremoniously dumped the dirt into a gravelike mound.

"That must be the new agrihood," I said.

"Progress. I loathe it. Aside from indoor plumbing and washing machines."

"Not to mention heated car seats."

"And the Internet."

We had it good — something it was all too easy to forget when trapped in the day-to-day grind. Something my mother and I had almost lost in an explosion. I squeezed my eyes tight for a moment, then opened them and took slow, deep breaths to calm myself.

We passed a dairy farm, and I wrinkled my nose at the acrid smell of manure.

We drove another mile, and Cora turned down a rough paved driveway. A black-and-white patchwork of cows lounged in pastures behind white wooden fences. A red barn surrounded by silos like fortress turrets rose from the flat earth.

"Officially," Cora said, "we're here on Ladies Aid business."

"Which is . . . ?"

"We've asked Dean to speak to our organization about the benefits of raw milk."

"Ah."

"I'm sure you'll find a way to subtly work your questions into the conversation."

I wasn't, but it was an introduction, and I'd take it. "Don't say anything about the car bomb."

"Why not?"

"I want to see if he gives anything away."

We parked beside a white-painted farm house and stepped from the Cadillac. The sun had begun to sink, and I shivered. I should have brought a thicker jacket.

A bulky middle-aged man with light brown hair and deep furrows around his eyes emerged on the porch. His nose was squashed like a boxer's. He wore a thick forest-green vest over his plaid flannel shirt, its sleeves rolled to the elbows. He blinked, as if surprised. "Mrs. Gale?"

She waved. "That's me. This is my friend, Maddie Kosloski."

"Come on in."

We followed him inside the farmhouse. In spite of the darkening skies, the entryway seemed to glow. The polished wood floors reflected off the stark white walls hung with antique farm implements — a wooden yoke, a drill spud, a Grim Reaper's scythe.

Dean Pinkerton plunked into a chair at a primitive-style dining table. A manual typewriter sat on top of it beside a messy stack of papers.

"Still writing your poetry?" Cora asked, taking a seat.

"Why would I stop?" he said. "You've heard about the Cowboy Poetry festival in Elko, Nevada?"

We nodded.

"I'd like to get a dairyman poetry festival going here."

"Do many in the Dairy Association write poetry?" I asked.

"You'd be surprised. Now about that talk, Cora. How long do you want me to speak for?"

He and Cora discussed the details, and I examined the photos on the walls of Dean with various dead animals. Holding up a trio of ducks. Kneeling beside a deer . . . and holding a complicated-looking bow in one hand.

NINE

Pulse speeding, I looked away from the hunting photos. The man knew how to hit moving targets with a bow and arrow. And farms used to use explosives for removing stumps and such. Could Dean still have some lying around?

I swallowed. Maybe interviewing a murder suspect near a wall of rusty farm implements hadn't been the best idea.

"Maddie?" Cora said.

"Sorry. What?" I asked.

"You said you had some questions?" she asked.

"Um, right," I said. "I think it might be helpful to discuss people's objections to raw milk head-on. I heard some members of the Dairy Association objected to your selling the milk?"

"Crony capitalism!" Dean slammed his meaty fist on the table and we jumped in our seats. The typewriter dinged faintly.

"The other dairy farmers don't want competition, and they're using force to squash the newcomer."

I hunched my shoulders, making myself a smaller target. "Force?"

His broad face darkened. "What do you think happens if they get their new regulations and I can't sell my milk? First they'll fine me, and if I don't pay, they'll send armed government regulators to toss me in jail. And all because the other farmers are too lazy to be competitive. That's the way government works these days — big companies use it to squash the little ones who might cause trouble in the future. Who do you think funds all those political campaigns?"

"Was the local Dairy Association funding any political campaigns?" I asked.

His eyebrows pinched together. "The association wasn't, but you can bet Bill Eldrich was."

"Whose campaign was he funding?" I sat up straighter in the wooden chair.

Dean deflated. "Tabitha Wildes', for starters. He said it was because her husband was in the association, but I knew better. Having a town councilwoman in his pocket was good for business."

In little San Benedetto, that seemed over

128

the top. But if Dean's business could be shut down, then the stakes were high for him.

A violet scarf slipped from Cora's shoulder and she bent to pluck it from the wood floor. "In fairness, Bill and Tabitha have done good things for the local dairy farmers. Lots of small farmers around the state are selling out to developers. That hasn't happened here, thanks largely to their efforts."

"It will," Dean said, expression gloomy.

I tried to maneuver us back on topic. "But you're able to sell your raw milk currently?"

"With proper labeling," Dean said, "raw milk is legal in California. But localities can create their own rules. Did you want to pick up your order today, Cora?"

"If it's no trouble."

He ambled from the room.

"Did you know he hunts with a bow and arrow?" I asked in a low voice and nodded toward the trophy wall.

She pursed her lips. "No, I didn't. Do you want to ask him about it?"

My gaze darted to the farm implements. I honestly didn't.

Dean returned with a wire carrier containing four milk bottles. "Here you go."

I took a deep breath and plunged in. "I

was at the Christmas Cow right after it burned. My mother was guarding it. I stepped on a wooden arrow, but the arrow that killed Mr. Eldrich looked like it was made of metal or something." I nodded to the photos on the rough wood wall. "I see you hunt. Do you need different kinds of arrows for different kinds of bows?"

He stilled. "Is that why you're here? You think I shot Bill?"

Gulp. *Maybe.* "No, of course not."

"Well, I didn't." He folded his arms over his broad chest. "And I don't appreciate getting sandbagged."

"No one's sandbagging you," Cora said. "Everyone knows it was a student prank gone wrong. Of course Maddie's upset. It was her mother, our president, who was in the crossfire. It was lucky Fran wasn't killed. And flaming arrows! Can you imagine?"

He grunted. "Anyone can make a flaming arrow. You can get instructions off the Internet."

"Bill wasn't killed with a flaming arrow," I said. There hadn't been scorch marks around his chest wound. Just lots of blood. I rubbed my jaw. If it had been an accident gone wrong, I realized, he would have been hit by a flaming arrow just like the cow was.

"I didn't kill Bill Eldrich."

"If we thought you'd killed him," I said, "we wouldn't be here." Or at least sensible Maddie wouldn't. "And I'd be asking you questions like, where were you at the time the Christmas Cow was burnt?"

Dean glared.

"I'm only curious about the arrows," I said weakly. I should have known getting his alibi wouldn't be that easy. "That's all."

"I was home in bed when the cow was set on fire. As to the arrows, it isn't a question of wood or carbon. It's about the weight. If you're hunting, you need an arrow with six to eight grains per pound of draw weight — that's the weight your bow can pull. For target practice, you can go lighter."

"Target practice . . . Aren't those archery targets usually set on straw?" I asked.

"Yeah. Usually."

And straw was what the cow had been made of. The cow had been target practice.

Bill Eldrich had been hunted.

Cora returned me to the darkened sidewalk in front of the museum. The iron street-lamps had flicked on, illuminating its brick facade.

I walked inside, and Leo and I dealt with a flurry of last-minute sales.

"Learn anything?" Leo asked as he made change.

"Mmm," I said, and wrapped a delicate green fairy. Dean had looked like a great suspect, and he hadn't given us an alibi. I suspected he didn't have one. According to Cora, he was single, so there was no wife to vouch for his presence in the early a.m.

Handing a nurse in blue scrubs a black gift bag with the fairy inside, I ushered her from the museum. I flipped the sign to *Closed.*

"Is that everyone?" I asked.

"I think so." Leo strode from behind the counter and checked the other rooms. "Yep." He returned to the counter. "We're alone."

"Thanks for taking over this afternoon. You can head out. It's my turn to clean up for the night."

"Thanks." He grabbed his motorcycle jacket off a hook in the wall and hesitated. "Maybe I should wait."

"For what?"

He just looked at me.

"Oh. No, it's fine. You go."

He stood for a moment, shifting his weight, then nodded and slipped out the door.

GD cat howled from his perch on top of

Gryla's papier-mâché cave.

I braced my fists on my hips. "I know you like him better. But he can't hang out with you all night."

GD dropped from the cave and prowled toward me.

The bell over the door jingled, and I stiffened. I hadn't locked the door? Maybe the museum was under a curse. "I'm sorry. We're . . ." I turned and trailed off.

Detective Slate leaned against the counter. "Bad timing?" His navy business suit was slightly rumpled, and I wondered if he'd been on a stakeout.

"No." Relieved, I smiled so hard my cheeks hurt. "Hi, Detective."

"I think by now you can call me Jason."

"Okay, Jason," I said, pleased. "Have you learned anything new about the bomb?"

"No, and even if I did, I couldn't tell you. But nobody's taking this lightly. We'll find whoever's responsible. Maddie, are you sure you're all right?"

"I wasn't hurt."

"That's not what I'm talking about," he said.

I drew a shuddering breath. "All I can think about is what might have happened to my mom. But she's okay, and you're protecting her."

"Not personally, but she's got protection."

"If you're not here to talk about the bomb, then why are you here?"

His expression turned grim. "I'm here about your investigation."

My insides quivered. Dammit, I'd known this was coming. He'd told me not to investigate, and I'd asked questions anyway. He had every right to be annoyed, but someone had tried to blow up my mother. And me!

GD cat sprang to the counter. His green eyes glowed.

I cleared my throat. "I'm sorry, but —"

Slate held up his hand. "This is getting serious, Maddie."

No kidding. My mom was under police protection, and her car was even deader than the Christmas Cow. My arms dropped to my sides. "I know. With everything that's happened, you must be furious."

"Of course not. I can't blame you for this cowbell business. Who would have guessed it would set off such a firestorm, no pun intended?"

"Firestorm? You've lost me. What are you talking about?"

"Dispatch has been getting calls all day from people hearing the bells. They're convinced they'll be next to die. The chief is going nuts."

I sank onto the stool. "You're talking about the curse." That explained his sudden interest in it. "Why didn't you tell me about this earlier?"

"Because it's ridiculous. By any chance have you come across new information on the bells?"

"No . . . there's just the curse," I said slowly. What else was there to know?

"Since you and I have managed to solve two ice-cold cases, the chief has put me on this one."

"I thought you were investigating Bill Eldrich's murder?" As was I; something an honorable person would confess to. But after the attempt on my mom's life, I couldn't afford honor. I studied the tip jar beside the register.

His smile was slow and sensual. "I'm a good multitasker."

Warmth flickered in my core. "But what are you multitasking? The cowbells are probably the most ridiculous curse story in the history of curse stories. What does your chief expect you to do about it?"

"Put a lid on it."

"Does San Benedetto have a psychic police force I don't know about?"

"It does now, and you and I are it. We

135

need to calm things down. Telling people the curse is silly isn't doing the job. I've convinced the chief if we can get to the bottom of the curse, we can debunk it once and for all."

That would *not* be good for business. *Selfish!* I mentally slapped myself. Besides, even if the curse was debunked, I could PT Barnum something out of the normal old bells. "Are you just saying this to distract me from my mom's car blowing up? Or is this curse hysteria really a problem?"

"Right now the panic is at level yellow — mildly annoying. But it's wasting police and dispatcher resources. If we go to orange or red, that will be a problem."

Yikes. "I'm sorry, I had no idea."

He laid his hand atop mine on the glass counter. "You had more important things to worry about. We'll get the guy who set that bomb."

My breath caught, his touch warming me. Our gazes locked, and I noticed the amber flecking his brown eyes. Slate and I kept meeting under the worst circumstances, but there was something about him —

The door jangled open and Laurel strode in on a blast of frigid air. Her tight navy pantsuit, the color almost a match for Slate's, hugged every muscled curve. Her

136

blue eyes sparked with annoyance.

I slid off the stool and kept the counter between us.

Jason jerked his hand from mine. "Is something wrong?"

She glared at me. "No."

Would Laurel ever get over our high school hostilities? 'Twas the season for forgiveness and goodwill toward men. And hopefully toward irritating paranormal museum owners.

"So what are you doing here?" Jason asked mildly.

"Following up with Kosloski on the bombing today."

"You've got my notes," he said.

"Right."

They stared at each other.

GD hunched, ears twitching, eyes tracking Laurel.

I scooped up the cat. He hissed and bit my hand, and I set him quickly on the floor. GD howled, an unearthly sound that prickled my scalp.

Laurel started and edged toward the door. "The Wildes told me Kosloski was asking a lot of questions about the murder."

Jason turned to me. "Oh?"

"It might have come up in conversation," I said, my mouth going dry.

"It sure did," Laurel said, "since you were playing detective."

I winced.

"Maddie told me she'd spoken with the Wildes about the possibility their son might know something," Jason said.

Laurel's mouth pursed and there was a long silence.

I released my breath. She must not have heard about my chat with Dean or she would have said something by now.

"How long are we going to keep an officer outside her mother's house?" Laurel finally asked, brisk. "We don't have the resources to play bodyguard."

"Let's give it another day," Jason said, "and then reassess the situation."

My stomach clenched. *Reassess?* Someone had tried to kill my mom!

Laurel gave him a long look, then nodded and strode from the museum. The door bammed shut.

"You okay?" he asked.

"I'm worried about my mother. It sounds like the police protection isn't going to last."

"I'll do my best to keep it in place. But Laurel was right about our resources being thin. Maddie, we'll do everything we can."

"I know, and I appreciate it." Biting my lip, I looked away. "So," I said brightly, "the cowbell curse got started in the '80s. Can you find any police records on the deaths?"

"I'm not sure what we'll have, since none were designated as murders, but I'll check. So our curse investigation is on?"

"Sure. Psychic PI, reporting for duty." I saluted with two fingers.

His eyes narrowed. "And you're *not* investigating the Eldrich murder."

"It's a small town," I hedged. "I can't really avoid the suspects."

"You've identified suspects?"

"Um. Well. There's Craig and his college buddies — a prank gone wrong. Or, if not, then it would have to be someone who wanted Mr. Eldrich dead."

Jason quirked a brow. "Your suspect is someone who wanted the victim dead. Really?"

When he put it that way, my deduction didn't sound all that clever. On the other hand, I didn't want him to know I was going to keep detecting. I *had* to investigate.

The door opened and I turned toward it, grateful to end the conversation.

Mason, my ex, strode into the museum, his blond hair tied back in a ponytail and his muscles straining the leather of his jacket. "Hey, Maddie. I saw your truck, and Belle said —" He clamped his mouth shut.

His gaze traveled from me to the detective. "Slate. Am I interrupting something?"

GD's ears swiveled.

The two men were a study in opposites: Jason Slate dark and tall with lean muscle, Mason Hjelm blond and built like a Viking, with arctic-blue eyes.

"No," Jason said. "I was just leaving. Maddie, if you need anything, let me know."

"Thanks," I squeaked. I cleared my throat.

Mason and I watched him leave.

"What's going on?" he asked. "I heard your truck was blown up, but it's sitting outside."

I frowned. If Belle had told Mason I'd asked about her winnings in the Christmas Cow betting, he would have led with that. Or would he?

"Not my truck, my mom's car," I said. "How'd you hear about it?"

"Are you kidding? It's all over town." He shifted his weight. "Belle said you spoke with her yesterday. Why?"

I stalled, wondering how much to tell him. "Do I need an ulterior motive?"

"No, of course not. But I notice you're not really answering me."

"I'm a little surprised you're asking me and not Belle," I said slowly.

"I did ask her."

"Then you have your answer." But I got the feeling he didn't. Was Belle keeping her bet hidden from Mason? I gnawed my lower lip. "I was in the beauty parlor with my mom, and everyone was talking about the Christmas Cow fire and where they were that night . . ." I trailed off, hoping Mason would fill in the blanks about Belle's whereabouts.

He didn't.

"Pretty crazy stuff," I said. "You must have smelled the smoke from your apartment. In fact, you probably had a bird's-eye view. You can see the park from your place, can't you?"

"Yeah," he said. "The sirens woke me up."

"I'll bet Jordan and Belle got a real show." And if they were home, then Belle was in the clear.

"I didn't get out of bed," he said.

Rats! I could have just asked him directly, but something stopped me — cowardice.

"What's Christmas in San Benedetto without setting a giant straw cow on fire, right?" I asked. "Belle must think we're nuts."

His jaw clenched. "She's not confiding in me, but I think San Benedetto is a little too small for Belle. Anyway, I'll let you get back to work." He nodded and strode out the door.

GD cat sneezed.

"Something's up between those two, and I'm not getting in the middle of it," I announced to the cat. Even though a part of me still wanted to protect Mason. I shook myself. That ship had sailed, sunk, and rotted on the ocean floor. His relationship with Belle was none of my business.

GD sprang from the counter to the checkerboard floor. His source of entertainment gone, he slunk to the Gryla exhibit and curled up beneath the ogress.

I locked up, swept up, and pulled up my notes on the cursed cowbells. It *was* odd that every member of the Christmas Cow committee had died within a year of bringing those bells back from Sweden. The business about them hearing the bells before they died had to be an urban legend. Hearing cowbells in a town with its own Dairy Association isn't exactly unusual, especially since two of the original committee members were in said Dairy Association. But the two Ladies Aid members and the city council member who'd died were a little harder to explain.

The bookcase slid open and Adele walked into the museum. She whipped her apron off and hugged me, then stepped away. "Is it true about your mom's car?"

I nodded.

"Thank God you're both all right. How can I help? Does your mom need to borrow a car? My parents have an extra they don't use. It belonged to my grandmother."

"I'll let my mom know, but I'd rather keep her grounded and under police watch as long as possible."

"It's as bad as all that?" she asked bleakly.

"Worse." I studied my friend. Her skin looked drawn, and several strands of black hair streamed inelegantly from the bun at the nape of her neck. "It looks like you had a rough day too."

Adele laughed shortly. "It can hardly compare to yours."

"What happened?"

She unknotted the bun and shook her blue-black hair free. "Nothing important. I was supposed to go Christmas shopping for Harper at lunch but there was no time. We've had a waiting list today for people to get in, which is fantastic. But I had to beg one of my waitresses to come in on her day off, we lost three vintage teacups, I still have no idea what to get Harper, and my feet are killing me."

"Lost?"

143

She gave me a look. "That's a euphemism for *broke.* Have you gotten anything for Harper?"

"A deck of Italian tarot cards and a new book on the Italian folklore traditions. Since she's Italian." Adele didn't know that Harper was a strega, practicing her witchcraft on the sly, and Harper was super-paranoid that word would get out and ruin her reputation as a hard-headed financial whiz. If it hadn't been for a murder case we'd gotten involved with earlier in the year, I wouldn't have learned about it either.

"Urgh," Adele said. "Those are perfect. Why didn't I think of that?"

"Because you don't work in a paranormal museum?"

She rolled her eyes. "But I'm in here often enough."

"So . . . time for a girls' night out?"

"Are you sure you're up for it?" she asked anxiously.

"I desperately need it."

"Then I'll call Harper."

We met Harper at our usual watering hole, a local microbrewery called the Bell and Brew. The place was packed, but Harper had managed to snag a booth behind the giant copper vat. I suspected the host had a crush on Harper, who was a Penelope Cruz clone.

She scooted over in the red Naugahyde booth to make room for Adele. Three beers sat on the table, the mugs still frosty.

I sat and grabbed mine, raised it. "To Friday."

"To you and your mom escaping a bomber." Harper toasted.

We clinked mugs, and I drank deeply. "Though I'd rather not talk about the bomb," I said, "if it's okay with you." The more I thought about it, the more frightened I became. Better to just move forward and deal with it.

"All right," Harper said, her green eyes sympathetic. Her usual pinstripes had been exchanged for an emerald turtleneck. "But one question first. Are you holding up?"

"Barely." Adele ran through a litany of woes — from smashed tea cups to a flooded toilet.

Harper folded her arms, a resigned look on her face. But I knew Adele was rambling to distract me from my own problems, and I appreciated it.

"And then this one" — Adele jerked her thumb at me — "nearly gets blown up!"

"Which I'd rather not talk about," I repeated. "Adele, go on."

She smiled knowingly. "The tea room is doing well. Our Christmas menu is a hit, especially the ginger cinnamon scones and sugar plum fairy tea. And . . ." She raised her brows.

"And what?" Harper asked.

"I saw a certain detective in the museum after closing hours," she said.

"Slate?" Harper asked. "Did he have any news about the bomb?"

"No." I sipped my beer. "He thinks we need to research the cowbells, and —"

"That doesn't sound like normal police activity." Adele propped her chin on her hands. "Do tell."

My face warmed. "It's just business."

"Curse research when there's a bomber on the loose?" Harper looked skeptical.

"I guess people have been calling the police station about the cursed bells," I said.

Adele coughed into her beer. "About the cowbells? Are you kidding me?"

"I'm only telling you what Jason said." I raised my hands, palms out.

"Jason?" Adele smirked. "You're on a first name basis?"

"She ought to be," Harper said, laughing, "considering she's the SBPD's best customer."

"I am not. Now, focus." I snapped my

fingers, slippery from the beer mug. "Cow-bells."

"So Detective Jason Slate wants your help researching a curse," Adele said. "And you don't find this the tiniest bit convenient?"

I flipped my hair over one shoulder. "It's incredibly inconvenient, since I'm also try-ing to figure out who blew up my mother's Lincoln and nearly killed us both. I think he's just trying to distract me from the bombing." But was that all it was? Frown-ing, I stared into my beer mug. Had I imagined the spark between us? My body grew heavy. Of course I had. I'd only broken up with Mason a few months ago. I wasn't ready to get into a new relationship.

"I just thought one of you might know more about curses than I do," I muttered. What I really wanted was Harper's help, but I couldn't say that out loud.

"Well, I don't know anything," Adele said. "But Harper's a secret witch. She might."

Harper's cheeks went white, then dusty rose. "How did you find out?"

"Oh, please." Adele waved her hand dis-missively. "Dieter told me."

"Dieter! How did Dieter know?" Harper asked.

"His lips are sealed, and so are mine." Adele gave her a look.

"I'm sorry," Harper stammered. "I should have told you."

"Forget it," Adele said. "And spill. Curses."

Our witch friend shifted in the booth. "What do you want to know?"

"How do curses work?" I asked. "If I'm going to debunk the bells, I need to know the basics."

"Most people think that it's all psychosomatic," Harper said. "If you think you're cursed, then you start making yourself ill, or causing your own accidents."

"Like a reverse placebo effect?" I asked. The way Herb had been panicking over the bells, I could easily see him making himself sick.

"Or . . ." Harper said.

We leaned closer. A chill shivered my skin. "Or?"

"Or the object is in fact used to hold and channel negative energy toward its victims. In this case, the easiest way to deal with it is to destroy the cursed object."

"Destroy the cowbells?" I asked, aghast. "They're historical!" I'd paid a lot of money for those bells. They were perfectly good bells!

The hostess led a trio of men in cowboy hats past our booth. Their gazes lingered longingly on Harper.

"There are some people who know how to neutralize objects through a binding spell," Harper said. "And if you're a magician yourself, you can always change the energy. I mean, energy is just energy. It's like a painting. You can paint something lovely or awful, but paint is paint. It's not inherently good or bad. A magician can change the negative energy to positive, so that the object actually sends out good vibes."

"Okay," I said. "That's interesting, but we're not dealing with magicians here. I need an answer I can use." I drummed my fingers on the table and made a disgusted sound. "Herb."

"What about him?" Adele asked.

"He said he knew a guy who could bind the bells better than he had." I hated to waste money, but I had promised Slate I'd try to fix this. Then I perked up. Idea! I could hold a public binding ritual. Invite the papers. Yeah, that could work. The bells had already been in the news. Local reporters might go for a follow-up story. "But how can I make it Christmas-themed?" I muttered.

"What are you talking about?" Adele asked.

I explained about the public binding ritual.

Harper groaned and braced her forehead
on her fist. "This museum is turning you
into a marketing monster."

"Christmas comes but once a year," I said.
"I need to make the most of it."

"That's what I'm afraid of," Harper said.

TEN

"Come again." I smiled, handing the customer her black paper bag. She jingled out the front door and passed in front of the sidewalk window. A thick fog obscured the street outside, making for a suitably spooky winter morning.

I scanned the street for suspicious cars, then the main room for impending disasters. GD stared intently at a trio of three creepy dolls on a pedestal. Tourists snapped pictures of him "detecting ghosts." People meandered into the Fortune Telling Room, milled about the main room, exclaimed over the Christmas fairies in the Gallery.

Leo bustled behind the counter brandishing a red-and-green-striped fairy with sparkly wings. "We're going to need to restock these fairies."

"I've already contacted the artist. She's going to make a delivery tomorrow."

"Have you called Herb about the binding thing?"

I'd been avoiding it. But I owned a paranormal museum, so it was time for me to cowgirl up. "On it."

I turned to the wall phone and made the call.

"Yes?" Herb whispered.

"Hi, Herb, it's —"

"Don't say my name! Someone could be listening."

I rolled my eyes. "It's Maddie. I wanted to follow up about that specialist you mentioned, the one who binds cursed objects?"

"I'm glad you've come to your senses. The cowbells are driving me crazy. Every time I hear one, I nearly jump out of my skin. Mother is furious."

"Your mom?" I edged closer to the bookcase behind the counter, giving Leo more room as he rang up a deck of tarot cards for a portly woman with red hair and a broad smile.

"I've already broken a crystal platter and two water glasses. My colleague can come by the museum tomorrow."

"Tomorrow?" I yelped. "But that's in one day."

"Exactly."

"But I want to invite the press, make this public."

"Oh," he said, "I don't think he'll agree to that."

"He has to. The whole point of this stupid ritual is to calm things down."

"Stupid? With that attitude, how do you expect the ritual to succeed?"

"But if people don't know the curse has been removed —"

"Bound," Herb corrected.

"Whatever. The panic will continue."

"My colleague's leaving for Belize on Monday. We do the ritual Sunday or not at all."

"There must be someone else who can do it?"

"Not as well as he can."

GD slunk across the checkerboard floor and hopped onto the counter.

I blew out my breath. "All right. It's only the local press. I'll get them here." I could make this work on short notice.

"I told you, he won't like it if the press are there."

"Does he want to get paid?"

There was a long silence. "And speaking of getting paid . . ." Herb named a figure high enough to give me a nosebleed.

I squawked. "Are you kidding me?"

153

"If you want him to come tomorrow and conduct the ritual before an audience, yes."

GD butted his head against my elbow braced on the glass counter. I ruffled his fur.

"Fine," I said. "Can you get him here by four?"

"That is not a problem."

"I'm trusting you, Herb," I said warningly. "He'd better be on time."

"Have I ever let you down?"

I stared at the ceiling. "No." Herb was loopy and paranoid and overpriced, but he'd never left me hanging.

"Tomorrow at four o'clock then. Expect him to arrive at three thirty to prepare for the ritual."

"Will do. And thanks."

I hung up and called my mom.

"Hello, Madelyn. Laurel was very upset yesterday. What did you say to her?"

"Laurel?" I shifted, uneasy. "Why were you talking to Laurel?"

Two customers strolled inside.

"She stopped by the house to ask more questions about the Christmas Cow assault and the bombing."

My eyes narrowed as I rang up two tickets, bumping elbows with Leo behind the counter. He struggled with wrapping paper and tape.

"What kind of questions?" I asked, making change.

"Oh, you know. And the police are still outside my house. They say they want to keep me under watch for at least another day or two."

My scalp pricked with alarm. Only a day or two? Did they think they'd have the bomber in custody by then? Because that did not seem typical of police work.

"Was there a reason you called?" she asked.

"I need your help." I handed the customers their tickets and a museum brochure.

"Of course, dear. Have you learned anything new in our investigation?"

"Not since the meeting with Dean. Cora said she'd fill you in."

"She did, dear. But I was hoping you would."

GD meowed. Absently, I petted him.

He nipped my hand.

I jerked away, smothering a curse. When would I learn?

"Sorry," I said, checking my hand. As usual, he hadn't left a mark. "It's been a little crazy. People are taking the cursed cowbells seriously, and it's causing panic."

155

"I've heard."

"You have?" I asked, surprised.

"Ladies Aid was involved in the original Christmas Cow. Our president and a member of the committee were at the airport to accept the bells from our Swedish sister city."

I frowned at Leo. His hand encased in tape, he handed a bag to the red-haired woman. They struggled briefly as he attempted to peel the tape from the paper, and the bag came away with a faint tearing sound. The customer smothered a laugh and walked out.

"I'd like to talk to you more about that later," I said into the phone. "But in the meantime, I've hired someone to remove the curse. At a public ritual."

She *tsked.* "Are you certain this is the right approach?"

"I know there's no such thing as curses, but people believe it, so we need to set their minds at ease."

"What if your ceremony feeds their delusion?"

"At least it will be the delusion that the curse has been bound," I said. "It's a happy, harmless delusion."

Two more customers walked in.

"Hmm," she said. "How much is this going to cost you?"

I rang up the tickets. "More than I'd like, but if I can get some press to attend, then not only will word get out that the bells are curse-free, but I can get publicity for the museum."

"And you need my help getting the press there."

"Would you mind?" I handed over tickets and a brochure to the middle-aged couple.

"Not at all. I'm going stir-crazy cooped up at the house. I can't go anywhere without those police officers. They're lovely young men, but you know how it is."

"Not really."

"So to keep myself busy, I've been baking up a storm. The policemen outside are happy, but I'd rather be doing something more useful."

"So you'll do it?" I asked.

Bored, GD slunk off the counter and into the Gallery.

"Certainly," she said. "This town is important to me. I want to see this silly curse business put to rest."

"Here's the challenge." I cringed, making a face. "The curse removal will happen tomorrow."

She sucked in her breath. "Tomorrow?"

"At the museum. Four o'clock."

"All right. I think I can get some local reporters there. But you need to talk to Laurel. I don't know what's happened between the two of you now, but she's very upset."

"Sure, right. We'll sort it out. Thanks!"

"I know you will, dear. Merry Christmas!" My mom hung up.

Smiling, I turned to Leo. "So that's that. The curse guy will do his thing at four, and the press will be here."

"So how do we prep for the event?" Leo asked, peeling tape from his hand.

"Prep?" I said blankly.

"There will be people standing around watching, right? Do we need to have food? Chairs? Should we rope off the area? Put a flyer in the window? What about the people on our electronic newsletter list? Do we invite them?"

I groaned. I'd just created mounds of extra work for us during the busiest month of the year. "No food. No chairs. Yes to the cordon. Adele used those velvet rope things for her grand opening. Could you ask her where she got them? I'm assuming they were rentals. And I'll pull together the flyer and the e-newsletter invite." It was such short notice, I doubted many people would come. But as long as some press showed

158

up, this could work.

"On it." Dropping the wad of tape into the garbage bin beneath the counter, Leo slipped through the bookcase and into the tea room next door.

I got busy on the computer. Between handing out tickets and making change for purchases, I typed up a flyer and email announcement.

Leo returned with a photocopied invoice. He slid it across the counter.

Silent, the cat leapt onto the counter and sat on the paper.

I pulled the warm invoice from beneath his furry butt. GD meowed, indignant.

"That's the contact info for the rental place and the cost," Leo said.

I scanned the invoice and nodded. "Looks good. Can you take care of this?"

"Sure." He grabbed the paper, pulled a cell phone from the pocket of his black jeans, and dialed.

The front door opened, bell tinkling. I straightened, pasting a smile on my face. "Welcome to the . . ."

Craig's mother, Tabitha Wilde, hesitated in the open door and scanned the throng of visitors.

My stomach knotted. I hoped she wasn't still upset by our last encounter.

She walked inside. Beneath her chic electric-blue parka, she wore a narrow cream-colored skirt and ankle boots. "Hi, Madelyn. I'd hoped to speak with you, but this looks like a bad time." Her olive skin darkened. "Somehow I lost your phone number. Maybe we can make an appointment for later?"

"We don't need to do that." Something cold wriggling in my chest, I motioned to Leo. Town councilwomen rarely dropped into the museum. Had Craig confessed to his mother? "Now is fine," I assured her. "I was ready for a break. Maybe we could pop into the Fox and Fennel, where it's quieter?" It was still early, so it wouldn't be too crowded.

Her shoulders dropped and she smiled. "That sounds fine."

I slid off my high seat behind the counter. "Leo? Do you mind?"

He nodded, still on the phone, and took my place.

We walked through the bookcase door into the tea room. Women crowded tables covered in elegant white cloths. Twinkle lights coiled around the curtain rods, setting the gauzy, vanilla-colored curtains aglow. Glittery pale aqua, green, and pink ornaments hung from artfully arranged boughs of long-needled pine. Mistletoe hung in clumps along the walls on pale green ribbons.

Adele, her black hair again in a neat bun, moved behind the counter with its bamboo-paneled wainscoting. A *Fox and Fennel* apron hung over her neck and was tied about her hips.

I walked to the counter. "Adele?"

She turned quickly, a brushed-nickel tea canister and scooper in her hand. "Oh. It's you. Hi!"

"Is there a table for two we can grab?"

"If you can find one, feel free to take it."

Tabitha and I roamed around, finally seizing an empty table squashed into a corner. A teardrop-shaped glass lamp gleamed above it.

Tabitha removed her coat and draped it over the back of a modern-looking wood chair.

A harried waitress also in an official apron bustled to our table. She handed us menus and an elegant card of thick, off-white paper. "Our holiday menu."

"Thank you," Tabitha said brightly. She perused the menu. "Oh, this sounds delicious. I hadn't meant to eat, but . . . Do you mind?"

My stomach rumbled. "Not at all." Anxious, I watched her study the menu and wondered what this was all about.

The waitress returned.

"I'll have the orange cranberry biscuits with the strawberry jam. And . . . Madelyn, how do you feel about frosted cranberries?"

"I feel confident that I'll like them."

"And the frosted cranberries," she continued. "And the Sugar Plum Fairy tea."

"I'll have the crème brûlée tea and gingerbread cake," I said.

"That comes with orange-nutmeg whipped cream," the waitress said. "Is that all right?"

Could orange-nutmeg whipped cream possibly be wrong? "That's fine."

The waitress hurried away.

"So, Madelyn, how on earth did you get involved in the paranormal museum?" Tabitha asked.

"It's a funny little job, but I love it," I said, enthusiasm bubbling inside me. As stressful as self-employment could be, at least my mistakes were my own. And the museum had come a long way since I'd taken it over.

"I saw the fairies in the window. They're adorable."

I fiddled with the silverware. "They're made by a woman in Auburn."

We made small talk, and I wondered again

when she'd tell me why she'd come to see me.

And then the food came, and I stopped caring about her motives. The gingerbread cake was warm and soft, but firm enough to dip into the bowl of orange and nutmeg-spiced whipped cream. I closed my eyes in ecstasy. Adele's baker had outdone herself.

Tabitha pushed a bowl of sugar-coated cranberries toward me. "Have one."

I took a sip of tea to clear my palette, then popped a cranberry into my mouth. Sheer decadence.

"You must be wondering why I asked to see you." Tabitha turned her teacup on its small plate.

"I assume it had something to do with the Christmas Cow."

She shook her head, her gold hoop earrings bouncing against her neck. "No, it's about the bombing."

"The bombing?"

"I feel terrible about what happened. You were nearly killed right in our driveway, and we had no idea someone was tampering with your mother's car while we were inside. I've already made this offer to your mother — if you had to go to the hospital, or you had any damage to your clothing, I'd like to pick up the bill."

I sat back in my chair. "That's kind of you, but I couldn't accept. You weren't responsible." The only reason I could imagine for Tabitha to make this offer was that she suspected her son was guilty. "I think everyone's going on the assumption that whoever blew up my mom's car was one of the people involved in the attack on the Christmas Cow."

"And that's the problem." Tabitha's mouth compressed.

"What do you mean?"

"The police seem convinced that Craig was involved in that cow business. He wasn't," she said quickly. "Yes, he and some friends of his joked about lighting the cow on fire, but that was all. They never actually did anything."

"You must be relieved." But she obviously wasn't, or she wouldn't be talking to me now.

"I am. I can tell when my son is lying. He's telling the truth. He and his . . . *friends* had nothing to do with the cow. And he certainly wouldn't know how to make a bomb."

But would he? There was all sorts of nasty stuff on the Internet.

Tabitha's full lips curled. "So he couldn't have set that bomb. It was simply bad luck that he stormed out of the house when he did. I understand how suspicious the timing must seem."

It did look suspicious. But Craig wasn't the only one who'd disappeared during our conversation. Tom had left the room as well.

My grip tightened on the teacup. If Craig or Tom wasn't the guilty party, then who was? Had someone followed us to the Wildes'? I hadn't noticed any tails, but I hadn't exactly been looking either. And even if I had been, I wasn't sure if I'd be able to catch one.

"What's wrong?" Tabitha asked.

"None of this is adding up. I have a hard time believing the shooting at the Christmas Cow was a prank gone wrong."

Her hand clenched on the teacup. "So do I! If that awful Oliver hadn't shot his mouth off . . ."

"Oliver?"

The councilwoman shook her head. "Oliver Breathnach. He's always getting into trouble and dragging Craig along with him. Who would have thought his stupid joke would have made such trouble for his friends?"

"Breathnach?" I'd heard that name before, but where?

"He's Kendra Breathnach's son. She's the

developer?"

"Oh, right." I'd met her in the beauty parlor where Belle worked. "So Oliver gets into trouble a lot? Do you think he was involved in the attack on the cow?"

"I wouldn't put it past him." Tabitha frowned into her cup. "But it doesn't matter anyway. Like I said, an attack on the cow was all hot air on Oliver's part."

I wondered if Oliver would shoot his mouth off to me. Absently, I rubbed my arm. "But the alternative, that a group of men conspired to kill Bill Eldrich, doesn't make sense either. And who would have wanted to kill him? Even though Dean Pinkerton was upset about the raw milk business, do you think he was angry enough to kill?"

"How would you feel if someone tried to legislate you out of business?" she asked.

A waitress bustled past, her black skirt swishing.

"I'd be pretty angry," I admitted. Angry enough to start setting bombs? "But is there anyone else you can think of who might have had it in for Bill?"

Tabitha sipped her tea. "There is someone," she said slowly. "She was furious with Bill, but like you, I have a hard time imagining her killing over this."

166

"Over what?"

She leaned back in her chair. "The president of the Wine and Visitors Bureau."

"Penny?" I asked, surprised. "What did she have against Bill?"

"It was my fault, in a sense." Tabitha's dark brow furrowed. "There was some extra tax money available from Measure C. We allowed the local nonprofits to apply for it. Originally, the Dairy Association and the Wine and Visitors Bureau had put together a joint proposal. But later, Bill put in a separate proposal for the Dairy Association alone. The tax committee felt the money would have more of an impact if it went to one organization, and it went to Bill's."

"And Penny blamed him," I said.

She picked apart a scone. Crumbs scattered across the white tablecloth. "I guess he didn't tell Penny about his solo proposal until after the voting. If she'd had any idea, I'm sure she would have put together a standalone proposal for the Wine and Visitors Bureau."

"So she felt betrayed," I said.

"I overheard them after the council meeting. She wasn't exactly shouting, but she was quite literally shaking with rage."

Penny of the grape cluster earrings? Enraged? "That's hard to imagine." I sipped my tea, sweet and spicy with a hint of plum.

"She takes her position at the Wine and Visitors Bureau seriously. You may not know this, but before Penny took over ten years ago, all we had was a wine association. She found the funding for the building and turned it into a tasting room. I have to say, she's done a wonderful job promoting San Benedetto wines. Without her work, we wouldn't have nearly as many tourists as we do today. Your museum can thank her for that."

"When did this happen?" I asked. "The argument about the funding, I mean."

"October."

No wonder I hadn't known any of this. In October, I'd been embroiled in a murder and paying zero attention to town politics. "So not that long ago," I muttered. After two months, would Penny still have been angry enough to kill?

ELEVEN

Tabitha left me at the tea room, and I finished my tea and gingerbread cake beneath the twinkle lights. I wiped the crumbs into a mound on one side of the white table cloth, then pulled out my cell phone. Not knowing Oliver's phone number, I called his mother's office.

"Kendra Breathnach, Breathnach Estates. How can I help you?"

"Hi, this is Maddie Kosloski from the Paranormal Museum."

There was a long pause. "Oh, yes. We met in the beauty parlor. How can I help you? Are you looking for a donation?"

"No, we don't really do donations." Aside from GD's tip jar, but that was for kibble only. I thought fast. I really wanted to talk to her son but I wasn't sure I wanted to let her know that. "I'm calling on behalf of Ladies Aid. About Bill Eldrich."

"Oh?" Her tone turned cautious.

"I didn't know him well" — or at all — "and I was hoping you could give me some insight into the man."

"Why?" Her voice sharpened. "Aren't the police investigating?"

"Yes, of course. But there've been some inconsistencies in the dealings between Ladies Aid and the Dairy Association that need to be cleared up," I babbled. I knew my mom would back me on this, and she was the president of Ladies Aid, but even I had no idea what I was talking about.

"Inconsistencies? But I'm not in Ladies Aid or the Dairy Association."

"I'd rather not get into it on the phone. Can we meet? Maybe this evening?" When her son was home?

"I'm about to leave the office for the afternoon." A heavy sigh. "Why don't you come by my house tonight?"

"Thanks." I pumped my fist in the air. Victory! "Is six o'clock okay?"

"Sure," she said. "Do you know where it is?" She gave me the address and we hung up.

A teenage girl walked into the tea room, the bell on her Santa hat jingling.

A woman shrieked. China shattered. The tea room fell into a weighted silence.

"The cowbells!" the matronly woman

gasped. "I heard them. Here!"

The teenager had frozen in the doorway. Face pale, eyes wide, warring between fight or flight, she fingered the end of her long red knit cap. "It's only my hat."

The woman rose and threw her cloth napkin to the table. "How was I to know? I thought this tea room was supposed to be a haven, a safe space. Bells! Here!"

Like everyone else in the tea room, I gaped, torn between embarrassment and fascination.

The teen backed up, bumping into the closed door. "But . . . it's Christmas."

The older woman jerked her jacket closed. "Those sound exactly like cowbells. You should come with a trigger warning."

The teen's shoulders crumpling inward. "I'm . . . I'm sorry."

Adele hurried forward. "No harm done," she sang out. She took the young woman's elbow and led her to an empty seat at the counter. "It was an easy mistake to make. Mrs. Wordsworth, can I get you more tea and another scone?" She bustled to the lady's table and got her back into her chair, bending to say something to her in a low voice.

Gradually, the chatter in the tea room rose to its normal levels.

Adele returned to the counter and spoke to the teenager. Soon, both were smiling and nodding. Then she stalked to my table and plopped into the chair opposite.

"You've got to do something about those cowbells," she grumbled. "In the last two days, there's been a fifteen percent increase in broken crockery. The town is panicking."

"Don't worry. I've got it all under control."

Her eyes narrowed. "How, exactly, do you have it under control?"

"The plan I told you about last night. Herb's bringing in a specialist to de-curse . . . I mean, bind the cowbells." I rubbed my jaw. "He'll be here tomorrow. We're inviting everyone on our email list, and my mom's going to get some local reporters to cover it. So the whole town will know that the cowbell curse is over and done with."

"It's not enough," Adele said bluntly.

I blinked. "What do you mean, it's not enough?"

"The curse is bigger than one of Herb's silly magical rituals."

"You think I should ask Harper to help?"

"Of course not," she replied. "But everyone is really afraid. Why should they believe your binding, or whatever Herb's planning, works?"

"You and I aren't afraid. It's the people who are superstitious who are worried. And I'm thinking the sort of person who believes in curses is the same sort of person who believes someone with magic powers can stop a curse."

"I hope you're right."

"I am." But doubt twinged through my veins.

"What?" Adele asked. "What's wrong?"

"Nothing." Folding my cloth napkin on the table, I scooted from my chair. "But there's something you can do to help."

"Oh?" She canted her head.

"Find out how much money Belle made off her Christmas Cow bet."

"You know Dieter takes his client confidentiality seriously." Adele drummed her manicured nails on the white tablecloth.

"I know there's an ongoing murder investigation, and he'd rather deal with me than the police, and someone tried to blow up my mom."

"Playing hardball, are you?"

"Playing desperate. Please Adele, I need to know."

She sighed. "I'll see what I can learn."

"Great. Thanks. I'd better get back to the

museum." I paid and hurried through the bookcase into the museum.

Leo stood behind the counter, the wall-phone receiver pressed to his ear. "There are lots of cows in San Benedetto," he said, "and plenty of them wear cowbells. It's not an unusual . . . . You heard the bells when you were walking into a store on School Street? Was there a bell over the door?"

I glanced at the bell over our own door. "What's going on?" I mouthed.

He put his hand over the receiver. "Someone's asking about the curse," he whispered.

I pointed to my chest. Did he want me to talk to them?

He shook his head. "There's no reason for the curse to have reactivated, but we're doing a binding spell tomorrow . . . . Because we had to hire a specialist . . . Yes . . . No, I don't — Yes . . . Yes . . . All right, I'll let her know." He hung up.

"What was that about?"

"Another curse call."

"Another? How many have we received?"

"A half dozen or so. Mind if I take my break?"

"No, go ahead," I said weakly.

I settled in behind the counter and got busy taking tickets and making change. The curse was just a silly story. I bit the inside of my cheek. Wasn't it?

The museum kept me too busy to wonder much if my curse-ending plan would succeed. Besides, I had flyers to make and an invite email to send out and panicked cowbell hearers to soothe.

My fist tightened on my pencil. Who the heck had dreamed up cowbells as death omens?

I dropped the pencil to the counter. Whoops. I was supposed to be looking into exactly that question for Detective Slate. Though if all went well, tomorrow's curse-binding ceremony would calm the town and the question would be moot.

Finally I ushered the last visitor out the door, locked it, and flipped the sign to *Closed.* I sagged against the counter and glanced at GD. He'd coiled possessively around the tip jar and slept, purring. At least I assumed he was asleep. For GD, closed eyes could be a ruse leading to an attack.

"Why am I the only one you bite?"

His black ears flicked.

I pushed the broom around the linoleum floor, ran the feather duster over the exhibits, and scuttled out to my truck, parked in the fog-shrouded alley.

The lights from Mason's second-floor apartment made long shadows of the dumpsters. I fumbled my truck keys, and they clattered loudly on the pavement. Stomach tightening, I glanced up again at Mason's square windows.

The best way for Belle to make sure she won the Christmas Cow bet would have been to set the cow on fire herself. But she hadn't lived in San Benedetto long enough to rustle up a posse of gingerbread men. Unless she'd brought in some out-of-towners from her former life. Had she offered to share the winnings with them? What *were* her winnings? I'd heard the money could get pretty big. Not lottery big, but big. Certainly big enough for her to move out of Mason's and get her own place. Assuming she wanted to.

I stepped into my truck and rolled down the alley, not liking the way my thoughts were running. Mason was a big boy, and Belle was none of my business. Besides, Mason had good instincts. He wouldn't share his apartment with an arsonist. Right?

Main Street was a Christmas wonderland of twinkle lights, its shop windows sparkling in their holiday bling. Wreaths of holly hung from doors and around the iron streetlamps. We might be snow-free, but the fog cast a mysterious London gloom and I imagined chestnut sellers and ragged boys in top hats racing down the street.

I made a turn, passing the Sugar Hall Bakery. A tall gingerbread house surrounded by prancing gingerbread men and women filled its window. It would be a long time before my mom could stomach gingerbread men again.

I smacked my head. My mom. I'd promised to come by for dinner. I glanced at my watch. It was almost six. Even with stopping by Kendra's, I'd only be a little late. And my mom would forgive my tardiness if I arrived bearing intel.

Kendra lived less than a mile from the Wildes' house, so she was easy to locate. Her home was a two-story, gabled, Tudor-style manse in a new subdivision. The lawns all had the same manicured look, with brick or flagstone driveways, and the houses were all half-timbered on the second floors. I expected a Shakespearean festival to sprout from a lawn at any minute, but that would be too gauche for the neighborhood's discreet white twinkle lights gleaming through the thickening fog.

I parked on the street. Zipping up my black parka, I walked up the flagstone path to the arched front door. There were no cars in the driveway, and my hopes of roping her son into this conversation fell.

A lion's head door knocker scowled at me. I grasped the ring between its teeth and knocked.

A minute later, Kendra opened the door. She was barefoot and chic in expensive jeans and a white blouse. Simple gold hoop earrings nearly vanished in the gold of her hair. Her brown eyes widened. "Maddie!" She blinked. "I'd forgotten you were coming."

"Is this a bad time?"

"No, no. Come in." She stepped aside.

Feeling underdressed, I entered the elegant foyer. A massive display of white poinsettia decorated a round table. "Should I take my shoes off?"

"If you don't mind."

I pulled off my tennis shoes and tugged down the toe of my left sock, trying to obscure the hole. I hadn't planned on anyone seeing it when I'd dressed that morning.

She escorted me into a plush, white-on-white living room. A Christmas tree decked in designer red and gold scraped the high ceiling.

"What a beautiful tree." I sank deep into the soft white couch. It was wide and my feet dangled, my big toe sticking from the sock. I crossed my ankles, hiding the view of my chipped nail polish.

"Thanks. Can I get you something to drink? Tea? Coffee? Hot buttered rum?"

"No thanks." I glanced around, looking for signs of her son. "I'm headed to my mother's house for dinner later."

"Ah yes, you said you were an emissary for Ladies Aid." Kendra sat in a wing chair across from me. "That there was some unfinished business about Bill Eldrich you thought I could help with? I'm really not sure how I can."

"There's a controversy about whether the Christmas Cow tradition should continue." Maybe if I got her talking about the cow, we'd naturally slide into the arson and her son.

"You mean — whether to rebuild it this year?"

The sock rode down my toe. Ears hot, I coiled my left leg beneath me, hiding my foot under my thigh. "Yes, and in future years."

"It's not a decision I'm involved with."

"But you are a prominent member of San Benedetto. You're building a new neighborhood."

She toyed with her hair. "I do feel community involvement is important."

"I've heard that Bill Eldrich was insistent the cow be built this year, in spite of a lot of opposition," I said. "But he was the head of the Dairy Association . . ." I shrugged, doubtful she'd be able to fill in the blanks. This had been a bad idea. I should have just asked her for Oliver's number.

Her smile was pained. "He could be quite determined. It's ironic that the cow he pushed so hard for killed him."

"How well did you know Bill?" I asked, surprised I might actually learn something from her. Had I accidentally stumbled onto an information source?

"Not very. I saw him at community events, of course. And my company has bids on several dairy farms, which Bill wasn't happy about, but I don't think he blamed me."

"Why did he care if you bought someone's farm?"

"Because the world of agriculture is changing. Small dairy farms are going away, being consolidated by major corporations that can operate them more efficiently."

I rubbed my hand lightly over the velvety sofa arm. "It is sad to see them go."

"Change is inevitable. That said, I certainly hope they don't all go away. The farms add to the character of the town —

180

not as much as the vineyards, but still. It's important for people to stay in touch with where their food comes from. That's why I'm so excited about our new vineyard-centered development. We're breaking new ground, both literally and figuratively."

"Oh?"

"The idea of an agrihood isn't new, of course. But by building the community around a communal vineyard instead of a farm, we're hoping to attract a more mature level of home buyers."

"You mean retirees."

She grinned. "Exactly."

"Harvest isn't easy," I said. It was back-breaking work. I couldn't imagine a bunch of citified septuagenarians harvesting grapes.

She stared fixedly at me. "Hiring younger people to assist with the harvest has been factored into the community fees. It will be well worth the price of producing wine that residents have bottled and tended them-selves. But you said there was some out-standing business with Ladies Aid?"

"Yes. There's been a story going around that kids from the local junior college were involved in the prank on the Christmas Cow."

"The arson, you mean," she said darkly.

181

I bit the bullet. "And that your son, Oliver, might know something about those involved."

Her face smoothed. "Know something?"

I remained silent and attempted an enigmatic look.

She jerked to her feet. "Are you accusing him of being involved?"

"No. But if this was a prank gone bad —"

"If? Are you saying it wasn't a prank? That it was intentional?"

"I have no idea, but if —"

Kendra Breathnach paced in front of the red-and-gold tree. "Isn't it more likely someone who was betting on the cow set it on fire?"

"That's a possibility," I said. "But if it was a prank, it's in the students' best interests to come forward voluntarily. The police are looking hard at this."

"Who told you my son was involved?"

"It's not important —"

"Who told you?"

"The easiest way to clear this up is to ask your son."

"My son was home in bed the night the cow was set on fire."

"How can you be sure?" It was unlikely she'd watched him while he slept — or pretended to sleep.

"I'm sure. And if the police ask me, I'll tell them the same thing. My son had nothing to do with that arson."

"Is your son home?"

"No," she said coldly. "He's at Lake Tahoe, skiing. It's his winter break. Why are you really here?"

"I'm doing an informal survey of people associated with the Wine and Visitors Bureau and the Dairy Association about the future of the cow."

"Because it sounds like an interrogation. And my son is none of your business."

A bead of sweat trickled down my neck. "Of course not. I'm sorry. I didn't mean to cause offense. There's a college student working at the museum, so I've got some sympathy for them. I'm sure none of the attackers planned to hurt anyone."

Kendra's mouth pinched. "To answer your survey question, I think the Christmas Cow is one of San Benedetto's biggest attractions. It would be a shame to see it go."

"Then that's all. Thank you!" I bounced off the couch and race-walked into the foyer.

She followed me to the paneled wood door.

But my speedy exit was thwarted. I hopped on one foot, trying to wedge the other into my sneaker. I squatted, knotting

183

my shoes. "Will the winery development also be Tudor-style?" I asked.

"No. Tuscan."

"Sounds great," I said brightly and straightened. I edged out the door. "Well, Merry Christmas!"

"Goodbye." She slammed the door shut.

Not-quite-running to my truck, I jumped in and drove to my mom's ranch-style house.

In the front yard, three reindeer fashioned out of grapevines and wrapped in twinkle lights glowed, giant red bows around their necks. My headlights flashed on the white picket fence and an empty police car parked outside.

Empty? Where were the cops?

Skin prickling, I parked beneath an oak and crept up the brick path to the front door. My mom owned a lot of acreage that she'd let revert to the wild. She said she liked the privacy. But now the acres of dark and tangled shrub seemed threatening.

I tried the knob.

The door was unlocked.

I swallowed, my pulse accelerating. True, my mom never locked the door. But under the circumstances, her lax attitude toward security worried me. And where were those cops?

Slowly, I swung open the door and sidled inside.

"No!" my mom shrieked.

Breathless, I sprinted into the kitchen and skidded to a halt.

My mom bent double, laughing.

Two police officers sat around the gray granite island munching pfeffernüsse cookies, powdered sugar drifting onto their blue uniforms.

Dieter leaned against the counter, mug of hot cocoa in his hands. He quirked a brow. "Hey, Mad."

"Dieter." I willed my heartbeat to slow. "What's going on?"

"Just an impromptu holiday party," my mom said. "Pfeffernüsse?" She offered me a plate.

"Thanks." I took a cookie. Pfeffernüsse was one of my favorites, even if it did leave me covered in powdered sugar.

"What brought you here?" she asked. "Not that I mind."

"I thought we were having dinner tonight," I said, disappointed.

She shook her head. "I forgot. We got caught up in telling stories, and the time flew."

I glanced around her country-kitsch kitchen, with its distressed off-white cabinets and missing cabinet doors. Trays and boxes of cookies filled every available counter space. "Maybe we should order in?"

"Marvelous idea," she said. "What do you boys want for dinner?"

The cops shook their heads. "We can't," one said. With smooth cheeks and an earnest expression, he looked like he was barely out of high school. "We should get back to the car. Thanks for the hot chocolate, though."

His partner's face fell, but he nodded. "Rules." They walked out.

"Dieter, would you order Chinese?" my mom asked. "You know what everyone likes. And Maddie, could you help me in the project room? I need your young eyes for some sewing I'm working on."

"Sure," I said and followed her into the project room that had once been my bedroom. Plastic boxes sat neatly stacked along industrial-looking shelves. My childhood flower-print curtains still hung in the window. "What's Dieter doing —"

"What did you learn?" my mom whispered.

I rubbed the back of my neck. "What?"

"The investigation! Surely you got *some* detecting done today?"

"I talked to Tabitha again, and she pointed

186

the finger at Kendra Breathnach's son, Oliver, as one of the gingerbread men."

"You've got powdered sugar on your chin, dear."

Whoops. I wiped it off.

"But did you talk to Oliver?" she asked.

"No, I talked to his mother, the agrihood developer."

"You should have talked to him. Really, Madelyn, what were you thinking?"

"But —"

"Never mind." She fiddled with her turquoise necklace. "Did Kendra tell you anything?"

"She said Oliver was home in bed that night, but I don't know how she could be sure. It's a huge house. It wouldn't be hard to sneak out after his mom went to sleep." I fingered my old curtains, wondering why she'd kept them.

"And Kendra's divorced, so he'd only have one parent to evade. What else? You said you followed up with Tabitha?"

"She followed up with me. She offered to pay for any damage from the bombing."

"She called me as well, and I told her not to bother. Insurance is dropping off a rental car tomorrow, and they'll take care of getting a permanent replacement. But she's afraid her son set the bomb."

"Or her husband."

"What are you two up to?" Dieter asked from the doorway.

I started guiltily. "You caught us gossiping."

His eyes narrowed. "Maddie, can you help me get something out of the truck?"

"Your truck?" I asked. "What do you need?"

He smiled determinedly. "Can you help or not?"

"Sure! Sure, sure, sure." I followed him out of the house.

He stopped beside his rickety truck. "Look, I like your mom and all, but she's starting to wig me out," he hissed.

"Not enough for you to turn down free Chinese food."

"She already knows Belle won the cow bet." Dieter's breath misted the night air. "What more does she want?"

"To know how much money Belle won?"

"Sorry, babe. I draw the line at financial information."

"You're a bookie, not a financial advisor." Harper was sticky about client privacy too.

"There are people who would say there's no real difference."

"Dieter, it's my mom. She was nearly killed in that bombing."

His suntanned face creased. "Look, I can't tell you how much Belle won, but I can tell you she needs the money. And the more your mom pokes her nose into this, the more danger she'll be in." He reached into the truck bed and grabbed an extension cord, then thrust it into my arms. "You've got to shut her down, Mad."

If only I knew how.

TWELVE

I left Dieter to my mother's tender mercies and forgot about him by the next morning. Between the museum's usual Sunday crowd, the calls of frantic tinnitus sufferers, and the impending binding of the cowbells, I'd been forced to skip lunch. I'd also caught myself giving parked cars a wide berth in case one suddenly exploded. That made me cranky.

Jason Slate prowled into the museum. He paused before the counter, his brown eyes twinkling. Beneath one muscular arm, he carried a manila folder. He wore a thick black coat over his suit and looked good enough to eat. It was almost unfair.

My irritation fading, I steadied my cartwheeling heart.

"A binding spell?" He slid my flyer onto the glass counter. "Really?"

"It's simple psychology." I admired the flyer, then returned to wrapping a silver fairy for my elderly customer. Her gray head barely cleared the top of the counter. I suspected elf heritage.

"Don't you mean parapsychology?" he asked.

I smirked. "Smartass."

"Young lady!" My customer's marshmallow brows rose. "Such language! And to an officer of the law."

"Sorry." I handed her the fairy. "And happy holidays!"

The elderly woman sniffed and tottered from the museum.

"Anyway," I said, "curses are psychosomatic. This binding ritual should un-psycho everyone."

"I wish you'd talked to me first," he said.

"Why?"

"Someone who knows how to set bombs tried to kill you and/or your mother."

"And you think the event might be a target," I said, aghast. Why hadn't I considered that? Was I putting people in danger?

"It probably won't be, but I'll be sticking around to make sure everything goes smoothly."

"The ritual was a last-minute event. I doubt there will be many people."

"No offense, but let's hope not." Jason set the manila folder on top of the flyer. "And

191

on another topic, here are those case files you asked for."

"You found stuff on the cowbell-related deaths in the '80s?" I hoped it wouldn't turn out to be a wild bell chase. But we wouldn't need the files once the town believed I'd bound the curse. "And the bombing? Have you learned anything?"

He shook his head. "Sorry. Have you had lunch?"

My stomach rumbled and I checked my watch. It was after one. "No. Between the Christmas rush and the ceremony at three, I've been swamped."

"Want to grab a bite? We can go over these files together before your show starts."

"Is this part of your guard duty?" I figured the only reason he'd ask me out was because he had to.

"No, this is me hungry."

"Then sure!" I quickly returned to earth. "But I can't. Leo isn't back from his lunch . . ."

Leo, carrying a shopping bag, hurried through the front door. "Hey. Sorry I'm late," he said, panting. "I can take over." He sidled behind the counter.

My assistant's appearance was enough to make me believe in fate. "I guess I'm free for lunch after all."

"How about the Book Cellar?" Jason asked.

The place was a little dark for perusing police files, but they had an excellent prosciutto and Brie panini. And the idea of having a candlelit lunch with the handsome detective wasn't wholly unappealing. Who was I kidding? It was totally appealing.

I grabbed my purse. Jason held the door for me, then followed me onto the brick sidewalk.

It was one of those cloudless winter days that snap at your cheeks. My spirits rose, even if I had to trot to keep up with Jason's long strides. He waited for a slow-moving Buick, giving me time to catch up, and then we crossed the street.

He held the door to the Book Cellar for me, and we walked through carpeted aisles scented with books and down the steps into the dimly lit cellar. Empty wine casks lined its walls. The bar and restaurant buzzed with conversation.

At a corner booth, I shrugged out of my pea coat. Jason hurried to help me, his fingers whispering across the back of my neck. I shivered and hoped he didn't notice.

We ordered, and he opened the manila folder on the red tablecloth. "Maybe it would be easier if we sat on the same side," he said.

"You're probably right." Casually, I slid out of the booth and sat beside him.

"Okay," he said, "we had five committee members when the Christmas Cow tradition started and the town was gifted the cowbells from our sister city in Sweden. All of them were dead by the following December."

"Were any of the deaths suspicious?" I asked.

"We're looking for proof there's no curse, remember. Not proof of murder." A corner of his mouth quirked. "But no, none were suspicious or we'd have more detailed reports."

"So what have you got?" My elbow brushed his and a tingle of energy flowed between us.

Or had I imagined it? Was I making up a fairy-tale romance because I'd lost Mason?

Jason slid a coroner's report toward me. "Hansel Braff, aged sixty-seven, height five-foot-ten, weight two hundred and eighty pounds. Died of a heart attack the January after the first Christmas Cow — which survived the season, by the way."

"Which is why they kept building the cow each year."

"Right. The arson didn't begin until the early 1990s. But that's got nothing to do with our curse issue."

"Hansel Braff was the driving force behind the Christmas Cow," I said, reciting the bells' placard from memory. "He was a Swedish dairy farmer. He traveled to our sister city in Sweden to receive the bells. People who believe in the curse say the first to touch them was the first to die."

"Next up was Heidi Durian, aged seventy-two." Jason's suit jacket sleeve brushed my hand as he passed me another report. "We have a bit more on her, because she died in a car accident. She drove her Honda into an oak during a bad storm in February."

I scanned the documents. "She was the president of Ladies Aid and met Hansel at the airport upon his return from Sweden."

"Where I suppose she fondled the bells."

"Who wouldn't?"

He grinned.

"Joking aside," I said, "second to encounter the bells, second to die. It is a little spooky." This lunch was just business, two colleagues getting together. Just business . . .

"You've been spending too much time in your museum."

"I've been spending all my time in my museum."

The waitress arrived with our drinks — iced tea for me and coffee for the detective. She bustled away.

"Third to die," Jason said, "was another member of Ladies Aid, Kamilla Shapira. Aged fifty-eight, she had a stroke in March and a history of high blood pressure. Her husband found her at home and called 911. She was pronounced dead at the scene."

He handed me that report, and I skimmed it.

"It all seems normal," I said, "but her death was when people started rumbling about a curse. She drove Hansel and Heidi from the Sacramento airport to San Benedetto."

"You've been doing a lot of research."

"For my cowbell exhibit. I should do more, but it's been so busy at the museum. Hopefully the binding ritual will calm things down. Are you still sure you want to come?"

"I'd better," he said, grim.

I straightened. "You're not really expecting trouble, are you?"

"Not expecting it," he said, "no."

"But?"

"We're getting more calls at the station, not less, since your flyers went up around town."

Brow furrowing, I sipped my tea. "At the

museum too. The panic seems to be catching."

"Why now?" he asked. "Those bells have been around for decades. Sure, Mr. Eldrich's death was dramatic, but why would people connect it to the curse?"

My appetite fled. "There was the newspaper article. And maybe just because this was the year the bells were brought out of cold storage?" In my defense, the museum is packed to the rafters with supposedly cursed and haunted objects. Nobody had ever freaked out before. How was I to know the bells would set off such a brouhaha?

"It's not your fault."

"Thanks," I said, not believing him. The worst of it was, I really didn't want to give up the bells. So this afternoon's binding ceremony had better work. "But the curse — which never really existed, of course — has only ever struck people on the original Christmas Cow committee. Why would anyone else think they're in danger?"

"People are irrational. We like to think we're driven by logic, but we're creatures of emotion."

"That's what Harper says."

"Your friend the financial adviser?"

"Yeah. She says all decisions are emotional. We just rationalize them later." Like

197

my decision to go out to lunch with Jason, even though we didn't really need to go through these police files together. "Okay, who was the next to die?"

Expression startled, the waitress set our plates on the table. A spinach leaf dropped from my plate onto the red cloth. "Can I get you anything else?" she asked.

Jason looked to me, and I shook my head. "No, thanks," he said. "We're good."

She scuttled away.

I took a bite of my sandwich, and my appetite returned. Hot melted Brie and prosciutto heaven. Which immediately jammed between my teeth, dammit. I should have known not to order it on a date. Not that we were on a date. This was purely professional. "Next?" I asked, hand over my mouth.

"Why are you covering your mouth?"

"Because I've got prosciutto teeth. Avert your gaze."

He stared down at the file. "Next up was another dairy man, Rudy Saarisland. He was eighty-nine, died of a heart attack in the hospital that May. All I've got on him is a death certificate." He handed it to me.

I glanced at it. "I couldn't find any record of when he first encountered the bells. Things get murky after the airport pickup.

And the last person?"

"The last to die was a member of the town council, Sigfried Tassi, aged thirty-six."

"Young. How'd he die?"

Jason bit into his panini, chewed, swallowed. "Electrocution. His new boom box fell into the bathtub. That was in June. His wife, Jennifer, called 911, but he was pronounced dead at the scene."

"Is Jennifer still around?" The current hysteria must have been bringing up all sorts of unpleasant memories for her. The poor woman.

"I don't know. Why? Do you want to talk to her?"

"I wonder how other family members feel about the revival of the curse story. It must be painful." And my fault. I'd always considered my museum harmless fun. But was it?

"Considering the ages of the people who died, I'd bet she's the only surviving family member. But I can check into it, if you want."

And suddenly I did want to talk to Jennifer. Maybe it was true that all decisions are emotional. But if the curse was causing someone real pain, I'd have to mothball the cowbells.

"If the binding ritual doesn't cool things off, yes, I think I'll need to speak with her.

199

And talk to any others who might still be around."

I looked up. Jason watched me intently, and my face warmed. "I still have prosciutto in my teeth, don't I?"

"You're prosciutto-free."

"Then what?"

"Nothing. Assuming today's ceremony doesn't work —"

"Why wouldn't it work? It'll work."

"But if it doesn't, what's your next step?"

"Talk to the older folks in Ladies Aid and the Dairy Association." And the fact that the dairy folks might offer insights into Bill Eldrich was wholly coincidental. If I happened to uncover any clues to his death, I'd turn them over to Slate like any good citizen. "They might remember some detail about what got the curse started that will help us defuse it."

"*If* the binding ceremony fails to convince the town they're safe."

"Right."

He nodded. "Let me know if you do decide to visit the old-timers. I'll come with you."

In spite of the panini weighting me down, my stomach fluttered. "You will?"

"And make sure the curse is the only thing you're interrogating them about."

I deflated. "What? That isn't fair."

He raised a brow. "Isn't it?"

"Just what are you accusing me of?"

"Did I accuse you of something? Why are you being so sensitive?"

"Finish your panini. I've got a curse ceremony to organize."

THIRTEEN

Velvet ropes cordoned off the bells, and a crowd of tourists pressed close. Detective Jason Slate had vanished into the throng. GD perched on the tippy-top of Gryla's papier-mâché cave and surveyed the room.

"What do you expect this ceremony will accomplish?" A bored-looking female reporter from Sacramento moved her digital recorder in front of my mouth. Attention from Sacramento was big-time for the museum, but all I could feel was relief that the press hadn't discovered it was my mother's car that had gotten blown to smithereens. I'd much rather talk about haunted cowbells than the bombing.

Mike, the young reporter from our local paper, leaned closer. He was probably more interested in the hottie from Sacramento than the curse-removal story, but I'd take what I could get.

I cleared my throat. "My hope is that the

cowbells, which are an important part of San Benedetto's history, will once again become objects of fun and interest rather than objects of fear."

"How does this ritual work?" Mike asked.

"Maddie!" Herb waved frantically from the Fortune Telling Room. The overhead lights glinted off his thick glasses. "Maddie!"

"I've been told it will both cleanse the object and bind any remaining paranormal energy," I said.

The carrot-top from Sacramento angled her head, her expression skeptical. "But how does it work?"

"That's a question for our specialist. Um, will you excuse me?" I slipped through the crowd.

Herb backed into the Fortune Telling Room and bumped into a case filled with Ouija boards, tarot cards, divining rods, and other tools of the trade. He slithered around the lightweight Victorian séance table in the center of the room and gripped a door on the tall spirit cabinet against the wall. A poster of Houdini glowered down at him.

"There's a cop here!" he whisper-shouted. He stepped into the cabinet, sat on the bench inside, and folded his arms.

I glanced through the open doorway at

the milling throng. Now was not the time for Herb's paranoia. "We've got a big crowd," I said, my voice soothing. "And the police are getting a lot of calls about the bells. They want to make sure everything's okay. Now where's your curse-removal specialist?"

"He'll be here. He's just picking up some holy water." Herb swallowed nervously. "This might cost more than I projected."

My eyes widened. "More?" I stepped forward.

Herb grabbed the door handles and slammed the spirit cabinet shut, barricading himself inside.

I pounded on the doors. "Get out of there. I'm not going to hurt you, and that cabinet's an antique."

"What about that cop?" His voice floated, a spectral hiss, through the closed wooden doors.

"And what do you mean cost *more*? How much more?"

He cracked open a door. One beady eye, monstrously magnified by his glasses, peered out. "The normal method for dealing with a curse as dangerous as this one would be to destroy the bells. At the very least, you'd bury them or sink them in a river."

"What?!" I yanked open the cabinet doors.

He raised his hands in a warding gesture. "But I knew you wouldn't want to do that. These are historical objects, after all. So I came up with an alternative solution — a binding box."

"What's that?"

"It's perfect for the museum, and a historical object in and of itself. It's been magically consecrated, with protective wards on all sides, and it's quite old."

A couple stuck their heads inside the Fortune Telling Room, saw me glaring at the spirit cabinet, and edged out.

"If the bells are in a box," I said, "how is anyone going to see them?"

"Xavier and I worked that out. We replaced the lid with glass and inked a powerful sigil onto the inside of the glass to maintain the wards. All you'll need to do is clean the outside of the glass regularly with a vinegar and holy water mixture."

I ground my teeth. "How much more?"

"A bargain at five hundred dollars."

"What?!"

"Xavier refused to hold the ritual unless he was sure it would work. This was the only other way to get him to agree."

"An extra five hundred dollars!"

"Think of it as more than a box, but as a new and exciting exhibit for the museum.

The original sigils were drawn onto the box by a nineteenth-century shaman, a priest, and a rabbi. It came from the Black Forest!"

"There are shamans in the Black Forest?" I asked, intrigued in spite of myself.

He folded his hands in his lap. "Shamans are everywhere. You really should learn more about your magical history."

"But . . . five hundred dollars more," I said weakly. We'd been doing well this month, but I fully expected January to be a dead zone. And I'd promised Leo a bonus. Still, I didn't see how I could get around it. The museum was packed, and the natives were restless and expecting a show. "You shouldn't have agreed to it without asking me first," I muttered.

Sensing my defeat, he clambered from the cabinet. "You won't regret it. This artifact is a work of art. And I've kept the box's original lid, so you can display that as well or resell it later. I was a little concerned that by replacing it with glass, and turning the box on its side for display, it would lose some of its efficacy. But we've cast the appropriate spells, and we managed to scare up another rabbi and priest to bless it. Fortunately, Xavier is a shaman."

"Of course he is." I groaned. This was

Herb's revenge because I'd refused to buy that stupid magic mirror.

"He assures me this will work. So, if you can you write me a check for the box . . . ?"

"Herb —"

"It was the only way I could get Xavier here. He takes his work very seriously. And if you want the town to believe those bells are safe, you need him."

"Herb —"

"No box, no ritual."

I looked around the muttering crowd in the next room. I couldn't back out now. Not after I'd charged for tickets. "We'll discuss this later."

"Fine, but I really do need that check up front. Xavier bought the binding box himself, and if he's not paid up front —"

"Fine!" I stormed from the room. Weaving between spectators, I bumped into Harper.

"Whoa." She brushed a speck of paranormal museum dust from the lapel of her suede blazer. Beneath it she wore a camel-colored turtleneck sweater and matching scarf. She flicked her luxuriously long hair over one shoulder. "What's wrong?"

"Herb's holding me up for another five hundred bucks. I have to put the bells in a binding box." It sounded ridiculous spoken aloud.

"I was wondering how they were going to get around burying or destroying the bells," she said.

"You mean the binding box idea is a real thing?"

A woman knocked into me from behind, and I grabbed a display case to steady myself.

"I've never seen one," Harper said, "but I've been doing curse research on your behalf. They're real."

"You've been researching?" I clutched her arm. "You're amazing!" I knew she'd be able to help.

"I'm no expert on curses," she said. "But you got me curious."

The red-headed reporter bore down on us.

"Let's talk later." I skittered behind a display case and bumped into a middle-aged woman in an old-fashioned violet cloche hat. "Sorry."

She turned and disappeared into the crowd.

Shrugging, I circled to the counter and edged behind Leo, who was selling tickets. I grabbed my purse from beneath the register and hastily wrote out a check, any profits

I'd hoped for from the event evaporating. At least I still had potential publicity to make it worth my while.

On the other side of the counter, Herb snatched the check from my hand. "This will do."

"So where is he?" I asked.

The front door opened, bumping a woman from behind, and a tall, cadaverous man with a salt-and-pepper goatee slithered into the museum.

"That's him," Herb said.

Expression leery, the man approached the counter. "Good afternoon," he said in a crypt-deep voice.

Ants crawled up my spine.

"May I presume you are Madelyn Kosloski, proprietress of this paranormal museum?" he asked.

"She is," Herb said. "Maddie, this is Xavier." He handed the man the check. "We're ready to start whenever you are."

"I'll need some assistance with the salt," Xavier said.

"Salt?" I asked.

"The barrel is rather heavy," the cowbell exorcist said.

"Salt?" I repeated.

"I can borrow the dolly from the tea room," Leo said, handing off change to a customer.

"That would be excellent, young man," Xavier said. "I'm afraid I had to park a few blocks away. The street is quite crowded."

Leo looked at the bookcase, saw people packed against it, and hurried out the front door and around to the tea room.

"Salt?" I bleated again.

"Burying the bells in salt is part of the cleansing process," Xavier said. "Since your bells are attached to that large tree-shaped iron form, I've packed a wine barrel with salt. We can put the bells in the barrel for the ritual. How fortunate that it's a sunny day."

True. I doubted I'd have had half this crowd if we'd gotten rained out. "So to bind the bells, you put the bells in the barrel, and then you put the bells in the box?" I asked. Balderdash.

Outside, Leo knocked on the glass half of the museum's front door.

Xavier nodded. "I shall return shortly, and we can begin the ritual. Please ask everyone to be quiet." He left.

I stared at the chattering crowd, and my stomach twisted. We'd better not be over fire code capacity. Counting heads, I walked to the bells and unhooked the red velvet rope that cordoned off the area. The people closest to the barricade quieted, and the silence rippled eerily outward.

I stepped behind the rope and scraped a hand through my hair. "Welcome to the Paranormal Museum." My voice cracked and I cleared my throat. "As you may have heard, today we'll be conducting a binding ritual on San Benedetto's famous cowbells."

I glanced toward the front door. "The bells were donated to San Benedetto by our sister city in Sweden the same year we introduced the Christmas Cow. The San Benedetto Christmas Cow was a nod to our sister city's Yule Goat," I said, stalling. Where was Xavier? "The origin of the Yule goat is unclear. It may stretch back to pagan days, when the Norse god, Thor, was believed to ride across the sky in a chariot drawn by goats."

Mason Hjelm walked past the front window. The big Viking paused and looked in, his expression puzzled, then grinned and continued on.

I swallowed. "Later folk depictions of Father Christmas showed him riding a goat. Today these straw goats are most frequently seen in Scandinavia as Christmas ornaments." Ugh. I was making the supernatural sound dull.

"What about the cursed bells?" a man

shouted.

I cut a nervous glance at the door. "There are stories of curses throughout history. The curse of Tutankhamun is perhaps one of the most famous. But I believe our cowbells are unique."

Jason caught my eye and frowned.

"However," I said quickly, "I've been working closely with the bells and nothing has happened to me. The curse is history. The town has nothing to fear." The whole point of the museum was the creepy and paranormal — I couldn't say the supernatural was *all* bunkum.

"Then why are you bringing in a curse remover?" another man asked.

"Excellent question." Really excellent question. Excellent, excellent, excellent. I forced a smile and struggled for an answer. "First, since this is a paranormal museum, I thought it would provide a unique opportunity to see this type of ritual in action. And second, because even though the bells are perfectly safe, extra protection can't hurt."

The front door opened and Xavier walked inside.

My shoulders sagged with relief. Then I frowned. Where was Leo and the salt barrel? Since I'd run out of things to say, I

212

motioned toward the corpselike Xavier. "And this is our specialist who will be conducting the ritual. Xavier, would you like to say a few words?"

Gravely, he approached the bells. I unhooked the rope and allowed him entrée, then slipped out and hooked it up again.

Jason nudged my elbow. "Nicely done."

"Thanks," I whispered and wiped my brow. With all the bodies crammed into the museum, the room had gotten hot. And I'd lost my body count for the fire code.

Xavier rubbed his hands together. "Thank you for coming. I'd like to ask you all to focus your positive energy on the bells throughout the ceremony. And I would also ask for silence. This work requires concentration." He turned to face the bells. Bowing his head, he clasped his hands together. His voice boomed. "Father in heaven . . ."

A motion at the corner of my eye caught my attention, and I glanced toward the front window. Leo was hopping on the sidewalk and blowing into his hands.

"Problem?" Jason said in a low voice.

"I hope not." I made my way through the throng to the door and slipped outside. Leo stood beside a wine barrel positioned upright on the brick sidewalk. Two massive sacks of salt sat beside it.

Rubbing my arms against the cold, I peered into the open barrel, about a quarter full of salt. "What's going on?"

"He said to wait with the barrel and the salt here."

"All right. Thanks." I ducked inside. The museum was strangely silent aside from a faint swishing sound. I pushed my way to the front and stopped beside Jason.

Xavier stood with a glass spray bottle covered in strange markings. They looked like they'd been drawn on with felt-tip pen. He squirted the bells with what I hoped was only water. I'd have to give them a good polishing when he was done so they didn't rust.

"Holy water," Jason muttered.

I relaxed.

Xavier lifted the iron form off its hook on the wall. Holding the bells high, he marched toward me.

Hastily, I unhooked the velvet rope.

The crowd stepped aside, murmuring.

I hurried to get in front of Xavier and opened the front door, wedging it open with my foot so the crowd could hear.

Xavier held the bells to the sky. They clanked, brass glinting in the sun. "The cleansing power of sunlight," he boomed, and I jumped. "May it break and dissolve all hexes, curses, and negative energies attached to these bells and their iron form." He plunged the bells into the barrel. "Young man?"

Faces pressed against the museum window. People spilled onto the brick sidewalk.

Leo helped him lift one of the sacks, and they poured more salt into the barrel.

I jammed my sleeves to my elbows and pulled them down again. If those bells were damp from the holy water, what would the salt do to them? Xavier and Leo dumped in the second bag, covering the bells completely.

"Now, son." Xavier came back into the museum and stepped inside the velvet rope. Leo wheeled the wine barrel behind him.

Hastily, I scooped up the discarded salt sacks from the sidewalk and followed.

Xavier raised his hand over the barrel. "Like the holy water, this salt has been consecrated. Holy water is a vehicle for purification. Salt, a pure mineral of the earth, is able to receive and hold both positive and negative energies. By placing the bells in salt, I have broken any negative energetic contact between the curse and the bells. Now, to ensure that contact is not renewed, I shall place the bells inside a consecrated binding box."

Whoa, whoa, whoa. Not without getting all that salt off first! I edged through the crowd and grabbed the feather duster from behind the counter.

Herb marched forward and handed what looked like a shadow box across the velvet barricade to Xavier.

"Young man?" Xavier asked. Leo straightened. "Would you please hold the binding box for me?"

Leo's Adam's apple bobbed nervously. "Sure."

Xavier hinged open the glass side of the box. A mysterious-looking symbol had been drawn on it in black marker.

And then the crowd closed ranks and I couldn't see anything. Frantic, I waved my feather duster in the air, hoping Leo would notice.

A hand grasped my arm. I turned and was nose to nose with Jason. My lips parted.

He released me. "Need some help?"

I stepped away, feeling myself flush. "Thanks." I let him guide me. The crowd magically parted for us, leaving us a clear path up to the cordon.

Xavier lifted the bells from the barrel. As I'd feared, they were encrusted with patches of salt. He turned away.

"Leo!" I hissed, and handed him the

duster. He passed it off to Xavier.

Xavier blinked, but nodded. Chanting something incomprehensible, he whisked the salt from the bells and onto the checkerboard floor.

I could clean that up later.

Intoning in Latin, Xavier carefully placed the bells into the box. They fit perfectly, seeming to hang on some sort of inside hook. I had to hand it to Herb. He may have snuck in a whopping extra charge, but he'd delivered a quality show.

Together, Leo and Xavier hung the box on the wall.

Leo stepped away. Xavier shut the glass front and raised his hands in a final benediction. "Strengthened by the intercession of angels and all heavenly spirits, I cancel all negative energies connected to these objects. I declare these bells bound!"

A thick silence fell.

I found myself holding my breath, and I slowly released it. So that was it. The curse was —

A woman shrieked. "Something bit me!"

My hands clenched. *GD!* I whipped my head around, searching for the cat. It wasn't like him to bite a customer, but the crowd might have upset him. Finally, I spotted the cat perched on top of Gryla's cave.

He stared down at me. His whiskers twitched with amusement.

Another woman squealed. "Ow! I'm bleeding! I've been bitten too."

"It didn't work!" someone shouted.

Xavier turned to frown at the bells, safely inside their binding box. "It *is* working. I can feel it."

The crowd swayed like an ocean tide. Someone jostled me and I staggered, nearly falling to the floor.

"Everyone, stay calm," Jason said. "It's probably just the cat."

We needed to get both exits open ASAP. "Leo," I shouted. "Bookshelf!"

He climbed over the velvet barricade and forced his way through the crowd.

I pushed through the masses to the front door and flung it wide.

People stampeded from the museum.

Glass smashed and I winced. The flow of people emptying onto the sidewalk became a stream, and then a trickle, and then it was just me and the open door.

Shaken, I stumbled into the museum. A display case lay on its side. A starburst of broken glass glittered on the linoleum floor. The bronze skull rocked to a halt beside my feet.

Leo and Harper leaned on opposite sides

of the open bookcase door. Leo's face was pale. "Wow."

I bent and set the skull on the counter.

Adele stormed through the open bookcase, her hands on her aproned hip. "What happened? What was that all about?"

"Emergency exit." Jason scanned the room. "Thanks for helping out."

She hadn't helped out, but the compliment seemed to mollify her. She smoothed her apron. "That's another three tea cups broken. But at least no one was hurt. Was anyone hurt?" she asked anxiously.

"I don't think so," Harper said.

Muttering and rubbing their chins, Xavier and Herb craned their necks at the bells. "It's working," Xavier said. "I don't understand what happened."

Harper straightened up off the bookcase and walked to the bells. Her eyes narrowed.

"There must be more than one cursed object in this museum," Herb said. "It was probably that bronze skull that attracted the dark spirit. That plus the energy of the crowd would have been powerful."

"Or the throwing knives," Xavier said. "I get a bad vibe from those."

The two reporters, their blazers askew, hurried over to the exorcists. "What happened? Why did the ritual fail?" the redhead from Sacramento asked.

"It didn't fail." Xavier's salt-and-pepper brows drew downward in a scowl.

"Says you," I muttered.

Harper waved a hand over the bells, her expression thoughtful.

Jason gripped my shoulder. "You tried."

Glum, I nodded and surveyed the destruction. Two haunted photos had been knocked from the wall, shattering glass and frames. A creepy doll lay on the floor. I picked it up and smoothed the skirt. "I guess it's back to Plan B. More research into how to debunk the curse."

"I thought that was Plan A," he said.

"It might have been your Plan A," I said, "but I hate having to debunk my own exhibits." I motioned toward the exorcists and the reporters, at Xavier stabbing his finger at the bells. "No one believes that binding box is any good!" And I'd paid five hundred bucks for it.

"It was a noble effort," Jason said. "You were right about the problem being psychological. The so-called 'bites' were probably mass hysteria."

"Thanks." I walked him to the door. "But I think I've made things worse."

We stepped onto the sidewalk. Sunset was

on its way, and the sky had turned a dusky blue.

He smiled. "No one was hurt. We'll figure this —" He suddenly shoved me sideways and I ricocheted off the wall.

A gray sedan jumped the curb and whizzed past. There was a sickening thump. Jason flew into the brick wall and fell hard to the sidewalk.

FOURTEEN

"Oh my God." I knelt beside Jason, limp on the sidewalk. Lightly, I ran my hands over him, checking for any blood or bones out of place. Something seemed wrong with his shoulder. Blood streamed from a cut on his head, making scarlet ribbons down one side of his face.

He groaned and sat up, and his dark skin turned gray.

"Don't try to move," I said.

The sedan squealed around a corner.

Leo and Adele ran onto the sidewalk. "Mad, are you hurt?" Adele asked.

"No, but Jason is."

The two reporters banged out the front door, and Herb and Xavier followed. The reporters whipped out their cell phones and took pictures.

"Stop that," I said, shrill.

"What's going on?" Herb asked, and then he caught site of Jason. The little man's eyes rolled up in his head and he fainted. Xavier and Harper leapt forward, catching him beneath the shoulders and lowering him gently to the brick sidewalk. Harper loosened Herb's bow tie.

"What happened?" the reporter from Sacramento barked.

"Adele," I said, "call 911! Tell them an officer's been hit by a car."

She raced into the tea room next door.

Fear and anger tangling inside me, I examined Jason's head. The cut didn't seem deep, but it was bleeding like crazy. "Leo! First aid kit."

He ran inside the museum.

"Detective," the red-headed reporter asked, "do you think this was an attack by the same person who killed Bill Eldrich?"

"Will you shut up?" I snarled.

"I'm only doing my job," she said and snapped another photo.

Leo skidded back out the door and wrenched open the ancient first aid kit. "What do you need?"

Scrabbling inside the dented metal box, I pulled out a gauze pack. I ripped it open and pressed it to Jason's forehead. It darkened with blood. The gauze wasn't enough. "Get the cheesecloth from the Gallery."

Leo raced back inside.

"It's only a cut," Jason said.

"Be quiet."

"What about Herb?" Xavier fanned the paranormal collector.

My brain stumbled. What did you do for someone who's fainted? "Put something under his head. Keep him warm."

But Harper had already done that. Her suede blazer was draped over Herb's torso, and her thick scarf was folded beneath his head. "He'll be all right," she said. "Take care of the detective."

Xavier sat back on his heels and scratched his salt-and-pepper goatee. "This curse is worse than I thought."

Mike, the sandy-haired local reporter, squatted beside me. "Can I help?"

Panic welled in my throat. "I think he's dislocated his shoulder —"

"I'm sitting right here," Jason said tartly.

"— and head wounds always bleed like crazy. I think it looks worse than it is." But who knew what sort of damage had been done to Jason internally?

Leo returned with plastic bags of the cheese cloth. Kneeling, I ripped open a bag in quick jerky motions. My bloody hands stained the white cloth. I laid it against Jason's forehead and prayed the only injuries he had were the ones I could see.

A siren wailed in the distance.

Jason was alive, and the ambulance was on its way, and I was not going to give in to my fear.

A blue muscle car screeched to the curb. Laurel leapt out and sucked in her breath. Knocking me sideways, she took my place beside Jason. "Slate. What happened?"

"Hit and run," Jason said. "First three letters on the license plate were XSH."

"What color?" she barked.

"Gray," I said.

"Blue," Adele said.

"I thought it was green," Leo said.

"You two were inside," I said. "How could you see anything?"

"Through the window," Adele said.

"It was gray," Jason said through gritted teeth.

Laurel cursed and raced to her open car door, bumping into paramedics on their way up the sidewalk.

I scuttled away and let the professionals take over. Then I remembered I had another guest in distress and hurried over to the two exorcists.

Herb groaned and sat up. "What happened?"

"You passed out," Xavier said.

"What? Why?" Herb glanced at the blue-shirted paramedics, at the blood dripping down Jason's chin. His eyes rolled up and he sank to the sidewalk again.

"He's got a phobia about blood," Xavier said, apologetic.

"So he became a collector of haunted objects?" Harper asked.

White teacup in hand, Adele knelt beside me. She handed me a cloth napkin. I wiped my hands and realized too late I'd ruined the white fabric. Customers from the tea room clustered in its open door.

Herb twitched and sat up on his elbow.

"Tea?" Adele walked to him and extended the delicate cup.

"Thank you." He reached for it, noticed the paramedics, and sagged.

"Oh no you don't," Harper said, shifting sideways to block his view. "Herb, you will not faint!"

Color flooded his cheeks and he straightened, then took the cup from Adele. "Thank you, miss."

Adele glanced toward the tearoom. "I'd better return to my customers."

"Thanks for everything." I rose to hand her the napkin, remembered the bloodstains, and crumpled it in my hands. I glanced at the paramedics. They still huddled around Jason, blocking him from view.

Smiling tightly, Adele walked to her tea room. She gently shooed in the gawkers and closed the front door behind her.

Herb raised a bony finger. "The first thing I want to say is, this was not my fault."

"What wasn't your fault?" I asked, stumbling to my feet.

"Those bells are now bound," Herb said. "I've checked the energy around that box, and no negative energies are entering or escaping. The bells had nothing to do with that man getting hit." He slurped his tea.

"Oh," I said. "It's okay. I knew that." The maniac behind the wheel was responsible and no one else. Except for maybe me. Me and my stupid idea to hold an exorcism for cowbells I'd never believed were haunted in the first place. So much more could have gone wrong. What if someone had been trampled? What if Jason was hurt worse than I thought?

"I can't explain the bites that people claimed to experience," Xavier said, "but Herb's probably right — there's another object in your museum that's causing the problem."

Harper shook her head and looked away.

"Now if you like," the exorcist continued, "I can examine the museum and determine which objects are problematic. I charge two

227

hundred dollars an hour."

I closed my eyes and prayed for serenity. But when I opened them, Xavier and Herb were still there. "I don't think that will be necessary," I said, "but thanks for the offer."

They shrugged. Xavier helped Herb up and they walked into the museum.

The paramedics wheeled in a stretcher, gouging a chunk out of a nearby plum tree. They helped Jason onto it, and I jogged over to them.

"Is he going to be all right?" I asked as they raised the stretcher.

"I'll be fine." Jason grasped my hand.

"Jason, I'm so sorry." I blinked rapidly. "If I hadn't held this event —"

"This isn't your fault, Maddie."

"Ma'am?" one of the paramedics asked. "We need to go."

"Sorry." Releasing Jason's hand, I followed them as they loaded him into the ambulance and shut the rear doors.

Back on the sidewalk, I rubbed my face. Cops in blue uniforms strode about the rooftop opposite.

Someone grabbed my shoulder and spun me around. Laurel scowled down at me, her neck muscles cording. "What happened?" Her short blond hair was rumpled as if she'd escaped a windstorm.

"Jason and I walked outside," I said, voice flat. "Someone drove up onto the sidewalk and hit him." And Jason had shoved me out of the driver's path.

"What was Slate doing here?"

"He was here for the event. What were you doing here?" Laurel had arrived awfully quickly. Almost as if she'd been surveilling me.

"What event?" she asked.

My shoulders hunched. "A ritual to de-curse the cowbells."

She blew out her breath. "Tell me that lunatic Herb wasn't involved."

"He's inside."

She turned on her booted heel and strode into the museum, stopping just past the doorway. "No he's not."

"Maybe he's in the Fortune Telling Room." I squeezed past her. Herb and Xavier were nowhere to be seen. "He likes to hide in the spirit cabinet."

Leo sat on the barstool behind the register. "Where's Herb?" I asked.

He shrugged. "He and his friend left through the tea room. You know how he feels about cops."

Laurel cursed and charged to the book-case. "Where's the damn secret lever?"

"On the book that says *Open.*" I trotted to her side, but she'd already opened the case. She ran into the tea room and down the elegant hallway that led to the alley.

Leo stared at me. "Is the detective . . . ?"

I swallowed. "Detective Slate will be okay." I only hoped it was true.

Not even Harper and Adele were able to cheer me up after the disaster. Once I'd cleaned up the museum, all I'd had the heart to do was go home and eat pizza. The only good news I got before going to bed was a call from Slate, reassuring me that all he had was a dislocated shoulder and a few stitches in his skull.

I hadn't been reassured. This was my mess from start to finish. I'd bought the bells, publicized the curse, and had the bright idea of a public binding ritual.

The museum was closed on Mondays, but that morning I went to work anyway. My first project was to scrub at a blood stain on the sidewalk — Jason's blood — with my ragged mop. I squeezed out the dirty water and rubbed the mop across the bricks. Spots of blood flecked the brick wall as well.

GD, observing from the open doorway, sneezed.

"Sure," I said. "It's easy to criticize when

230

you're not doing any work."

The cat yawned and retreated inside the museum.

Thirty minutes later, I peeled off my rubber gloves and studied the area. I'd gotten rid of most of the stains, along with several pieces of hardened gum. If I looked hard, I thought I could still see blood. But I doubted anyone would be crawling around Sherlock Holmes–style inspecting the brickwork.

The wall phone jangled. Forgetting the museum was closed, I hurried inside and answered it. "Paranormal Museum, this is Maddie speaking."

"I heard bells," a man whispered. "And something bit me last night. Is it true?"

My gaze clouded. "Is it true that you heard bells and something bit you?"

"Is it true that you made the curse worse?"

"No. The curse is not worse." I winced. Now I was rhyming? "The binding ritual worked. My experts assure me that everything is fine."

"But I heard bells, I tell you."

"It's ten days until Christmas. Bells are ringing everywhere. I've got one over my door. Who is this?"

He hung up.

Atop the antique cash register, GD me-owed.

"Don't start." My grand plan to cool the town's fears had crashed like the Hindenburg. "How am I supposed to debunk a curse?"

GD sneezed and dropped to the floor. He swaggered to Gryla's cave and vanished beneath the ogress's skirts.

"Fat lot of help you are."

Okay, forget the curse. Someone had tried to blow up my mother and run Jason and me down — someone who had killed Bill with a bow and arrow. And since anyone could have tried to run us down, and, it seemed, blow us up too, I was left with only the arrows as a clue. Penny at the Wine and Visitors Bureau had been an almost-Olympic archer. And according to Tabitha Wilde, she had had a motive to kill Bill Eldrich. I had a hard time picturing Penny as an arrow-slinging killer, but I couldn't ignore this lead. Dean Pinkerton was also handy with a bow and arrow, but it was easier to annoy Penny.

I locked up the museum and squinted into the crisp morning light. On the sidewalk, the plum trees were barren. Green cords of unlit twinkle lights wrapped around their silvery-gray bark.

I walked past Mason's motorcycle shop. In its window, Belle adjusted a holly wreath over the headlight of a cherry-red Harley. It was a gorgeous bike — even I could admire its lines — but I had zero desire to ever get on one again.

I slowed to a halt, and our gazes met. Deliberately, Belle turned her back.

She had reason to be peeved with me, even though I hadn't spilled the beans to Mason about her secret Christmas Cow bet. Or was it a secret? Just because Mason hadn't brought it up didn't mean he didn't know about it. Maybe he was keeping mum to protect her. Or even to protect Dieter. I still wasn't clear on the legality of the contractor's betting service, but I was pretty sure it fell on the wrong side of the law.

I got into my pickup. It coughed, and I drove off.

The Wine and Visitors Bureau was also closed on Monday mornings. But I knew the not-so-secret entrance, a metal door in the brick side wall. And I knew Penny would be there. She was always there.

I rapped on the cold metal. It clanged hollowly beneath my knuckles. Blowing into my hands to warm them, I waited.

The door creaked open and Penny peered out.

She opened the door wider and tugged down the hem of her holiday sweater. It managed to incorporate wine bottles, goblets, and howling holiday wolves. "Oh. I thought you were a delivery."

"Can I come in?"

"Sure." She stepped away from the door.

I walked into the dimly lit hall and shivered.

"Since it's only me today," she said, "I didn't bother turning on the heat. Come into my office. I'm running a space heater there."

I followed her into the room stacked with boxes and brochures. Penny lowered herself into a swivel chair behind her desk, and I shifted a stack of wine maps from the chair opposite and sat.

"What can I do for you?" Penny asked.

"You heard what happened yesterday at the museum?" Lowering my head, I studied her. I'd invited Penny to the binding event, but she'd been conspicuously absent. True, it had been a last-minute thing, but Penny was usually on hand to support me. After all, my museum was an associate member of the Wine and Visitors Bureau.

Her lips pressed together. "Terrible. I was sorry I couldn't make it, but now I'm glad. No offense."

"None taken." I faked a smile. "Did you have a conflicting appointment?"

She eyed me. "A family matter. I read in the papers that the detective's injuries weren't life threatening."

"Yes. The car grazed him. But you do know how much damage an arrow can do when it hits."

She straightened in surprise, her grape earrings tangling in her gray hair. "How would I know that? All I've hit are targets."

"Well, you know more about it than I do," I said peevishly.

"I had no reason to want Bill or anyone else dead."

"Oh?" I cocked my head.

"What's that supposed to mean?"

"I heard you and Bill were at odds over some tax funding."

"At odds?" Penny's ample chest heaved. "He stabbed the Wine and Visitors Bureau in the back. I was furious when he submitted his own bid on behalf of the Dairy Association. If it wasn't for him, I'm sure the bureau would have gotten the extra funding. He sank that opportunity. It was pure greed. Fear and greed."

"So it's true," I said unhappily.

"Yes, I was angry. But not angry enough to kill him. Not over a government grant."

235

All my instincts said Penny was no killer. But my instincts had also told me a public exorcism was a good idea. Clearly, my instincts were the Benedict Arnold of trustworthiness. "All right," I said. "Then who did hate Bill enough to kill him?"

She rolled a pencil between her fingers. "I couldn't say."

"Penny, Bill's dead. A policeman could have been killed. If you know anything, you have to come forward."

"I don't know anything."

"But you suspect something?"

She didn't respond.

"Please," I said.

She stared at a metal bookshelf stacked with wine boxes. "There were some odd . . . currents between Bill and Tabitha at the last meeting. I'm not sure if you've met her. Tabitha Wilde is one of our town council representatives."

"We've met. Which meeting was this?"

"The Christmas Cow committee meeting."

I relaxed in my chair. "Interesting. What do you mean by 'odd currents'?"

Her round shoulders lifted and dropped. "I'm not sure how to explain it. Normally they were quite at ease with each other. But that night, something seemed strained. They wouldn't even look at each other."

"Do you have any idea why?"

"If I did, I'd tell you. Or I'd tell the police if I thought it had any bearing on what's going on."

"Did anything else happen between them?"

"Not between Bill and Tabitha, no," she said slowly.

I sat forward, my knees brushing an open cardboard box. "Between Bill and someone else?"

"At our last meeting, I overheard something between Bill and Kendra."

"Kendra Breathnach? The developer? She's not on the committee."

"No," Penny said, "but she donated the straw for the Cow. Didn't you see the sign thanking her company for its sponsorship? You must have seen it at the park. It's quite prominently displayed."

"Right." I vaguely remembered a sign getting knocked down by the fire department.

"At any rate, it sounded like an argument, but I can't be sure."

"What were they saying?"

"Something about zoning. They were standing outside the Wine and Visitors Bureau after the meeting. I thought everyone had left and was locking up. I think I startled them."

"Who was talking about the zoning?" I asked.

"Kendra. Her voice was quite sharp. Maybe it was nothing. It was a cold night, and it had been a long meeting. All our nerves were frayed, except of course your mother's."

I made a mental note to ask my mother about the so-called tension. I'd need to follow up with Kendra and Tabitha too. Not liking the idea, I rubbed my temple. "When was this?" I asked.

"December 5th." Penny regarded me speculatively. "There is one other thing."

"Oh?"

"I only bring it up because . . . well. Maybe I shouldn't bring it up at all. I have tremendous respect for your mother."

"My mother?" I straightened. "What do you mean?"

"I know she had nothing to do with this. She'd never cause problems for your museum."

I tapped my fingers on the arm of the chair. "Penny, what about my mother?"

"There seemed to be something between Bill and your mother as well."

"He thought guarding the cow was beneath him," I said. "My mom wanted him to set an example and help out."

"No." Penny pursed her mouth. "I don't think that was it at all."

"Oh? Then what?"

Penny colored. "It's none of my business. I'm sure I was wrong."

"Penny, just tell me."

"It's only that . . ." She flushed more deeply. "I was under the impression that Bill and your mother were dating."

FIFTEEN

Hands tight on the wide steering wheel, I cruised toward downtown. My mom and Bill Eldrich? It couldn't be true. My mom would have said something. I'd have known if she was seeing someone.

Wouldn't I? I tugged at the seat belt, suddenly uncomfortably tight across my middle.

If Laurel ever found out about this so-called relationship, she'd think my mom had a motive.

Maybe Penny was wrong. The president of the Wine and Visitors Bureau had pretty much admitted she was guessing.

Twisting my hands on the wheel, I slowed, bumping across the railroad tracks. Enough speculation. My mom and I were adults. If she was hiding a relationship to protect me, then that couldn't be very nice for her. I'd tackle this head-on and put the whole business to rest.

After lunch.

I pulled into the parking lot of my favorite taqueria. A rack of newspapers hung by the open double doors, and I grabbed the local paper.

HIT AND RUN AT PARANORMAL MUSEUM, the front page proclaimed. I winced.

Shuffling forward in the line along the counter, I read the article. It mentioned something Jason had not: he was now on medical leave. Did that mean Laurel was in charge of the Bill Eldrich investigation? I rolled my shoulders. At the bottom of the page was a tag to turn to page three for another story about the museum.

"Next," the Hispanic woman behind the counter called out.

I stepped to the register and ordered a veggie burrito. The checker gave me my number and I went to collect green salsa from the bar, then to stand in a corner and read while I waited.

I flipped to page three and winced. *FAILED EXORCISM CAUSES MASS PANIC.*

"Number twenty-seven!"

Shielding my face behind the paper, I grabbed the red plastic basket from the counter and scuttled outside.

While my burrito cooled in its foil wrapper, I sat at a wooden patio table and forced

241

myself to read the article.

An attempted exorcism at San Benedetto's Paranormal Museum caused mass
panic after observers reported being bitten
by an invisible entity.

The museum was attempting to remove
the curse from the town's haunted cowbells, which are reputed to have caused
the deaths of the original Christmas Cow
committee members.

"Curses of this sort can be bound," said
local expert Xavier Landau. "It's important
to cut the psychic link between the curse
and its victims."

However, the "psychic link" appeared not
to have been broken. At the closing of the
ceremony, at least two participants claimed
something bit them, causing a sudden
panicked rush from the museum. No other
injuries were reported.

"At least they didn't blame the cat," I
muttered to the small black birds hopping
about my feet. But the article had done me
no favors. Not that I deserved any. It was
sheer luck no one had been hurt in the
stampede.

I ate my burrito, tossed the remains into
the garbage can, and got into my vintage

pickup. Penny had given me two good leads: Kendra and Tabitha. It was time to follow them.

Kendra's office was closest, a low, 1950s-era building with floor-to-ceiling windows. Its mid-century-modern lobby was decorated with turquoise sofas, orange ottomans, and fluffy white rugs. A young brunette looked up from behind a glass table and smiled.

"May I help you?" she asked. A wreath with matching turquoise ornaments hung on the wall behind her.

"I'm here to see Kendra."

Faint twin furrows appeared between her brows. "Who may I say is here?"

"Maddie Kosloski." I straightened my jacket. Would Kendra even talk to me after our last encounter?

"One moment please." The young woman picked up a phone and angled her chair away from me.

I studied a watercolor of a new development, oddly elongated people strolling along tree-lined paths.

The receptionist hung up and rose, smiling brightly. "This way, please." She led me down a wide hallway to an oak door. Knocking twice, she opened it. "Ms. Kosloski is here to see you, Ms. Breathnach."

243

Expression impassive, Kendra rose from behind her glass desk. "Thank you, Sally." She tucked her blond hair behind one ear and motioned me to an orange chair.

The receptionist nodded and left, closing the door softly behind her.

Kendra flecked an imaginary piece of lint off her crisp white blouse. She wore jeans and a blazer, and I could tell neither had come from the bargain shops I haunted. "Is there something I can help you with?"

"First, I'm sorry about the other day."

Kendra sat back down in the turquoise-leather chair behind her desk. "So you're not trying to pin the blame for what happened at your museum yesterday on my son?"

My cheeks tingled with warmth. "I assumed Oliver was still in Tahoe."

Her smile was wry. "Yes, he is."

But Tahoe was only two hours away. Oliver could have easily returned to cause trouble. I shifted in my chair. "This has gone beyond a college prank gone wrong."

"No kidding. It looks like the killer's targeting holiday events."

My head rocked back. I wouldn't have exactly called the binding ritual a holiday event. But could she be right?

"Maybe, but someone also blew up my

244

mother's car when we were leaving the Wildes' house," I pointed out.

"So you think you were the target yesterday?"

I drew a slow breath, remembering Jason pushing me sideways, the blood. "I don't know why I'd be a target."

"You've been asking a lot of questions." Kendra cocked her head, her blond hair falling loose over her shoulder. "Maybe the killer thinks you're close to an answer."

I looked out the picture windows. Cars inched past on the street outside. "Not close enough," I said. "But my mother and I have each been in the line of fire twice."

"Why are you here?" she asked, brusque.

"I'm sorry to keep bothering you, but you knew Bill Eldrich. Why might someone have wanted him dead?"

"Even if I knew, why should I tell you anything? You're not the police."

"Maybe that's reason enough," I said. "I heard there was tension between Bill and Tabitha Wilde at the last committee meeting. Did you notice anything?"

She gave me a long look, and her lips pursed. "I did."

"Do you have any idea what it was about?"

"You said you were at the Wildes' house when someone attacked you?"

I nodded.

She rubbed her chin. "Then I suppose you should know, though I dislike gossip."

"What gossip?"

An odd expression crossed her face, a mix of shame and curiosity. "That Tabitha and Bill were having an affair."

Weirdly disappointed, I blew out my breath. No outsider really knows what goes on in a marriage. But I liked Tabitha, and I didn't like the idea of her as a cheater. Did her husband know? Did her son, Craig?

Kendra canted her head, studying me. "And now I suppose you're wondering how I know?"

I shook myself. "How do you know?"

"I saw them together at Lake Tahoe. I was consulting on a lodge project. They were holding hands, and obviously . . . well. They didn't see me. At least I don't think they did. They never spoke to me about it, and I never brought it up. It's none of my business." She gave me a repressive look, but I was done with feeling shame over my role as a busybody. I was already marinating in guilt for my role in the museum near-disaster.

"Have you told the police?" I asked.

"As I said, it's none of my business."

"I think you should. Detective Slate is in

charge of the investigation."

"After getting hit by a car? That seems unlikely."

My heart plummeted. She was right. They'd put him on leave, and that made Laurel the lead detective. She was a decent cop, but she detested me. Jason had always been a moderating influence, reining her in when her temper got the better of her. "Then it will be Detective Hammer."

"I'll tell her if you think it's important," Kendra said, dismissive.

"I do." Now even more depressed, I rose and walked to a massive watercolor on the wall. I had to ask Kendra about her own conflict with Bill, but I wasn't sure how to start.

"Is there anything else?" she asked.

I squinted at the watercolor: a map of homes surrounding a vineyard. A squad of dairy farms encircled the whole development, and I wrinkled my nose. On a hot summer day, those dairy farms made quite a stink. "Is this the new vineyard housing development?" I asked, stalling for time.

"Our agrihood, yes. We got final approval to rezone the land from agriculture to residential at the November town council meeting."

"Congratulations."

She smiled, and I thought it was the first genuine smile I'd seen her wear. "The framing work will start in two weeks."

"Will the cow pastures be part of the agrihood?"

"Those are privately owned," she said, her voice clipped. "We expect the type of people who'll be interested in living in an agrihood will consider the nearby fields a bonus, though we can't promise that the farms will be there forever. The only thing eternal is change."

"I thought it was death and taxes."

"Is there anything else?"

I turned to her. "I heard things were tense between you and Bill at the last meeting."

She waggled her expensive navy pump. "Who did you hear that from?"

"There were several people at the meeting—"

"Penny." She leaned forward, her expression sharpening. "Penny said that, didn't she?"

"Does it matter?" I'd watched enough *Magnum PI* to know you never gave up one source to another source.

She laughed harshly. "You don't have to say anything. I can tell. Did Penny tell you that she and Bill were once romantically involved?"

"Penny and Bill?" Penny of the crazy sweaters and grape-cluster earrings? Was there anyone over fifty Bill hadn't dated? "I hadn't heard."

"It's not as surprising as it sounds. Bill was quite the ladies' man."

Suddenly I wanted this conversation over. "Okay, well, thanks." I laid my business card on her table. "Even though your son wasn't involved, he might know something. Please ask him to call me if he gets a chance."

Her smile was wintery. "He's skiing. Don't hold your breath."

I hesitated at the office door. "By the way, where were you on Sunday afternoon between four and four thirty?"

"Home. Alone. As I said, Oliver is in Tahoe."

So she had no alibi for the hit and run. "Thanks again." I hustled out of the office.

My jaw tightened. I couldn't avoid it any longer. I needed to talk to my mom.

I pulled into my mother's driveway and parked my pickup beneath the big oak. A metal ladder leaned against its trunk. I squinted into the sunlight streaming through its branches.

Impervious to the cold, Dieter clung to a wide branch and wielded a circular knife.

His jeans rode down his hips, and his ripped T-shirt rode up his stomach as he stretched for a bunch of mistletoe.

Two policemen stared up at him.

"Dieter?" I asked. "Do you need any help?"

"No, Mad K, I got this." He reached for the cluster of mistletoe, wobbled, and grabbed the branch for balance.

I sucked in a quick, terrified breath. "Dieter —"

"I can do it," he insisted.

"Well, scream if you fall," I said. "I'll call 911."

"911 is here," one of the cops said.

"Right," I said. "Then carry on."

I strolled up the winding walk, past the straw reindeer and barrel-hoop snowman and a new-looking Lincoln SUV, and walked inside. I shut the door and the wreath rattled against it. Following the scent of baking flour and sugar, I made my way to the kitchen.

My mom slid sugar-and-spice cookies off a baking sheet onto wire racks.

"Yum," I said. I reached for a cookie and she smacked my hand with the spatula.

"Ow!"

"I have to frost those," she said. Her short

hair was rumpled. Flour smeared one of her cheeks.

I rubbed my hand. "Need help?"

"What I need is to get out of here." She gestured at the kitchen piled with plastic and metal cookie containers. "The insurance company paid for a rental car, but what's the point when I'm a prisoner in my own house?"

"Is Ladies Aid having a bake sale?"

"Not this year." My mother slumped against the gray granite counter. "Maybe my police escort will let me take them over to the old folks' homes. Not everyone is allowed sugar, but these are just too many cookies."

"There's no such thing as too many Christmas cookies."

"What have you learned? Have you gathered any more clues?"

Dieter strolled into the kitchen and dropped a bundle of mistletoe in the sink. "Here you go, Mrs. K. What's next?"

"Madelyn was just going to tell me what she'd learned about our killer."

Grinning, Dieter folded his arms and lounged against the counter beside my mom. "Oh, she is?"

"Don't say anything, Mom," I warned. "He's probably got a bet running."

"Dieter wouldn't do that," she said. "Dressing up like Santa to murder someone . . . I still can't believe it. And you could have been killed yesterday, Madelyn. And poor Detective Slate. Have you spoken with him? Is he all right?"

"I called. He says his arm is in a sling. I guess they've put him on medical leave."

My mother's lips flattened. "So Detective Hammer is in charge?"

Dieter whistled. "That changes the odds."

I frowned at him. "You'd better be joking."

"It's a pity cats can't apologize," my mom said. "Between you setting her hair on fire —"

"I didn't!"

"— and GD breaking her foot, that detective isn't well disposed toward you."

"GD broke her foot?" Dieter shoved aside a tin of cookies and braced one elbow on the counter. "I thought that was an urban legend."

"He didn't." I glared at him. "It was a weird accident."

"It's a pity," my mom continued, "because Detective Slate clearly likes you."

My cheeks warmed. "What?"

"Well, it's obvious to me," my mom said.

"You're dating Slate?" Dieter asked.

"Does Adele know?"

"Who said anything about dating?" I asked. "He's helped me with some research on stuff in the museum, that's all."

"What sort of research has he been helping you with?" Dieter grabbed a warm sugar cookie off the plate and shoved the entire thing in his mouth, scattering crumbs across his ripped tee. My mother did not smack his hand with a spatula.

"Certain of my haunted objects have been connected to deaths," I said, intentionally vague. I didn't want to give the cowbell curse any more traction. "Detective Slate has access to the police archives."

"Yeah," Dieter said, nodding. "He's totally not into you."

I sucked in my cheeks. "It's not as if he's been kept busy investigating homicides in San Benedetto." Not until recently, at least.

"Speaking of homicides, what have you learned?" My mom brushed the back of her cheek with her hand, widening the smear of flour.

Wary, I glanced at Dieter. But he could keep his mouth shut when it mattered. "Kendra said Tabitha and Bill were having an affair, and that Penny had once dated Bill. And Penny said things between Tabitha and Bill, and between Bill and Kendra, were tense. But Kendra said Penny was lying because of her old fling with Bill."

"It sounds so high school," my mom said.

Dieter snorted.

"But if Bill and Tabitha were having an affair," my mother continued, "it might show he had undue influence over where that tax money went. As a town councilwoman, Tabitha held sway when it came to funding decisions. If she was capable of being corrupted in this instance, perhaps she was in others too."

"Whoa." Dieter straightened off the counter. "Corrupted? You mean like bribes?"

"Young men are so innocent." My mother pinched his cheek, and to my amazement, he grinned.

"But if Tabitha was taking bribes," I said, "that's no reason for her to kill Bill."

"Unless someone was blackmailing her," Dieter mumbled, spewing crumbs. "Maybe someone's got evidence."

"Or maybe nothing's going on," I said. "All we have is Kendra's word that Tabitha and Bill were an item."

My mom shook her head. "No, I suspect it's true. It would explain a lot about their relationship. When I saw them together, they always seemed a little too close for comfort, laughing and touching each other's arms.

Sometimes I wondered how Tabitha's husband could be so calm about it all. Perhaps he wasn't."

"So you noticed something going on between them too?" I asked. "Why didn't you say anything?"

"I wasn't certain," she said. "But now that I know I wasn't the only one who noticed something odd, there's no sense in being discreet. What else did you learn?"

"What else?" I glanced at Dieter. I couldn't ask my mom about her dating Bill with the contractor hanging around.

"I know there's something else," she said. "You have that guilty look in your eyes."

"I don't have a guilty look. There's nothing for me to feel guilty about. You asked me to investigate, and now I've made most of the local women in positions of power mad at me."

"You're not investigating because I asked you to."

"I'm not?"

"You're investigating," my mom said, "because you're good at it."

Dieter nodded. "The odds are totally in your favor."

I glared at him.

"Besides," she said, "someone's shot the cow, blown up my Lincoln, run down a

255

perfectly good detective, and ruined your ritual. Kosloskis don't take that sort of thing lying down."

I reached for a cookie, and her eyes narrowed. Slowly, carefully, I withdrew my hand and cleared my throat. "The ritual was ruined before Detective Slate got hit by that car."

"What happened?" Dieter asked.

"I'm not sure," I said. "A woman said something bit her —"

"GD?" my mom asked.

"No, he was on top of the holiday ogress cave the whole time. I think having all those people in the museum freaked him out."

"Imagine," Dieter said dryly.

"And then another woman said she was bitten. And someone shouted that the curse was still on, and there was a panic, and everyone ran out of the museum. Herb and Xavier insist the curse has been removed, but no one's taking them very seriously."

"Including you," my mom said. "Maybe that's the problem. People know you're a skeptic."

I clawed my hands through my hair. "The reason I don't believe in curse exorcisms is because I don't believe in curses. This is nuts."

"No, it's human nature," Dieter said.

"The idea of malign influences is embedded in our caveman DNA."

We stared at him.

"What?" he asked through a mouthful of cookie.

My mom turned to me. "Now what aren't you telling us?"

"Telling you?" My pulse accelerated.

"Spill it," she said.

"Yeah, Mad, spill it," Dieter said.

"Dieter doesn't want to hear this stuff," I said. "Let's bundle up the mistletoe and we can talk later."

Dieter braced his chin on his fists, his blue eyes wide. "Au contraire, mon frère. I am busting with interest. Does Slate know you're running an off-the-books PI firm?"

I grabbed a cookie before my mom could object. "Says the man who's running an off-the-books bookie firm."

"Children, enough," my mother said. "Now Madelyn, say whatever it is you haven't been saying. And Dieter, stop teasing Madelyn."

I shuffled my feet. "Um. Well. Penny said you were dating Bill. Recently." It would have to be recently. My mom was still a relatively newish widow.

Dieter snorted. "And you believed her?"

My mother sighed. "Penny is cannier than

I give her credit for. I certainly didn't tell anyone, and I'm sure Bill didn't."

We gaped at her.

"Way to go, Mrs. K!" Dieter raised his hand for a high five.

She frowned and he dropped his hand, stuffing it into the pocket of his jeans.

"Then it's true?" I asked.

"He asked me out, and I said *yes*. This was before I was president of Ladies Aid, you understand."

"What does Ladies Aid have to do with it?" I asked. "Is there a rule against the president of Ladies Aid dating the president of the Dairy Association?"

"Of course not," my mother said. "But I hadn't worked with Bill very closely up until that point, which is why I agreed to go out with him. Then I discovered he thought real work was beneath him."

"How many dates before you figured it out?"

"Really, Madelyn. I don't think that's any of your business."

"Well, no, but —"

"I don't sit home in suspended animation waiting for my children to return so I can bake them cookies." In a gentler voice, she added, "I miss your father terribly. No one will ever be able to replace him. But it's

258

rather lonely in this big house. And I am an adult."

I thought about the huge changes that had happened in her life after my father died. Selfishly, I'd just assumed everything was working out for her. "It's okay," I said. "I mean, it's great. I'm not upset. And it's none of my business even if I was. I'm just . . . surprised."

"When I became president this fall," she continued, "my life got busy, and Bill and I drifted apart. Romantically, I mean. We were working with each other quite regularly. But if he was having an affair with Tabitha Wilde, I wonder when it started? He seemed a bit distant when we were dating, but I thought that was just his character. Maybe he was seeing her then and using me as a beard."

"No way," Dieter said, indignant.

She patted his hand. "What I don't understand is why Madelyn hasn't been given a police guard after yesterday's attack."

"Oh, that's easy," Dieter said.

We turned to stare.

"I talked to the cops outside." Dieter bit into another pfeffernüsse. "They said Detective Hammer wants to keep an eye on Mad personally."

■ ■ ■ ■

The next morning, I drove past fields blanketed in pewter fog. My gaze flicked to the rearview mirror. If Laurel wanted to keep an eye on me personally, she was keeping her surveillance covert.

I shrugged my shoulders in my fleece-lined jacket and checked the rear-view mirror for the *nth* time. Two could play at this game.

The museum was closed on Tuesdays too. It's just not a big day for visiting wineries or paranormal museums. But Internet sales happen daily, and I needed to ship some orders and feed GD.

First, though, I wanted to talk to Penny again. The Wine and Visitors Bureau would be open this morning, doling out tastings at the bar to any tourists disappointed by the dearth of open wineries. And Penny *had* seemed to be trying to divert suspicion from herself yesterday. I couldn't ignore her archery background.

I slowed as a VW Bug pulled from a vineyard into the road. The VW sped forward, its engine sputtering, and careened around the corner of a barren apple orchard.

I didn't actually know where any of the

suspects had been on Sunday afternoon. Kendra said she was home, but there was no one to verify it. Penny said she'd been called to a "family matter." And I had no idea where Tom and Tabitha Wilde or their son Craig had been. And then there was Dean Pinkerton of the unpasteurized milk. And Belle, the mother of my ex's child.

My grip tightened on the wheel. I had too many suspects.

All right. *Think.* Was Kendra a suspect? I'd initially approached her because Oliver might have been involved. Now it seemed that he wasn't, but there'd been odd currents between Kendra and Bill, according to reports.

A crow skimmed low over the road. I braked, barely missing it, my head rocking forward. Nerves officially wracked, I drove on.

What about Belle? She could have set up the cow burning to win the prize money, and one of her hypothetical confederates accidentally killed Bill. Then, to make it seem like someone had intentionally killed Bill, since she'd had no motive to do that, she manufactured some mad conspiracy and attacked the museum event — conveniently located by her apartment.

All in all, it seemed a little much.

I turned onto a wide road leading into town. The fog was thicker here, the nearby vines invisible, and I slowed, keeping an eye out for wildlife.

Tabitha, now . . . she'd been helpful. Too helpful? If anyone was trying to throw suspicion on others, it was her. She was clearly worried Craig might have been involved. The offer to pay for the damage from the bombing smelled like a payoff.

If it was true that she and Bill had been having an affair, and her husband or son found out, would either of them have killed Bill Eldrich?

I pulled into the Wine and Visitors Bureau's misty driveway. Penny's Honda was parked in her private space, toward the back of the educational vineyard. In the small plot, barren vines twisted along metal wires. I backed into a visitor's spot, hopped from my truck, and shut the door.

A sound — a smothered cry — floated through the fog.

I froze, head cocked. "Hello?"

Something thudded softly from the direction of Penny's blue Honda.

The hair lifted on my arms. "Hello?" I called again.

No answer.

My heart thumped. "Laurel, I hope you're

around," I muttered.

Swallowing hard, I crept toward the sound. "Hello? Is someone there?"

Soft gulps and gasps and snuffling emerged from the other side of the blue Honda. For a moment I wondered if I'd stumbled across an animal in distress. I forced my leaden legs to move forward and rounded the rear bumper.

Through the fog, I saw a bulky figure hunched against the small car.

Relieved, I exhaled and trotted forward. "Penny?" I squatted beside her. She was crumpled against the car door. In her white parka and ski cap, she looked like a melting snowman. "Penny, what's wrong?"

She raised a shaking finger and pointed toward the grapevines.

I stared into the swirling fog and saw . . . more fog. Straightening, I walked toward the front of her car.

A chill wind lifted my hair and parted the mist. Something pink fluttered on the ground.

Automatically, my legs moved forward toward the pile of clothing. I stopped, mouth slackening, disbelieving.

Tabitha Wilde lay on the ground, her eyes staring at the blank sky, an arrow in her chest.

SIXTEEN

I gasped and staggered backward, banging into a wine trellis. My sleeve caught on a wire. Frantic, I disentangled myself, ignoring the ripping sound, and rushed to the side of the Honda for cover. I knelt beside Penny. "Have you called 911?"

She clasped her mittens and shook her head. "Is it . . . ? It's really her, isn't it?"

"It's Tabitha Wilde." I pulled my cell phone from my jacket pocket. Hands shaking, I dialed.

"911, what's your emergency?"

"This is Maddie Kosloski. I'm at the Wine and Visitors Bureau with Penny . . ." Suddenly I couldn't remember her last name. "We've found a body. Tabitha Wilde's been shot with an arrow. She's dead in the educational vineyard."

"I'm sending help now," the dispatcher said. "Are you sure she's not breathing? I'd like you to double check."

I nodded, then realized that the dispatcher couldn't see the gesture. "Okay. I'll check again."

Reluctant, I left the shelter of Penny's car and walked slowly into the grapevines.

I knelt beside Tabitha's body. Blood soaked her pink dress, her coat, the ground. I pressed two trembling fingers to the side of her neck. Dew dampened her skin and the collar of her pink coat. Her flesh was cold.

So was mine.

I pressed harder and felt no pulse. No breath rose and fell in her chest. No spark of life lit her brown eyes. "There's no pulse," I croaked into the phone. "Her body's cold."

The phone slipped from my grasp. I fumbled to pick it up. The call had disconnected.

I trotted to Penny and sat beside her against the Honda. "Are you all right?"

Penny nodded, knocking the back of her head against the door. Wincing, she rubbed her knit cap. "She's dead, isn't she? This is really happening."

"Yes." I grasped her hand and squeezed lightly, her mittens soft beneath my palms. "How long have you been here?"

Her breath came quick and shallow. "Not

long, I think. I got out of my car and saw what I thought was a pile of rags in the vineyard. I went to pick it up — sometimes kids dump things here. And it was her. Tabitha. And an arrow. And then all I could think was to hide, but the distance from here to the building seemed so far. And then you were here."

Laurel's Mustang roared into the parking lot and screeched to a halt, lights flashing on its front dash. The detective, big, blonde, and badass, stepped from the car. So she *had* been nearby.

I rose. "Laur— Detective Hammer? Over here!"

She strode toward us. "Where is she?"

I pointed to the vineyard.

Laurel brushed past me. A few minutes later, she returned. "What happened?"

"I got here about five minutes ago and found Penny. She's the one who discovered the body, Tabitha —"

"I know who it is," Laurel snapped.

Penny stared blankly ahead, her eyes wide, her doughy face pale.

"Penny?" I knelt beside her and looked up at Laurel. "I think she's in shock."

Laurel snorted and stalked to her car. She returned with a thick blanket and we draped it around Penny's shoulders.

"Let's get her off the ground," Laurel said.

I should have thought of that, dammit. We helped Penny up and got her into her car. She sat, shoulders hunched, legs dangling out the driver's side open door.

Laurel's smile was mirthless. "Once again, here you are at the scene of a crime. What exactly *were* you doing here, Kosloski?"

"I came to get more wine map brochures," I lied.

"Isn't today your day off?" Laurel asked.

"Which made this the perfect time to run errands."

"Where were you last night?"

"I ate dinner at my mom's, and then I went home around nine. Alone." If she'd been surveilling me, she'd know that. For once, I'd have a police alibi.

"Go sit in your truck," she said.

"Okay." Meek, I returned to my pickup. I knew the drill. She'd want to question Penny without me listening.

Two squad cars, a fire truck, and an ambulance crowded into the parking lot. Their red and blue lights turned milky in the fog.

Keeping my hands below the dash, I texted my mother. *Tabitha murdered — arrow.*

Mother: *Where?*

Me: *W&VB.*

Mother: *Gather evidence.*

Me: *Can't. Laurel here.*

Mother: *Evade & observe.*

My mouth flattened. Evade and observe? How?

Someone knocked on my window. I yelped and dropped the phone.

Jason Slate quirked a brow, but his brown eyes were unreadable.

I rolled down the glass and fumbled around my feet for my phone. "You're here! Are you off medical leave? How's your shoulder?" I stammered. But the questions answered themselves. His arm was in a sling, and he wore a running jacket and jeans, so he was off duty.

"I'm fine. I'm still on leave."

"Did they find the person who hit you?"

He shook his head. "The car was abandoned. It had been stolen. No prints."

My stomach lurched. Stolen. Belle had once tried to steal Mason's car. Could she have . . . ?

"What are you doing here?" he asked.

"Oh." Awkward, I cleared my throat. "I came for brochures and found Penny by her car. She found Tabitha. I called 911. Laurel — I mean, Detective Hammer — is here."

"Okay," he said. "Why are you really here?"

"Really here?"

His mouth pulled downward. "Maddie . . ."

"Okay!" My breath quickened, my cheeks growing warm. "According to gossip, the Christmas Cow committee was a hotbed of romance and Bill Eldrich the local Casanova. Both Penny and Tabitha may have been involved with him."

"So you came to interrogate Penny."

"I wouldn't say *interrogate,*" I muttered. If I'd been a better interrogator the first time around, I wouldn't have had to return to find Tabitha's body. "But I was surprised Penny didn't come to the binding ritual on Sunday. She comes to all my events," I babbled. "And what with her being an almost-Olympic archer —"

"We know."

"You do?"

"The first thing we did was look for archers among our suspects."

My face warmed. Right. Because the police weren't dunces and neither was Jason.

"Slate!" Laurel stormed past the emergency vehicles. "Are you questioning my suspect?"

He stepped away from the truck door. "Nope."

"Because you're on leave," she said. "You're not supposed to be here or listening in on the police radio."

I watched them covertly. It was one thing to bite my head off, another to tell off Slate. Was she feeling insecure about her control over the investigation?

"Come on, Laurel," he said. "I was in the neighborhood and thought —"

"What?" Her jaw jutted forward. "That I'd need help? That I couldn't handle this?"

Oh, yeah, she was insecure. Embarrassed, I studied the vines clinging to the Visitors Bureau brickwork. A breeze ruffled their dying leaves.

"What were you thinking, Slate?" she asked.

"That we're partners," he said.

She glanced at his sling. "I get that this is personal for you. But that's why you can't be here."

"Right." He backed away. "If you need anything —"

"I won't call." Laurel folded her arms across her chest and watched him amble into the fog. She turned to me. "What are you looking at?"

"The vines . . ." I gestured vaguely toward

the building. "Nothing."

"What did you say to him?"

"The same thing I said to you."

She glowered. "Elaborate."

"He asked me what I was doing here. And I asked him what he was doing here. And I told him I was here for brochures." Guilt reared its ugly head, and I stuffed my hands in my jacket pockets. I couldn't withhold evidence. Not even from my high school bully. "But I did hear some interesting gossip about the Christmas Cow committee. Tabitha and Penny might have been dating Bill Eldrich." I could withhold *some* evidence. If I told her about my mom's few dates with Bill, it would only muddy the waters.

"So you came to play detective."

"No!" I laid my hand against my heart. "I would never do that. How's Penny?"

"None of your business. Now take me through your story step by step. What time did you arrive?"

"It's not a story —"

"Kosloski!" Her neck corded.

"I think it was around nine fifteen."

"And then?"

"I heard what I thought was a sob and something heavy falling. The sound seemed to come from the Honda, so I walked over

271

and found Penny. She told me . . . Well, she didn't tell me anything. She was too shaken. But she pointed toward the vineyard, so I walked in and found Tabitha. Then I called 911."

A chill blast of air stirred the fog and ruffled Laurel's blonde hair. I shivered and pulled my jacket tighter.

"Did you touch anything?" she asked.

"The dispatcher asked me to make sure if Tabitha was alive or dead, so I tried to find a pulse in her neck."

A muscle jumped in Laurel's jaw. "So the answer is *yes.* We'll find your DNA all over the crime scene."

"Not all over. The dispatcher told me to double check. If she was alive, maybe we could have saved her."

"She's obviously been dead for quite some time."

"Quite some time? So what do you think? Since last night?" I'd researched this before; body temperature drops on average one and a half degrees per hour. Tabitha had been cold. But it had been a cold night, so that would have sped up the process.

Laurel growled. "I'm the detective. I ask the questions."

"Sorry."

"And the only way you're a part of this

investigation is as a suspect."

"What?" I gaped. "I'm not a suspect. How am I a suspect?"

"Anyone on the scene for the discovery of two bodies is a suspect." Laurel stepped closer, forcing me to crane my neck. "And Kosloski, that means you." She smiled. "You're coming with me."

SEVENTEEN

Laurel didn't cuff me, but I could tell she wanted to. I spent my entire day off at the police station, and most of it was spent waiting in a cinder-block interview room. But I wasn't arrested, and they let me go late that night.

The next morning, tired and irritated, I dragged myself from bed and drove to the museum.

GD hissed at me from atop the ogress's cave.

"You didn't go hungry yesterday," I said, filling his bowl with kibble. "Adele fed you."

He howled, an unearthly sound that set my teeth on edge.

"Fine. I'm sorry I didn't do it myself. Okay?"

The black cat's tail lashed.

A bunch of online orders awaited me, so I got busy boxing garden gnomes and porcelain fairies and ghost detecting equipment.

At nine, a short column of teenage boys had lined up outside the door. I flipped the sign in the window to *Open,* knocking down a handful of fake snow in the process, and unlocked the front door.

The boys streamed inside. I kept an eye on them as they migrated to Gryla's cave. It had become a hot selfie spot, and GD photobombed every single picture.

More customers poured in and congregated around the bells. The wall phone rang.

I eyed it, then sighed and plucked the receiver from its hook. "Paranormal Museum, this is Maddie speaking."

"Is it true about the curse?" a man asked, his voice raspy.

"No."

"No?"

"No."

"Then why do you have the bells in your museum?

"Historical interest."

Silence.

The caller hung up.

Shaking my head, I replaced the receiver. It wasn't my fault if the whole town was nuts. Was it?

I glanced out the window to the street outside. Holiday shoppers ambled past, their arms full of paper shopping bags.

My legs twitched. Was Laurel outside somewhere watching? I suddenly felt exposed behind the thin pane of glass.

The wall phone jangled.

I growled, then grabbed the receiver. "Good morning," I said through gritted teeth. "This is Maddie at the Paranormal Museum. The bells are officially uncursed."

"Maddie, this is Kendra Breathnach."

The developer? I adjusted my hoodie's collar, which seemed intent on strangling me. "Hi. What's going on?"

"I read . . . I just read about Tabitha in the paper. Is it true she's dead?"

Lungs tightening, I lowered my head. Poor Tabitha. And her family . . . what must they be going through? "Yes."

"And you found her?"

"Penny did. I was next on the scene."

Kendra's breath hitched. "I can't believe it. I've known Tabitha forever. We were in scouts together as children. This is awful. Did the police say anything to you?"

Two customers strolled in, and I pointed at the ticket price sign on the back of the register. The man dug a wallet out of the rear pocket of his chinos.

"No," I said. "They asked a lot of questions but didn't tell me anything."

"But the papers said she was shot with an

arrow, like Bill."

"Yes. It looked that way." I made change and handed over two tickets and a brochure.

"What were you doing at the Visitors Bureau?"

I shifted the receiver beneath my chin. "I had to get more wine maps. We've been going through them faster than I expected."

"Yes, the Christmas season . . ." Kendra trailed off and cleared her throat. "Well, I'll let you get on with your day. I suppose I should call Penny. She must be shaken up. Take care of yourself." She hung up.

Rubbing the back of my neck, I replaced the phone. The call seemed odd. Kendra and I hadn't exactly parted on bad terms when I'd barged into her office, but they hadn't been good either. The opportunity to hear what had happened from someone who'd been on the scene must have been overpowering for her. Was she still worried her son might take the fall?

More customers trickled in. I made small talk, handed out tickets, boxed packages to mail.

At noon, Leo strode into the museum. He whipped off his black leather jacket. His *Paranormal Museum* long-sleeved tee looked brand new, and I wondered if he washed his clothes or just bought new ones. He went through a lot of our T-shirts.

"Sorry I'm late." He dropped a newspaper on the counter. "There's been another murder."

"I know." I glanced at the paper — Tabitha's murder was front-page news, but I didn't need to read the article; I'd been on the scene. I checked my watch. "And you're not late, so . . . apology not accepted."

He tapped the paper. "Why kill Craig's mom?"

"I don't know. But Tabitha and Bill knew each other and were both on the Christmas Cow committee. Have you talked to Craig?"

Leo's ears turned red. "No. Where do you want me?"

"Cash register." I edged aside, grabbing the box I was packing with fairies. Leo slid behind me, taking the seat behind the register.

The wall phone rang.

Bracing myself, I answered. "Paranormal Museum, this is Maddie speaking."

"This is Mike from the *San Benedetto Times.* We met on Sunday?"

I winced. "Hi, Mike. What can I do for you?"

"I was hoping for a comment. Tabitha Wilde makes the second Christmas Cow committee member who's died —"

"Been murdered," I interrupted.

"Do you believe that your attempt to bind the curse failed? And since you're the new owner of the bells, do you feel you're in danger after the hit-and-run outside the museum?"

My throat tightened. "I think that the power of any curse is people's belief in it. The bells were not the cause of Bill and Tabitha's deaths. Whoever was responsible will be caught by the police."

"But what about you? Do you feel under threat?"

Not with Laurel lurking in the shadows surveilling me. "Not at all," I said loudly.

Customers turned to stare.

I turned toward the window and lowered my voice. "I have every confidence in the skills of my curse binders."

"Thanks." Mike hung up.

Leo handed a guest change and turned to me. "Another person afraid of the curse?"

"Newspaper."

"It'll blow over," he said.

I laughed hollowly. "Will it?"

The front door jingled open and Cora Gale marched inside. Two elderly ladies trailed behind her in a flurry of rose water and talcum powder. They clustered around the old-fashioned cash register, their expressions intent.

"What are our assignments?" a short, rail-thin woman rapped out.

I rubbed my temple. "I'm not . . . assignments?"

"Hello, Leo, Maddie." Cora's mid-length gray hair was bound in a ponytail. Layers of thin coats and scarves wafted around her zaftig body. "Maddie, your mother sent us." She shot the short lady a repressive look. "To assist with your . . ." She lowered her voice. "Investigation."

My stomach dropped.

"We're Ladies Aid," chirped the third, a portly woman with steel-gray curls. She wore sensible shoes and a thick pink coat that reached to her knees.

"She knows that," Cora said. "This is Dolores." She motioned toward the plump woman. "And Rosalind." She nodded to the thin one. "I understand your movements are, er, limited due to a police presence. Your mother thought we could act as your eyes and ears."

"Spies!" Dolores's gray curls gave a little jump.

"Detectives," Rosalind corrected with a wheeze.

"So?" they asked in unison.

Leo covered his mouth with his hand and

280

turned away.

"Thanks, but I don't think that's a good idea." I had enough arrows on my conscience. I didn't need these three getting hurt. "The police are investigating, and —"

"I heard Detective Slate is on leave," Cora said.

"Yes," I said, "but Laurel Hammer knows what she's doing."

Cora's brow arched. "Does she?"

"That's not fair," I said. "She's a good cop. She saved the museum from burning down, even though she really hates me."

"Hmm." Cora didn't look convinced. "Be that as it may, your mother asked us to investigate, and so we will, with or without you."

Thinking hard, I let my gaze wander the museum. Two young girls with a selfie stick posed in front of those damned cowbells. The cowbells . . . Maybe my mother's friends could help out.

"Actually," I said. "I do need a research — I mean, detective team."

"Excellent," the tall one said. "What do you need?"

"There may be a connection between what happened in the 1980s — the cowbell curse — and what's happening today," I lied. "I need to know everything I can about

281

the people on the original committee."

Cora nodded. "We'll compile complete dossiers. It shouldn't be difficult — we were all around at the time. Several of us knew them."

Win-win. The ladies would be happy investigating something with no danger attached, and I could focus on investigating the murders. They also had a better sense of local history than me, so I could tick the box on my to-do list about interviewing past Ladies Aid members.

I pointed to the bells. "To get you started, on the placard there's a short write-up about the curse and the people who died."

The three marched to the cowbells, retrieved three sets of reading glasses from around their necks, and peered at the cardboard sign. One pulled a cell phone from her purse and snapped a photo.

"Thanks for that," Leo said in a low voice. "For a minute I thought you were going to ask them to do some real detecting."

"They can't get into trouble researching the bells." My scalp prickled and I glanced at the three, arguing beside the cave.

Leo frowned, shifting in his seat. "Right." We stared at each other.

"It'll be okay," I said. "Mrs. Gale is sensible."

"And a good person."

"Exactly." A widow and an empty-nester, Cora had taken Leo under her protective wing after his parents had died. "I respect her. And I really do need help researching this curse. Those women might not have been active in Ladies Aid in the '80s, but they have a better chance of getting to the truth than I do."

Leo straightened. "I'm in."

I fumbled with a piece of tape, which had looped and stuck to itself. "In with the curse research?"

"No, the murder cases." He shrugged, looked out the window. "It was Craig's mom."

Leo had lost his own parents at a young age. It was something I was sure he'd rather not have had in common with Craig.

I nodded, brisk. "It's time we talked with the other members of the gingerbread gang. Any idea who they might be?"

"Everyone's clammed up."

A customer walked in. Leo sold a ticket and handed out a brochure.

"But they can't be involved in the deaths," he said. "Not after Craig's own mother was killed."

"Probably not," I said slowly, wrapping the last box in brown paper. "But they're witnesses. And I wonder if someone learned of their plans and decided to piggyback arson with a murder." I crumpled the tape and threw it in the garbage bin, then wiped my palms on my jeans.

"You think Santa Claus was the outside killer?"

"That's my guess." My mom still hadn't forgiven that bit of sacrilege. "But if you want to help, figure out who was in the gingerbread gang."

I taped the brown paper shut. Double-checking the customer's address, I block-printed it on the mailing label, weighed the package, and printed a stamp.

What was I doing? Just because I'd gotten lucky before, why did I think I could help solve this crime? Jason had nearly gotten killed, and poor Craig had lost his mother . . . My nostrils flared, heat rushing through my veins. And people knew things they weren't telling the police. I couldn't give up yet. But I needed help, and from someone who actually knew what they were doing.

"I've got to drop these in the mail," I said. "Do you mind if I leave you here?"

"Nope. Go ahead."

"Thanks." I bundled the packages into a big red sack my mom had given me and lugged them down the elegant hallway to the alley. With my hip, I pushed open the heavy metal door and trudged to my pickup.

Belle Rodale, swathed in an electric-blue parka, chucked a plastic trash bag into the dumpster. She dropped the lid and it clanged shut.

My muscles stiffened. I opened my passenger door and shoved the packages inside.

She brushed her palms off on her jeans and approached me.

Leery, I shut the passenger-side door and waited.

"Hey." Belle brushed a hank of long auburn hair behind one ear.

I glanced at my pickup, then at the door to the concrete stairwell, then to the windows to Mason's apartment above. "Hi."

She shifted her weight.

"Do you need something?" I asked.

She hesitated. "You didn't say anything to Mason about my bet."

"No."

We eyed each other, the tension stretching like a worn rubber band.

"That was cool of you. Thanks." She turned and walked into the stairway to the second-floor apartment.

I stood unmoving. Had it been cool of me? I was one of those people who were keeping information from the police. Was I aiding and abetting a criminal? But I couldn't believe that the mother of Mason's child was a killer.

I slid into my red truck. Watchful of the holiday shoppers determined to hurl themselves beneath my tires, I drove slowly to the post office.

I parked on the street and groaned. A line streamed out the post office door.

Edging past the line with my ginormous sack of stuff, I bumped my way to the bin. I jammed the boxes inside and waded through the crowd. Pausing on the brick sidewalk, I dug my cell phone from my pocket and called Jason.

He answered on the third ring. "Maddie?" His voice was low and intense. "Is everything all right?"

"I'm fine." My hands were strangely slick on the phone. "How are you feeling?"

He laughed. "I feel like I was hit by a Buick. Any news on the curse?"

"Three associates of mine are compiling dossiers on the original committee members for us to review."

"Associates?"

"Ladies Aid. Some of these women were around when the curse went down in the '80s. They have memories of the victims."

"Victims? They all died of natural causes."

"I mean curse victims," I corrected. "Not murder victims." Why *had* I called them victims? "If you're still on leave, are you free for lunch?" And even though it wasn't going to be a date, I felt my face warm, my pulse beat faster.

"I am, and I am. What are you thinking?"

I thought of the least romantic place in San Benedetto. "How about the Wok and Bowl?"

"Should I pick you up from the museum?"

I checked my watch. I still had plenty of time to kill. "That would be great. See you around noon?"

"High noon it is." He chuckled and hung up.

I returned to the museum and took tickets, answered questions, sold paranormal tchotchkes. Leo and I worked smoothly together. I couldn't imagine managing the crowd without him. But some day he'd move on to bigger and better and higher-paying things. I needed to be prepared for that day.

At noon, Jason walked through the door, a camel-colored coat over his shoulders like a cape. In his navy sweater and jeans, he looked good, and I repressed a grin.

"Ready?" he asked.

In answer, I grabbed my purse from beneath the counter and followed him to his cop sedan. He opened the passenger door for me.

"You don't need to do that," I said. "You're injured."

"I'm not helpless."

One-handed, he drove to the bowling alley and parked in the lot. We walked side-by-side toward the glass front doors. The last ten feet, he sprinted ahead to open one for me. "After you."

My ears went hot. "Thanks." And I'd thought chivalry was dead.

The bowling alley was shake-rattle-and-rolling. Bowlers knocked down pins to thunderous shouts. Waitresses in poodle skirts swished past.

We found a booth in the corner. A waitress dropped off a menu and swirled away in a froth of crinoline. Jason and I made awkward small talk and ordered.

"How are you holding up?" he asked after the waitress had left.

I looked at the Formica table. "I feel terrible about Tabitha. Her son is just out of his teens."

"You knew her well?"

"Not really. I think she was worried her son might have been involved with the

288

Christmas Cow and my mom's car being bombed. She offered to pay for the damage."

He crossed his arms. "She did?"

"But Craig couldn't have been involved." I folded an empty sugar packet into thirds. "I can't imagine him killing his own mother."

"It's been known to happen."

"Not here."

His gaze drilled into me. "Are you pumping me for information?"

"I thought I was giving you information," I said carefully.

"Is that why you wanted to have lunch?"

"No." I dropped the sugar packet onto an empty saucer. "I never properly thanked you."

"For what?"

"For saving me from that car that hit you. Did you get a look at the driver?"

"No," he said. "I realized what was happening too late and could only think of getting you out of the way and then getting the license plate."

I bit the inside of my cheek.

"What?" he asked.

"Was it my fault?" I blurted. "What if they came to disrupt the event? What if someone else had been hurt?"

Jason laid his hand on mine, and my pulse jumped. "If I'd thought your event was a real danger, I would have asked you to shut it down."

"You're not in trouble, are you?"

"Getting hit in the line of duty covers a multitude of sins. I'll be okay. And I told the chief about your plans for the ritual when I saw the flyers. We all believed the risks were low."

"Oh," I said in a small voice. I cleared my throat. "Do the police think I'm a target?"

He frowned. "They're not consulting me. I'm on leave, remember? I'm off the investigation."

"That must sting." Especially when Laurel had told him to mind his own business.

"It's the right thing to do," he said.

"Where was that car stolen from? Unless it's confidential," I said quickly.

His eyebrows rose. "Are you interrogating me?"

"What? No way."

"Just because I'm off the investigation doesn't mean I can be your inside man."

"I wouldn't dream of asking." Except I *had* asked.

The waitress arrived with our food, and we fell silent.

After she left, I prodded at my kung pao

chicken. "Would you mind if I asked a police procedure question?"

"Shoot."

"What do detectives do when they're stuck in an investigation?" I asked.

"What do I do?"

"Even better."

"I go back. Look for what I've missed."

"But what if you have too much evidence?"

He sipped his coffee. "There's no such thing."

He was right. The problem wasn't too much information. The problem was I hadn't figured out how to sift the meaningless from the meaningful. But there had to be meaning in the madness.

All I had to do was find it.

EIGHTEEN

"No," I said, phone cradled between shoulder and ear. "There's no more curse. It's a historic curse. It's history." I wrapped a pack of tarot cards in tissue paper, slipped it into a paper *Paranormal Museum* bag, and handed it to Leo.

He passed it across the glass counter to the customer, a college-aged strawberry blonde. "Come again," he said, longing in his voice.

"But my husband says he hears bells," the caller said. "There are no Christmas bells in our house. We're not near a cow pasture. Something's going on."

I stared out the window. My pale reflection stared back. It was only four thirty and already it was growing dark outside. I massaged my temple. "If there was a curse, it ended in the '80s. Now the cowbells are just cowbells."

"Then why do you have them in your

museum?"

"Historical interest."

"But the papers said —"

"The papers are looking for an angle to dramatize recent events."

"But two people from the last committee are dead. And other people are dying too."

The skin prickled on the back of my neck. "Others? Someone else was shot by an arrow?"

"No, but haven't you checked today's obituaries?"

"Obituaries?"

Leo bent to pull a crumpled newspaper from beneath the counter and handed it to me. I unfolded it and found the obituaries.

"The curse is real. I'm sure of it." She hung up.

Pulse accelerating, I studied the obits. All two of the recently deceased were well past seventy and had died of natural causes. "People are attributing every single death to the curse."

Leo folded his arms. "At first I thought people's reaction to the bells was funny. I was sure wrong about that."

I dropped the paper on the counter and scraped both hands through my hair. "This has to blow over soon."

The wall phone rang, and I groaned.

"Want me to take it?" Leo asked.

"No." I sighed. "With little power comes ridiculous responsibility, etc., etc." I plucked the phone from the receiver and smiled, forcing good humor into my voice. "Good afternoon. This is Maddie at the Paranormal Museum."

No one responded.

"Hello?" I smoothed the front of my long-sleeved *Paranormal Museum* tee.

A long, drawn breath.

"Hello?" I said, less certainly.

"This is Craig."

I frowned, confused. Craig? Who . . . And then I remembered: Tabitha and Tom's son. "Craig Wilde?"

"Yeah."

"Craig, I'm so sorry about your mom. How are you doing?"

"I need to talk to you."

I straightened on my seat. "I'm listening."

"Not on the phone. Can you meet me?"

I cut my eyes toward the door. This was not a good idea. I was pretty sure Tabitha's son wasn't our killer archer, but there's a grand canyon between "pretty sure" and "certain." Still, I couldn't pass up this opportunity — not with cops stationed outside my mom's house and Slate off the case. "When?"

"In an hour, at the swimming hole."

"It's a little dark out there —"

"Come alone." He hung up.

Pursing my lips, I replaced the receiver. I was not going alone.

"What's wrong?" Leo asked.

"Craig wants to meet me at the swimming hole."

"I'll come with you."

"That would be —" I smacked my forehead. "Dammit."

"What's wrong?"

"I'm supposed to meet Craig in an hour. We've got that speaker coming at six to set up for." As a lure for repeat customers, I'd started a weekly speaker series in the Gallery area. I hadn't been confident I'd be able to keep the speakers coming, since the topics were always connected to the weird and paranormal, but there were a surprising amount of paranormal writers, surrealist poets, and persons with interests in the strange and unusual all too happy to give short talks. Tonight we'd booked a fairy shaman.

"Look," Leo said, "I think Craig's an okay guy, but you can't go alone."

"And I won't." I dug into my pocket for my cell phone. Mom would be perfect for this. She was great with the younger generation. Plus, she had a police escort.

"And you can't bring your mom."

Considering, I sucked in my cheeks. "No, I can't." Her police escort might scare Craig off.

Would Adele let me borrow Dieter? Nah. If the college students had burned the cow, I didn't want the bookie who'd managed the bets in on the conversation.

Palms going damp, I dialed Jason's number.

"Twice in one day?" the detective rumbled. "Do I smell desperation?"

"I need you. Your help!" My face heated. "Sorry. I mean —"

He chuckled, his voice low and warm. "What's going on?"

"Craig Wilde asked to meet me. I think he wants to talk about the assault on the Christmas Cow. Can you come along?"

"Maddie, this is called interfering with an investigation."

"No it isn't." I'd looked that up online earlier in the year and was careful to stay within the rules. "Besides, you're a police officer, and I'm telling you. He called me and wants to talk. He didn't say why. There's nothing illegal or interfering about us talking. And whenever I've learned anything useful in the past, I've always turned it straight over to you. But he did ask to meet in a kind of dark and secluded spot, and I don't like the idea of going alone."

There was a pause. I drummed my fingers on the top of the ancient cash register.

"Where exactly?" Jason asked.

I also didn't like the idea of him telling his partner. Would he do the right thing or keep Laurel out of it?

"We're supposed to meet at five thirty," I hedged. "I can pick you up. Just tell me where."

There was another long silence, then, "532 Cabernet Drive."

"I'll be there in fifteen minutes. Thanks." I hung up and checked my watch. "I'll be back by six thirty. Are you okay setting up on your own?"

Leo nodded. "It's only putting out folding chairs and the projector. I'm good."

"Thanks." I clapped him on the shoulder. Leo was already scheduled to work tonight's speaker series, so I felt no guilt about abandoning him. Grabbing my thick pea coat off the wall hook, I hurried through the bookcase and down Adele's narrow hallway. I burst through the heavy metal door to the alley and bumped into a solid wall of leather-clad Viking muscle.

Mason grasped my shoulders, his arctic eyes crinkling. "Hey, you all right?"

"Fine!" We were close enough to kiss, and suddenly I remembered the feel of his mouth on mine, the roughness of his cheek. I swallowed, breathless. "What are you . . . ?" I started noticing more than his tight T-shirt and slim hips. He didn't have a garbage bag in his hand for the dumpster. His motorcycle was parked outside the rear door to his shop. And he didn't need to go through Adele's place to get to the street, since he had his own entrance from his store.

"I wanted to ask you something," he said and released me.

"Oh." My gaze darted about the alley. I could play this casual. "What's up?"

"It's this curse business." He crossed his arms over his broad chest. "It may not be real —"

"It's not."

"But it's got Belle rattled. Especially after someone was run down outside your museum."

"Detective Slate."

His gaze slid sideways. "Yeah." He grimaced.

"A lot of people are worried," I said, unsure why I felt I was tiptoeing through a

298

minefield.

He shook his shaggy blond head. "It's more than that." He hesitated.

"Then what is it?"

"Belle's been acting strange, skittish. You know anything about that?" An odd expression, somewhere between suspicious and hopeful, crossed his rugged face.

"We don't talk much," I said.

His gaze narrowed. "She said she doesn't like having a haunted museum right beneath our apartment."

Our apartment. Disappointment tightened my stomach, and that feeling was wrong for so many reasons. I'd walked away so Mason and Belle could sort things out for the sake of their son. That things were working out for them now was good news. "So she's staying?"

He blew out a gusty breath. "I'm not sure."

My stupid, traitorous heart leaped with hope. And that was wrong too. "Anyway, I'm researching the curse now, so that I can debunk it."

His smile was bleak. "I'm sure you'll figure it out. You always do." He hesitated, as if he'd say more, but then he turned and walked up the steps to his apartment.

Unsettled, I got into my truck and drove

down the alley. Mason and I had broken up only two months ago, so mixed feelings were probably normal. I'd been attracted to Jason Slate since we'd first met nearly a year ago, but was I looking at him now as rebound guy? Because he deserved better than that.

I drove beneath the adobe arch marking the exit from downtown and turned right on a residential road.

Maybe nothing would happen between Jason and me anyway. Maybe the detective wasn't interested in me at all, and my crush — eesh, I had a crush — was one-sided. I'd just go slow and see what happened.

What if nothing happened?

What if something happened?

By the time I pulled in front of his neat lemon-yellow house, I'd worked myself into a full-throttle panic. Did I . . . ? Did he . . . ?

His front door opened, silhouetting his lean, muscular figure. And then the detective trotted down the short flight of porch steps and across the manicured lawn.

I leaned across the seat and unlocked the pickup's passenger door. Jason slid inside and fumbled with the old-fashioned seat belt one-handed.

"Need a hand?" I asked.

His navy parka slid off his left shoulder and he exhaled heavily. "If you don't mind."

I held the locking mechanism. He pressed the seat belt into the lock and our fingers brushed.

A tingle of electricity raced up my arm. My mind might be saying "go slow" but my hormones hadn't gotten the message.

"Where are we going?" Jason adjusted the parka over his left shoulder.

I started. The question was taking on metaphysical dimensions. "Swimming hole." I revved the truck and pulled away from the curb.

His dark brow furrowed. "There's a swimming hole in San Benedetto? What about the lake?"

San Benedetto had a small man-made lake surrounded by a park. I never went there. "The swimming hole is where all the cool kids go. You have to hike to it, and it's private."

"Gotcha. Why does Craig want to talk to you?"

"He didn't tell me. Maybe he has something to say but isn't ready to talk to the police." I glanced at the detective. His face was chiseled in the darkness, and there was something comforting in having him beside me. "He told me to come alone, but I'm not stupid. If Craig wants to talk to me, I'd like to give him the opportunity. But if he sees you, I'm not sure he'll open up."

"I'm certain he won't."

"Oh?"

"Detective Hammer and I worked the good cop/bad cop routine on him after your mom's car got blown up. I was the bad cop."

I tried imagining Laurel as the good cop and failed. "Okay. So how do you want to do this?"

"The kid doesn't strike me as a killer, either. I'll keep close but out of sight. If anything feels odd, yell. I'll come running."

"Will do." Pleased, I rolled my shoulders. I'd taken a risk calling the detective. He could have made me cancel the meeting, or insisted I bring in Laurel. But he'd done neither.

I turned down a dirt road, bumping along it until I reached an old oak. Three cars were parked beneath the gnarled tree.

"Doesn't look like Craig came alone," Jason said.

"No." I killed the ignition. The headlights blinked out, washing us in velvety night. The pickup ticked, the metal cooling, contracting. I clenched the keys in the pockets of my pea coat and they dug into my palms.

"You sure you want to do this?" he asked. "I can go instead."

"Craig wanted to talk to me." I stepped out of the truck and let my eyes adjust to the night.

"Flashlight?" Jason asked.

"I don't need one." A three-quarter moon turned the landscape of oaks and high frozen grasses into a charcoal silhouette. I buttoned my pea coat, turning up the collar.

"Which way?" he asked.

I pointed to a trampling of grass: the path.

He grunted. "Lead on. Let me know when we get close, and I'll fall back."

We walked along the flat ground. The silhouettes of barren oaks twisted like misshapen giants. The ground swelled, rising, and there was the faint trickling sound of running water. "The swimming hole is just over the rise," I whispered.

He nodded and slowed.

I continued alone and plodded up the small hill. My skin pebbled from the chill, or paranoia, or both. The world was cold and still, except for the soft sound of running water and the crunch of my footsteps on the trail. I crested the rise.

Below me, the swimming hole, really a wide bend in the creek, glittered in the moonlight. Low brush squatted around a narrow band of beach. It was a secluded spot, perfect for serial killers or vampires.

I walked down the slope, gravity pulling me along. "Craig?"

No one responded.

I reached the stretch of bare earth. The water lapped, sluggish, against the shore.

Eyes wide, I scanned the brush but saw no one.

Branches rustled behind me. I jumped and spun around.

Three masculine figures stepped from behind the brush.

NINETEEN

I tensed. "Hi, Craig." Please let it be Craig and not a merry band of murderers. I didn't see any bows in their hands, but there was a lot I couldn't see.

Water lapped gently against the shore. Something plopped into the water, and my muscles squeezed. But it had only been a fish.

"Hey," Craig said. His voice was roughened, I guessed by grief. His bulky parka made him seem small and vulnerable, and for a moment I saw his mother in him — the soulful, umber eyes and dark complexion.

The muscles between my shoulders relaxed. He wouldn't hurt me. "Who are your friends?"

"No names," said one of the men, a broad-shouldered blond with a thick five-o'clock shadow. Like his two friends, he also wore jeans and a parka.

I angled my head. The blond looked too old to be a college student. So did his companion.

They approached, surrounding me. Not liking that, I edged away, backing up to the water. "You said you wanted to talk?"

"Are you alone?" the other stranger asked. He wore glasses and was small and narrow, with a full dark beard that screamed *compensating!*

"You told me to be." I forced confidence into my voice. "You're all students at the junior college?"

"Yeah," the bearded one said. "Why?"

"No reason." But these students had to be at least as old as I was. "I take it you three are the gingerbread gang?"

They glanced at each other.

"We didn't shoot that guy," the beefy blond said.

"Then what happened?" I asked.

A branch cracked and they spun, their heads turning.

"Is someone out there?" Craig asked.

"It's probably an animal," I said, my heart rabbiting.

The blond walked to the top of the rise and scanned the horizon. He shook his head. "I don't see anyone." He returned to the group.

"Why did you want to talk to me?" I asked Craig.

"We didn't kill Bill Eldrich," Craig said.

"But you were all there, at the cow, that night?" I asked.

"Not all of us," Craig said. "I mean, we three were all there, plus Oliver, but he wouldn't come tonight."

"Oliver," I said. "Kendra Breathnach's son?"

"Yeah."

"All right," I said. "You were there. And you shot up the cow. What happened next?"

"It was supposed to be a prank," Craig said. "Students from the college try for the cow nearly every year. We weren't the only ones who'd talked about going for it."

"But you did more than talk," I said.

Craig nodded, his brown eyes morose. "We knew they had a webcam, so we got costumes from the theater department. Fred—"

"No names," the bearded guy barked.

Craig's shoulders hunched to his ears. "One of us had a contact there. We thought the gingerbread men would be funny."

"Who was Santa?" I asked.

"No one," Blondie said. "There was no Santa. It was the four of us, with four gingerbread men costumes. We've got no idea where the Santa came from."

So I'd been right, and Santa had taken advantage of the students' attack. But had he known about it in advance, or had his presence been a coincidence? "What kind of bows were you using?" I asked.

"You know," Blondie said, "the usual kind,"

"Recurve bows," Craig said.

"And the arrows?" I asked.

"Wooden," Craig said.

"You all used wooden arrows?" Bill had been killed with an arrow made of some sort of modern, not-quite-metal material.

They nodded.

"Okay," I said. "Santa showed up. What happened next?"

"The cow caught on fire and we took off," Craig said. "We agreed it would be a quick in-and-out job. Even though we had costumes, we knew the cow would be guarded. We didn't want to hang around for the show."

Something rustled in the bushes, and we all twitched.

"An animal." Fred (I think) scratched his chin beneath his beard.

"And what was Santa doing?" I asked.

They looked at each other.

Fred shrugged, his narrow shoulders

hunching. "I noticed him, but I wasn't really watching him."

"Anyone else see what he was doing?" I asked.

They shook their heads.

"Did you tell anyone you were going to attack the cow that night?" I asked.

"No," Craig said heatedly. "We didn't."

"What are the odds that Santa would show up with a bow and arrow at the exact same time your team did?" I asked.

"We didn't tell anyone," Fred insisted.

"Then how could someone have found out?" I asked. "Were you meeting about it in public?"

"No," Craig said.

"And don't you find it suspicious that Oliver isn't here?" I asked. "Maybe he's the one who spilled the beans."

"Oliver didn't do this," Craig said. "He's not here because his mom sent him away. She knows he was involved and is freaked he'll go to jail."

"How did she know?" I asked.

"The same way my mom knew I was in on it, I guess." Craig laughed bitterly. "But my mom knew lots of things."

"What does that mean?" I asked.

Craig hung his dark head. "It means my mom was crooked."

Even in the dim light, the anger scrawled across Craig's face was plain. His two friends looked at each other and shifted their weight, their parkas rustling.

Fred grabbed Craig's arm. "Come on, man. You don't know that." His breath puffed in the chill night air. Moonlight glinted off his glasses.

Craig shook free. "What else could it have been? My mom was taking payoffs." His olive skin darkened.

"How do you know?" I jammed my fists into the pockets of my pea coat, an ugly feeling growing in my chest.

"I overheard her talking to Mr. Eldrich about some permits or something."

"Or something? What exactly did you hear?" San Benedetto seemed too small to have stakes worth bribing anyone over.

"Bill Eldrich was going to make a 'big donation.' " Craig put the last word in air quotes. A vein pulsed in his temple. "But I knew what they were really talking about."

"Where were you when you heard them?" I asked.

"At my mom's home office." The skin bunched around his umber eyes. "They didn't think anyone was around. This must be why someone killed her. It's got nothing to do with the cow fire."

"And you think the same person killed Bill Eldrich?" I asked. "Because of whatever they were discussing?"

"Maybe. I just know there's only one reason why anyone would want my mom dead." His voice broke, and a sliver of cold pierced my core. I wanted to step closer and comfort him but didn't think it would go over well.

But had Craig misconstrued what he'd overheard? Had Tabitha's relationship with Bill been romantic or criminal? "You need to speak to the police," I said. "Your mother's murder —"

"No way." Fred removed his glasses and polished them on the hem of his parka.

"The reason we're here is so *you* can tell the police, lady," the blond man said. "But no names."

Craig lowered his head. "It doesn't matter anymore."

"No cops." The broad-shouldered blond glared at Craig. "If Craig wants to confess, that's his business. We're out of it." He stalked up the slope.

Jason emerged from behind a tree. "Sorry, son. But you're all involved."

"Cops!" Bent low, the blond bolted left.

Jason moved to intercept. There was a blur of motion, and the detective went down.

"Jason!" I ran up the small hill.

Craig's two friends scattered.

Jason rolled to his feet and made a muffled sound. Wincing, he grasped his sling. His face looked strained in the moonlight. "Hell," he said through clenched teeth. "Why did I think I could do that?" He scanned the expanse of low ground, but the two had disappeared.

I looked toward the water.

Craig stood at the edge, shoulders slumped, and stared at the moonlight glinting off the dark pool.

I touched Jason's arm. "Craig Wilde is ready to talk."

The detective walked down to the swimming hole. I waited on the crest of the hill.

The two men spoke in voices too low for me to hear. Then Craig nodded and followed Jason up the hill.

The three of us returned to my pickup. In silence, we drove to the police station. I parked on the street, killed the engine, and reached for my seat belt.

"You should head home," Jason said to me. He glanced at Craig, who was crammed between us. "Craig approached me to confess, thinking I was still involved in the case."

Craig nodded, his lips pressed together.

I checked the dash clock. I had time to make it to the museum before the speaker series began, but I didn't want to leave Craig. It had just been a stupid college prank. Now two people were dead, including his mother.

"It's easier if we don't have to explain your presence," Jason said.

"All right," I said.

The men scooted from the truck.

I leaned across the seat. "Craig, it's going to be all right. Do you want me to call your father?"

"No." He hurried up the short flight of concrete steps to the police station. I wasn't sure which he was disagreeing with me over — whether it would be all right or if I should call his father.

"I'll make sure his father knows," Jason said.

Unhappy, I nodded and watched the two vanish into the police station.

Sun streamed through the tea room's gauzy white curtains. They fluttered, dreamlike. Diners spoke in low voices, a cheerful holiday buzz.

In the corner booth, I huddled over a cup of tea and a roast beef sandwich. It was two in the afternoon, but my eyes burned from a sleepless night. I propped my elbows inelegantly on the white tablecloth.

Across from me, Adele smoothed her knot of black hair. "And then what happened?"

"I don't know. I haven't heard from Detective Slate since they went into the police station." I yawned and raised the tea cup to cover my gaping mouth.

Adele frowned. "At least we know who was responsible for the cow."

"Did you find out how much money Belle made off her bet?"

Adele leaned forward. "Fifty," she whispered.

"Only fifty dollars?" That wasn't worth committing arson over.

"Fifty thousand."

I set my cup down too hard, rattling the plate. "Are you kidding me?"

"The Christmas Cow is serious business," Adele said. "People from all over the world place bets. And installing the webcam has only piqued the interest."

"What's Dieter's cut?"

Her gaze narrowed. "Why does that matter? Dieter had nothing to do with lighting the Christmas Cow on fire. You know who did it. The kids confessed."

I shifted in the booth. Santa's identity remained a mystery, but at least it couldn't have been Dieter. He'd have been smart enough to back off when he saw the gingerbread men attacking the cow. And I couldn't imagine him killing Bill Eldrich. "Only curious. That's big money, and I'm assuming there's some legal risk involved, since we're in California and not Vegas."

"Dieter and I don't talk about money." Adele's foot bounced. It baffled me how she managed her high heels, but when it came to fashion, pain would never slow her down. "Though I guess we should talk about it," she continued. "Did you know that money is the number one cause of divorce?"

I drew a quick breath. "Are you thinking of getting married?" Was I going to be a bridesmaid? I could imagine Adele's wedding in the vineyard — she'd only been talking about it since the fifth grade.

"No, of course not." She tucked in her upper lip. "But it's important for couples to be on the same page. At least I know that Dieter is a saver. He's actually quite frugal with his money."

"Mmm." I drew back against the booth. Fifty thousand dollars was motive enough for Belle. It was motive enough for a lot of people, especially for a woman who was broke and dependent on a man she hadn't seen in years.

And she hadn't told Mason she'd won the money. Why was she holding back? Was she waiting for the right time to surprise him, or was there something more sinister afoot? My hand tightened on the warm cup. Stop jumping to conclusions, Maddie. There was still no reason for her to shoot Bill.

"What's wrong?"

"Nothing. Thanks for finding out about the bet."

"It wasn't easy."

I grinned. Dieter couldn't deny Adele anything for long. He doted on her.

I grabbed the plate with the remainder of my sandwich. "I've got to get back to the museum. Can someone bring the bill over?"

"Your wish is my command." She slid from the booth.

I went to the bookcase and pressed the spine that said *Museum*. The bookcase slid open and I strode inside. Behind the glass counter, Leo simultaneously sold a ticket, talked on the wall phone, and taped a package shut.

Hurrying behind the old-fashioned cash register, I set down the plate. I completed the ticket sale and took the package from Leo's grasp.

"The rumor isn't true," Leo was saying to the caller. "Three paranormal specialists have confirmed that the cowbells have been effectively bound."

I frowned, worried. Three specialists? Did he know about Harper's secret life too? I finished taping the package and weighed it.

"No," Leo said. "No . . . Yes . . . I'm certain . . . Okay, have a good one." He hung up and blew out his breath.

"Another?" I asked, printing out the postage.

"This isn't going away." His dark brows slashed downward. "But your sandwich is."

"What?" I spun. The strip of packing tape pulled from its roller and wrapped around my fingers.

GD sprang from the counter, roast beef trailing from his teeth.

"GD!"

He scuttled beneath Gryla's skirts in the ogress cave.

Mournful, I stared at the two pieces of bread, watercress, and tomato he'd left. "I hope he gets heartburn."

"GD would need a heart first."

"So who's the third paranormal specialist?" I asked.

"What?"

Making a face, I peeled tape off my fingers. "You said three specialists had confirmed the cowbells were safe. Who are they?"

"Herb, that Xavier dude, and you."

Was I a paranormal specialist now? At least it was a more exciting job title than "project manager," my last one. Even though I'd been forced out of my old company, I was glad now that it had happened. I loved my wacky new career.

Was my mom right that I had a passion for crime solving too? I wasn't sure how I felt about that, because there was nothing entertaining about the crimes. A man was dead, my mom had nearly been killed, and Craig had lost his mother.

I slapped the tape on the next box. A part of me wished I'd never heard Tabitha might have been a corrupt council member. The other part was furious that someone had killed her. Corruption or no, she was a mother and a wife, and her family didn't deserve this pain.

The front door jingled open, and Cora and her two minions fluttered inside. They clustered around the counter in a flurry of violet perfume and scarves and rustling paper bags.

"We have something," Cora whispered.

I handed Leo the wrapped package.

Cora's voice dropped. "But it might be

best not to talk about it here." She fingered one of the filmy scarves around her neck and glanced hopefully at the bookcase. "Perhaps the tea room?"

"Seriously? You found something?" Could they have actually cracked the curse?

"You will be amazed," Cora said.

Leo sighed. "Go ahead. I've got everything under control."

GD edged from beneath Gryla's skirts and meowed as if placing an order.

"I won't be long." I walked to the bookcase and opened it, nearly bumping into an apron-clad waitress.

"Whoops!" She held up the bill. "Adele asked me to bring you this."

"Can you get us a table instead?"

She glanced at Adele. The tea room was packed, but Adele always held a table in reserve for emergencies.

Adele nodded.

"I think I can find something," the waitress said. "This way, please."

She led us to the table I'd recently deserted, then passed out menus and took the ladies' coats.

Cora sat and pulled a thick manila file from her purse. She slid it across the white tablecloth to me. "Those dossiers you wanted."

I thumbed through the files, and my head lowered in disappointment. The dossiers were helpful, and I'd have to read through them more carefully, but Cora's "amazement" comment had unrealistically raised my expectations. "This is great. Thanks. Look, order whatever you want. It's on me. I've got to get back to the museum to help Leo." I began to rise.

"Wait." Cora touched my wrist.

I sank onto my seat, hope blossoming in my chest.

"We found more," Dolores intoned.

"Much more," Rosalind said.

"What did you learn?" I asked, crossing and uncrossing my legs.

The waitress reappeared at my elbow. "Are you ready to order?"

"Oh!" Rosalind's blue eyes widened. "We haven't had a chance to look at the menu, I'm afraid."

"I know what I want to order," Dolores said, her chins trembling. "Your Christmas high tea."

"For me as well," Cora said, brisk.

"Christmas high tea?" Rosalind asked. "What's that?"

Expensive, I thought, mentally tallying my upcoming bill.

The waitress tapped her pen on her notepad. "A red velvet Christmas cupcake, two mini-scones with raspberry jam, a poached turkey-breast sandwich with cranberry and whole-grain mustard, and a cucumber sandwich with lemon-herb cream cheese, Scottish shortbread, truffles, and your choice of tea."

"Oh, I'll have that too," Rosalind said.

"And for your tea?"

"The sugarplum fairy," Cora said. "Dolores? Rosalind?"

"Me too."

"Me three!"

The waitress glanced at me.

I shook my head, and the waitress zoomed away.

"So." I cleared my throat. "Did you come across anything related to the origin of the curse? I want to be able to debunk it."

Cora shook her head. "Not about its origin in the '80s."

"Then what?"

"We know what started it up this month!" A triumphant expression lit up Cora's face.

My brow furrowed. "You mean the curse — as they call it — wasn't activated by me promoting the cowbells at the museum?"

"That might have been the trigger." Cora adjusted a filmy green scarf. "But it's not the cause of the panic."

"Then what is?" I asked.

"Jennifer Falls has been shooting off her mouth all over town that the curse has returned." Dolores shook her head, her gray ringlets trembling.

"A lot of people have been talking about the return of the curse," I said. "We're getting calls every day."

Cora leaned forward. "You don't understand. Jennifer Falls is the *source*. She's the one who started the rumor."

"How can you be sure?" I laid the file on the table.

"Because," Cora said, "we asked people where they first heard about the curse returning. Too many reports could be traced to her."

"You can't really blame her," Dolores said.

"Not with what happened," Rosalind agreed.

"You mean, her husband's death?" I asked. "I guess I could see where she'd be more sensitive, but that was a long time ago."

Cora tapped the file. "Obviously, you know her first husband, Sigfried Tassi, was one of the victims of the curse in the '80s. He was on the committee, the youngest member of the town council."

"Yeah, the one electrocuted in the bathtub," I said.

"Those ridiculous boom boxes." Dolores *tsked.*

"She's remarried," Cora said. "But I'm afraid she's gotten a little silly about it all. She's terrified she'll lose another husband to the curse."

"Why would she?" I asked. "He's not on the Christmas Cow committee, is he?"

"No," Cora said, "but he is a member of the Dairy Association, and he's been somewhat accident-prone lately."

"Well, thanks," I said. "Good work." I wasn't sure how this information helped — the proverbial cat was out of the bag. Even if Jennifer did recant her statements, how much good would it do? But maybe I could at least set her mind at ease. "I'll follow up with her."

"If you need any introductions," Cora said, "we can help. Jennifer is the only spouse from the original committee still alive today. All the others have passed."

"Thanks," I said. "I may take you up on that."

Rosalind tittered. "Please do. This was ever so much fun."

Dolores nodded. "Much more interesting than working the poker table at our last fundraiser."

"You worked . . ." I shook my head. Not important. "You said there aren't any other survivors I can talk to?"

"I'm afraid not," Cora said. "With the exception of Sigfried and Jennifer, the original committee were already quite elderly back in the '80s. They've all passed on."

"Quite elderly?" Dolores asked, indignant. "They were only in their seventies."

"Seventy was older back then," Cora said hastily. She shot me a look, her lips quivering.

"I'll talk to Jennifer," I said, rising and taking the folder. "Thanks."

"Be careful," Cora said.

I halted. "Why? You don't think the curse has sent her over the edge?"

"I think there are a lot of arrows flying around," Cora said. "And they seem to be headed in your direction."

TWENTY

I parked beside the police cruiser and strolled up my mother's brick walk. The straw reindeer raised and lowered their heads as if grazing, their bodies strung with tiny white lights. A Christmas tree twinkled in my mother's front window. I won't say no one does Christmas better than my mom, but she's pretty good at it. Memories of Christmases past crowded me, and I hummed a carol.

I knocked beneath the Christmas wreath and tested the knob. Predictably, the door was unlocked, and I walked inside. My mother rarely locked her door, and with the police in her front yard I guess she didn't feel the need to start now.

In her cozy living room, my mom slumped on the pale green couch, her feet on the coffee table, a Santa Claus blanket over her shoulders. The room was a Christmas monsoon of twig reindeer, pine cones, and tinsel. Swags of holly hung from the distressed-wood rafters. A red-rimmed plate of Christmas cookies sat on the table.

My mother clutched a steaming mug in her hands. Dark circles shadowed her eyes, and her makeup had worn off in patches. Worried, I checked my watch. It was only six o'clock, and she looked exhausted.

"Hi, Mom." I sat in the cream-colored wing chair opposite. "Rough day?"

She sipped from her mug and didn't meet my gaze. "Ladies Aid held an emergency meeting."

"About what?"

She lowered her chin. "The murders, what else? I understand you diverted the committee into researching the cursed bells?"

"Um. Yes."

She sighed. "I suppose it's just as well. There seems to be a strange nexus between the bells and the murders. They're heightening the panic. It's even reached Ladies Aid. I had to be very stern with Mary Hunter tonight."

"I see you still have police protection."

"It seems pointless. But they're concerned that other members of the committee may be targeted. Since I was on the scene when Bill was murdered, they think I'm a potential victim. I suppose you've got an escort as well?"

"Yes, but she's keeping out of sight." And my respect for Laurel's lurking abilities was growing. Though she hadn't interfered at the swimming hole. Why? Because she'd spotted Slate?

"Will you get in any trouble with her for investigating?" my mom asked.

"I haven't so far. I think she's waiting to see what I turn up so she can swoop in and take the credit."

"Madelyn —"

"I know." I raised my hands in a defensive gesture. "I shouldn't have set her hair on fire, and I didn't set her hair on fire. But this is a good thing. If Laurel's around, I can poke as many hornets' nests as I like and she'll be there to back me up if someone pokes back." But my stomach quivered with unease. What if Laurel wasn't around? No, she had to be. Dieter had said she was personally watching. And since when did I take Dieter's word as gold?

My mom sat up and the blanket slipped from her shoulders, pooling on the couch. "So where are we? Have you eaten?"

"Not yet." My mouth watered. My mother was a fantastic cook.

"I'll order Chinese." She grabbed her cell

phone off the coffee table and placed the order.

I smothered my disappointment. But she was probably too knackered from all her Christmas baking to cook, and the point of this visit was spending time together, not food. Still, Chinese again?

She hung up. "What?"

"Nothing," I said.

"You were telling me about the case?"

There was a knock at the door, and three uniformed officers walked inside. "We're changing shifts," one said. "This is Officer Parnel and Officer Rogers. They'll be taking over tonight."

"How lovely," my mom said. "Can I get you coffee? Hot cocoa?"

"Coffee would be great," one of the new officers said.

My mom bustled to the kitchen, and the cops and I eyed each other. I tapped my foot.

"Cream? Sugar?" my mom called out.

"Black please," the men said.

My mom returned with two full mugs. "Please feel free to freshen the coffee whenever you like. The pot's on in the kitchen. And the bathroom is down the hall, second door on the right."

"Thanks, ma'am."

The cops left.

"Last night I met with Craig Wilde," I said. "He confessed to setting the cow on fire."

She blew out her breath. "If you'd told me that a few days ago, I'd have wrung Craig's scrawny neck. But with his mother dead . . ." She shook her head, sorrow creasing her face. "What a terrible, terrible thing."

"I know." I scrubbed a hand over my jaw. If I'd pushed Craig harder, sooner, would Tabitha have died? "It's why Craig came forward. He knows the cow arson is muddling the investigation."

"Who else was involved?"

"I didn't get their full names, and they took off before Slate could grab them."

She arched a brow. "Detective Slate? I thought he was on leave?"

"I wasn't going to meet Craig on my own. And Jason seemed —"

"Jason? You're on a first-name basis?"

My cheeks warmed. "He was off duty. Calling him Detective Slate all the time was getting weird."

"Ah."

"There's nothing going on."

"Of course not. He seems like a very by-the-book sort of person. I'm surprised he allowed you to talk to Craig."

"Craig called me," I said. "I was only being a responsible citizen bringing Ja— Detective Slate along."

"Of course you were. So what happened?"

"Craig said he overheard a conversation — at his house — between his mom and Bill Eldrich. He said it sounded like she was taking bribes. But I wonder if he misunderstood?"

My mother sipped her cocoa. "Bribes."

"What would Tabitha have been taking bribes for?"

"Exemptions from regulations, favorable council decisions like that grant funding . . . Power corrupts, and even in a small town like this, there are temptations. And it *was* a bit odd the way the Wine and Visitors Bureau lost the funding at the last minute. Everything I'd heard indicated they'd be getting something, and then it all went to the Dairy Association."

"But bribes?" Ignoring my mother's pointed look, I rested my feet on the coffee table. "Bill wouldn't pay a bribe on behalf of the Dairy Association out of his own pocket, would he? It would have to come from the association. Wouldn't their bookkeeper have something to say about it?"

"I'm not sure," she said. "The Dairy Association does a lot of lobbying on behalf of its members. A bribe could be disguised — as a donation to a favorite charity, for example."

"A 'donation.' That's what Craig overheard."

"It might have been an innocent donation to an actual charity that he heard them talking about."

"All right," I said. "Let's assume it's true, and Bill was paying off Tabitha. Now they're both dead. Who would kill them? A third party to a bribe who wanted to keep it quiet? Someone angry that a bribe resulted in a council decision they didn't like?"

"If the latter, that points to Dean with his raw milk or Penny with her lost income for the Visitors Bureau."

"Why would Penny kill over that?" I toyed with the zipper on my hoodie. "She may treat the Visitors Bureau like it's her own, but —"

"But that's the point. The Wine and Visitors Bureau would be nothing without Penny. She was the one who got the funding for the building they have now. She started the wine tastings. She expanded the staff. It's her baby. But I have a difficult time imagining her committing murder too."

We mulled that over.

"There is, of course, another possibility," she said. "That Tabitha's husband, Tom, knew about her affair with Bill."

"And if she was taking bribes," I said, "he'd have to know about that too, wouldn't he?"

"He'd have little reason to kill his wife over some bribes, as despicable as that may be. But if he was hurt . . . angry about the affair . . . ?"

"Have you attended any of the town council meetings lately?" I asked.

My mom adjusted her squash blossom necklace. "Between the holidays and Ladies Aid, I haven't had the time. Why?"

"If there was something hinky going on, maybe we can figure out what it was from the minutes."

"The minutes only list the topics discussed, not the content of the arguments," she said, rising. "But who knows? I'll get my laptop."

She left the room and returned a few minutes later, the open laptop in her arms. She handed it to me.

I zipped to the town council's website and the meeting minutes. My mom was right. The minutes weren't terribly informative.

I did a web search for *raw milk* and Dean

Pinkerton's name and turned up a newspaper article on the conflict. "This is interesting," I said, skimming the article. "Tabitha Wilde is quoted in it."

"What did she say?"

"That it's the town council's duty to protect the health of its citizens, and the safety of unpasteurized milk is debatable. It sounds like she was planning on voting with team Eldrich."

"Do a search for Tabitha's name. See what else you find."

I did. Once I waded past the articles about her murder, it was all small stuff — an appearance at the annual Christmas Cow launch. A quote about funding for education. A plea to vote yes on a bond measure . . . "This is going to take a while."

The doorbell rang.

"That's the Chinese food." She stood up. "I'll get it. Keep looking."

I did and got nothing more out of my time than a fortune cookie. It read: *Ignore Previous Fortunes.*

Alone in my mom's kitchen, I tossed empty boxes of Chinese food into the bin beneath the sink.

My cell phone buzzed in the pocket of my hoodie. Frowning, I checked the number and my heart skipped a beat. Jason Slate.

"Hello?" Leaning against the granite counter, I studied the open-front cabinets with their display of red plates and mugs.

"Maddie, it's Jason."

"Hi. What's up?"

"Have you learned anything more about the curse?"

"My contacts in Ladies Aid believe they've found the source of the recent hysteria." Credit where credit was due.

He chuckled. "Ladies Aid, the true power in San Benedetto."

"Invisible and everywhere and super powerful, if you know how to use it."

"So who amped up the curse rumors?"

Yawning, my mother ambled into the kitchen.

"The wife of one of the victims from the '80s," I said.

"Jennifer Tassi?"

"She's Jennifer Falls now. She's remarried. Apparently her current husband's had a couple minor accidents recently, and she's been telling people she's worried the curse is happening all over again."

"Who is it?" my mother whispered.

I covered the receiver. "Detective Slate."

"May I?" She extended her hand.

"Mom," I hissed.

334

"Madelyn . . ." She waggled her fingers impatiently.

"Um, Jason, my mom wants to talk to you." Dread puddling in my chest, I handed her the phone.

"Detective Slate, this is Fran Kosloski. I wanted to thank you for saving my daughter's life. It was remarkably brave of you . . . Yes . . . Thank you . . . I understand you've been moved to curse duty . . . ? Yes . . . Yes . . ."

I shifted my weight and leaned closer, but I couldn't catch Jason's end of the conversation.

"Oh, I can arrange that," my mom said. "How soon would you like . . . ? Then tonight it is. We'll see you shortly." She hung up. "Detective Slate is coming over." She returned the phone to me and left the kitchen.

I tugged on the strings of my museum hoodie and trotted after her. "What? Why?"

She walked to her work room, cluttered with empty boxes marked *Xmas.* Opening a drawer in the battered desk, she withdrew a tattered phone book. "Because there's no time like the present. If you're going to talk to Jennifer Falls, you may as well do it now."

"I don't even know Jennifer . . ." I folded my arms across my chest. "But you do, don't you?"

"She's not in Ladies Aid. But we have crossed paths." My mother squinted at the open book. "My eyesight isn't what it used to be." She grabbed the phone on the desk and dialed. "Hello, Jennifer, this is Fran Kosloski . . ."

Rubbing the back of my neck, I returned to the kitchen.

If I was going to put a damper on this curse hysteria, talking to Jennifer was the next logical step. And if my mom knew her, all the better. But I wasn't sure whether my mom was pushing me toward ending the curse or toward Jason Slate. Either way, it was embarrassing. He would come over, and she'd grill him, and then he'd think that she thought we were an item.

I groaned and fitted the last dishes into the washer.

"You're all set." She strolled into the kitchen. "Jennifer's expecting you and Detective Slate." Her eyes widened. "He'll need a Christmas plate!"

"I don't think —"

"Nonsense. It's just good manners. Besides, I've given my police watchers plates." She peeled a lid off a plastic container and arranged cookies on a red and white paper plate.

Fifteen minutes later, the doorbell rang.

I bounded from the kitchen and opened the door.

Jason stood on the step. A thick blue scarf looped beneath the collar of the parka draped over his shoulders. His sling was white against his navy sweater. "Cold out tonight."

"Then you'd better come in, Zorro."

Grinning, he stepped inside, and I shut the door.

My mom bustled into the entryway bearing cookies. She thrust two plastic-wrapped plates into Jason's free hand. "One for you, and one for Jennifer and her husband." She bustled us out the door. "Have fun investigating!" She waved and slammed the door shut.

Jason's lips quirked.

"I'm not responsible for my mother," I said.

"I like her. And she's right. It is late at night for a police visit."

"Good thing you're on leave. At least we have cookies."

"I have cookies," he said. "You get your own." Chuckling, he strode down the pathway and past the nodding reindeer. He held open the sedan door for me and I got inside, reaching across to unlock his door.

"Do you know where we're going?" I asked when he slid behind the wheel.

"By now I think I know this town." He started the car and we drove off.

A car approached, its high beams on, blinding. Jason flipped his headlights and the car roared past.

"You say she's afraid for her new husband?" he asked.

"Right." I filled him in on what Cora had told me.

"He's a farmer?"

"He owns Falls Yogurt."

"Really?" Jason cast a quick glance at me. "I love that stuff."

"I know, right? Especially since they've started making Icelandic yogurt."

We chatted easily, and he let me steal a pfeffernüsse cookie.

Jason's sedan drifted to a halt in front of a small brick two-story house. He checked the address. "Either they live simply, or Falls Yogurt isn't as successful as I thought."

"My sources at Ladies Aid did imply Mr. Falls was frugal."

He grinned. "Are these confidential sources?"

"You better believe it." I unbuckled myself. "I'm not crossing that crew."

We walked up the darkened concrete path,

Jason carrying the cookie plate. On the porch, a light flashed on beside the simple front door. I rang the bell.

A few minutes later, the door opened, and a woman with graying hair gazed at us through the screen. "Yes?"

I stared, trying to remember where I'd seen her before.

"I'm Detective Slate," Jason said. "This is Madelyn Kosloski. I believe you were expecting us?"

"Of course." She pushed the screen door open, and we walked inside.

The wallpaper in the entryway was faded. A woman's violet-colored cloche hat sat on a hat stand on the dusty end table. Lightly, I touched the two faux-pearl hat pins sticking from its band.

Mrs. Falls shut the door and pulled her yellow cardigan more tightly about her slim frame. "Your mother said you had some information about the curse."

I snapped my fingers. "That's where I saw you. You were at the museum for the curse binding ritual."

She hung her head. "You probably think I'm foolish."

"No," I said quickly. What I felt was guilty for inflicting the stupid cowbells on the town. It had seemed so innocent at the time.

"I'd hoped . . ." She looked away, then motioned us into a white-painted living room with beige carpeting.

We followed her into the room, and she sat on a brown-and-green floral-print sofa. Jason and I sat opposite her on a matching couch. A row of antique women's hats, complete with veils and elaborate pins, lined the center of the coffee table. I felt like I was back in my college apartment. All that was missing was a poster of Magnum PI (sexy in any decade).

"The hats are lovely." I picked one up and something sharp pricked my thumb. "Ow." I set it down quickly.

"Sorry," she said. "The pins are sharp. So you wanted to tell me something about the curse?"

"Madelyn owns the paranormal museum," Jason said. "She's an expert in curses."

My mouth opened, closed. I was an expert? Oh, right. I was. I nodded sagely.

"Madelyn?" Jason prompted.

I cleared my throat. Time to step up, even if it did make me look like a fraud. "There's no curse."

Mrs. Falls blinked. "You mean the binding spell worked?"

"No, because there was nothing to bind," I said. "The ritual was authentic. We only did it to calm people down, and because the ritual itself was interesting. But there's no curse."

"But those deaths . . . and you were hit with a car outside the museum." She motioned to Jason's sling. "Right after the riot."

Whoa, whoa, whoa! "I wouldn't call it a riot —"

"That's exactly the point," Jason said. "Panic has inflated this so-called curse in people's minds. But there's no curse. There never was."

She laughed hollowly. "Tell that to my first husband. Every single member of that committee died within a year of receiving those horrible bells."

"What do you remember about that time?" Jason leaned forward as if to prop his elbows on his knees. At the last minute he pulled back, remembering his sling.

"It was terrible," she said. "All those people dying. At first, we thought the deaths were accidents, natural causes. And then people began to see a pattern."

Jason reached into his breast pocket and his parka cascaded off his shoulders. A flicker of annoyance crossed his face. He rummaged in the pockets and pulled out a folded piece of paper. "This is a list of people who died in San Benedetto during that period." He handed it to her.

"There were more curse victims?" she asked, paling.

"No. Take a look at it. I think you'll see they all had something in common."

She scanned the paper, her mouth pursing. "So many people. I didn't even know them."

"That's not too surprising. They were all over seventy-five, and you were a young woman."

She set the paper on the coffee table. "I don't see what you're getting at," she said stiffly.

"The average life expectancy in the 1980s was seventy-three and a half," he said. "All the victims, with the exception of your husband, were past that. The only curse they suffered was old age."

She blinked, her eyes watery. "But the curse — the museum. That woman's hand was bitten."

"The museum has a cat." I sent a mental apology to GD. There was no way he'd bitten those women. Sure, it was *possible* he'd nipped an ankle and then snuck back to his perch atop the cave. He'd bitten me often enough. But he'd never gone after a customer, and I didn't see how he could have reached anyone's hand. "People panicked."

Her worn face tightened. "Your cat bites people? And you let him around the public?"

"Do you remember how the story of the curse got started back in the '80s?" I asked, changing the subject.

She gnawed her bottom lip. "A newspaper article, I think."

I shook my head. There *had* been a newspaper article — I'd found it in my initial curse research. But the article had referenced fears whipping through the town. It had reported on the curse story, not started it.

"Have you heard about the placebo effect?" I asked.

"You mean, when people are given fake drugs, but the drugs work because people believe in them?"

"Exactly," I said. "Curses work the same way — a reverse placebo effect. They're not real, but when people believe in them, they sometimes come true. The more people think there's a curse, or even joke about it, the more likely it is that bad things will happen — or that people will blame everything that happens on the curse. The best thing you can do — for yourself and the town — is to stop talking about or even thinking about the curse."

"Have you ever tried to not think of something? It's impossible." Jennifer Falls raised her chin. "Maybe I have been a bit foolish. But Byron is the one in danger. A part of him believes in that curse. And like you said — if he believes it, it might still come true. That would explain all those little accidents he's been having. What if he's made himself clumsy?" She shuddered. "Do you have any idea how much machinery he works around?"

"The original curse only applied to people who were on the actual Christmas Cow committee," I said. "Your husband wasn't on this year's committee. All you need to do is explain that the curse — if it exists — doesn't apply to him."

"But Byron *was* on the committee," she said. "He attended the first meeting, then realized he wouldn't have time for it and quit."

Aghast, I sat back on the couch. "What sort of accidents did you say he was having?"

TWENTY-ONE

I passed two tickets and a brochure across the counter and smiled. "Here you go. If you have any questions about the exhibits, feel free to ask."

GD, seated on top of the antique cash register, meowed an agreement.

The middle-aged couple smiled, their eyes unfocused. They'd obviously already hit several wineries. I watched them weave through the crowd, then I returned to my to-do list. It only had two items on it: Byron Falls and Dean Pinkerton.

My lips pursed. Jennifer Fall's husband had had accidents. That disturbed me, especially if my cowbells were responsible. I wasn't sure I could talk him out of believing in the curse, but I had to try.

I also had to talk to Dean about Tabitha's vote on the raw milk controversy. But I probably wouldn't have time until Monday to tackle either of them. Fridays were almost always busy, and the museum would be hopping all weekend. Plus I didn't much like the idea of interrogating anyone after hours. My nighttime investigations rarely ended well.

The front door jangled and Leo walked inside. He peeled off his motorcycle jacket. Ketchup stained his black T-shirt. "Hey."

"Yo." My stomach growled, and I slid off my high seat. I hadn't eaten much breakfast and I was long past ready for my own lunch break.

"Anything I should know?" he asked.

"I asked the Historical Association to see if they could find more articles about the original curse. They may call."

"I thought we'd found the only article."

"I did too, but now I'm not so sure."

My cell phone rang in my hoodie pocket, and I fished it out and checked caller ID. It was my mom.

"Hi —"

"Madelyn, this is your mother."

"Mom."

"You'll never believe it, but I'm free!"

"Free?"

"They've decided I no longer need police protection, so —"

I straightened. "What? Why? Did they arrest someone?"

"I've no idea, but the police are gone."

Why would they dump my mother's protection now? Had something changed? "But why — ?"

"I thought we could do some sleuthing together. Dean Pinkerton needs a further talking to, and this time, I need to be there."

"I agree, but Fridays are tough for me." As were Saturdays and Sundays.

"Of course, dear. That's why I thought we'd pop over during your lunch."

My stomach's growl turned into a snarl. "Actually, I was about to get something to eat."

"Perfect." The front door swung open and my mother strode inside. She dropped the phone into the pocket of her quilted blue jacket. "I'm ready to go when you are."

"But I'm hungry," I whined.

"We'll use the drive-through. My rental is parked out front."

Leo grinned.

Urgh. If I didn't go with her, she'd go alone. Grabbing my scarf off the wall hook, I bundled up and followed her onto the sidewalk. Dodging holiday shoppers, I hustled to her rental Lincoln.

"Which drive-through?" I asked once we'd settled ourselves inside the giant sofa on wheels. It smelled like new car, and I ran my hand across the burled dash.

"Whichever you like, dear. But that burger place is on the way to Dean's. It would save time."

I sighed. "Burger place it is."

"Did you lose your police protection too?" she asked.

I glanced over my shoulder. A gray sedan followed two car lengths behind. "I don't think so."

"I would hope not, not after that attack in front of the museum. Clearly the killer has focused on you. Honestly, I don't know why they kept the police in front of my house for so long."

We drove over the railroad tracks. I barely felt them beneath the SUV's tires.

"You were on the Christmas Cow committee, and at the scene when Bill Eldrich was murdered," I said. "The killer might think you saw something or know too much."

"If I'd seen something, I would have told the police by now."

"The killer doesn't know that," I said. "If these murders do have to do with Bill and Tabitha being involved with bribes, maybe the murderer thinks you're waiting to blackmail him. Or her." And maybe going to visit Dean Pinkerton without backup wasn't the hottest idea. I thought of those rusty farm tools and repressed a shudder.

"That would be rather stupid."

"Maybe we should let the police take this interview."

"Don't be ridiculous," she said. "We don't have any proof Dean was involved. And if he is, or if he knows something, he's going to tell me. Bad enough that Bill and Tabitha are dead and my Lincoln has been reduced to shrapnel. Detective Slate could have been killed!"

"But don't you think —"

"Here we are!" She swung sharply into the drive-through and stopped in front of the menu. "What would you like?"

"Double cheeseburger and a medium diet cola."

"As if a diet cola makes up for all those calories."

"You were the one who suggested burgers."

"Don't tell me you were planning on eating anything healthier."

"Burritos are healthier," I said. "They're jammed with healthy beans and veggies."

"And cheese and sour cream."

"I always ask them to hold the sour cream." And add extra guacamole. Avocados are *good* calories.

A horn brayed behind us, and we edged forward to the intercom. My mom ordered and the Lincoln glided to the front window. "Don't mind me," she said. "I'm jealous you can still eat burritos. I used to love spicy food," she said sadly. "Now I can't stomach it. And you look quite nice. Have you lost weight?"

My eyes narrowed. "You're trying to distract me. Going to see Dean alone is a bad idea."

"I considered that and have got it covered. Dieter's going to meet us there."

I yelped. "Dieter? Why Dieter?"

"He's such a nice young man. And he'll do anything for Adele."

"What does Adele have to do with this? She's not coming too, is she?" I asked, my alarm growing.

"Of course not. It's still the lunch hour. How could she possibly leave her tea room? I simply mean, every woman deserves to be adored. And so do you."

I tugged on the seat belt. "This conversation is getting weird."

"Only because you don't want to have it."

"I'm not even sure what we're talking about."

The drive-through window slid open and a woman in a striped hat stuck her head out. "That will be $7.85."

I reached for my wallet, but my mom beat me to it and paid. She took the paper bag and handed it to me. The scent of cheeseburger filled the car. "May we have some extra napkins?" she asked, apologetic, and glanced my way. "It's a rental. I intend to return it in the same condition I borrowed it."

The woman handed her a sheaf of paper napkins and my mom passed them to me. We drove out of town, and I managed to eat my burger without ruining the leather seats.

My mother turned off at Dean's rutted driveway, and the scent of cow grew stronger. We cruised past green pastures. She braked, parking beside Dieter's rickety truck in front of the white-painted farm house.

Dieter, in a ski cap and sleek jacket, leapt to open my mother's door. "Afternoon, Mrs. K. Do you want me to come inside with you? Or should I just stand by your car and look menacing?"

"I think it's best if you wait here and menace," she said.

A black-and-white cow wandered to the fence and stared at us. The animal shook her head, her cowbell ringing.

Dieter saluted. "Sure thing."

My mom headed for the house, and I followed.

"Does Dean know we're coming?" I asked.

"I called last night and made an appointment."

"And you're only telling me this now?"

"I know how busy you are. He's a busy man as well, which is why we're catching him at his lunch hour."

We climbed the porch steps and I rapped on the door.

It sprang open.

Dean filled the doorway. He peered at Dieter, who waved in a very non-menacing way. "What's he doing here?"

"He's with us," my mother said. "May we come in?"

He stepped away from the door and we walked inside the airy, polished-wood entryway. Dean stopped in the foyer, arms crossed over his plaid flannel shirt.

My mother examined the antique farming equipment bolted to the wall. "How lovely. Are these from your farm?"

He rubbed the raven tattoo on the back of his neck. "Yeah. This stuff's been in the family forever."

"Such history," she said. "It must pain you to see so many small dairy farms going under."

"Mine won't. Specialization is the key."

"You mean selling raw milk?" I asked.

He nodded. "To succeed, we need to differentiate ourselves, target niche markets like raw milk." His mouth twisted. "But the big farms don't like the competition."

"No one ever does." The room was hot, and my mother unsnapped her quilted jacket, revealing a crisp, white blouse. "People think small towns mean small stakes, but when they're personal, they're quite high."

His green eyes flashed. "Like I said before, I didn't kill Bill Eldrich, if that's what you're getting at."

"It isn't," I said quickly.

His jaw clenched, and he glanced toward the front door. "What's this about?"

"Have you heard about anyone on the town council taking bribes?" I asked.

"Bribes?" His dark brows lifted. "No. But I guess it wouldn't surprise me."

"Farmers understand the world better than most, don't they?" my mother mused. "The nature of man is fallible."

"You're a philosopher," he said.

"Why wouldn't bribes surprise you?" I asked.

"Corruption is everywhere."

"Did Tabitha play a role in blocking the

sale of your raw milk?" I asked.

"It wasn't blocked," he said. "Yeah, she was leaning toward Eldrich's view, but no laws or regulations against it were ever passed. I'm still selling my milk." He scowled. "And yes, I know that could have changed. Their deaths were convenient for my business. But I didn't kill anyone."

"Was she always on Eldrich's side of the issue?" I asked. "Or did her opinion change?"

"It changed," he said slowly. "When I first started promoting the raw milk, the town council — including Tabitha — was supportive. Some of the other dairies in the association were interested too. Then Bill started lobbying, showing them the error of their ways." He shook his head. "The council won't do anything, though. Raw milk is still legal in California."

"So the change was entirely due to Bill's lobbying efforts?" I leaned one shoulder against the wood-plank wall.

"I thought so. The Dairy Association is important, and not just to San Benedetto. They carry weight." He shook his head. "But I can't see Bill paying bribes to get things done."

"Where were you last Sunday afternoon?" I asked.

354

"If you must know, I was at the farmers' market, selling gallon jugs of raw whole milk."

My mother and I glanced at each other. She nodded. Someone at Ladies Aid would be able to confirm or deny his alibi.

"Thanks, Dean," I said. "You've been helpful."

He saw us out, slamming the door behind us.

"He wasn't that helpful," my mom muttered. She stared across a pasture at the red barn.

"If we can confirm his alibi for Sunday's hit-and-run at the museum, we can take him off the list of suspects." Unless Santa had an accomplice.

Something buzzed past my ear and twanged into a white-painted support beam on the porch. I jerked away.

My mom gasped.

I stared, disbelieving, at the arrow quivering in the beam inches from my head.

"Get down!" Dieter shouted. An arrow struck his truck with a metallic ping and he scrabbled beneath the vehicle.

My mom grabbed my arm. We stumbled across the porch to a wooden picnic table. I knocked it on its side and we crouched behind it. Something thunked into the wood, and I swear the table moved from the force of the blow.

The front door creaked open and Dean stepped out. "What's —"

I opened my mouth to warn him. An arrow thudded into the door frame. He yelped and vanished into the house.

Two more arrows thumped into the table. "I think we can safely say Dean isn't trying to kill us." My mother's voice trembled.

Another thunk, and we yelped.

"Don't worry." I gulped. "Laurel will be here any second." Any second now . . .

"Why would she?" she asked, her face ashen. "Neither of us have called the police. Don't assume Dieter has."

Scrabbling in my pocket, I pulled out my phone, dialed 911. "She's been following me, remember?" I said, shrill. "She's probably circling around right now to nab whoever's shooting at us. All we need to do is keep them occupied."

Two more arrows hit the table.

"What the hell?" Dieter shouted from under his pickup.

"911, what is your emergency?"

I explained, gave the dispatcher the address.

"Are you in a safe place?" she asked.

Another arrow struck the table and I

winced. "Relatively."

"Take shelter. The police will be there soon."

"Thanks," I squeaked and hung up.

"Well?" my mom asked.

"The police will be here soon."

"That's not very helpful."

Behind the table, I made myself as small as possible. This was insane! I forced my breath to be steady, pushing away my fear and anger. I had to be calm, to think. And the more I thought, the more bizarre our situation seemed. "Does this seem efficient to you?"

"Hiding?"

"No, the shooting. The killer shot Bill Eldrich, a moving target, at night. He killed Tabitha. But his aim today seems erratic. Whoever it is isn't going to get to us as long as we're behind this table. The shooter is either trying to scare us rather than kill us, or —"

"He's keeping us pinned down." My mother's eyes widened. "What if there's a second shooter, circling us now?"

My breath burst in and out. To the right and left were open pasture, and only a few porch chairs to block us from a potential hail of arrows. "Let's move the table," I said.

"Where?"

"We move it in front of the door, use it to cover us as we go inside."

"That's clever, Madelyn." She grabbed a table leg.

I grabbed the other. We scraped the table across the porch. Another heave, and it lay in front of the door.

Staying low, I grasped the screen door, opened it, and shifted around it. Then I went for the wooden door. On hands and knees, the two of us backed inside. I slammed the door shut.

Dean sat against the wall by the door. "I called the cops."

"So did we." I glanced at the wall clock and hoped Dieter was safe beneath his truck. Adele would kill me if something happened to her boyfriend.

In the distance, a siren wailed.

"Oh, thank God," my mom breathed.

I edged the door open and risked a peek beyond the table. Dieter lay beneath his truck, his hands over his head.

"Dieter?" I shouted.

He waved, not looking up, and I blew out my breath.

A blue muscle car, its dash lights flashing, raced down the gravel driveway.

I sat hard on the wooden floor.

That was Laurel's car.

She hadn't been following me in a gray sedan. Laurel hadn't been watching me. My hands rose to my face.

No one was watching me except the killer.

Dizzying indignation spiraled up my spine and into my skull.

"I haven't heard any arrow strikes lately," my mom said. "Have you?"

"No." Why hadn't anyone been tailing me? Had my tail been called off when they pulled off my mother's? Of course it had. Why had I assumed otherwise?

"On the bright side," my mom said to Dean, "at least now the police will know you're innocent."

"On the dark side," he said, "we're getting shot at."

"Not anymore," I said. "The shooter's stopped."

Gun drawn, Laurel scuttled out of her car. She ran, bent double, to Dieter and knelt beside his truck.

He lifted his head, and the two exchanged words.

Staying low, she raced up the porch steps and jammed the table aside, skidded into the house. "Is everyone okay?"

"Yeah," Dean said.

"Where's the shooter?" she asked.

We looked at each other, shrugged.

"Since the arrows hit the front of the table," I said, "I'm guessing he was facing the house."

Laurel's gaze bored into my mother. "This *would* happen as soon as we pulled your police protection. What haven't you told us about that night Bill Eldrich was killed?"

"Shouldn't you be out trying to catch the shooter?" My mother fingered the squash-blossom necklace beneath the collar of her blouse.

"Not without backup," Laurel said. "Now talk."

My mom straightened against the wall. "I told you everything I saw."

"If you're holding something back, that's impeding an investigation," Laurel warned.

"I would never!" My mother's eyes flashed.

"Honestly," I said. "She wouldn't." My mom was a believer in fair play.

"How is it I always seem to find you interrogating our suspects?" Laurel asked.

"Dean is not a suspect," my mom said. "He couldn't have shot these arrows. He's been inside the entire time."

I nodded, admiring her ability to evade the question.

"Is anyone going to rescue me?" Dieter shouted.

"Cool your jets, Finkielkraut!" Laurel hollered. She glared at my mother and me. "What's he doing here?"

"Dieter works for me," my mom said.

"As what? Your butler?"

"He runs various errands and was kind enough to agree to pick Madelyn up and return her to her museum. Her lunch hour is nearly over, and Friday is one of her busiest days."

More police cars roared up the drive.

"All right." Laurel rose. "You three stay here."

"The butler remark was uncalled for," my mother muttered.

"It's a tense situation."

"You're feeling charitable today."

"I am." Strangely enough, I didn't enjoy my new awareness of my high school bully's insecurities. Sure, I knew most bullies were insecure, but I guess I was more comfortable with our usual roles.

Laurel walked outside and conferred with the uniformed officers pouring from the cars.

And then she arrested my mom.

TWENTY-TWO

I met my mother, rubbing her wrists, on the steps of the brick police station. "Really!" she sputtered, her cheeks crimson. "They fingerprinted me!"

The late afternoon sunlight was watery, and twinkle lights had flashed on in the plum trees along the sidewalk. Laurel hadn't kept my mother long. I suspected she'd done it more to scare us off than because she really thought my mom was involved in the murders.

I steered her to her rented SUV parked on the street. "At least they didn't charge you with anything."

"Fingerprinted!"

"Laurel's just trying to sweat you."

"I will not be sweated. No wonder you set her hair on fire. Not that I approve." Her expression turned wistful. "She did have such lovely long blond hair. Like a fairy princess."

Blech. I stopped myself from making vomiting noises just in time.

My mother stopped on the sidewalk as I walked to the driver's side door. "Where are you going?" she asked.

"You're upset. I thought I'd drive." I jingled her keys.

She puffed out her cheeks and opened the passenger door. "I don't suppose it matters."

I waited until she'd buckled in, and we drove off.

A police car pulled onto the street behind us.

The Lincoln's brakes were softer than mine and farther from my toes than I was used to. I made a whiplash stop on Main Street and our heads jerked forward.

"Sorry," I muttered.

My mother sighed.

I cruised past the museum and tried not to look at the crowds milling inside. Leo had stepped up like a champion again while I'd loitered outside the police station waiting for my mother. I felt like I was taking advantage of his holiday goodwill.

"I baked a casserole," my mom said, apropos of nothing.

I blinked. Had I daydreamed through a

critical part of the conversation? "Casserole?"

"For Tom and Craig Wilde."

Not liking where this was going, I ran a jerky hand through my hair. The killer had found us at the Wildes' once before. It wasn't such a leap to imagine it happening again. "I can take it over."

"Not on your life. We're going together. Now."

My stomach rolled. "Now?"

"After we get the casserole from my house."

"Mom, it's Friday, one of my busiest days . . ."

She shot me a hard look. "Even if we weren't investigating, it's our duty to both pay our respects. Tom and Craig are a part of this community, and that means something."

My shoulders hunched. She was right. And I could add an extra something to Leo's Christmas bonus to make up for all the extra time he was spending at the museum.

We drove to my mom's house. She strode inside and I waited in the Lincoln.

A murder of crows roosted in the oak tree. Heads cocked, they studied me as if waiting for something exciting to happen. One of the straw reindeer leaned at a drunken angle. I was just about to step from the car to straighten it when my cell phone rang. Adele.

"Hi, Ad—"

"Maddie, is it true? Dieter told me you three were attacked. What does the killer have against Dieter?"

"Hopefully it was only a case of wrong place, wrong time."

"But that's worse! Anyone can be in the wrong place at the wrong time."

Especially if they were near me and my mom. "I'm sorry, Adele. I had no idea anything like that would happen."

"Do you have any idea how hard it is to find a decent boyfriend these days?" She hung up.

I stared at the phone. At least she hadn't sounded too angry.

My brow wrinkled. Or was she?

Foil-wrapped casserole in one hand, my mom got into the car. She slid the dish onto the dash. "Let's go."

I started the Lincoln. "So what's the play here?"

"You're more experienced with this sort of thing. What would you do?"

"You already know my investigative technique."

365

"Yes, but I don't think asking questions until someone tries to kill you is terribly practical."

My grip tightened on the wheel. "I'm trying to change up that last bit."

She gnawed her bottom lip, biting off the beige lipstick. "Oh? Because it seems to be happening all over again. It's déjà vu. Someone trying to kill you, the return of the cowbell curse . . ."

Shifting in the leather seat, I pondered that. The feeling that someone wanted you dead was not a good one. "Or," I said, "we could back off and let the police do their jobs."

"Don't be ridiculous, dear. Someone's trying to kill us. We're American citizens. It's our duty to get ourselves out of this mess."

"Ask questions it is," I said.

We drove to the Wildes' house and parked in the circular drive. "Our" police car, back on protective duty (or trailing my mom), glided to a stop on the street behind us.

Lights glowed through the front windows of the gabled farmhouse. But the Christmas lights were off, and a weight of sadness descended in my chest. For the Wildes, the holidays would never be the same.

Feet dragging, I followed my mother up

the front steps. I rang the bell.

My mother nodded, a determined look on her face.

Behind the door, footsteps approached. The front entry snicked open.

Tom's chinos were rumpled, and the buttons on his blue shirt didn't line up. The widower's expression was haggard, his face nearly as gray as his hair. "Fran?"

She took his beefy hand. "Tom, we're so sorry for your loss. We came to pay our condolences and help in any way we can. I went through this not long ago myself, and I know how much there is to do after a loss. How can we help?"

"I honestly don't know." He backed from the door.

My mother stepped inside.

I trailed behind, satisfied to let her take the lead.

In the entry, Tom stopped short and stared at the unlit Christmas tree in the living room. "The police have Tabitha's body," he said, his voice dull, heavy. "I don't know when we'll get her back. We can't make arrangements until . . ." He swallowed.

"How frustrating for you both," my mother said. "How is Craig doing?"

"The police released him. I heard it was because of you. Thank you."

Surprised, I darted a look at my mother. "Under the circumstances, Ladies Aid and the Dairy Association decided not to press charges," she said. "Though I understand the fire department may be sending you a bill."

He laughed hollowly. "Craig will be working that off until he graduates. But it beats jail."

Balancing the casserole against her hip, she squeezed his hand. "Finding out who killed Tabitha and Bill is more important than this silly Christmas Cow incident."

He blinked. "Can I take that from you?"

She handed him the foil-covered baking dish. "It's for you. Truffled mac and cheese."

He ambled into a wide kitchen. Silently, we followed, watching him set the casserole dish on the central island. Dishes piled in the sink. Crumbs and wrappers littered the black granite counters.

"About Tabitha —" I began.

"Craig wasn't involved," he said quickly.

My brows drew together. "We didn't think he was. He came forward about the cow. I'm sure he wants to do everything he can to help the police catch her killer."

Tom grimaced. "Sorry. I've gotten too used to apologizing for Craig lately. He may not be perfect, but he loved his mother."

"Do you have any idea what Tabitha was doing at the Wine and Visitors Bureau?" I asked. I remembered how her coat had been damp with dew, her body cold.

"She got a call about an emergency meeting there regarding the Christmas Cow."

My mom cocked her head. "A meeting? When?"

"The night before she was found."

My mother shook her head. "We didn't have any meetings that night, emergency or otherwise. I'd have known."

"Someone called her," Tom said. "I heard the phone ring, and she told me why she had to go."

"And she didn't return afterward," I said. At least we were getting closer to time of death. "Did you call the police when she didn't return?"

His face darkened. "No."

"I'll bet the police considered that odd," my mother said, as if the police have the most outrageous ideas.

He hesitated. "Tabitha and I were having some problems." He stared at his hands. "Sometimes she liked to stay out."

"Stay out," I repeated, hoping he'd elaborate.

My mother's gaze turned thoughtful. "With Bill Eldrich?"

He rubbed his brow and stared at the carpet. "That's what I'd thought, but then he was dead, and she was away again that night, and . . ." He laughed, his voice harsh. "Can you believe I was relieved to think I'd been wrong about them? But I wasn't, was I?"

So he'd known about his wife and Bill. That gave him motive. For Craig's sake, I hoped Tom wasn't guilty. Losing one parent was bad enough.

"I suppose I should tell the police," he said. "But I know how it will make me look. If they focus on me, then they won't go after the real killer."

"They'll likely find out anyway," I said.

"It will look better if you come forward," my mother said.

He nodded, looking unconvinced.

The doorbell rang.

"Probably another casserole," he said. "I've got a freezer full of them. Just a minute."

It was a request for us to stay, but we trailed him to the front door.

Penny, grape-cluster earrings jiggling, stood in the doorway, a foil-wrapped baking dish in hands. "I'm so sorry for your loss," she said, extending the dish. "Please let me know if there's anything I can do."

370

Arms limp at his sides, Tom stared at her. "It's lasagna." She raised the dish higher.

"A guilt offering?" He laughed, his voice high and strained.

"No." Penny noticed us behind him and her cheeks pinked. "Tabitha and I had our differences, but I liked her. I never . . . Tom, this is awful. I feel terrible that I was short with Tabitha last time we met."

"Short? You practically called her a liar."

"I'd felt sandbagged, that was all." Penny moved aside a set of keys and set the lasagna on an end table. "The reallocation of the funding. I'd told myself nothing is set until it's official, but I wasn't expecting all the money to go to the Dairy Association."

"To Bill, you mean," Tom said bitterly.

"To the Dairy Association." She rubbed her neck. "I'm sorry I've upset you coming here. It wasn't my intention. Tabitha was a lovely woman. I can't imagine how terrible this is for you, but please believe I'm sincere when I say I want to help in any way I can." She nodded to us and left.

He closed the door and turned to us. "Now you know why the money all went to Bill. Undue influence."

"Are you sure?" my mother asked. "Can there be another explanation?"

"Tabitha thought she loved him." Tom

sighed. "Can you believe I thought she might have killed him? She knows how to shoot with a compound bow. We all do." He blinked slowly. "Now they're both gone."

"Did Craig say anything else?" my mother asked.

"Craig has nothing to do with this!"

"Of course not," my mother said. "But he may have some information that's important, even if he isn't aware of it."

"He doesn't know anything," Tom said.

"Could anyone else have had undue influence over Tabitha?" I had to ask, even if the question made my stomach writhe.

Tom paled.

"Not romantically," I said. "Financially."

"Financially?" His nostrils flared, his mouth flattening. "What are you saying?"

What was I saying? Tom's son had thought Bill was paying off his mother. Dean Pinkerton said he could easily believe bribes were involved, but he was a cynic where government was concerned. "I'm trying to understand who else might have had a reason to kill Bill Eldrich and your wife. Their only connections were town council business and the Christmas Cow committee, and . . ." I trailed off.

"Their affair." His broad shoulders slumped. "And if it wasn't a work thing, then the only person who'd have reason to kill them both would be me or . . ." His face turned ashen.

"Or who?" I asked.

"I can't live with this anymore," he said, his voice rough.

"Tom." My mother reached for him.

"I did it. I killed them both."

TWENTY-THREE

"And he just turned himself in?" Adele shouted over the roar of the jukebox. The light from the overhead pendant lamp glinted off the gold threads in her pink Jackie Kennedy–style blazer.

Throat sore from hollering, I nodded and took another sip of beer, accidentally nudging Harper with my elbow. It was our regular Friday girls' night out at the Bell and Brew. But nothing felt regular about tonight. I'd watched the police lead Tom away in handcuffs while my mother hugged Craig, who was too stunned to protest. I shook my head.

"So it's over." Beside me, Harper shrugged out of her leather jacket and three men at the bar paused, beer to their lips, to stare. All she was wearing was a simple white T-shirt, but for Harper, that was enough.

"I guess so." I tapped my finger on the damp table. "At least Laurel was happy."

The detective had actually smiled at me when she'd arrested Tom Wilde. It had been mildly terrifying.

"What's wrong?" Adele asked.

"Nothing." I took a quick sip of my holiday ale. It tasted faintly of pumpkin. "Tom Wilde was the only person I could figure who had a motive to kill both Bill and Tabitha, aside from Dean. And Dean couldn't have done it, because he was cowering in the house with us when we were getting shot at." But I hated this. I hated what Craig was going through. I hated that a family had been destroyed.

And for what? A stupid affair. Still, I wondered if Tom was telling the truth or if he was protecting his son. Craig had overheard his mother and Bill. The whole family knew how to shoot arrows, and Craig had been on the scene when Bill died.

"Now you and Detective Slate can focus on the cowbell curse." Adele adjusted her beer mug, centering it on its cardboard mat.

I groaned. "I never should have displayed those stupid bells. They just seemed perfect for the holidays."

"They are perfect," Harper said. "By which I mean they're not cursed."

"That's what you . . ." I sat up straighter in the red Naugahyde booth. "Wait. You mean . . . you checked them?"

"I asked her to after that disaster of a ritual," Adele said. "Her being a witch and all."

"I'm a strega," Harper said, "not a witch."

"Potato, po-tah-to," Adele said. "Your secret is safe with us. But this curse is out of control. The town needs your help."

"I'm not sure I can help," Harper said. "There's no curse. If Herb and his buddy's binding ceremony didn't convince people, what can I do?"

"This fake curse is bigger than all of us." I clutched my frosted mug more tightly. "Ladies Aid managed to track down the woman who's been driving the rumors. I talked to her, but I'm not sure I persuaded her we're curse-free. Besides, she said it's her husband who needs converting. It sounds like he's made himself clumsy worrying about a non-existent curse."

"So what are you going to do?" Harper asked.

I gulped my beer. "I'll talk to him, but I don't think this is something I can reason anyone out of. No one's reacting from reason. It's all fear and superstition, which normally is excellent for business, but now . . ."

"Business is down?" Adele asked, frowning.

"No," I said. "Business is booming. This is just the first time I've felt guilty about it."

The jukebox switched to a country lament, Patsy Cline falling to pieces.

"Don't," Adele said. "It's not your fault if people are going overboard. Everyone knows you can't take anything in that museum of yours seriously."

"Hey," I said, sucking in my cheeks, "I've got some nice antiques from the American Spiritualist movement."

"And let's not forget the creepy dolls," Harper said dryly.

"I wish I could." I hated those dolls, but they were a big draw.

Grinning, Adele braced her head on her fist. "Tell us about Detective Slate."

My face warmed. "There's nothing to tell."

"You like him," Adele said. "I could tell from the beginning."

"What's not to like? He's smart and honest and easy on the eyes."

"And single," Harper said.

"Definitely a selling point," I said. "But nothing's going on between us."

"Why not?" Harper asked.

"Mason, obviously," Adele said. "Don't

tell me you're still hung up on him?"

"We only broke up two months ago." I examined the red plastic basket of fried artichoke hearts. "I don't want to rush into anything."

"Ah ha!" Adele pointed at me. "So there is something to rush into."

"I never gave you this hard a time about Dieter," I grumbled.

"Your loss." Adele turned to Harper. "What do you think? Should we give her a break?"

"Watching her squirm is too much fun," Harper said. "When are you going to see him next?"

"I don't know." I dipped a beer-battered artichoke heart in ranch dressing and bit off half. The artichoke threads caught in my teeth. "And I don't think Tom killed Bill and Tabitha," I said, hoping to divert them.

"He confessed, didn't he?" Adele asked.

"Yes, but —"

"There you go," Adele said. "Honestly, I think you like it when people try to kill you."

I shuddered. "I don't."

"Why do you think Tom's innocent?" Harper asked.

"It just doesn't feel right." I washed down the artichoke with a swig of beer. "Yes, everything fits. They were having an affair, her husband knew it, and he killed them both. And I don't know who else would want to kill them both. But Craig overheard Bill bribing his mother, and that's odd enough to look into."

"That's what he *thought* he heard," Harper said. "Could he have misunderstood the conversation?"

"Maybe, but what if he didn't? What if the relationship between Bill and Tabitha isn't what we all think? What if there's another reason someone wanted the two of them dead?" I ran my thumb along the handle of the beer mug, feeling the ridge where the glass had been pressed together.

"Someone like Dean, whose raw milk business was being threatened?" Harper asked. "I thought you'd written him off as a suspect."

"I did, since he was trapped in the house with us when the archer struck. But if Tabitha was on the take, then she was probably getting money from more than one person. I mean, you don't stop at one bribe, do you?"

"That's a big *if*," Harper said.

"I checked the minutes of the last council meetings, but they don't record any details of the discussions." I snapped my fingers. "Dean and Penny must have been at some of those meetings. Their businesses were under discussion. Maybe they remember what happened."

"Well, you can't take Dieter to talk to them," Adele said. "He nearly got an arrow through the heart the last time he played bodyguard."

I rose from the table. "Don't worry. I got this."

"You're going now?" Adele asked.

"No time like the present."

"It's nearly ten at night," Harper said.

"They'll be up." I had to know. Craig's father was sitting in jail. We couldn't wait for the truth.

"No," Harper said. "This is exactly how you get yourself into trouble."

"But Tom Wilde —"

"Is safe at police headquarters and a confessed murderer," Adele said. "Harper's right. You can't go tearing off now to harass Dean and Penny. Dean will probably shoot you for trespassing, and you'll frighten Penny to death banging on her door at this hour."

"A late-night surprise interrogation is not the sort of thing to loosen people's tongues," Harper said. "What you need is a gathering of the suspects to hash things out. Like Hercule Poirot does."

"Hercule Poirot only calls the suspects together when he knows who the killer is," I said. "And I don't. But I'll wait for daylight."

Dieter, in a parka, ripped T-shirt, and jeans, slid into the booth beside Adele. "Hello, ladies."

We stared at him.

"Darling, it's girls' night," Adele said.

"And that's sacred," Harper said.

"Come on," he said. "I'm one of the girls, aren't I?"

"No," we said in unison.

He rubbed his shoulder. "But I was shot at," he said plaintively.

"Your truck was shot at," I said.

"I was nearby, protecting you and your mother when you were shot at. You at least owe me a beer."

"Fine." I waved at an aproned waiter. He hustled past to a raucous bachelorette party.

"Cool." Dieter released a gusty breath and slumped in the booth. "I'll take the holiday ale."

"Long day?" Adele asked him.

"I made the payout on the cow today."

Harper raised a brow. "It's been over a week since it burned. What took you so long?"

I tried to flag down another waiter. Unseeing, he strode past.

Dieter rumpled his shaggy hair. "Arson is serious business. I had to make sure the bettor wasn't involved."

I leaned forward. Dieter had been running a separate investigation? "And did you?"

He shrugged. "Sure. It was those kids who set the cow on fire."

My eyes narrowed. I looked between him and Adele. "How did you hear the students confessed? That hasn't made the papers."

He looped his arm across Adele's shoulders. "Sources."

"Adele?" How could she! "You *know* my investigation is confidential. What else did you tell him?"

"Everything?" She made a rueful face. "It's Dieter!"

"We're a couple," Dieter said, insufferably smug.

"Adele!"

"Sorry, Mad," she said. "But you put me in a bad spot. I can't keep things from him."

I blew out my breath. I couldn't expect Adele to keep secrets from her boyfriend. Not if she was serious about him.

"It's okay," I said. "No harm done, and it was a fair trade."

Dieter frowned. "What fair trade?"

Adele frantically shook her head, her black

hair rippling about her shoulders.

"Ah . . ." I stammered. "I misspoke."

Spots of color rose in his cheeks. He turned toward Adele. "Did you tell them the size of the payout?"

"She's one of my best friends," Adele said weakly.

"She's dating a cop!"

"I'm not actually dating . . ." I trailed off.

Dieter's eyes bulged. "That information is confidential!"

"What was I supposed to do?" Adele asked. "You wanted information on Mad's investigation. She wanted information on how much money was at stake. I couldn't tell one of you and not the other."

"But," he sputtered, "it's confidential."

Whoops. Time to exit, stage left. "The waiters are sure busy tonight." I slithered from the booth. "I'm going to get your beer from the bar."

"I'll come with you," Harper said quickly and followed.

I squeezed past a trio of cowboys and caught the bartender's eye. "One holiday ale," I shouted over the din.

He nodded and strode to the taps.

I turned to Harper, now neck-deep in grinning, lovesick cowboys. Honestly, did she use a magic potion?

My friend seemed to be enjoying herself, so I braced my elbows on the bar and watched the TV. A commercial for pillows came to an end, replaced by a local news show. The closed captioning scrolled across the screen.

WITH US TODAY IS XAVIER LANDAU, AN EXPERT ON CURSES.

Xavier? Herb's Xavier?

The lady newscaster, blond hair shimmering, turned to Xavier. It must be true about the TV adding ten pounds, because the bell exorcist looked less cadaverous than usual.

I leaned closer.

TELL US ABOUT THE CURSE. DO WE HAVE ANYTHING TO BE WORRIED ABOUT?

Xavier stroked his salt and pepper goatee. *NOT AT ALL. I CAN SAFELY SAY THE CURSE — IF THERE EVER WAS ONE — HAS BEEN BOUND.*

The newscaster's eyes narrowed. *IF THERE EVER WAS ONE? DO YOU MEAN THE MUSEUM IS PERPETUATING A FRAUD?*

I groaned.

Xavier shook his head. *NOT AT ALL. AND I AM QUITE CERTAIN THERE ARE SEVERAL OBJECTS IN THAT MUSEUM THAT BEAR FURTHER INVESTIGATION.*

SEVERAL? NOT ALL? the reporter asked. "They have historical value!" I howled at the screen.

Harper placed a hand on my arm. She pointed at the TV. "Is that the guy from the binding ceremony?"

"They're talking about the museum!" I looked up and realized I'd missed something critical, because now two middle-aged women in pastel twin sets had joined Xavier and the newscaster.

One woman raised her sleeve, displaying two small red punctures on her forearm. *SOMETHING BIT ME THAT DAY IN THE MUSEUM.*

The other woman nodded and raised her sleeve. The back of her wrist was similarly marked.

The newscaster turned to Xavier. *WAS THE CURSE RESPONSIBLE?*

He shook his head. *BITES ARE USUALLY CAUSED BY ANGRY GHOSTS OR DEMONIC ACTIVITY.*

The newscaster leaned forward. *THERE'S DEMONIC ACTIVITY AT THE PARANORMAL MUSEUM?*

"No, there isn't!" I shouted. "There's nothing demonic . . . Harper." I motioned toward the screen. "Tell them!"

"They can't hear you," she said.

I hung my head. "I can't believe this."

"Do you really need me to tell you there's nothing demonic at your museum?" She shivered. "Though those old dolls are creepy."

"But not demonic!"

"Look." She pointed at the TV. "He's saying it was probably a ghost."

I turned.

THANK YOU, the reporter said. THINGS ARE GETTING STRANGE AT SAN BENEDETTO'S PARANORMAL MUSEUM.

The show cut to the weather.

"GD probably freaked out in the crowd and bit them," Harper said.

"No way."

"He's kind of a jerk."

"Yeah, but . . ." I frowned. GD couldn't have done it. He'd been on top of Gryla's cave the entire time. I moaned. Was I liable for the bites? Would the women sue? "This is a disaster."

Harper tossed her long hair. "What's your favorite saying?"

"No publicity is bad publicity." But there was a first time for everything. "Whatever I do to try to calm things down, I just make things worse."

"Maybe you should stop trying."

If only I knew how.

TWENTY-FOUR

I drove home sober and alone. Sunk in thought about lawyers and lawsuits, I didn't notice the motorcycle parked outside my aunt's garage. I climbed the dark steps to my apartment.

A broad shadow detached itself from the landing. "Maddie."

I yelped and grabbed the wooden railing to keep myself from tumbling over. "Mason! What are you doing here?"

He wore his usual — black jeans, black leather jacket, black T-shirt. No wonder I hadn't spotted him — he'd faded into the night. His blond hair was in a shaggy ponytail. "Belle's gone," he said.

I walked up the remaining steps to the door and the overhead light flipped on. Mason's broad face was carved in misery.

"Gone?" I pulled my jacket tighter, a sour taste rising in my throat. "What do you mean?"

"She left with Jordan."

My pulse slowed. "Gone. You mean for good? Are you sure?" When Mason reconnected with Belle and Jordan, he'd opened his home and his heart. Belle couldn't just leave.

"She left a note. Do you have any idea where they went?"

"No. My God, I'm sorry." Confused, I shook my head, my body temperature rising. "Wait, why would you think I —"

"Because you've known something was up all along." He bit off the words. "I could tell something was up between the two of you. I thought it was because you're my ex and she's living with me, but after she left, I realized it had to be more than that."

I covered my mouth. "The Christmas Cow winnings."

"What winnings?"

A light went on in my aunt's house. My gaze darted to her front door, then to him. "Let's go inside." I unlocked my door and ushered him into my nautical-themed studio (my aunt's decorating). "Belle won this year's Christmas Cow bet," I said. "Fifty thousand dollars."

His blue eyes turned arctic. "And you didn't tell me?"

"I thought she'd tell you. I didn't

know . . ." that she would take the money and run. I looked at the closed front door. Was this my fault too? Why hadn't I just said something?

"She's got my son. My son!" He swiveled and punched his fist through the sheetrock wall.

I jumped, tensing.

Mason's hand was covered in grainy white bits of sheetrock. It drifted from the hole in the wall to the wood-beamed floor. He bent his head and breathed heavily. "Sorry. I shouldn't have . . . I'll pay for that. I'll go."

"Don't," I said. "I get it. You're worried about Jordan. But we know he's safe. Belle's taken good care of him in the past —"

"They were sleeping in a van."

"But she has money now, and I'm sure she's doing what she thinks is best. Have you called the police?"

"They can't help." He paced the narrow space between the wall and the blue-gray couch. "I only found out about my son's existence two months ago. I don't have any parental rights."

"How do you know that?" I asked gently.

"Because I know people who've been through this."

I could have told him hearsay wasn't legal advice and every case was different. Instead,

I asked, "Did Belle say anything that might have given you a clue where she was going?"

He reached into the rear pocket of his jeans and handed me a folded piece of paper. Rough-edged, it looked like it had been torn from one of Jordan's spiral-bound notebooks.

I read.

It's time for us to go. You've been wonderful, but I need some space to be on my own. I would have told you in person, but I was afraid I wouldn't be able to leave. Thank you for everything.

My throat squeezed. "That doesn't sound too bad."

He clawed his mane of blond hair. "She's got my son. They could be anywhere. I wish you'd told me about the money."

"I know. I'm sorry. I thought it was between you and Belle, and none of my business." I compressed my lips and looked at my tennis shoes.

He collapsed onto the sofa. "Three months ago, I didn't know I had a son. Now I can't imagine life without him."

I sat on the lounge chair across from him, my elbows on my knees. "I'm sure she'll get in touch with you once she's settled." I wanted to believe it, but parents left with their kids all the time. Mason didn't have formal custody, so this probably wouldn't be considered a kidnapping. But whatever it was, I'd played a peripheral role.

"She kept Jordan from me for years," he said bitterly. "Why would you assume she'd get in touch now?"

"Because you two have a relationship again. We could ask a friend of mine at the police department for advice. He must have a better handle on the laws than either of us."

Mason stared at me, his expression hollow. "Make the call."

Some of the tension leaked from the back of my neck and shoulders. I pulled my cell phone from the pocket of my jeans and called Jason.

"Maddie," he said, his voice warm. "Your museum's made the news again."

"And not in a good way. Jason, I'm at home. Mason's here. His girlfriend left with their son. He doesn't know where they are, and he's really worried."

"Is he sure she didn't just leave to see a movie?"

"She left a note," I said. "I wondered if

391

you might be able to help, give him some advice."

There was a long pause. "Your ex is at your house?"

"Yes."

"Why?" he asked.

Mason's girlfriend had left, and he'd run to me, his ex. I knew how this sounded, and I grimaced. "He thought I might know where she went."

"Do you?"

"I wish I did." There had to be a way to make this right.

Another beat, two. Then, "Why don't you hand him the phone?"

Relieved, I passed off the phone and went to the 1950s-era kitchen, where I made as much noise as possible brewing chamomile tea. Not that there was much to eavesdrop on. Mason's side of the conversation consisted largely of grunts.

Within a few minutes, he walked into the kitchen and laid the phone on the cracked tile counter. "He's coming over."

"Great!" I chirped. I opened a pale blue cupboard and extracted three mugs. "So he thinks he can help?"

"Mmm."

The teakettle whistled.

"Tea?" I asked.

Mason's smile looked forced. "No thanks." Slowly, he walked from the kitchen.

Wishing for something stronger, I poured myself a mug of tea and dropped in an extra teaspoon of sugar.

I felt awful. But in the middle of all the awfulness, I felt an odd sense of relief. I knew now that Mason and I were done. My only feelings for him were horrified pity, guilt, and a side dish of irritation. My aunt was going to kill me when she saw the hole he'd punched in her wall.

Footsteps rattled up the steps. Clutching my tea, I hurried to the door and flung it open.

Jason, his blue parka over his shoulders, stood on the steps, and the remainder of the tightness left my muscles.

He nodded, brusque. "Maddie."

I stepped away from the door and he walked inside. Rubbing his reddened knuckles, Mason rose from the couch.

Jason scanned the room, taking in Mason, me, the fresh roundish hole in my wall. He angled his head toward the front door. "Why don't we step outside and talk?"

"Fine." Mason strode onto the landing. Jason followed, shutting the front door behind them with his good arm.

Chastened, I returned to my kitchen and

wiped the counters, swept the floor, washed dishes. Had Belle left because she could, now that she had fifty thousand dollars in her pocket? Or was there a more sinister reason behind her sudden departure?

I thought of Belle's penchant for stealing cars, and my stomach twisted. But she had no reason to kill Tabitha. She wasn't the killer.

Outside, a motorcycle engine roared. I listened as Mason's Harley drove down the drive and turned onto the main road.

Jason strode into the living room. "Maddie? You okay in here?"

Wiping my hands on a dish towel, I emerged from the kitchen. "Fine. Thanks for coming over so quickly."

"What was he really doing here?" Jaw set, Jason eyed the hole in my aunt's wall.

"He wasn't thinking. He got it into his head I might know where she was going."

"Are you and Belle friends?"

I leaned one thigh against the arm of the couch. "No, but she lives over his shop, which is next door to my museum. We bump into each other."

"That doesn't explain why he came to your home at this hour."

"I learned Belle won this year's Christmas Cow bet — fifty thousand dollars. And then

I learned she hadn't said anything to Mason about it. And I guess I was a little awkward around them both. Mason picked up on it and jumped to the wrong conclusions."

Jason made a noise low in his throat. "Did he do that?" He pointed at the wall.

"Yeah." I traced my finger along the hole and chalklike dust drifted to the floor. I didn't see how it could be patched. I'd probably need a new piece of sheetrock. My aunt had given me the friends and family discount on the garage apartment, largely because she knew I'd take care of it. "He said he'd pay to get it fixed."

"Did he hurt you?"

"No." My hands curled in the damp towel. "He was upset about his son and punched the wall. That's it."

"Maddie, since you're his ex-girlfriend, your relationship is still covered under domestic abuse laws."

My face heated. Could this get any more awkward? "I don't care what the law says. Mason and I don't have a relationship. And the only thing he hurt was the wall and himself."

"Mason must think you do have a relationship for him to have come straight here when he discovered they were gone."

I gazed at him steadily. "Then he's wrong.

And the only reason he came here is because he's desperate and afraid."

"All right." Jason's posture loosened. "Judging from the note she left, I suspect she'll be in touch with him. But he won't bother you again any time soon."

I opened my mouth to say it wasn't a bother. But what had Jason said to him out on the landing? My face warmed again. "Thanks. I think she'll be in touch too." And I was willing to bet that Belle hadn't gone far. It hadn't been easy getting Jordan into a local school after the term began. She'd probably want to keep him in his classes. Though it was winter break, and the kids were out, and . . . I clutched the dish towel more tightly, bringing it to my chest.

"What's wrong?" he asked.

"Nothing. Thanks again for coming over. This definitely falls into the above-and-beyond category."

His smile was brief. "A cop's never really off duty. And I was in the neighborhood."

"Oh?" There wasn't much neighborhood around here. Just vineyards.

"It's late. I'd better go."

I walked him to the top of the steps. I wanted to say something, assure him that Mason and I really were over. But I didn't know how to without sounding desperate.

"Jason —"

"It's been a long day. Get some sleep." He trotted down the steps and to his sedan.

From the top of the stairs, I watched his taillights fade into the night.

TWENTY-FIVE

Yawning, I drove past burger joints and brick buildings. The road dipped beneath the freeway and into San Benedetto's industrial/agricultural area — corrugated iron buildings surrounded by vineyards. The early morning fog was oddly bright, reflecting rather than diffusing the sunlight. I squinted and flipped down the truck's visor.

My nerve endings twitched. I'd slept badly the night before, unable to stop thinking about Mason and Jason. Was I into guys whose names rhymed? Maybe I shouldn't have called Jason for help with Belle's disappearance. Now he thought Mason and I still had a connection.

Rubbing my burning eyes, I bumped over a railroad track. I turned right into a parking lot, my truck drifting to a halt beside a silo and a pickup nearly as old as mine. I might not be successful in my attempt to cure Jennifer Fall's husband of his curse obsession, but I was also curious about why he'd quit the Christmas Cow committee.

After wandering the parking lot for five minutes, I spotted a sign for the Falls Yogurt factory office. I didn't have an appointment, but Byron Falls was a small business owner, which probably made him a workaholic. I guessed he'd be here.

Opening the metal door, I walked inside.

A bulky man with gray hair stood behind a counter and thumbed through a stack of envelopes. An X of medical tape marked his temple. His jeans sagged around his hips, and his plaid shirt was worn. He glanced up. "Can I help you?"

"I'm Maddie Kosloski from the Paranormal Museum. I'm looking for Mr. Falls."

"Mr. Falls was my father. I'm Byron." He reached across the counter and gripped my hand. "If you're looking for a donation, though, I'm afraid I can't help you."

"Oh." I blinked, startled. He was the second person lately who'd assumed I'd wanted a donation. "No. It's about the cowbells."

His gray brows rose. "Cowbells?"

"The, er, cursed cowbells."

He stared at me.

I shifted my weight. "At the museum?"

"I'm sorry, what are you talking about?"

Was he too embarrassed to admit he believed in curses? I blundered on. "Back in the '80s, after the original Christmas Cow committee came into being, they received a set of cowbells hung in the shape of a Christmas tree from our sister city in Sweden." Say *that* five times fast. "When everyone on the committee died within a year, an urban legend started that the bells were cursed."

He snorted. "People aren't that smart, are they?"

I tugged on the drawstrings of my museum hoodie. "Anyway. The bells eventually went into storage. Two months ago, I bought them for my museum."

He thumbed through the mail, pulled out a white envelope. "And?" he asked, studying it.

I shoved my hands in the pockets of my jeans. "And now, because of the recent deaths of two other members of the Christmas Cow committee, some people are saying the curse has returned."

He shook his head. "Like I said, not that smart. Someone got angry at Bill Eldrich and Tabitha Wilde and killed them. That's no curse. That's a maniac with a bow and arrow."

"Yeah. That's . . . what I think." Hmm. I

shifted tactics. "I heard you dropped off the Christmas Cow committee?"

Byron grunted, still pawing through the mail. "Too busy."

"Is that the only reason?"

"It was too political."

"Political?" I asked.

"No one was there to get things done — no one except that Fran woman, who by the way is terrifying."

I smiled tightly. I couldn't interrupt a potential witness to defend my mother's honor. And he wasn't entirely wrong. "Did anything odd happen at the meetings you attended?"

"Odd? No. Just a lot of blah, blah, blah, people talking to make themselves feel important. I'm too busy for that."

"What were they talking about?"

"Who can remember?"

"You said it was too political," I reminded him. "Do you remember any of the political discussions?"

"That Penny woman was threatening to run for town council." Byron chuckled. "It really pissed Bill off."

"Why?"

"Who knows?" He held an envelope to the light from the window, then dropped it on the counter. "Bill had a short fuse — that's

401

probably what got him killed."

"Do you know who might have been upset with Bill and Tabitha?"

"Nope."

So much for that line of inquiry. "Anyway, as you seem to already have figured out, there's no curse."

"And you're going door-to-door telling people this?"

"Nooo." I swallowed, feeling foolish. "I heard you'd been having some accidents and might have thought they were curse-related."

He tore open a thick manila envelope. "Look, if you're trying to drum up interest in your museum, I've got no problem with it. I know what it's like being an entrepreneur. But you're barking up the wrong tree. I don't believe in ghosts or curses."

"Right." I shifted my weight. "Mind if I ask how you got that?" I pointed to the X of tape on his skull.

He picked at the bandage. "Fell off a ladder. It was getting wobbly. Should have replaced it sooner, but it broke on me when I was fixing a shelf on the stairs for my wife. Hit my head, and I've got no one to blame but myself."

"So, not curse-related."

He laughed. "The only curse is my wife's

obsession with filling our house with junk." He sighed and dropped his hand. "It's antique hats now. But if they make her happy, what am I going to do?"

"Did you hear we had a panic at the museum on Sunday?"

One corner of his mouth turned downward. "Saw it in the papers. Not too smart."

I wasn't sure if he meant the papers or the patrons or me, but it didn't sound like Jennifer had mentioned to him that she was there. "We were lucky no one was hurt in the stampede," I said. I lowered my head, studying him. Surely his wife would have said *something* about the madness? She'd been in the thick of the crowd.

"No one?" His brow wrinkled. "I heard a cop got hit by a car outside afterward. I guess you think that's down to your curse too?"

"No, a person committed that crime. So no one you knew was at the museum that day?"

He returned to the mail. "No one I know's got time for such foolishness."

I edged toward the metal door. "Okay. Well, thanks for your time."

He didn't look up as I backed from the office. I let the door clang shut.

Weird. Byron Falls sure didn't act like

someone worried about curses. If he was lying, he was pretty good at it. Was the curse entirely in Jennifer's head? I glanced over my shoulder at the closed metal door. She'd cared enough about the curse to come to the binding ritual at the museum, but she hadn't told her husband she'd gone. Filing my questions away for future research, I drove off in my truck.

I reached the museum ten minutes before opening and parked in the alley. The blinds to Mason's apartment upstairs were drawn. I stared up at the windows. Had Belle called?

Shaking myself, I unlocked the alley door to the tea room and went inside.

Adele looked up from behind the cream-colored counter and smoothed her chignon. Rows of burnished-nickel tea canisters lined the shelves behind her. Someone clattered in the kitchen, though the Fox and Fennel didn't open until eleven.

"Good morning," she said. "Want a cup of tea? On me?"

"No thanks." I yawned, my eyelids heavy. "How's it going with Dieter?"

My friend tugged down the front of her apron. "He's not upset anymore."

"I'm sorry I got you into hot water."

"You didn't. I should have told him I told

you, and he was being sensitive." She smiled fondly. "He really does take his clients' privacy seriously."

I braced my elbows on the counter and fantasized about stretching out on it. "He's trustworthy." In a weird, Dieter way.

She squeezed my shoulder. "You look tired. You're not still worried about that TV interview, are you? No one watches that show."

"No publicity is bad publicity, right?" Hoping it was true, I slouched to the book case and pressed the *Museum* spine. The secret door pivoted open.

"Maybe last night's interview will calm people down about the curse," she said.

"I thought nobody watched that show." I reached for the bookcase to pull it shut behind me.

"Maddie, I heard about Mason."

I turned, brow furrowed. "How did you hear about that?"

"Your aunt stopped by my parents' house on her morning walk. I was there for breakfast."

I rubbed my head. One of the drawbacks of living in my aunt's garage apartment was that she knew every move I made, even if she pretended not to. I was surprised she hadn't stopped by later to ask about the shouting, but she'd always been militant about giving me privacy. It was one of her better qualities. Being a huge gossip was one of her worst.

"Is it true Belle left with his son?" Adele walked from behind the counter and leaned one hip against it.

"It was true last night. I don't know what the situation is this morning."

She bit her bottom lip. "This isn't your fault. How were you to know she was going to take the money and run?"

"I should have known," I said, annoyed at myself. "There weren't a lot of good reasons to keep the winnings secret from Mason."

"But even if that were true, what could you have done? You and Mason broke up. You couldn't get involved in his relationship with Belle."

"That's what I keep telling myself. But when we broke up, I'd hoped we'd stay friends. And I don't think I acted like one."

She jammed her fists onto her slim hips. "Everyone says they'll stay friends but no one means it. Not right away, at least. And you two only broke up a couple months ago. Friends doesn't happen for at least a year."

"Right." Forcing a smile, I walked into the museum and closed the bookcase behind me.

GD slunk from the Icelandic ogress's cave and howled.

"Hold your horses." I poured kibble into his bowl and refreshed his water from my thermos.

He turned his back on me and ate, crunching sounds echoing off the linoleum floor.

I flipped the *Closed* sign to *Open* and booted up the computer. But instead of burying myself in the Internet, I drew from beneath the counter the manila envelope Jason had given me after our lunch at the Book Cellar. He'd told me the case files were cleared for the public, but it still felt like I was doing something naughty. I flipped through the pages and examined the records for the death of Jennifer's first husband, Sigfried.

There were actual photos in this one — well, photocopies of photos. I was glad they were in black and white, because looking at a naked dead man in a bathtub felt like a severe invasion of privacy. Fortunately the shower curtain had been pulled from its rings, covering any embarrassing bits.

The boom box was submerged in the water by Sigfried's feet, the cord extending from the outlet by the sink. Trying not to look at the body, I studied the boom box and the cord.

Had the portable stereo been balanced on the sink or on the tub? If it had fallen from the sink, it could have bounced off the edge of the tub and slipped inside. But placing the boom box in either place seemed really dumb.

The sink was old-fashioned and free-standing. It didn't sit inside a counter, and its edges were rounded. And it was a claw-foot tub without much of a ledge at all. The "foot" end was jammed against the wall, beneath the shower head, so something could have been balanced there. Still, if you were determined to listen to music in the bath, why not put the boom box on the toilet? Because it was on the opposite side of the sink and too far to reach if you wanted to change the station? I rubbed my face, too tired to make sense of it all.

The door opened, jingling the bell, and I straightened off the counter. "Welcome —"

Cora Gale floated inside, her thick burnt-orange shawl fluttering in the breeze from the slowly closing door. "Leo has a cold. He won't be coming in today."

She really had stepped into a mother-figure role with my employee. "I'm sorry to hear that," I said.

She waved off my concern. "It's only a cold. He'll be fine in a day or two. He wanted to come to work, but I told him you wouldn't want him passing his germs off to you and your customers." Reaching across the counter, she clasped my hand. "But how are you? I heard about the contretemps with your ex last night."

My toes curled. "My aunt told you?"

"No, Mrs. Rosewood."

Tingling swept my chest and neck. Mrs. Rosewood? Who the heck was Mrs. Rosewood? "Does the whole town know?"

"Not the *whole* town. What happened? Are you all right? I can't understand why Mason blamed you for his girlfriend leaving."

"He's worried about his son. And I don't think he blamed me. He came to me because we're friends."

"Hmm." She ran her hands across her beaded necklaces. "I heard you called the police."

"No, not the police. I mean, a friend who's in the police. I thought he might have some advice."

"And did he?"

"I don't know. They talked outside. I didn't want to get involved in something that personal."

"I can't say I blame you, dear." She rolled her shoulders. "Now, I didn't come here to gossip. Your mother is indisposed —"

"She's not sick, is she?"

"Sorry, poor wording. One of our more elderly members, Mrs. Tyre, fell and broke her hip. Your mother's at the hospital with her."

"Oh no."

"It happens when you get older. Not that you'll have to worry about that for a good long time. At any rate, your mother asked if I could provide you with any further assistance in your little problem."

"My problem?" Which one? There were so many.

"The curse?"

"Oh. Right." I glanced at the open folder on the counter. "I was just reviewing the first deaths, from the '80s."

Cora tapped Sigfried's photo and pursed her lips. "Terrible. I've never seen this photo before." She turned it to face her and shook her head. "What a ridiculous way to go."

"It does seem careless."

"He wasn't that way at all in his public life. Sigfried wouldn't have made it to town councilman at such a young age, otherwise. He was meticulous. Disciplined. But I suppose many of us wear two faces — public and private. And he did marry Jennifer, so he must have had a wild streak."

"Why do you say that?"

"She was gorgeous, vivacious, loved a good party and a good cocktail." Cora raised a brow. "I won't say all the men wanted her, but many did. Of course, Sigfried was going places, so it wasn't such a surprise when the two married, even if he was a dull fish. We all expected her to turn her hostess skills toward taking her place in the community."

"And she didn't?"

"No. For a politician's wife, she was remarkably disengaged from community events. Even today, when she's married to a dairy man, she's not involved in Ladies Aid."

The horror! I tried not to roll my eyes and failed.

Cora smiled. "Which I suppose you think is good sense on her part."

"Ladies Aid can get a little intense."

The door opened and a middle-aged couple strolled inside. Cora edged from the counter and I sold them tickets.

"Where are the haunted bells?" the woman demanded.

Tensing, I pointed.

She giggled. "What a kick!"

The two moved off.

"It seems the TV interview last night

411

hasn't hurt business," Cora said in a low voice.

"You saw that?"

"I don't sleep much. One of the benefits of age. The closer we get to dying, the more opportunity we have to enjoy life."

"You're not that close to dying."

"Closer than you are. At least I hope I am. I must say, I don't like the aura I'm seeing around you." She wafted her hand about my head and shoulders as if fluffing an invisible cloud.

"You see auras?" Repress, repress my inner skeptic. A group of twenty-somethings walked in and I sold more tickets.

"Of course I see auras," Cora said after they'd moved into the Gallery. "Yours is usually a lovely, iridescent sparkle. But there are all sorts of cords attached to you — other people are imposing on your energy field. If you like, I know an energy worker who can help."

"Maybe after the holidays," I said.

"Considering everything that's been happening, I'm surprised you're not taking this more seriously." Her lips crimped together. "I only hope after the holidays isn't too late."

So did I.

TWENTY-SIX

Exhausted, I locked the museum door and leaned against the counter. I wasn't sure what the interview with Xavier had done for the curse panic, but it had been a busy Saturday at the museum. And with Leo out with a cold, my blood hummed from the tension of single-handedly selling tickets, wrapping gifts, and answering questions.

GD glanced over his shoulder at me, then returned to his contemplation of the ogress in her cave. They'd obviously bonded, and I hoped he didn't pitch a fit when we removed her after the holidays

I was sweeping the black-and-white floor when the wall phone rang.

"Paranormal Museum, this is Maddie speaking."

Someone breathed heavily on the line.

"Hello?" I asked.

"It's Oliver," a deep voice boomed.

As if I was supposed to know who the

heck that was . . . I straightened, and my broom clattered to the linoleum.

GD hissed, one paw raised to strike. Fortunately I was nowhere near striking distance.

"Oliver Breathnach? Kendra Breathnach's son?" I asked.

"Right."

"Hi, Oliver. I'm glad you made it back from Tahoe safely."

"Yeah."

I waited. He'd called me, so I assumed he had something to say.

"Craig told me to call you," he said.

"Well, thanks. I understand you were at the Christmas Cow when —"

"Not on the phone. Can you meet me tonight? My house?"

Oh no, hell no. No more solo witness interviews and especially not at night. "Oliver, if you saw anything that night, the best people to talk to are the police, especially now that Craig's father is in custody."

"I can't talk to them. My mom would kill me if she found out what I'd done. Look, Craig said it was important I talk to you. If you don't want to talk —"

"No," I said quickly, "I'd love to talk. I'll be there in an hour."

"Cool." He hung up.

GD hopped onto the counter and coughed up a fur ball.

"Gross!" Beneath his critical gaze, I cleaned up the mess.

"I know I shouldn't go," I chattered. "Craig's dad confessed. There's no sense in me playing detective."

The cat washed one paw.

"But I'm not sure it's over. It wouldn't hurt to tie up the loose ends."

GD planted his paw on the cash register and yawned.

"Okay, maybe I don't want to believe Craig's father is the killer. Or Craig for that matter. Obviously, Craig's dad is protecting him. But what if Craig's innocent and his father is doing it all for nothing? And if Craig really is guilty, then he could hurt someone else and needs to be off the streets."

GD rolled onto his back and in a swift motion, lightly bit my hand.

I studied the two pale white marks. "Or I could clear your name."

The cat meowed and hopped off the counter, returning to Gryla's cave.

I called my mom. "Hi, Mom. It's Maddie."

"Yes, I know. Your name comes up on my screen. How are you, dear? I would have stopped by, but things got rather hectic with Ladies Aid."

I braced my elbow on the cash register. "Cora told me about Mrs. Tyre's broken hip. How is she?"

"Her hip is still broken, but she's as stubborn as ever. How are *you*?"

"Fine." I'd no doubt my mom had heard about Mason's visit last night. Everyone else had. "Oliver Breathnach called. He wants to meet at his house in an hour."

"So he's finally back from his ski trip?"

"He said Craig told him to talk to me, but he wants to keep the conversation private. It sounds like his mom doesn't know that he was involved in the cow attack."

"And so he wants to meet at the house his mother lives in?" she asked. "He's either a liar or not the sharpest knife in the drawer."

"Maybe she's working late. Anyway, do you want to come along?"

"I'll meet you there."

"See you then. Bye." I hung up. With my mom's police escort returned, I didn't imagine Oliver would be much of a threat. I also didn't hold out much hope he'd have useful information. We'd already talked to the other members of Team Cow. But, no stone unturned and all that jazz.

I finished sweeping and restocked the Gal-

416

lery, then I locked up and left. My truck sputtered. After a breathless moment, the engine roared to life. Maybe the lifting of the curse had cured it, but I'd take it to the garage for sure once the holidays were over.

Muttering a prayer to the truck gods, I turned onto Main Street. Christmas lights twinkled on the barren plum trees. A few pedestrians strolled the brick sidewalks, pausing to check menus and peruse shop windows.

Past the San Benedetto arch, I turned left into a residential section. The yards between the homes widened. I drove past the turn-off to the Wildes' house and my heart grew heavy. I didn't hold out much hope Oliver would have information to clear both Craig and his father. But I had to try.

A few long blocks farther, I turned the pickup into Kendra's development and parked on the street in front of her brick Tudor home. The windows on the upper story were dark, but the Christmas tree glowed in the front window.

Headlights illuminated my truck cab, and my mother's rented SUV pulled up behind me. Her lights cut off.

Stepping from my pickup, I scanned the empty street. Where was her police escort?

She got out of the car and locked it with

her fob. "I'm sorry to say, you can't be too careful these days."

"You still leave your front door unlocked."

"That's different," she said. "No one bothers with my neighborhood."

"Where are your police?"

"My police? I don't have police."

"The guys who were watching you."

"Oh, they left this afternoon."

I muttered a curse.

"Madelyn. Language."

"I called you so we'd have police protection."

She folded her arms. "And I thought you wanted your mother."

"I do, but . . . the police would have been useful."

We walked up the flagstone drive.

"I checked in with my contacts at Ladies Aid," she said. "Three people saw Dean selling his raw milk at the farmers' market at the time your bell-cursing event was going on."

"De-cursing," I said. "I guess that leaves him out of the running."

"Which we already suspected, but it's best to be thorough."

"Do you know Oliver?"

"No," she said. "But he's, what? Twenty? Hardly a match for the two of us."

"Maybe in a battle of wits, but if he's our archer —"

"He couldn't be." She stepped up to the front door and rang the bell. It echoed faintly inside the house. "He's been in Tahoe."

"So his mother says," I said darkly. "Tahoe's only two hours away."

"You have a very cynical view of human nature. And that's something else I wanted to talk to you about."

I stiffened.

"I heard —"

The front door opened and a lanky man with blond hair stared out at us. His lips were chapped, his rugged face wind-burnt. I put him at over thirty. Oliver's stepdad? Did he have a stepdad?

"Yeah?" he asked. He wore jeans and a rumpled sweatshirt with a comic book hero on its front.

"I'm Maddie Kosloski. This is my mother, Fran."

"You didn't say you were bringing your mom."

"Say?" I stuttered. "Wait. Are you . . . Oliver?"

"Yeah. Who'd you think?"

We stared at each other.

"May we come in?" my mother asked.

419

Oliver stepped outside and shut the door behind him, herding us into the driveway. "This way." He walked across the paving stones and opened a gate on the other side of the garage. Its hinges creaked ominously.

My mom and I glanced at each other, shrugged, and followed him through the gate.

Fishing a set of keys from his pocket, he unlocked a side door to the garage. "More private." He reached through the door, flipped on a light, ambled inside.

A drum set stood in one corner and a computer with what looked like a sound setup sat on a table nearby. Wires snaked across the thin gray carpet. A second door stood shut, presumably leading into the house. Why hadn't we used that entrance?

"You've got a band," I said.

He shrugged and pulled out a folding chair, sat.

My mother raised an eyebrow.

Hastily, he rose and unfolded two more chairs for my mother and me. Then he jammed his hands in his pockets, his fists clenching and unclenching. "What have you heard?"

I sat on the cold metal chair. "That you and a group of your college friends set the Christmas Cow on fire."

He scowled. "But you didn't hear it from me. I laid low, like we agreed. But someone blabbed, and now none of the guys will talk to me."

"Not all of them," my mother said, taking a seat beside me. "You talked to Craig."

His neck corded. "All he'd say was that I needed to talk to you. So I'm talking to you. What's going on?"

"A man was killed there that night," I said.

He shook his head. "I didn't know about that. Not until I got home."

"When did you leave for Tahoe?" I asked.

"The morning after the cow fire."

"Cow arson," my mother said tartly.

He ignored her. "My mom had gotten me tickets for the slopes the week before — some special deal."

"And you didn't check the Internet for news about the cow?" I studied him carefully.

"Why?" he asked. "I knew who set it on fire."

"You weren't the least bit curious about what people had to say?" my mother asked.

His chin dipped. "Maybe I did read something."

"But you decided to stay in Tahoe," I said.

"I didn't know anything. If I'd seen who'd shot that guy . . ." He looked away.

He probably still wouldn't have said anything. Not if one of his buddies was responsible. "All right," I said. "Tell us what happened that night."

Oliver heaved a sigh. "We met here, like we'd planned."

"Not at the cow?"

"We stored the costumes here." He glanced around the garage. "And we did our planning here between sets. If I'd known . . . we wouldn't have done it."

"And where are the costumes now?"

He shrugged. "We got rid of them."

"Okay, so you met here," I said. "Then what?"

"We took two cars to the cow and lit it up. We ran to where we'd parked the cars —"

"Where was that?"

"A few blocks away, on the street in front of the bank."

"And then?" my mother asked.

"Then we went home. The next morning, I left for Tahoe."

"That didn't leave you much time to ditch the costumes." The cold from the concrete floor seeped through the soles of my thin tennis shoes, numbing my toes.

"I took mine to Tahoe and tossed it in a dumpster behind my hotel."

"Clever," my mom said. "Which hotel were you at?"

He gave us a name, and my mother nodded. "They may not have views of the lake, but it's close to Squaw Valley," she said.

"I had a great view," he said. "And it's near Northstar."

"Of course," my mom said. "My mistake."

I eyed her. My mother knew Tahoe like the back of her hand. She was checking if Oliver was lying or not, and apparently he'd passed the test.

"Having a hotel room and lift tickets doesn't prove you were there," I said.

He swatted at the air. "You think I'm lying? Why would I do that?"

"We believe you." My mother crossed her legs and the metal chair squeaked. "You've obviously been spending a good bit of time on the slopes. But we still need evidence."

"I've got receipts from restaurants and stuff."

"You keep receipts?" I asked, surprised.

His face turned the color of a brick. "My mom said she'd reimburse me for food if I brought back receipts."

"Let's see them," my mother said.

"I'll be back." He strode from the garage.

She peeled off her knit gloves. "Madelyn, there's something I need to tell you."

"Mmm?"

"I am so glad you moved out."

I stared.

"Don't get me wrong," she said. "I hated seeing my birds leaving the nest. And then I see the birds that never leave and realize I'm lucky."

"It's a tough economy," I said, sheepish. I'd gotten the deal of the century on my garage apartment, so I was in no position to criticize.

"Hmm. How old do you think he is?"

"Twenty-eight? Thirty?" More? I guessed more.

"And he's still in college. Not grad school, *college.* Even if that man-child saw something," she said, "he's not going to admit it."

"Probably not. But he did call me. He wants to talk about something."

"He wants to get off the hook with his friends."

The door leading into the house opened, slamming against the wall. Kendra stormed into the garage. "How dare you interrogate my son!"

My mother rose. "Hello, Kendra. How nice to see you again."

The developer flipped her blond hair over the shoulder of her red power suit. "You two have no right to be here. Leave or I'll call the police."

"You should," I said. "I'm sure they'd like to talk to Oliver and clear some things up."

"There's nothing to clear up," she said. "He wasn't involved with that stupid prank."

Oliver slunk into the garage. He blinked rapidly. "Actually, Mom, it was sort of my idea."

Kendra's lips whitened. "Stop talking."

He hunched his shoulders. "We didn't think anyone would get hurt."

She sank onto one of the folding chairs and pressed her palms to her eye sockets. "This can't be happening." Her head snapped up, her brown eyes flashing. "A man was killed! Do you have any idea how much trouble you could be in?"

"I didn't do it," he whined. "I didn't see anything. We were aiming at the cow. It was pretty hard to miss. The thing stands thirty feet tall."

"Stood," my mom corrected.

Kendra rose and paced the garage. "All right. All right. We'll deal with this. I don't know what the penalty is for arson, but I'll talk to Ladies Aid and the Dairy Association." She looked hopefully at my mother. "Maybe they won't press charges."

"There is the matter of Bill Eldrich," I said.

"Which was awful, but Tom Wilde confessed to that murder." Her voice rose. "My son had nothing to do with it."

Oliver handed a wad of crumpled papers to my mother. "Here are those receipts."

"Aren't you glad now I asked you to keep them?" Kendra asked him.

My mother smoothed them out and raised them to the overhead light. "Yes, they're receipts from Tahoe for the days in question. On your mother's credit card." She passed them to me. I thumbed through them and nodded.

Kendra snatched them from my hands. "I still don't understand what you're doing here."

"I called them, Mom."

"You called . . ." She pressed a manicured hand to her chest. "You wanted to talk to them and not me?"

He rumpled his blond hair. "Craig said —"

"Craig said! I suppose if Craig told you to jump off the Golden Gate Bridge, you'd think it was a good idea too. He was behind this whole cow business, wasn't he?"

I fought back a nervous grin. How many times had I heard that line from my mom growing up?

"No, Mom, I told you. It was my idea."

The developer moaned. "This is all my fault. If I'd waited to divorce your father, I could have spent more quality time with you rather than working late on my business."

"Mom, it's all right."

"It is not all right. You caused damage to private property. And even though you had nothing to do with it, a man was killed. We need to talk to the police and clear this up. Now who else was involved?"

His tanned forehead wrinkled. "I'm not going to narc on my friends."

"Oh yes you are, young man."

He shook his head. "I'll admit to what I did, but none of us hurt Mr. Eldrich. If the other guys want to come forward, that's up to them. I'm not telling who they are."

"But I can guess," his mother said. "They're all in your band, aren't they?"

I cleared my throat. "Going to the police is a good idea. We'll leave you to it."

Kendra walked us to the door. "I apologize for flying off the handle. It's just . . . he's my only son. I guess I can be overprotective."

My mother smiled. "Of course you are. But it was just a silly prank. There was no reason for them to think things would go so horribly wrong."

The two of us walked outside and paused by her car door.

"Just a silly prank?" I asked.

"Hardly." She sniffed. "It was a rotten thing to do. Ladies Aid and the Dairy Association won't press charges, but those boys will face a huge bill from the fire department. Otherwise some other idiots will do it again next year."

"Good luck with stopping them," I muttered.

"Cynicism is unattractive. Now, I heard about this business last night with Mason."

Of course she had. I blew out my breath, leaving a trail of mist in the chill night air. I was only surprised she hadn't brought the topic up sooner. "It was nothing. Mason was upset, and —"

"He came to your house."

Warmth crept across my cheeks. "He thought I knew something about Belle's disappearance."

"But you didn't."

"Of course not!"

"Which Mason should have known."

"He wasn't thinking straight."

She sighed. "At least I don't have to worry

about you getting on a motorcycle with him again."

"You never had to worry about that." Motorcycles terrified me.

"Madelyn, what happened between Belle and Mason isn't your fault. But you need to decide where you stand. You said you'd broken it off with Mason, but obviously there's still an emotional connection. For both your sakes, you need to move on."

"Believe me, I have." My chest tightened. Hadn't I?

TWENTY-SEVEN

I sprawled on my sofa, the room awash in gray Monday morning light. My brain ached. Yesterday I'd had to extract a kid stuck in Gryla's cave while GD howled. Someone, who shall remain nameless because no one admitted to the crime, knocked over a display of Christmas fairies. And the heater had gone on the fritz, dropping the museum to sub-zero temperatures.

The remote control dropped from my limp hand and clattered to the laminate floor. As much as I wanted to, I couldn't sleep away my day off, not with Craig's father still in jail. I was more convinced than ever that there were puzzle pieces to these murders that needed to be set in their proper place. And with Jason out of commission, I didn't trust my arch nemesis Laurel to probe deeper.

Also, while the museum might be closed, GD's stomach never shut down for business. I had to feed and water the cat.

Sighing, I tied on my sneakers and drove to the museum.

GD was suitably ungrateful when I discharged my cat-owner duties. After a futile attempt to pet him, I left, driving through the morning fog to the Wine and Visitors Bureau.

The place was closed until noon on Mondays, but Penny's Honda sat parked, dusty and dismal, in the lot. The bureau's red tile roof was cloaked in low fog. Mist twisted, wraithlike, through the educational vineyard, and I shivered.

Stepping from the pickup, I adjusted the collar of my museum hoodie beneath my thick black vest. I wasn't worried about Penny bashing my head in and burying me in the educational vineyard. Maybe she *was* good enough with a bow to shoot Tabitha, ditch the weapon, and then pretend to discover the body, but grandmotherly, grape-cluster-earringed Penny couldn't have been the one to lure Tabitha to the Visitors Bureau.

I walked to the arched side door and rattled the knob.

Locked.

I called Penny from my cell phone.

"Wine and Visitors Bureau. This is Penny

speaking. How may I help you?"

"Hi, it's Maddie."

"What can I do for you?" Her voice cooled.

"I'm outside. Can I come in for a quick chat?"

There was a long pause. And just when I thought she was going to turn me down, she said, "Of course. I'll be right there." She hung up.

I waited.

Bolts rattled, and the portal edged open.

She peered out, her gray curls trembling. Seemingly satisfied, she nodded, her Christmas-ornament earrings bobbing. A fluffy reindeer pin was stuck to her *Kiss My Glass* sweatshirt. "It's been a day for surprise guests." She opened the door wider and stepped aside.

"Oh?" I walked into the narrow hall lined with wine crates.

Dean, in a thick down vest, emerged from Penny's office, and we both stopped short. He rubbed his squashed nose.

I curled my arms around my waist. Dean wasn't a member of the Wine and Visitors Bureau, not even at the associate level. "Hi," I said. "What brings you to the Visitors Bureau?"

"I'm looking to become an associate

member." He shifted his weight, his bulk knocking into a stack of cardboard wine crates in the hall. They wobbled, and he leapt to steady them.

Associate member? My eyes narrowed. "For your dairy farm?"

"I'm going to start doing tours," he said, lining up the edges of the boxes and not looking at me. "And I sell directly from the farm, so it's a good fit for tourists."

I canted my head. That explanation made some sense, and Dean couldn't be our killer. But my paranoia was running amok.

"Why are *you* here?" he asked.

"I'm out of vineyard maps," I lied.

"Again?" Penny asked. "We just gave you some."

"Things have been crazy since the news stories on the cowbells. Which aren't cursing anyone, by the way," I said quickly. "I mean, they're cursed, so to speak, but they're totally harmless. There once was a curse but not anymore. Now the bells are just of historical interest."

Penny stared over her spectacles. "My grandson turns into a motormouth whenever I catch him doing something he shouldn't. He thinks if he talks faster, no one will notice he's not being honest."

My cheeks warmed. "The bells are a sore

433

spot," I said. "And I've learned something about Tabitha's death I'd like to ask you both about." I glanced at Dean. The police frowned on doing joint interrogations — something about contaminating witness statements.

Good thing I wasn't a cop.

"You learned something?" Penny asked sharply. "What?"

"Someone called Tabitha the night before we discovered her body in the vineyard. She told her husband that the caller said there was an emergency meeting about the Christmas Cow, here at the Visitors Bureau."

Penny frowned. "Emergency meeting? We didn't have any meetings here that night."

"Where were the meetings normally held?" I asked.

"Here, actually. We have space for meetings in the main room."

I nodded. In an open room to the left of the counter was a circle of comfy chairs for wine tasters, and the space sometimes doubled as a meeting place for small community events.

"But I would have known if there was a meeting." She braced one elbow on a stack of wine boxes. "I would have had to unlock the doors."

"That makes sense." But the call Tabitha received had to have come from someone connected to the Christmas Cow committee — someone she trusted. "There's something else. Have either of you attended any town council meetings recently?"

Penny and Dean glanced at each other across the narrow hallway. Penny spoke first. "Three months ago, I spoke at city hall, pitching the Wine and Visitors Bureau to receive that tax money."

"I was there two months ago, when the anti-raw milk regulations were proposed," Dean said.

"What else do you remember about those meetings?" I asked.

Dean rolled his eyes. "Are you kidding? It was all I could do to stay awake until it was my turn to speak."

"The meeting I attended ran long as well." Penny's lips compressed.

"Do you remember what else was discussed?" I pressed.

Penny tapped her chin with a crooked finger. "Let's see. The tax money — lots of nonprofits were pitching for their share, including Ombudsman Services, the library, and the arts council. And of course there was the zoning issue for that new agrihood community. I actually spoke on behalf of that as well." She glowered. "Maybe that was why Bill Eldrich turned against me."

"Bill was against the agrihood development?" I asked.

"Oh, not the development itself," she said. "Those were all vineyards. Sad to see them go, but that part went through fairly smoothly."

"Then what?" I asked, leaning closer.

"The area around the development," she said. "It's dairy pasture. Kendra was hoping to buy up all that land and convert it to homes or a park. But it isn't zoned for residential. They ended up tabling the motion on the zoning for that."

One side of Dean's mouth curled. "They couldn't reach an agreement on that at the meeting I attended either."

"So Kendra's project is stalled?" I asked.

"Heavens no," Penny said. "She got the zoning approved for the agrihood itself. Getting the land around it shouldn't make a difference one way or another."

But wouldn't it? I massaged the back of my neck. As much as I liked dairy products — and I really do like dairy products — cows make a big stink, especially on a hot day. They can be noisy too. Not everyone wants to live near livestock.

A breeze drifted down the narrow corridor

and I zipped my vest higher.

"How did Tabitha vote on the expanded zoning?" I asked.

Penny turned and pressed her hand to the exterior door, as if satisfying herself it was shut. "I don't remember."

"She was against it," Dean said. "Got into a hot discussion with another council member about it."

"Do you remember anything else?" I asked. "Anything odd happening at the council meetings?"

"The only thing odd is that anybody goes to them," Dean said. "It was like watching paint dry. Oh, wait. There was one hot moment. A hairdresser was mad that she had to get relicensed or pay some business tax fee or something. Tabitha pretty much told her the rules were the rules. They really got into it."

"A hairdresser?" My chest tightened. "Was her name Belle Rodale by any chance?"

"I don't remember her name," Dean said, "but she was a real looker. Tall, slim, long reddish-brown hair?"

I sucked in my breath. Belle. She'd had a motive to kill Tabitha after all.

Since GD had made it clear I was persona non grata on this fine frosty morning, I

437

drove home.

Ignoring the lure of the couch, I booted up my laptop at my cracked kitchen counter and drew up a bar stool. Then, shivering, I went to my room and slipped on a pair of fingerless gloves. As much as I loved the cheap rent, my aunt's heater was barely making a dent in the winter cold.

I glanced through the floral-print curtains at the fog bank. Wind rustled the tree branches and the mist parted, revealing my aunt's house next door. The fog soon reformed into a solid, gray wall, and my nearest neighbor vanished from sight.

Was it possible Belle had killed both Bill and Tabitha? My heels bounced on the barstool's spindle. Even to kill Tabitha, Belle would have had to be insane. Mason would have known if she was off-balance. I couldn't imagine he'd let a crazy woman live with him.

My fingers froze, poised over the keyboard. Unless he'd been keeping her close to protect his son.

I shook my head. Was my mom right? Was I worrying about Mason more than I should? No. I knew now I wasn't in love with him, but I did want things to work out for him.

My screen flickered to life, and I searched

438

the Internet for Tabitha Wilde.

LOCAL COUNCILWOMAN
FOUND DEAD

San Benedetto Councilwoman Tabitha Wilde was found murdered this morning. The San Benedetto Police Department has yet to offer a possible motive for the crime, though they have released information that she was killed by an arrow similar to the one that killed Mr. William Eldrich at the town's Christmas Cow conflagration.

The body was discovered outside the San Benedetto Wine and Visitors Bureau. A Visitors Bureau employee called the police after finding the body.

Tabitha Wilde joined the City Council on December 31, 2013, serving the town of roughly 25,000.

"She was a wonderful person," said Robert Cross, who joined the City Council at the same time as Ms. Wilde. Cross also said that his brother graduated from high school with Ms. Wilde. "Tabitha was a positive force on the council," he said. "She will be missed."

Wilde leaves behind a husband, Tom Wilde, and a son, Craig Wilde.

Neighbor Helen McKenna told the San

Benedetto Times that she had known Ms. Wilde well in the fifteen years she had lived next door. "I can't wrap my brain around this. She was a huge part of the community."

I scanned the Internet some more. There were a few later articles about the murder, short updates saying nothing new. I frowned and re-read the first article.

I sat up straighter. Wait a minute. Something was missing. I didn't know what it was, but something . . .

A motorcycle rumbled up my drive. The engine cut, and I looked up.

My cell phone rang. I dug it from my jacket pocket and answered without looking at the screen.

"Hello?"

"It's Mason. We need to talk."

TWENTY-EIGHT

I leaned back on my seat and the barstool rocked alarmingly. Hastily I leaned forward again. One-handed, I clutched the fractured kitchen counter for balance.

"After the way I acted the other night, I can't blame you if you don't want to see me. But I'm downstairs. Can I come up?"

"You weren't as bad as you think you were." I hopped to the linoleum floor and strode through the living room to open the front door. Below me, Mason, clad head-to-toe in black leather, leaned against his Harley. His helmet dangled from one hand. I waved and hung up.

He trudged up the steps to the landing.

"I'm sorry about what happened," he said, his blue eyes morose. "And I'm sorry I punched a hole in your wall."

"Look, about that —"

"I talked to Dieter. He said he'd fix your wall and send me the bill."

I pulled a smile. "Thanks, but —"

"You were right to steer clear of Belle and me," he said. "I get it. It would have been weird if you'd gotten involved in our problems. And you and I both need to move on."

"Mason, I'm trying to accept your apology."

"Oh." He brightened. "Well. Thanks."

A cold breath of wind stirred my hair. "Come inside. It's freezing out here." I backed into the apartment and he followed. "Have you heard anything from them?"

His rugged face broke into a smile. "Yeah. She got an apartment in Sacramento. They're good. And I'm still a part of Jordan's life."

Relieved, I reached for his hand. Then I remembered myself and drew away. "That's fantastic news."

"She'd just freaked out about how fast things were moving. One minute I didn't know I had a son, and the next we were all living together like a happy family."

"It's enough to throw anyone for a loop," I agreed.

His ears turned red. "I'm not sure where this is going with Belle, but I'm grateful I have the chance to find out." He shuffled his booted feet.

"That's great. Have you seen them yet?"

Because while I was happy for him, I was also in suspicious amateur detective mode. Belle could have called him from anywhere and said she was in Sacramento.

He nodded. "I stopped by their new apartment. It's in a decent neighborhood. And I told your Detective Slate everything was fine."

"He's not my Detective Slate."

Mason winced. "I screwed that up for you, didn't I? He thinks we've still got something going."

"I don't know what he thinks," I said. "But if it's meant to be, it'll be." Urgh. Now I was quoting my mother.

"No, Mad. If it's meant to be, you've got to go after it."

I smiled, rueful. "When did you turn philosophical?"

"Having a kid really does change your perspective."

"I'm glad you and Belle have a chance," I said. "You deserve it." I only hoped Belle did too.

I stood on my mom's doorstep and banged the knocker encircled by a Christmas wreath. The late afternoon sunlight slanted low, breaking through the clouds, and the wreath's holly leaves glistened.

443

Suddenly I felt lighter. I was nearer to a solution — and not just for the murder. I really was over Mason.

"It's open!" my mother shouted.

I strolled inside.

"Is that you, Madelyn?" she called from the kitchen. The scent of baking pumpkin and spices filled the house.

"It's me." I walked into her kitchen. Flour lay in drifts across the granite counter. The red-and-white room was cheerful any time of year, but the scent of baking pies took me back to Christmases long past. And this Christmas would be upon us in two short days. I hugged her. "How's it going?"

She blinked. "Fine, dear. I'm baking pies for our shut-in members."

"Need help?"

"You're too late. They're in the oven. All I need to do now is clean up."

"That I can manage." I grabbed a sponge and wiped down the granite counter.

She planted her fists on her aproned hips. "You're in a good mood."

"Mason stopped by today."

She canted her head. "Madelyn, you're not —"

"He found Belle in Sacramento, and they're moving forward with their lives, together it seems. He's hopeful."

"And you're all right with that?"

I brushed the flour into my hand and dumped it in the sink. "Yep. 'Tis the season for family reunions. He deserves it."

"That's very mature of you."

"Also, he's hired Dieter to fix my wall." Which meant I wouldn't have to.

"Good news all around, except for Craig, whose father is sitting in jail."

I cringed at her faintly accusatory tone.

"Have you learned anything that might clear his name?" She flicked a wet cloth across the counter.

"We don't know if Tom's innocent. He did have motive and opportunity to kill his wife and Bill Eldrich."

"And Belle had fifty thousand motives to set that cow on fire," my mom said. "Can you really tell me Bill might not have gotten hit by one of her stray arrows? Though she had no reason to kill Tabitha."

"Actually," I said, "she might have. Belle and Tabitha got into it over some licensing issue for hairdressers at a town council meeting."

"Where did you hear that?"

"From Dean Pinkerton, who's the only person we can cross off the suspect list. He couldn't have shot arrows at us when we were at his house."

"Unless he had a co-conspirator."

I shook my head. "This has the feel of a lone archer to me. We can account for all four of the gingerbread men. The killer had to have been Santa."

She shuddered. "Don't call him that. The killer was only *dressed* as Santa."

I glanced at the collection of Santa figurines on the ledge above the kitchen sink. "Someone lured Tabitha to the Wine and Visitors Bureau for a bogus Christmas Cow committee meeting. Dean wasn't on the committee. If he was trying to lure her there to kill her, he'd need a different excuse."

"We only have Tom's word that that's where she was going. Even if he was telling the truth, who's to say that Tabitha was honest about the call? She was having an affair with Bill, and she'd lied to her husband about that."

"But Bill was already dead." I pried open a blue cookie tin and grabbed a pfeffernüsse. "If she was off for a romantic rendezvous, whom with?"

"I can barely imagine Tabitha having an affair with anyone, much less finding a new lover right after the old one died."

Unless her new lover had killed them both? Shaking my head, I took a bite and licked powdered sugar from my lips. We had to stick with the facts, and we had no evidence a new boyfriend had been in Tabitha's life. "I hate to bring this up, but what about Craig?"

My mother blanched. "No. It would be monstrous. Besides, how would Craig have known that Bill would be at the Christmas Cow that night?"

"Who managed the guard schedule?" I finished the cookie and brushed sugar from my fingers.

She picked up the tin and replaced the lid. "Cora did, and we circulated the guard duty roster among the Dairy Association and Ladies Aid members who participated. But I don't see how Craig could have gotten hold of it." Her brow wrinkled. "Or Tom, for that matter. We didn't send the list to his wife."

"It might be another point in Tom's favor."

"Or not," she said. "The list might not have been public, but it wasn't exactly private either. It wasn't the sort of information I thought we'd need to keep confidential. And Bill was complaining to everyone who'd listen about his guard duty."

"Then there's Kendra Breathnach."

"Kendra?" My mom's blue eyes widened. "What did she have against Bill?"

"She wanted to expand her development

into the dairy pastures." I gazed wistfully at the cookie tin in her arms. "Bill and Tabitha blocked that."

"But she has her development — that agrihood thing."

"And it's surrounded by dairy farms. You know how they smell in the summer."

My mom wrinkled her nose and set the tin on top of the humming refrigerator. "Surely people who move to the country will expect to be around livestock."

"But they might not understand what that really means until it's too late."

"This won't get Tom out of jail." My mother folded her arms. "What else do you have?"

I rubbed my cheek with the flat of my hand. "The only suspects we're left with are Belle, Tom, Craig, and Kendra. Unless you can figure out some Agatha Christie way Dean could have arranged for us to be shot at while he was cowering inside the house with us." I straightened. Oh, damn. Damn!

"What's wrong?"

"The newspaper article!" My pulse hammered in my skull, my breath quickening.

"What article?"

"The one about Tabitha's murder. Dammit, I know who killed them both."

"Why is that a bad thing?" My mom

pressed her palm to her apron. "Unless . . . it isn't Tom or Craig, is it?"

"It's a bad thing because there's no way I can prove it." And then I made a fatal mistake.

I told her everything.

Twenty-Nine

Tuesday morning. The museum was closed
for the day, and I stared vacantly at my
aunt's bookshelf of nautical instruments. I
bounced my stockinged foot. How could I
trap the killer without my prior irritate-
them-until-they-try-to-kill-me approach?
Seriously, there had to be a better way.

The logical person to call for advice was
Jason. Maybe I should have called him last
night. But I didn't have proof, and he was
still on medical leave.

I was *not* going to call his partner. Laurel
would either laugh or threaten me with
interfering in an investigation. And I certainly wasn't going to poke the bear and try
to get the murderer to confess. That sort of
thing never ended well.

At loose ends, I bundled up in a *Paranormal Museum* hoodie and down vest and
hurried down the steps to my pickup. It
coughed, sputtered, died. I pumped the gas

and turned the key again. The truck wheezed and fell silent.

Cursing, I lowered my head to the wheel. The lingering morning fog spiraled around my truck.

I called a tow truck and then an Uber driver, and arrived at the museum way past GD's breakfast time. The cat looked up from a sunny patch on the glass counter and hissed.

"Sorry I'm late." I unwound my scarf and draped it over the cash register.

He flicked his tail and growled, a ridge of black fur rising along his spine.

Hastily I fed him, then pulled my clipboard from beneath the counter and scanned the inventory list. My forehead wrinkled. The Christmas fairies were nearly sold out. But we were closing in on the big day. There was no time to order more.

Clipboard beneath my arm, I strolled into the Gallery and turned on the twinkle lights to cheer myself up. Delicate fairies spiraled from the ceiling, danced atop display cases, frolicked in drifts of fake snow. But there were empty spots that needed filling.

The front door opened and I froze, heart thumping. I was sure I'd locked the door.

"Maddie?" Jason called.

My heart beat faster. "In here." I strolled

into the main room.

Purring, GD rubbed against Jason's leg, depositing black hairs on his jeans. The detective knelt and stroked the cat's fur with his good arm. Then he rose, adjusting his sling. "Hey."

"Hi." Relief fizzed inside me. Jason was here. We could finally talk, and the first thing I wanted to talk about was my theory on the murder. But something in his expression stopped me. "What's going on?" I asked. "Is something wrong?"

There was a long, brittle silence. Two deep lines appeared between his gold-flecked eyes. "I guessed you would think something was wrong after the last time we met. I'm here to say I'm sorry."

"Sorry?"

"I know I was brusque the other night, about you and Mason."

I raked my hand through my hair. "There *is* no me and Mason. There hasn't been for months."

"I know."

"You do?" I asked, relieved.

"I was angry the other night, but not at you."

"Oh." I shrugged to hide my confusion.

"What?" he asked.

"If that was you angry, you hid it well."

And that seemed like a good thing. Between the museum, my mom, Herb the paranoid paranormal collector, and Ladies Aid, a drama-free relationship would be heaven.

"You can't lose your temper when you're a cop. But it leaked out the other night when I saw that hole in your wall." He stepped closer. I could feel the warmth radiating from his body, smell his musky scent. "You've thrown me off-balance, Maddie. After the divorce, I thought I was done with relationships, but . . ."

My breath caught.

He smiled, wry. "You've got the strangest look on your face. Should I go?"

"No," I said quickly. "Please stay." My face warmed. "Assuming being off-balance isn't always a bad thing."

"Not in this case," he rumbled. Gently, he pulled me into the circle of his uninjured arm and kissed me.

I melted against his broad chest. My legs trembled, and I clutched his parka for balance.

We drew apart, breathless.

"At least I can kiss you now without any police ethics violations," he said.

"Ethics are important," I agreed, pulse pounding. And now was the time for me to tell him what I suspected.

But then he kissed me again, and I forgot all about newspaper articles and murderers.

GD gagged, expelling a hairball.

Pulling away, I glared at the cat. He'd timed that.

"Sorry." I sighed. "I need to clean that up." Because I couldn't kiss Jason next to one of GD's hairballs festering on the black-and-white floor.

Jason braced his good elbow on the counter and watched, grinning, while I cleaned up. "I've been doing more digging into that curse," he said.

My feet as light as one of Adele's cream puffs, I returned the broom to its black-painted cupboard. "I didn't think there was much left to dig into. We talked to Jennifer Falls. I spoke to her husband —"

"You did?" Jason straightened off the counter, and his cop face dropped into place like a mask. "What did he say?"

I sat on my barstool behind the counter and rested my hand on the glass. "Byron Falls denied all knowledge of and interest in the curse. And I believed him. He seems a lot more practical than Jennifer's first husband. People said her first husband was a sensible, driven guy, if a bit of a cheapskate. But only an idiot would put an electrical appliance on the bathtub ledge."

"I talked to one of the cops who worked the bathtub scene." Jason's mouth drew into a straight line. "He's retired now. He said he hadn't liked writing it up as an accident. It looked too pat — his words. But there was no evidence of foul play."

GD sank his fangs into my hand.

I yelped, springing from my seat. Scowling, I rubbed the two faint white marks. "What was that for?"

And then my mouth fell open. The jolt of pain had got my brain firing. "The hat pins."

"What?"

"Jennifer Falls was here wearing one of her old-fashioned hats the day of the curse removal." My words tumbled over each other. "There were hat pins in it. She could have used them to make those marks on the women who were attacked."

GD growled.

"I always knew you didn't do it," I said to the cat, then looked up at Jason. "But if I'm right . . . I can't be right. There must have been other ways those two women could have been bitten. Because why would Jennifer intentionally promote the curse?"

Jason's eyes glittered. "What else did you hear about her first husband?"

"He was a miser. Jennifer liked to party and presumably spend the money. You don't think . . ." My eyes widened. "Could she have killed him? Is that why she's pushing the curse? To shift attention away from the real cause of his death?"

We stared at each other.

"I'm jumping to conclusions, right?" I asked.

"Right." But he rubbed his jaw.

I laid my hand beside his on the counter. "Jason, nothing's changed. She remarried the same type of guy. She still has a motive. What if she's not talking up the curse just to cover for a decades-old murder?"

"She's using it as cover for a new one."

My head spun. Had Jason and I actually stumbled upon a murder in the making?

"I've gotta go." He strode out the door, knocking into Leo and Cora Gale coming in. "Sorry." He raced down the street.

"Good goddess." Cora floated into the museum on a current of scarves. She smoothed her windblown gray hair. "Is everything all right?"

"What's his hurry?" Leo set his motorcycle helmet on the counter. His black leather jacket was zipped to his chin.

I swore. Dammit, I hadn't had a chance to tell Jason what I'd learned about the arrow murders. "He has a hot lead. What are you two doing here?"

"Christmas shopping for Leo's cousins," Cora said.

"You've got cousins?" I asked. I didn't think Leo had any family left after the death of his parents, and I was glad he did.

"They're in Eureka." He shrugged. "They invited me for Christmas, but I'd rather stay here."

"However, it's an excellent excuse to reconnect with family," Cora said. "And it's only polite to arrive with host and hostess gifts. Especially for a holiday dinner. We saw the lights on and thought we'd stop by. What are you doing here on your day off? And with the police detective . . . ?" Her brows arched, coy.

"He saw the lights on in the window too, and with everything that's been happening . . ." I turned to Leo. "Are you feeling better?" I was desperate to change the subject.

He sniffed. "Yeah. I can work tomorrow. Hey, I parked my bike in the alley — do you mind?"

"Of course not," I said.

A pained look crossed Cora's face at the mention of the motorcycle, and I shot her a sympathetic look. It unnerved me every time I saw Leo get on it.

"Leo," she said, "perhaps one of those

fairies would make a nice hostess gift?"

Leo rolled his eyes. "Do you mind, Maddie?"

"I never say no to a sale." Even if he did get an employee discount.

While they perused the Gallery, I locked the front door and unlocked the cash register. A few minutes later, they emerged with a delicate blue-and-white fairy.

"This one doesn't suck," Leo said.

Cora rolled her eyes. "He's in a mood."

Leo's brows lowered. "I don't want to drive to Eureka."

"It is a long drive on a motorcycle," I said innocently as I rang up the fairy. "Maybe he could use some company?"

"Company?" Cora asked. "Well, I suppose I . . . But I wasn't invited."

Leo brightened. "They said I could bring a guest."

"Well." She fussed with a filmy violet scarf. "My children aren't coming to visit this year. They're busy with their own families. So I *could* come. But I'm sure your cousins meant for your plus-one to be a younger friend or a girlfriend."

"They said *guest*," he said, gruff. "Besides, you're family too."

She blinked rapidly. "Oh. What a lovely idea. Then I'll go with you to Eureka. And now I need a hostess gift too. I have to buy some wine."

"I'm surprised you don't have a cabinet full of it." I drew wrapping paper from beneath the register and spread it atop the counter.

"Good wine," she amended.

The wall phone rang and I reached for it. "Paranormal Museum, this is Maddie speaking."

"Madelyn, this is your mother," she said, her voice strained.

Phone cradled to my ear, I packed the fairy in its box. "Hi, Mom. What's up?"

There was a long pause.

"Mom?" I waited. "Mom . . . ?" Had her phone battery died?

"I have your mother." The voice was mechanical, like one of those voice-scrambly things you hear on TV shows. The hair on the back of my neck lifted. "If you want to see her alive again, come to the corner of Walnut and McKay."

The gears in my brain locked. "What?"

"Come alone. If I see any police, your mother dies. You have fifteen minutes."

"But —"

The voice hung up.

I swayed, dizzy. "Keys."

"Madelyn, you're white as a sheet," Cora said.

"Leo, I need the keys to your bike."

"What's wrong?" he asked.

"Kendra Breathnach's kidnapped my mother."

THIRTY

GD leapt onto the museum's counter and touched my hand lightly with his paw. He angled his head as if concerned, and hysterical laughter bubbled in my throat.

I swallowed it down.

"Kendra Breathnach?" Paling, Cora tugged on her scarves. "Kendra? The developer?"

Stomach roiling, I grabbed my black vest off the wall peg and slipped into it. "There's no time to explain. Leo, keys." Cora would argue or insist on coming if I asked for her car keys, and I knew Leo's bike was close.

He tossed them to me and I caught them in both hands.

"You two have to tell the cops what's happening," I said. "Try to get through to Detective Slate." I scribbled his number on my yellow pad. "He's no longer in charge, but he'll make sure the police take action."

Cora shook her head, her loose, gray hair

461

tumbling around her shoulders. "But —"

"I'm on it." Leo pulled his cell phone from the pocket of his leather jacket.

"Not yet," I said sharply.

His dark brows pulled downward.

"Kendra said no police." In a shaky hand, I scrawled the address on a piece of paper. "This is where she told me to meet her. Give me fifteen minutes before you call the cops."

"Maddie," Cora said, "I understand how you must feel, but —"

"It's my mom. I have to go." Breaking free, I raced to the bookcase and pressed the hidden latch.

It swung open.

"Maddie!" Leo shouted.

I turned, and he tossed me his helmet.

"Thanks." I raced down the tea shop hallway and nearly knocked a waiter flat.

"Wait! Maddie!" Cora shouted behind me.

I burst through the metal alleyway door.

Belle jerked up short, but not quick enough for me to avoid her. I ricocheted off her shoulder.

"Sorry." I brushed past the hairdresser.

Belle turned, her brown eyes wide. "Maddie, I have to tell you —"

"Glad you're back," I said. "Can't talk now."

Cora ran into the alley. "Maddie, you can't go alone!"

An elderly woman shook her cane at me. "Young lady —"

"Sorry!" I jumped onto Leo's motorcycle.

"But Maddie —" Whatever Belle would have said was lost when I roared down the street. No experience is wasted. *Thank you, Mason, for teaching me to ride. Let me be quick enough to save her.*

I drove as fast as I dared, at the edge of the acceptable limit in town. But once I reached the open fields and straight country roads, Leo's bike flew, and I claimed the center of the road.

Horn bleating, I veered around a truck loaded with onions. I'd eaten up too much time explaining things to Leo and Cora. But they were my insurance now that they knew the truth.

I hit a pothole. The shock jolted my bones, snapping my teeth shut.

Cora and Leo would follow my instructions and tell the cops. And no matter what happened — *nothing would happen, my mom would be fine.* But Kendra had already killed two people, all because she wanted the area around her development to be rezoned. Bill Eldrich had wanted to save those dairy farms. He had influence over Tabitha —

they were having an affair — and Tabitha had backed him, signing her death warrant.

I roared past an orchard, its skeletal branches scraping the bottom of the low fog. The engine's vibration rattled through me.

Kendra wouldn't hurt my mom before I arrived. She'd wait to make sure I was in her clutches. She had to. My eyes burned, and I told myself it was due to the onion truck.

Kendra must have overheard the boys planning the attack on the Christmas Cow — all the planning had happened in her garage — and she'd decided to take advantage.

I screeched around a corner, my rear wheel skidding, one foot on the ground, and narrowly avoided a vineyard signpost.

Why had it taken me so long to figure out it was Kendra? She'd asked me about my finding Tabitha's body at the Wine and Visitors Bureau the morning after the body was discovered. But my role hadn't been in the paper. Only the cops and my mom and Penny knew I'd been on the scene, and I couldn't imagine Penny telling her. The only way Kendra could have known was if she'd been there too.

A gust of wind buffeted me from the side,

and I felt the bike tilt beneath me. I jerked upright, over-compensating, wobbled, and continued on.

What the hell had my mom been thinking, confronting Kendra?

I knew what she'd been thinking — that none of this was evidence. So she'd confronted Kendra to get some.

I sucked in deep gulps of air, steaming the helmet's visor, and tried to calm myself. It didn't matter how this had happened. What mattered was what happened next. I could stop this. I had to believe that or I'd never pull it off.

I passed the sign for the agrihood. The nearby fields had been scraped clean of vegetation, leaving flat, barren tracts of earth. Ahead, the street signs for Walnut and McKay came into view, and a construction site littered with equipment.

The bike skidded to a stop beside a trailer. Expecting an arrow at any moment, I knocked the kickstand into place and swung myself off the seat.

Before me was a deep, muddy pit the size of a building — for a parking garage? A swimming pool? An excavator rumbled at the edge of the pit, its bright yellow paint nearly blinding against the iron gray sky. Its arm angled away from the pit, but no one manned the machine.

Overturned mounds of dirt, like graves, littered the field. *I'm not too late. Please, don't let me be too late.* A sickening tug in my gut pulled my attention toward the sad mounds of earth, ideal for dumping a body. I swallowed a hard lump and looked toward the trailer. Kendra wouldn't be lurking in a dirty pit. And Kendra was the one I wanted.

I ripped off the helmet and set it on the bike. "Mom?"

No one answered.

I slunk to the trailer. My back to the corrugated metal, I edged around its side. I scanned the open ground, reached up with one hand, and rattled the door handle above me.

Locked.

My chest ached. I jammed my hands beneath my arms. *Mom, where are you? Safe, safe, she had to be safe.* Kendra had chosen the perfect daytime murder site. No one was around. I stared at the grumbling excavator.

Nausea clutching my throat, I hurried, bent double, to the excavator.

No body sprawled in the pit beneath its arm. My legs wobbled with relief.

I clambered into the excavator's seat and turned the key. The machine coughed and its rumbling stopped. Silence fell like a shroud across the development.

From my vantage point, I could see more gaping grave holes. *Not graves, stop thinking about graves.*

A murder of crows shot from behind a pile of dirt. I started. Their cawing shattered the air.

"Mom?" I croaked. Slithering from the excavator, I stumbled toward the mound of earth the crows had abandoned. A piece of fabric fluttered in the breeze.

She's not there. It isn't her. A smell, sour and cloying, rose from the opposite side of the mound. Throat tight, I circled around the small pile of earth.

A garbage bag, sliced to ribbons. Rotting food and cardboard spilled from its black plastic.

And that was all.

I blew out a shaky breath.

So where was my mother? Kendra had lured me out here, presumably to put arrows through us both. What was she waiting for?

I prowled the development, skulking around mounds of dirt, past empty pits. "Mom?"

Kendra was playing with me. With *us.* My mom was still alive. She had to be.

Blood pounded in my ears. "I'm not taking another step!" I screamed. "I know you're here. Show yourself!"

My shouts fell flat, absorbed by the loose earth.

The door to the trailer opened and my mom tumbled out, her hands raised.

"Mom!"

I raced toward her across the uneven ground.

Kendra emerged on the trailer steps. "Some detective. You can't even figure out how to open an unlocked door."

THIRTY-ONE

Hands raised, my mother walked forward.

My knees buckled and I nearly fell. She was okay. I wasn't too late. Kendra marched ten feet behind my mother. She held a complicated-looking bow with wheels and cables. It was aimed at my mother's back.

My mom shook her head.

I rushed forward and hugged her.

"Really, Madelyn. What were you thinking? You should have called the police. And was that a motorcycle I heard you arrive on? You know how dangerous they are," she said, her voice thin and shaky.

"It's okay," I said, then louder: "Kendra, the police know everything. Don't add two more murders to your jail sentence."

She tossed her head, her blond hair dancing in the breeze. A quiver of arrows was strapped to her back, the strap rumpling her thick navy blazer. "Why not? What does it matter at this point? Besides, I went to all the trouble of digging your graves." She nodded to the excavator.

"What happened with Tabitha?" I asked, stalling and edging in front of my mother. "We know why you killed Bill Eldrich. It was the zoning, wasn't it?"

My mom stepped sideways, making a target of herself again.

Kendra sneered. "My demographic is wealthy retirees from urban areas. They don't want to live next to a bunch of cows. Bill was in the way, after I'd invested all of that money — mine and others'. He had too much influence over Tabitha."

Delay. Delay and figure out some way to get out of this. But what? I hunched my shoulders, trying to make myself smaller. "Why shoot Tabitha? Was she going to keep blocking your purchase of the dairy farms? Or did she figure out you'd killed Bill?"

"Kendra panicked," my mother said. "She's been following you all along, and she got nervous when she saw us talking to the Wildes."

"Got nervous?" I asked. "She tried to blow us up!"

"She knew Craig might blow the whistle to you about Oliver's involvement. And she lost control when Tabitha began putting the pieces together."

"It wasn't panic," Kendra said. "Tabitha knew I had a motive and the know-how. We learned to shoot together in scouts. She collared me outside my office last week. It was clear from her questions she knew too much."

"So you lured her to the Visitors Bureau with a phony meeting?" I stepped in front of my mom. She immediately shifted right, and my nostrils flared. Would she stop making herself a target?

One corner of Kendra's mouth angled upward. "I told her I'd see her after the committee meeting that night. She was so panicked about forgetting a meeting, she didn't bother to check if it was legitimate."

"And then you followed me to the Visitors Bureau," I said. "That's how you knew I was there when Penny found Tabitha's body."

Kendra drew back the bow.

"Leo and Cora were with me when you called the museum," I said. "They've called the cops. They'll tell them all about you and this kidnapping."

Kendra froze, the arrow drawn, poised. "You're lying. Your museum is closed today. No one else was there when I called."

"They stopped by when they saw me inside," I said. "Of course I told them about

471

your call. I wasn't taking any chances after you set that bomb in my mom's car. Did you get the explosives from your construction site?"

"Where else? Maybe I overreacted, but I didn't like the questions you were asking. But I was careful today. I used a voice-changing machine. You couldn't have known it was me."

"I knew," I said. "Just like my mom did."

"I do hope you know where you're going with this," my mother murmured.

"All you could have told them was that you heard a voice over a machine." Kendra tossed her hair. "Your friends won't be able to prove it was me."

"I didn't tell them you used a machine to distort your voice," I said. "I told them you called, and that you'd kidnapped my mom. By now they've told the police everything, and given that you tried to run down one of their detectives with a stolen car, the police are out for blood."

"Then I've got nothing left to lose." Kendra drew the bow string back farther.

"Stop that!" a quavering feminine voice called out.

Belle Rodale and the old lady I'd nearly flattened in the alley ambled around the corner of the trailer. They moved at a glacial pace, the old woman leaning heavily on Belle's arm.

I gaped. "Belle?"

"Cora told us what was going on, and I volunteered to follow you. I figured I owed you." Belle angled her head toward the old woman. "Mrs. Pagliochi drove. Sorry it took us so long." *Slow,* she mouthed.

Kendra didn't lower her bow. "I've got plenty of arrows. Get over there."

"I don't think so, young lady." The older woman's voice quavered, but the stare over her spectacles was long and hard. "We've had quite enough murder in this town. Now put down that bow."

There was a blur of movement and something zinged past me, burning my cheek.

I gasped and clapped my hand to my face. Warmth trickled between my fingers.

"That was a warning shot," Kendra said. "Now get over there."

To my horror, she'd already nocked a new arrow to the bow. It was aimed straight at me. Damn, she was a good shot, I thought, depressed.

"Mrs. Pagliochi is right," Belle said. "Everyone knows what you've done. Even *I* knew, and I'm not from around here. You may as well give up."

"What will your son think when he learns

473

the truth, Kendra?" my mother asked.

"Leave my son out of this," Kendra snarled. "I'm doing this for him!"

Cora strode around the side of the trailer. Her long pastel scarves fluttered in the breeze. "There you are!"

I moaned. Cora too? At least she'd had the sense not to bring Leo.

"Now stop this, Kendra," Cora said.

"Stop telling me what to do!" Kendra shrieked.

"You might as well drop the bow," Cora said. "I've called the police and told them what you're up to and where you are. They're on their way."

"I told her to come alone," Kendra said, her brown eyes wild. The bow shook. "Alone!"

My mother gripped my shoulder. "But that's not how a community works. We take care of ourselves, and we take care of each other."

"And we don't like people shooting up dairy farmers and town councilwomen," Mrs. Pagliochi warbled.

"You people are crazy," Kendra shouted.

A gray Volvo roared down the road and skidded into the drive. Oliver, Leo, and Harper jumped out.

"Mom!" Oliver shouted. "What are you doing?"

The bow wavered. "If we don't get the new zoning," Kendra said to him, "we'll lose everything."

Oliver's lanky frame sagged, anguish scrawled across his sunburnt face. "Is it true?"

"I gambled all we had on this development and more," Kendra said.

Her son shook his head, his face paling. "Not the development. I don't care about the money. You killed those people? Mom, you need to stop."

A siren wailed.

Harper's lips moved, and her fingers made a quick gesture. Wildly, I thought she might be cursing Kendra.

"Oliver, get in the car and go home." Kendra's bow dipped.

Tearing my attention from Harper, I grabbed my mom's arm and focused on Kendra's bow hand.

"No, Mom," Oliver said. "I'm not going anywhere."

Kendra burst into tears.

"Is this a private party?" Dieter asked. His hand gripped Adele's as the two strolled toward us. A long line of cars roared down the road.

"The entire town knows what's going on out here." Adele brushed a hank of her silky black hair over one shoulder. "Cora announced it in my tea shop." She turned to me. "Though you should have told me."

"Things were happening fast," I said. Something glinted on Adele's finger. "Is that a . . ." I shook myself and refocused on Kendra and her deadly bow.

"You're engaged," my mother said, not sounding at all surprised. And suddenly, I knew what secret of Dieter's she'd been holding over his head. "Congratulations."

"Shut up, shut up, shut up!" Kendra's fingers slipped.

Time slowed.

I swear, I tracked the arrow in flight. Followed its trajectory. Pushed my mother aside. Another bolt of heat grazed my shoulder and I cried out, tumbled to the ground.

Then time resumed its normal gallop. People were shouting, running.

"Madelyn!"

I sat up and clutched my shoulder. No arrow protruded from my jacket but the shoulder was torn, and my hand came away spotted with blood.

My mom sat back on her heels and gulped. "Oh, thank God."

I looked at Kendra. Oliver had wrapped his arms around his mother in a restraining hug. The bow lay in the loose dirt.

Police raced toward us.

Harper squatted beside my mother and I. "You two okay?" she asked.

"Harper?" I blinked. "How?"

"I ran into Leo outside the museum. He suggested we collect Oliver along the way."

I saw Adele and her mother embracing. Mr. Nakamoto clapped Dieter on the back.

"You're bleeding," Harper said.

"It's only a scratch," my mother observed as she helped me to my feet.

"Yeah," I said. "A scratch." I'd ask Harper if she'd cursed that arrow later, when my mother wasn't around. Not that I believe in curses, but that shot had been terrifyingly close.

Cars lined the road, filled the driveway to the development. Waitresses in poodle skirts from the Wok and Bowl. Dean Pinkerton, arms akimbo, glaring at Kendra while Laurel cuffed her. Women from Ladies Aid directing traffic.

Mason roared up on his motorcycle. He ran to Belle and swept her into his arms.

Herb stepped from his battered yellow bug. Gawping, he removed his coke-bottle glasses, cleaned them on his shirt tail, and replaced them on his nose. Penny shook her head, her grape-cluster earrings quivering with sorrow. The owner of the Bell and Brew stood with his hands on his hips. A cluster of ghost busters I knew milled around the worksite. I won't say the whole town had turned out, but it was well represented, and I laid a hand over my heart.

My vision blurred. I'd spent most of my adult life away from home — first in college, then working overseas. Because of my wandering, I'd never felt a part of a community, hadn't even known what I'd missed until this moment. "All these people risked themselves to help us."

"Unlikely," my mother said. "Most came to gawk at our little disaster."

My highfalutin' reflections crashed to earth. "We're like the Christmas Cow."

"But some came to help," she said. "And that matters."

I looked around, searching the crowd for Jason.

He wasn't there.

THIRTY-TWO

I sat alone in the police station's cinder-block interview room and eyed the table. A metal bar for handcuffing prisoners protruded from its top.

And since I'd been sitting there a long time, my thoughts wandered to my truck. Because the truck had stalled, I hadn't been on the spot when the cow was attacked. Because it had stalled again, I'd been forced to face my fears and jump on a motorcycle to save my mom. So many little things had happened — like a museum door that strangely opened when Jason showed up — and I'd assumed they were random. It was almost as if a benign force had been showing me the way.

Nah.

I crossed my arms and leaned back in the metal chair. They couldn't keep me here much longer. Not even Laurel could find something to charge me with today. I shifted. Could she?

The heavy metal door opened and Jason strode into the room. He carried a thick manila folder beneath his good arm.

I rose, the room suddenly seeming brighter. "Jason."

"I heard what happened," he said, pulling me into a one-armed embrace. He touched the tape on my cheek where the arrow had grazed me. "Are you okay?"

"I'm fine. Has Tom been released?"

"Yes, though he may be in some trouble for that false confession."

"He was trying to protect his son. What are you doing here?"

"I'm back on duty."

I studied his chiseled, dark-skinned face. His brown eyes snapped with electricity. "Something's happened," I said. "Aside from my mom getting kidnapped. What is it?"

"When I left you today, I drove to the Falls' house." He dropped the file folder on the desk and papers spilled out. Some I recognized — old documents from the deaths in the 1980s. "When I got there, Jennifer Fall was tipping her husband head-first out a second-floor window."

I gasped. "Did you —"

"I arrived in time to stop her. The doctors

480

think he was drugged. She tried to claim she was pulling him back inside, but we've got her. You stopped more than one murder today."

"*You* stopped her."

"But I couldn't have done it without you." Jason exhaled, a long and contented sigh. "We make a good team."

"I think so too," I said slowly, warming. My parents had been a team. Team was good. Especially when my teammate was standing so close I could feel the energy radiating from his lean body. Especially when my teammate was crazy sexy. And especially when he was good and honorable and kind. I swallowed. "So Jennifer did kill her first husband in the '80s."

"She's not admitting to it, but we're reopening the case. Husband number two is still pretty groggy, but we've already got enough from him to put her away."

"Why did she do it?" I asked. "For his money?"

"That's what we think. And we've impounded those hat pins as evidence and called the two women in who were supposedly bitten at your museum. The hat pins look like a match for the supposed bites."

"So she revived the curse for cover."

"Pretty crazy, right?" Jason shifted his

weight. "But I've got some bad news for your museum. I saw those women talking to a reporter outside the station. I think the press is going to run with the fake-curse angle."

"It doesn't matter if the bells are cursed or not. As long as there's a story and GD is cleared, people will come to see the museum."

His hands fell to his sides. "If I'd known about Kendra, I wouldn't have left you alone there today."

"How were you to know? You saved a man's life. My mom and I are okay. It's all good." And for the first time in a long time, I believed it was all good. The museum would be successful. The people I loved would be happy, and so would I.

"I can't tell you how I felt when I returned to the station and heard the calls coming in about you."

"Calls? Plural?"

"Half the town called to report the kidnapping." He grinned. "Worst-kept secret ever."

I'd been a little annoyed at how word had spread about Mason's visit to my apartment. But a wildfire-like spread of gossip wasn't so bad when confronting a killer. "That's life in a small town."

"I suppose Laurel's already told you that

you shouldn't have raced after your mother," he said.

"The phrase *interfering with a police investigation* may have been said a few dozen times." But since there hadn't been a police investigation of Kendra until after Cora called the police, I wasn't worried. Much. I rubbed the back of my neck. What jury would convict me for trying to save my mom?

"I suppose you want out of this place," Jason said.

Now that he was here, I was in no hurry. But I nodded.

"You're free to go." He smiled at me and began gathering the scattered papers. "The DA will no doubt have more questions later, but you know the drill."

I hesitated at the door and turned. "Jason?"

He looked up. "Yeah?"

"You know, we could maybe go out some time and talk about things that aren't crime-related."

He took my hand and pulled me toward him. "I'm counting on it." And he kissed me.

My head whirled, my knees going weak.

He released me and we both stared at each other, dazed. Our relationship had been moving so slowly, I'd almost missed what it was becoming. But I wouldn't take it for granted again.

Jason cleared his throat. "You'd better get out of here before Detective Hammer changes her mind. She really wants to charge you with something."

"You know where to find me." I floated out the door and into the grim linoleum hallway. My mother and I were alive. Kendra wouldn't be shooting anyone else. And Jason . . . as far as I was concerned, today was a Christmas miracle.

In the reception area, my mom sat ramrod-straight in a plastic chair. When she saw me, she leapt to her feet. "Madelyn, thank heavens. I was beginning to think they were going to charge you for interfering. You shouldn't have come for me."

I hugged her. "Of course I was going to get you."

Gently, she pushed me away. "No, I mean you really shouldn't have. You could have been killed."

"But we weren't."

"This was all my fault." My mom looked away, her hands curling inward. "Ironically, if I'd been more like Kendra, you would have been safe."

"A greedy killer?"

"A greedy killer who made sure her son had an alibi by keeping those Tahoe receipts." She jammed her hands in her jacket pocket. "And I thought she was just coddling Oliver."

"What happened?" I asked. "How'd she get hold of you?"

"I went to ask Kendra where she'd heard that you were on the scene when Tabitha was discovered. I wanted you to be out of it and safe."

"So instead of me annoying the killer until she tried to kill me, you thought you'd do it?"

"I wasn't trying to annoy her, just trip her up and get something we could use. I guess I wasn't as subtle as I thought. I never believed Kendra would insist on dragging you into her net. But I should have. You were the one out front, asking questions. She assumed if I had the answers, so did you."

"Mom, I helped you investigate because I wanted to. I probably would have gotten involved in any case." And in that moment, it was true. "Let's grab some eggnog."

We walked out of the station and paused on the brick steps. I drew a deep breath. The fog had dissipated, and the night wasn't *quite* thick with stars — we were too near the city lights of Sacramento for that. But there were lots of them, and they went on forever.

ABOUT THE AUTHOR

Kirsten Weiss writes paranormal mysteries, blending her experiences and imagination to create a vivid world of magic and mayhem. She is also the author of the Riga Hayworth series. Follow her on her website at kirstenweiss.com.

The employees of Thorndike Press hope you have enjoyed this Large Print book. All our Thorndike, Wheeler, and Kennebec Large Print titles are designed for easy reading, and all our books are made to last. Other Thorndike Press Large Print books are available at your library, through selected bookstores, or directly from us.

For information about titles, please call:
  (800) 223-1244

or visit our website at:
  gale.com/thorndike

To share your comments, please write:
  Publisher
  Thorndike Press
  10 Water St., Suite 310
  Waterville, ME 04901